The *Soles* of Cyrus Eblis

Mark Macedonia

St. Polycarp Publishing House

The *Soles* of Cyrus Eblis

Cover Image: *Shutterstock / Voluroi*
Chapter Heading Images: *Shutterstock / alex74*

ISBN: 1-947707-80-9
ISBN-13: 978-1-947707-80-1

Library of Congress Control Number: 2018946437

Published by St. Polycarp Publishing House
www.stpolycarppublishinghouse.com
info@stpolycarppublishinghouse.com

Printed in the United States of America

CONTENTS

CHAPTER 1

alem Massachusetts, September, 1831

S "It seems an unlikely day to conjure up ghosts," mumbled the old man. The response provoked a curious look from the younger male seated next to him on the perch of the open, horse-drawn chaise. "The sky is so bright and so blue today," the old man continued, closing his eyes in recollection. "A warm soft blue as was the color of her bonnet the first day I set eyes upon her." He opened his eyes and turned toward his travel companion. "Such a cruel irony is the finality of death."

"How do you mean, father?" asked the younger gentleman.

"For although I am overcome with a great emptiness at the loss of a dear friend, I am comforted with the belief that her soul has been delivered into the hands of the Creator. I shall miss her."

"It was a beautiful service," replied the young man, preoccupied with clutching the reins, guiding the mare's steady trot as it pulled the bouncing chaise over cobblestone streets.

"She was a special lady," the old man paused to reflect. "Lived a long life, she did."

"Salem has changed much since you brought me here as a boy," recalled the young man. "So many homes."

"Yes, Joshua, but it is still Salem...still timeless...still dark and mysterious. Her gabled roofs and spires beckon thee to days gone by."

"I can see the church, father."

The old man peered upwards and gazed upon the colorful foliage canopy that lined the streets. "Autumn is New England," he said with a pleasant sigh. Through the breaks in the tree branches he could distinguish the steeple of the red brick church. "Another block or two," he determined.

The chaise slowed at an intersection alive with pedestrians and a variety of horse drawn vehicles. "Stop here for a moment," the old man instructed. His eyes widened. "It was here...here on this corner."

"What was here, father?"

"The seven gabled Turner home stands just down the street facing the sea," he explained pointing. "It was here as a lad that I listened to the tale from an old sea dog. It was here that it all began for me that day, so many years ago." The old man stared off into the distance locked in a memory.

"You have many fond memories of this place?" Joshua asked.

The old man returned from his reminiscence and looked at his son. "I have many memories...not all of them very fond," he said with a grin bespeaking of a man with a secret. "Let us proceed to the church."

With a sigh, Joshua snapped the reins and the horse resumed its trot pulling the chaise another block. The vehicle came to rest before a large red stone building with a gabled rooftop sloping toward the north, adjoined with a tall steeple rising high above the roof that dominated the structure. The building's religious significance shown in the large white Christian cross that was positioned against the façade and centered above the middle of three long stained glass windows. The oak door of the church had been set below the windows and the carved wooden sign planted in the front yard revealed the identity of the house of worship...*Immaculate Conception.*

Joshua turned toward his father. "A Catholic church? Father, did you bring me here to tell me you've changed your denomination?"

The old man smiled. "Come, Father O'Brien is expecting our arrival," he said gingerly climbing down from out of the vehicle with the support of a cane.

The two men proceeded up the narrow stone walkway to the front steps of the church. "It looks to be a new building," Joshua remarked, adjusting his stride to slow his pace with that of his father's.

"Six years. It was built in eighteen twenty-five," his father responded quickly.

At the top of the steps, both men removed their stylish top hats and Joshua pulled the large wooden door open allowing his father to pass through. As the door closed behind them, he followed the old man inside the church, temporarily blinded by darkness that was broken only by a half dozen symmetrical streams of sunlight penetrating stained glass windows at the sides of the church.

Joshua stood in the rear of the church trying to adjust his eyes to the sudden darkness before he recognized the resonance of his father's cane against the wooden floor moving away from him. He peered down the center aisle of the church that split uniformed rows of wooden pews and realized that his father had continued on a path down the center of the building toward the altar.

"Father?!" Joshua called out in a loud whisper; but to no avail.

"It's all right," a voice assured, originating from a figure appearing suddenly from out of the shadows across the room to Joshua's left. The man moved in Joshua's direction pacing through a row of pews dressed in a long sleeved, close-fitting, black garment skirted at the feet with a high stiff white neck collar.

"Father O'Brien?" Joshua deduced.

"Yes," he smiled reaching Joshua with hand extended.

The two men shook hands and then Joshua remembered his father, turning to see him now standing upon the altar beside a marble table, dwarfed by religious images painted on the wall behind him. A large wooden crucifix was centered above the altar flanked by two stone statues—one of the Virgin Mary and the other of Joseph the Carpenter.

"You must be Joshua Caleb Pratt," the silver-haired priest acknowledged reclaiming Joshua's attention. "Your father has mentioned you often in our correspondence. I dare say you're younger than I imagined."

Joshua chuckled politely. "I'll take that as a compliment, Father, but I am thirty-three."

Suddenly pounding echoed about the church, temporarily interrupting their conversation. Immediately Joshua focused his attention to where the altar was positioned and watched as his father pounded the end of his cane against the diamond-shaped sandstone set in the

3

center of the marble-laid floor in front of the sacred table. "Father!" Joshua gasped.

Red-faced with embarrassment Joshua turned back toward Father O'Brien. "I don't know what's come over him?!"

The priest continued to smile. "It is all right. After all, your father's generosity allowed for the construction of this church—God won't mind if he beats on a stone."

Joshua was surprised. "My father built this church?"

"He owned the land on which this church stands and donated it to the Diocese."

Joshua brought his hand to his chin with a bewildered look.

"You are surprised?" O'Brien asked.

"Somewhat...you know my father is a member of the Second Congregation Church—I don't understand this connection with the Catholic Church? I mean it's all very strange," Joshua admitted. "I'll be honest with you. We were raised in a very strong Christian home, but my family spent very little time in church. It wasn't something my parents emphasized. So I'm not really sure why my father has brought me here today; he has never spoken of this particular parish. We've come directly from a funeral, but my father insisted we stop here before departing for home. He was quite adamant about it you know... I couldn't refuse."

"Perhaps he has a secret he wishes to share?" the priest replied with a smile.

"He has been very cryptic today," Joshua replied, "Well I guess I had better find out. Excuse me," He turned away from the priest and began pacing down the center aisle toward his father.

The old man had ceased his assault on the stone, stepping from the altar, and began a pace down the center aisle for a few steps before meeting his son.

Joshua turned back toward Father O'Brien to be certain the priest still maintained his distance at the back of the church and well out of earshot from the two of them before addressing his father. "Father I'm very confused," Joshua began. "The priest has told me you once owned the land upon which this church is built. Is this true?"

The old man grinned. "You doubt the word of a man of the cloth?"

"Well...." Joshua stammered. "No...but..."

"Father O'Brien!" the old man called, looking beyond Joshua. "May I have some time alone here with my son?"

"Of course. I shall speak with you later," the priest replied and disappeared within the shadows at the rear of the church.

"Sit down, my son," the old man instructed pointing to a pew.

Joshua reluctantly dropped down in the pew and his father slid in beside him.

"My friend's untimely departure has brought me to Salem today. Her unfortunate passing has called attention to my own mortality," the old man began, pausing to take a breath and gather his thoughts before continuing. "As you know, although you were born and raised in the state of New York, I have my roots in New England—in fact, here in this very town of Salem. My devotion and honesty toward my family and friends has been incessant and I have endured seventy-seven good years marred only by the grim misfortune of outliving a wife whose love bore me seven children." The old man glanced up at the crucifix above the altar and then back at his son. "You and your brothers and sisters will someday inherit a small fortune—money I accumulated as a proprietor of a brewery. But did you know that when I was a lad I spent my days as a journeyman in the art of shoemaking and eventually became a shoemaker?"

"I believe mother told me that at one time," Joshua revealed. "Father I don't like the tone of this conversation...after all you are in good health."

The old man smiled and ignored his son's concern. "And I am very much intrigued by religion and a portion of my income has been donated to churches of various denominations. It is a gesture of my deep conviction to faith and righteousness."

"But you and mother never placed much emphasis on attending church? I remember you once saying organized religion restrains the soul?"

The old man grinned. "Yes...I did. Didn't I?"

"So you've built other churches?" Joshua inquired leaning forward.

"No. This is the only church built on land I once owned."

"Why Catholic and not Protestant?"

"Timing," the old man responded. "Please let me continue."

Joshua sighed and leaned back in the pew.

"Throughout my life I have been privy to many a momentous

event from the birth of American democracy to the wondrous engi-
neering feat that is the Erie Canal. I have witnessed the terms of
seven presidents and inhaled the suffocating smoke from gunpowder
as our nation plodded through two wars with Britain. I have tasted
the fruits of liberty provided by the Constitution and listened to the
political discourse on equality—all the while Uncle Sam continues to
add stars to the American flag at the expense of the Indian and black
slave. I have felt the power of industry, and the sudden rash of inven-
tions has given me a glimpse of the future. In spite of such stirring
occurrences, it is the recollection of my confrontation with one
called..." the old man paused and gripped his son's right arm. "I have
not uttered his name in many years..." he swallowed hard, turned away
from Joshua, and peered at the altar. "The one called *Cyrus Eblis*," he
uttered quickly before turning back toward Joshua. "It was my
confrontation with *Eblis* that has done the most to chart the course of
my existence."

The old man's tone was more serious now and he released his hold
on Joshua's arm. "My childhood was cast in a time when skepticism
bred ostracism. The long shadow of suspicion would quickly envelop
those eager to share an unusual experience or strange encounter. Thus
on an unforgettable night many years ago, a trio of friends pledged an
oath of secrecy, vowing never to reveal the following experience while
all remained among the living. Instead we decided that the burden of
recording the macabre events of our youth would fall upon the last
surviving member of our trinity. God help me—for I am that person!"

Joshua turned to see if the priest still stood at the rear of the
church, but found him to be gone and then turned back to his father.
"You're serious, aren't you father?"

"I have never been more serious. What I am about to tell you may
seem fantastic and the imaginative product of a man stricken by years;
but as your father, I can only give you my word on the authenticity of
the events and implore you to remain patient with the story I have to
tell. Do I have your attention?"

Joshua nodded. "Yes...of course, father."

"And so I begin...," the old man said, slumping against the back of
the pew, "...as if slumbering back into the midst of a bad dream. As I
remember, I was a boy of thirteen when first hearing the legend of the
beast of Cape Hatteras; although I must admit that I've acquired a

deep respect for the validity of such folklore and use the term legend loosely. It was with the recital of the Cape Hatteras story that the experience with *Cyrus Eblis* began for me—a nightmarish chapter of my youth worthy to be recounted around the dying embers of a fireplace on a stormy autumn evening. Sometimes there exists a fine line between myth and reality...I crossed that line in the autumn of seventeen sixty-seven..."

CHAPTER 2

Salem, Massachusetts, 1767

S I recall that September afternoon as unseasonably chilly, brought on by a biting gale blowing from out of the east that whisked the bob wig from atop Master Hammond's bald head as he stepped briskly past the blacksmith shop. Before the fuller could retrieve it, the wind set the brown wig down upon a hot iron outside of the shop. Instantly the stylish horsehair became engulfed in flames causing some of the passing townsfolk to laugh aloud as Hammond stomped upon the burning hairpiece. Turning away from the spectacle, I grabbed a tight hold of my tricorn as I felt it lifted by the breeze and continued in the direction of the wharf. The wind made it a perfect day for sailing and I realized the force of the gale would surely place the *Lucky Star* in port well ahead of schedule.

It was the third Friday of the month and when finished with my schooling I would accompany my father, William, on his trip to the wharf where he would purchase a cask of molasses brought north by the *Lucky Star.* A popular product of the West Indies, the thick syrup would be distilled to produce rum. For at one time, my father owned one of the largest distilleries in Salem; but the King's tax on sugar and the impending Townshend Acts, which would place duties on other goods imported into the colonies—such as molasses—weighed heavily on such a business. Soon it became much too expensive to operate a distillery on the continent. This injustice forced my father to open a tannery and make his living by selling the cured animal hides as leather to shoemakers, harness makers, and saddlers in and about the town of Salem. On occasion, he still enjoyed making the rum for his own pleasure and as a way of earning a few extra pounds from local taverns. My father never passed up a chance to purchase the thick syrup that arrived in the port of Salem; but on this day he was taken ill and had entrusted me to complete the monthly ritual alone.

The streets of Salem pulsated with life as was usual for a Friday afternoon. Tuesday and Friday were market days in the town when those farmers who lived farther inland would bring their goods to peddle in Salem. The variety of products to be found on these two days of the week brought scores of interested buyers and sellers out into the dirt and cobblestone streets of the New England port city.

I could taste the saltwater carried by the wind as I proceeded down Derby Street and past the seven gabled Turner home facing south across the harbor. Gripping the reins with each hand, the grocer Wrigglenecke gave me a frown from his perch at the front of an empty two-wheeled cart as I tried to keep pace with his trotting black nag. His annoying stare discouraged my youthful persistence and I slowed my pace to a stroll watching the horse and cart pass me by. It was at the intersection of Derby and Turner Streets that I noticed a group of children quickly drawing to a circle around an old man seated upon a wooden crate. The center of interest was Old Red, a venerable character whose age could not be certain; although there were some musing about who wagered that each line of his wrinkled forehead represented a decade, and I counted eight of those lines. Despite such presumptions, his thick untidy beard and the auburn hair that crept out in all directions from underneath his soiled tricorn, had yet to be completely usurped by the encroaching gray—hence the nickname of Old Red.

When the old man eased his ailing body down upon the crate with the help of a staff of birch, all those gathered round knew a story was sure to spill from his lips. For Old Red had spent most of his youth on a frigate compiling such a backlog of tales that it seemed a generation could slip by before he might repeat one.

Curiosity got the better of me that afternoon and although I realized the *Lucky Star's* molasses would be sold to the first buyers at the wharf, I hedged my way into the circle of children to get a gander of Old Red.

The old man pulled down on his close-fitting woolen jacket and sat facing the ground, tugging at his loose breeches as the children's chatter diminished to a whisper. Slowly lifting his head, he turned it deliberately about his eager audience, revealing bloodshot eyes that made contact with those of each one of us, commanding our attention like the beacon of a lighthouse. Passing the sleeve of the left arm across his weathered lips, the old sailor leaned forward supported by the staff that he clutched with both hands.

"When I was a lad in Bristol, England..." Old Red began in a raspy voice with an antiquated tongue that spout a seaman's lingo, "...thar came to be much excitement one day with the capture of the pirate, William Kidd. I believe twas seventeen hundred one...aye...I am certain of it. Shortly afore Captain Kidd was sentenced to be hanged he reflected upon some of his pirating. Kidd's days as a buccaneer were few unlike the endeavors of many of his crew, and he told the followin' tale that had been passed down to him by one such mate called 'Shank'. In Kidd's own words, the mate—who earned his nickname with a talent for tyin' the sheepshank knot—began his career as a cutthroat with a band of pirates that preyed upon vessels in the waters of the Carolinas.

"Off the coast of that which is called North Carolina these days, thar exist a number of narrow strips of islands aligned like the curved horns of a demon," Red paused to etch the description in the dirt with the end of his staff. "These islands were the favorite haven of pirates who used the shiftin' sands of the deceptive coastline and the suddenness of nature's fury to lure many a vessel laden with European treasures, to their doom—much like a spider traps the unsuspectin' insect in her invisible web.

"One such island be named Cape Hatteras and twas thar in the year sixteen hundred ninety-one that the band of pirates happened upon..." Old Red paused and lowered his voice to a whisper. "...the beast of Cape Hatteras."

I listened intensely as Old Red spun his yarn, enthralled by each and every image that he painted with vivid detail. He was a master bard, constructing his story with the aid of facial contortions and vocal variations that reflected the mood of each piece of the tale.

Before too long he had succeeded in hijacking his youthful audience far from the port of Salem, whisking us away with his words to another time and place steeped in mystery and suspense.

Old Red's eerie account centered on an English galleon christened *Aeshma* that wandered aimlessly off the coast of the Carolinas before being overtaken by buccaneers. The marauders were hoping to find the ship carrying gold and silver, but to their surprise and disappointment the vessel was void of such booty. More disturbing proved to be the mental and physical condition of the small number of crew members aboard the ship—thin, frail, ghostly pail, and listless as though they were locked in a trance. Upon further inspection, the vessel began to reveal a violent and grisly recent history as the pirates found the bloated corpses of four officers hanging from the mainyard that supported the rigging and topmast. The evidence of carnage expanded to the poop deck where the buccaneers were horrified by the discovery of a great many severed human body parts littering the ruddy blood-stained floorboards, scattered around a large wooden crate with its lid tossed aside. The pirate captain cautiously examined the inside of the box and found half buried in a bed of sand, an alabaster cylinder the size of a cask. Strange wedge-like characters could be found on the outside of the strange container. Its lid had been removed and the cylinder had been emptied.

After pressuring the drowsy crew of the galleon, the pirate captain found a sailor with the courage and energy to speak. The tormented seaman recounted how the *Aeshma* had set a course home for England from an excursion in the Middle East where it had picked up the cylinder—an object of antiquity; but east of the Azores the voyage home turned treacherous when a ferocious storm blew the ship off course. Days later the return of calm seas revealed the vessel's new location to be off the coastline of North America, and it was at this point, the sailor explained, that the crew began hearing strange voices originating from inside the cylinder. The message from the voices appeared foreign and undecipherable, terrifying the crew who were warned by a passenger—a doctor of science—not to remove the lid. In spite of his warnings, the frenzied sailors—already overwrought after having survived the storm—pried opened the cylinder and unleashed an invisible beast whose presence afflicted the souls of each crew member turning shipmate against shipmate.

Old Red's audience—myself included—had swallowed the bait. With widened eyes and a whimsical grin, the aged teller of tales readied to reel us in with the gripping conclusion.

Red described how, as if on cue, the conclusion of the sailor's bizarre account coincided with a steady ocean gale that howled as it blew across the deck of the galleon. The direction of the wind drew the pirate captain's attention back to the poop deck where a shadowy figure clad in a long black hooded robe suddenly appeared from out of thin air. When the figure slowly lifted the prolonged bony fingers of both hands and pulled the hood of the robe down exposing a head of scraggly white hair and the wrinkled face of an elderly woman, the pirate captain screamed, "Witch!" Overcome with fear, the buccaneer rushed the old hag who glared at him from behind stark, cavernous eyes, cracking a smile tarnished with rotted teeth. She belted out a high shrill just as the captain ran his cutlass through her midsection with such momentum that it drove her backwards until she disappeared over the side of the vessel.

Suddenly the ocean surface began to churn with the fury of a caldron and the black water erupted into a sea of crimson. The captain dropped his cutlass and gripped the railing with both hands as the steady gale whipped into a tempest. With a thunderous roar, the ocean parted and up from its depths surged a hideous snake-like behemoth whose size towered twice that of the ship's main mast. The serpent's head equaled the length and width of a cannon and its long, scaly mid-section supported a half dozen wriggling tentacles—each stretching the length of a pulling boat.

Numb with fright, the captain was unable to pull himself free of the railing in time to prevent one of the tentacles from wrapping itself around his body with a vice-like grip. The slimy appendage hoisted him from the deck, and with the serpent hissing the captain belted one final scream before disappearing within the frothing jaws of the beast as it submerged beneath the ocean surface.

At some point the galleon had caught fire. The flames began to spread rapidly across the wooden vessel, forcing the other pirates and those left of the *Aeshma's* crew to abandon ship by leaping overboard. The decision proved fatal for most, as the monster resurfaced from the depths and turned its sights on the helpless seamen. Using its tentacles as a fisherman skillfully maneuvers his net, the serpent

plucked each unfortunate lad from the water and consumed them—
one man at a time.

Old Red finished the tale by explaining how the pirate Shank and a
handful of others managed to escape the fury of the beast and safely
reached the beachhead. Dazed and horrified, the buccaneer recalled
standing on that dark shoreline and listening to the terrifying shrieks
of shipmates as they were being snatched by the creature's tentacles.
When the gut wrenching cries could be heard no more, Shank
watched the burning sail of *Aeshma's* topmast disappear beneath the
waves. The serpent roared, equaling the bark of ten lions, then hissed
with the force of a hurricane, before submerging for the final time.
The beastly hiss produced a frigid whirlwind that blew past the pirate,
rustling the tree line at the edge of the sand. From that day forth,
Shank believed something sinister blew ashore that evening that
would forever curse the continent.

CHAPTER 3

The clomping of horse's hoofs redirected my attention away from Old Red and I raised my head to see the grocer Wrigglenecke's cart passing by; but now his cart moved in a westerly direction away from the wharf and was loaded down with barrels. *The Lucky Star! I've missed the Lucky Star!* Pushing my way out of the group of children, I pulled the tricorn from my head and began a sprint toward the dock. In between each breath, I cursed myself and cursed Old Red for telling such a thrilling story and in my haste I nearly knocked the widow Mulhern to the ground as she stepped from the bakery, while exciting Banard Smith's two Irish Setters into chasing me for three blocks.

When I reached the wharf, I found it surprisingly sparse for a Friday afternoon. The *Lucky Star* rested in her usual location moored to the dock, with only a few of the ship's hands lingering about the pier, and with hurried feet I approached an unkempt, rough-looking man standing near one of the ship's wooden ramps. "Sailor!" I exclaimed, out of breath. "I would like to purchase a cask of molasses!"

The man gave me a curious glance. "Sorry lad. She's empty."

"Just one cask, please!" I persisted.

"What's the matter, son? Do you have cotton in yer ears?" he replied with a scowl. "I said we're all out of it. I can't give ya what I don't have."

Once again, I cursed under my breath. *My father is going to whip my behind.* I rubbed my rear-end envisioning what pain lie ahead of me once I returned home empty-handed. The dread of punishment quickly gave way to thoughts of what would become of my father's confidence in me, and this seemed to hurt more than a good whipping could. He entrusted me to obtain the molasses on my own, and I had let him down.

It was then that I noticed the second merchant ship in port and in particular, her name board depicted by painted carvings at the stern. She was called *AESHMA*. The eerie coincidence of her name startled me for a moment; however, as I was unfamiliar with the word, I could not be certain that Old Red's pronunciation matched the spelling of the frigate's name. Nearly comparable in size to an English galleon, the frigate lacked the richly decorated stern of the English ships of the line. The merchant vessel appeared weathered and rickety, and not a soul could be seen aboard her decks.

Still angered by the fact that I had no molasses to bring home, I scoffed at the vessel's strange name and pulled the jacket collar tighter around my neck as the air grew colder. Placing the tricorn back upon my head, I sunk my hands deep into my pockets and started back in the direction of town.

By the time I retraced my steps to the intersection of Derby and Turner Streets, the group of children had gone although Old Red could still be found seated on the wooden crate. I approached the bearded old man and watched as his feeble hands worked at dissecting the core of an apple with a dull jack-knife.

When Red realized I stood over him, he raised his head. "What tis it, lad? Another story? Maybe tomorrow, aye. This old body of mine is plenty tired."

"The *Aeshma*," I replied. "How is it spelled?"

"The spellin'? Now, that be a curious question. Let me think...?" He pondered for a moment and grinned. "*A* as in apple...*E* as in eye...*S* for the serpent that slithers on by. *H* as in heaven...*M* as in man...*A* for the angel with the serpent in hand."

Amused by the clever lyric, I repeated it once to myself. "It's in the harbor!" I revealed.

Red lost his smile. "I'm not humored, lad. Now run along."

"I saw it old man! It's in port!"

"Son, it tis unlucky to name thy vessel after one lost at sea. The *Aeshma* rests in Davey Jones's Locker. Thou hath just imagined her in port. Now be off with ya!"

I was disappointed that Old Red refused to believe me, but realized it was of no use to argue with the stubborn old sailor. With a disgusted sigh, I turned away and proceeded in the direction of the marketplace.

Upon reaching the center of the market, I stopped in front of Wrigglenecke's grocery and grasped the coins inside my pocket, realizing that my only alternative was to purchase a cask of molasses at a higher price from the grocer. Fear of embarrassment caused me to deliberate in front of that store for some time before I dropped my head and reached for the door handle. Suddenly a large crash followed by angry voices emitting from the alley adjacent to the store persuaded me to release my grip on the handle, and I stepped to the side of the building to peer down the alley. Standing in between his cart and a broken cask of molasses oozing the thick, dark syrup over the cobblestone, was the red-faced grocer scolding his young son. At that moment, all thoughts of purchasing the molasses vanished, for behind the cart lie the forest. I began scheming on how I might make off with a cask under the cover of the autumn brush.

Whatever power influenced my decision, it did not take long. Soon I found myself positioned in the edge of the forest behind a large hemlock—only a few feet from the cart and its precious cargo. The woods were rumored to be haunted but it didn't seem to matter. Nothing seemed to matter. I don't know what came over me. I wasn't a thief—in fact, before that moment I had never stolen anything in my life; but the opportunity to make amends for my mistake clouded my senses. Besides, I was confident that Wrigglenecke surely would not miss one cask of the thick syrup.

I watched carefully as the grocer and his son worked in shifts unloading the casks, which proved to be a manageable task, for the smaller concave-shaped barrels contained a quarter of the contents found in a keg. Father and son would hoist a barrel on their shoulder and carry it inside the store, remaining out of sight for several seconds before reappearing for another load. This would be enough time for me to grab a container and disappear into the woods.

The grocer stepped back outside and marched toward the cart.

Wrigglenecke was surely an unusual name but never did a title fit the physical description of a person so well. For when the grocer shuffled to the wagon, his long, slender neck would twist, causing his head to bob from side to side as though it were the crow's nest of a ship swaying above the deck. I watched as Wrigglenecke reached out for a cask, lifting the barrel from the cart and began moving in the direction of the grocery. Stepping out from behind the tree, I dashed toward the wagon, hoisted one of the heavy casks onto my shoulder and lumbered back behind the hemlock. I waited until Wrigglenecke's son came and went, before advancing farther into the woods, scurrying behind another large tree. After the grocer had gathered an additional cask, I wandered off into the forest under the cover of the thick brush.

Breathing heavily and struggling with the weight of the cask, my guilty conscience fueled a brisk pace along a narrow path littered with leaves. Whisked with the bright colors of autumn, the painted foliage glistened in the rays of the late afternoon sun where streams of light pierced the canopy of branches and sprinkled the forest floor. Dodging overgrown limbs that had reclaimed the path, I would occasionally turn my head to be sure no-one followed me and take a moment with each step to reposition the sagging barrel that grew heavy in my arms. The serenity of the forest was broken as I plodded through the brush snapping twigs and crunching dry leaves beneath my feet; but I didn't hear this. What I heard were the trees. As a soft breeze rustled the branches of the quaking aspens, their leaves fluttered and emitted a rhythmic chant that I could only distinguish as WRIGGLENECKE…WRIGGLENECKE…WRIGGLENECKE.

My pace quickened, and suddenly, as if someone had reached up from out of the earth and grabbed my ankle—there was the root. It crept across the path, partially buried under the leaves and hidden from my view. I tripped over the offshoot of a lofty elm, lost the grip on the cask of molasses and hurled face down to the path, closing my eyes as my face and stomach thumped against the hard surface. When reopening my eyes, I rolled over on my back and confronted a terrifying sight. The figure of a man stood above me silhouetted by rays of sunlight, and although at first he remained faceless, I was certain it must be Wrigglenecke.

I jumped up and turned to run, but felt a pull on my arm that held me fast in one spot. "Let me go!" I cried out and turned toward him; but to my surprise, I could see the man standing a few feet in front of me with his hands folded across his chest—he did not have a grip on any part of my body, yet I could not move.

Overcome with fear, I continued to try and gain my release from whatever mysterious force held me by shifting my weight in the opposite direction of the stranger. And then without warning I was free; but my momentum had forced me to tumble to the ground again. I turned to look up and this time found an extended hand hovering over me adorned with a ring of gold on each finger that featured the longest fingernails I had ever seen on a man's hand. Reluctantly I reached for his hand and the stranger pulled me to my feet.

At that moment, I realized he was not Wrigglenecke and I marveled at how mistaken I could have been to confuse the tall stranger with Salem's grocer. The man who helped pull me to my feet wore a bronze complexion uncharacteristic of the pale New Englander. Exhibiting a stoic expression, he sported a youthful, handsome face—a perfect face—clean-shaven with not a scar or blemish to be found.

"You are bound for home?" the stranger asked, slowly relinquishing his hold on my hand. Only at that moment did I realize what an icy cold hand it was. "Perhaps I remind you of someone else—someone that is obviously feared?" he continued with a deep sonorous voice. "Might this have something to do with the cask?" he inquired glancing at the barrel on the ground resting on its side. The stranger looked back at me flashing an incriminating grin.

I tried to avoid a response and stooped over to examine the cask, finding only minor damage as one of the hickory hoops that bound the staves of the barrel had snapped, breaking away from the container.

When my glance returned to the stranger, I gazed upon his most striking physical feature—his eyes. At first I thought the dimly lit forest had created an illusion, but the longer I stared the more evident it became that the man's right iris matched the color of a clear blue afternoon sky, while his left was as dark as molasses.

"Is it damaged?" he pried.

I shook my head from side to side and proceeded to brush the dirt and leaves from my clothing before bending over to retrieve my tricorn.

"Such a lanky young man. You would be but a morsel for a hungry old wolf," the stranger added with a broad grin.

Finally I could hold my tongue no more. "I do not know you."

The stranger continued to emit a perpetual smile. "What is there to know...Benjamin?"

I was surprised. "How do you come by my name?"

The man reached out, snapped the end of a branch from a tree with his left hand and held it out in front of his face, twirling it slowly. As I studied the turning stem, the soft light of the forest produced a sparkle as it struck the mourning rings of gold that lined each prolonged finger of his hand. Clad in a frock of charcoal-grey cloth that extended just below the knees before exposing stockings of fine grey wool, the stranger brushed the end of the branch against his white neckcloth. "Your father is a tanner and you are his lone son," he revealed. "Tell me Benjamin, it must be difficult to grow up alone without the companionship of a brother or sister. No-one with whom to share the pleasure of youth. No-one to share in secrets and game. Do you miss your brother?"

My brother? How could he know of him? I ignored the question. After placing my tricorn back on top of my head, I reached down to retrieve the cask.

The stranger pressed the edge of the branch against the underside of his large brimmed circular black felt hat, lifting the headdress to the top of his forehead. "Ah...I've opened an old wound. Forgive me, young Benjamin."

I hoisted the cask onto my shoulder and looked up at the stranger who continued to smile. His thick and tidy head of raven-black hair was pulled back away from his face and tied with a narrow black ribbon at the nape where it fell from underneath the hat.

"What be your name?" I asked brashly.

"My name? Forgive me again, young Benjamin. I become so enchanted with the lives of those with whom I stumble upon that, often, I assume that they are just as familiar with me," he explained with a sardonic grin. "Please allow me to introduce myself...I am *Cyrus Eblis.*"

"I am sorry sir, but I am not familiar with that name."

"Sir?" Eblis replied amusingly. "I have yet to be knighted by the king. Indeed I am not a sir; merely a title—man-made verbosity created for the sole purpose of separating race, class, and gender. Why is a noble called noble and a peasant called peasant?"

I thought I best answer. "A noble is rich; a peasant is poor."

"Exactly! The difference is but a few thousand pounds. If one is not a *goodman*—born to till the soil, then he is a *gentleman*—educated and learned in the art of stealing the hard earned wages of the *goodman*. And if one is a *mister*, then he commands the right hand of the law, using his powers as the magistrate to enforce the cycle of disparity that binds us all to an uneventful existence. For the lack of a few thousand pounds a man is condemned to a life of misery—toiling with his hands from dawn to dusk and never feeling the soft touch of silk against his weathered skin," he said as he brushed the end of his neckcloth against his chin, "...or the cold, solid weight of sparkling gold around his fingers." Eblis again flashed the fingers adorned with gold. "That's the curse of human nature—the abhorrence with thoughts of equality. Someone must always have the upper hand. Inequality breeds greed and where there is greed, young Benjamin, there is deceit," he continued glaring at the cask of molasses, "And where there is deceit, young Benjamin..." he paused and gently laid his hand upon my shoulder, "...there is I."

"You are the constable?!" I surmised with a trembling voice. "I promise I shall return the molasses!"

Eblis chuckled, lifted his hand from my shoulder and tossed the stick away from his other hand.

"Benjamin, I am not a constable, nor do I think you should return the molasses. You've done the proper thing," he persuaded, leaning slightly forward to look me in the eyes. "Old man Wrigglenecke will surely never miss one cask of molasses. Your father will be proud of your effort...I am proud of you."

I was hardly comforted by his approval of my actions, for they seemed such odd words coming from a stranger. *Could he read my mind? How does he know of my anxiety with my father over missing the opportunity to purchase molasses? How did he know of my theft of the cask? How did he know of my brother?* Then strangely, as I stared at the stranger, the pupils of his eyes began to dilate as does ink in a pond and then each began to spin. Soon I found myself engulfed by the rapid rotation of the dark circles, drawing me inside as if gripped by two bottomless whirlpools. Only when the cask of molasses slipped slightly from my shoulder did the hypnotic spell break, returning me to the forest.

I was alarmed. "It's getting dark..." I stammered. "I must go sir...I mean..."

"Cyrus Eblis," he corrected, pulling himself upright with his hands at his hips. "Oh how darkness exudes such fear. It is out of darkness from whence man first came and it is into darkness that he shall retire," Eblis babbled. He was so full of himself—inflating his ego with an endless torrent of opinions and reveling in my obvious fear. "Allow me to walk a little farther with you since I am bound in the same direction," he offered, much to my dismay. "But first, let us erase all doubt about to whom this cask of molasses now belongs." Eblis pulled a large knife from out of his coat and handed it to me. "Carve your initials in the cask," he commanded.

I set the cask down and gazed at the knife that rested delicately in the palm of my hand. Twice the size of a Jack-knife, the polished blade was dazzling. I stared at my reflection in the pristine steel where a brilliant wavy pattern had been etched and admired the decorative blade protruding from a smooth handle crafted of curly maple.

"Do you fancy the blade?" Eblis beamed.

"I've never seen the likes of this before," I replied.

"It is one of a kind, young Benjamin. Forged of the purest of flames."

Gripping my fingers around the handle of the knife I carved the letters BP into the flat wooden surface of the top of the cask and handed the tool back to Eblis.

"What is done, is done," Eblis barked with outstretched arms. "The cask is now the property of Benjamin Pratt."

I hoisted the barrel back upon my shoulder and we began our trek through the woods with Eblis taking the lead along the path. I was now truly frightened of my situation alone in the woods with this eerie stranger and began to feel as though I were being punished for my theft. Our conversation ceased and I welcomed the quiet, praying the end of the wooded path would soon reveal itself, while Eblis pushed along humming an unfamiliar but hauntingly hypnotic tune. At one point I dared to stop along the path hoping he would continue ahead unaware of my abrupt halt; but as I stopped, Eblis stopped. He never turned around. He just stopped and waited for me to move as though he had eyes in the back of his head. Unnerved by this, I resumed my steps and like the reflection in a mirror, Eblis resumed his.

Then suddenly Eblis halted. He focused his attention on a nearby oak, snatching several dry leaves from a branch and crushed them in his hand. "Ah...autumn!" he exclaimed whirling toward me with his fist clenched. "It tis the season of the dying! As the air grows cooler, the leaves begin to select their colors before parting from the security of the branch. How it warms me so!" Slowly he opened his fingers and displayed the crushed leaves in his palm and to my surprise, instantly the leaves burst into flames, curling into ashes against his pink flesh. Not once during this exhibition of black magic did the smiling Eblis appear to be in any pain. Clenching his fist once more, he extinguished the flame and finished the bizarre demonstration by brushing the ashes from his hands.

I was amazed and petrified by Eblis' magic and my only response came as an attempt to lessen the burden of guilt which grew so heavy in the shadow of this man. "I didn't mean to steal the molasses!"

"Don't spoil the moment," Eblis retorted. He turned away from me and continued his pace through the woods.

At first I did not or rather, could not move until the startling caw of an unseen bird broke my rigidity.

When I rejoined Eblis, I began to wonder what interest he had in the forest? As if reading my mind, he replied, "You are curious to what brings me to the woods? It is an anniversary, young Benjamin...an annual pilgrimage." The tone of his voice grew more serious and I more frightened.

"Anniversary...?" I stammered. "What forest has an anniversary?"

"All in good time, Benjamin."

"What is your trade?" I persisted with trembling words.

Eblis scoffed. "Trade? I'm a manufacturer, young Benjamin. I manufacture...*soles*."

"You are a shoemaker?" I attempted to clarify.

Eblis stopped and turned his head just slightly, glancing back at me with one eye and casting a wide grin. "Why of course, Benjamin," he acknowledged before resuming his steps and his humming.

The path on which we tread grew steeper as we climbed a hill, and a few moments later we stepped into a circular clearing dominated by a large oak tree. The towering tree sprung up from out of the center of the clearing with its partially exposed roots spreading out in all directions from the massive trunk like the probing tentacles of a great octopus. Half-way up the trunk, the two lowest branches with the thickness and length of the center beam to a house, extended outward and supported the lesser branches that coveted the clearing in the form of an oval roof.

I stopped and watched as Eblis stepped beneath one of the branches. He scoured the limb for a moment before turning toward me. "Young Benjamin, come hither."

I should run now! But my legs will not move! Feeling helpless, I reluctantly stepped underneath the branch.

"Do you see?" he asked pointing up at the large limb hovering overhead and well out of the reach of an average sized man.

I followed his arm until I noticed scores of large gashes notched into the side and top of the branch. *What does it mean?*

Eblis looked at me with widened eyes. "Why, this is the hanging tree from which the witches of Salem met their fate seventy-five years ago—this very month," Eblis described with a chilling smugness.

"Gallows Hill!" I gasped. My legs trembled. "The witches?! We should leave here now! My father told me to steer clear of this spot lest the spirits of those witches follow me home!"

"Twenty executions, Benjamin. Nineteen hangings and one who was pressed to death. It was such a dark time," Eblis described with delight. He seemed to be enjoying himself, all the while my heart raced. "And the corpses?" he continued. "Look around, Benjamin. For their bodies were thrust into shallow holes—discarded like the acorns of this mighty oak."

"This is the anniversary that brings you to this forest?!" I barked with disgust.

"Yes, Benjamin. Exciting, isn't it? Tell me," he began to ask with an inquisitive glare, "do you know of any witches?"

"Not...one."

"Pity. For they're quite a devoted lot. Perhaps you shall make the acquaintance of one someday?"

"I don't believe in them."

"I wouldn't be so quick to dismiss their existence," he cautioned.

"Of course many of the legends of daughters of black magic sailing before a full moon on a broom handle, or stirring a bubbling caldron with a slimy toad, are but that—legends. The real witch is a state of mind, Benjamin, and that can be very powerful. For after all, dark witchcraft is but a human attempt to establish contact with...well... with you know whom," Eblis baited with a broad grin.

"The devil?"

"Devil is so trite," he said annoyingly. "Human beings are but animals; transfixed to the present like sheep in a pasture. The human mind has the power to transcend the present and soar far from reality. Those who believe themselves to be witches are but imprisoned souls craving release from an earthly life of little substance—like sheep tied to the land." Eblis slowly encircled the trunk of the oak, gliding his hands over its bark as if it were a sacred object. "Benjamin, in sixteen ninety-two most of those twenty souls were victims. The true messengers of Satan were the accusers and executioners themselves—those who expelled so much energy in creating the hysteria. For it was they who unknowingly contributed to a heightened awareness of the prince of darkness. It is this awareness that feeds *him*."

"You know much history of these woods," I remarked with trepidation.

Eblis snickered and started a slow approach toward me. Still frozen with fear I could not flee; but as the stranger drew closer I summoned up the courage and strength to match his steps with backward steps of my own.

"Yes, Benjamin. I know much about those dark days of yore. I can see them as plain as you now see me. Do you know how?"

I breathed heavily and shook my head from side to side.

"I was here, Benjamin!" Eblis hissed. "Here in sixteen ninety-two on the very soil that you now stand!"

"How can it be?!" I challenged, still backing my way out of the clearing.

"Are you frightened?" Eblis retorted. "Fear is a sign of weakness."

I couldn't respond.

Eblis laughed. It was a deep menacing laugh and seemed to echo about me.

I continued my retreat until a gentle brush against the back of my shoulder impeded my movement. My breathing stopped and my heart pounded, so I dropped the cask at my feet and closed my eyes. My adrenaline surged and I whirled around with such force that my tricorn flew from my head as I swung my arm to combat whatever now blocked my withdrawal. I opened my eyes just as my arm shattered the branch of a small tree, bringing a sense of momentarily relief, but then remembered Eblis. As I turned back around, black clouds had rolled in across the sky obscuring the day's final rays of the setting sun as a sudden burst of wind whipped the leaves in the clearing into a colorful vortex obstructing my view of the stranger. I held my arms over my face to shield my eyes from the whirling debris tossed about by the cyclone which had now completely swallowed Eblis.

"Until we meet again, Benjamin Pratt!" the dark stranger called out from within the cyclone. I grabbed hold of a tree trunk as the entire clearing seemed to be spinning in a dazzling display of colors as the whirlwind produced a vacuum sucking all loose objects into its center.

And then just as suddenly as it had come up, the dark clouds passed overhead, re-emitting the fading sunlight. The wind ceased, allowing the leaves to float effortlessly to the ground as a disquieting hush fell over the forest. As mysteriously as he had appeared, *Cyrus Eblis* was gone.

I released my grip from the tree trunk and my trembling legs buckled, dropping me to my knees. Taking a moment to gather my thoughts, I remembered the cask of molasses and began searching the ground around me, looking out over the clearing to locate my tricorn; but the barrel was nowhere to be found. It had disappeared along with Eblis.

CHAPTER 4

My father had never heard of *Cyrus Eblis*, insisting instead that he was a product of Old Red's storytelling and a poor excuse for missing the chance to purchase molasses from the *Lucky Star*. It proved to be as severe a scolding as I had anticipated; although I deliberately neglected to include my theft of the molasses in retelling the day's events. My father vowed that it would be a long time before he would ever again entrust me with such a task, and in his anger lost control of his tongue by reminding me that I lacked the qualities that made my late brother Jordan such a responsible and dependable young man. The mentioning of my brother's name brought tears to the eyes of my parents. It was especially painful for me, unleashing memories of the events surrounding the tragic accident two years before.

Despite the onset of winter and the steady decline of his health, my father took it upon himself to make the trip to the port of Salem for a cask of molasses. Each trip burdened me with guilt. I continued to accompany him, taking the opportunity to search the streets for the stranger I encountered in the forest. I examined hundreds of faces and explored the shops of the few shoemakers in Salem; but there was no sign of *Cyrus Eblis*. I began to convince myself that maybe the events were all a bad dream.

Three months had passed when suddenly on Christmas morning, my father died of consumption. He was thirty-five. My mother and I were devastated. My father's patriarchal grip dominated our meager existence in Salem and his judgment, guidance, and work ethic proved to be a constant force that molded our daily lives. We were ill-prepared for the emotional and economic burden that his passing bestowed upon us. My mother lacked the knowledge and desire to continue the operation of the tannery and I was too young and inexperienced to inherit the business.

On a bitter cold and snowy morning, we buried my father in the graveyard behind the lofty wooden steeple of Salem's meetinghouse. A small group of family and friends gathered to bid farewell to William Pratt, laying him to rest alongside my brother, Jordan.

Standing ankle-deep in the wet snow, I gripped my mother's hand as two men shoveled earth atop my father's pine coffin, while the minister read a passage from the Good Book. I didn't cry; but listened to the words of the Bible with my head bowed, numb from the cold and the sadness that surrounded me. Then there was silence. The preacher seemed to have stopped in mid-sentence, so I raised my head to see the clergyman's lips moving and watched his breath in the cold air; but I couldn't hear the words. The world around me had grown mute. Suddenly the eerie muteness was broken by the whisper of my name. It echoed about me, but originated from nowhere. Glancing around at those who stood above the open grave none appeared to take heed. I turned my head to look over my shoulder and there in the distance loomed the dark figure of a man positioned in between two headstones, wearing a circular brimmed hat. My mouth grew parched and for an instant I was unable to move. Something inside told me it was the stranger—*Cyrus Eblis.*

Sensing my discomfort, my mother turned toward me. "Benjamin, what is it?" she asked breaking the silence.

I swallowed hard. "It's him...the man from the forest!"

My mother followed my stare and lifted her eyes in the direction of the stranger. "I see no-one."

I could still see him and continued my glare across the graveyard. "But mother! He's there! What does he want?!"

My mother placed her cold hand to the side of my face and gently turned my head toward her. "Oh Benjamin, you're all I have. Don't trouble me so," she said with eyes welled with tears.

When I looked behind me again the stranger was gone.

The clergyman closed the Bible and paced toward my mother. Upon reaching her, he took my mother's hand and consoled her with a few brief personal thoughts. She wept softly as the minister gave her a gentle hug and turning in my direction, acknowledged me with a nod and a tip of the tricorn before walking away. She and I remained at the gravesite in silence until the coffin had been completely covered with earth. When we turned away from the plot, I could see my father's older sister and her husband—locked arm in arm—trudging through the snow in our direction.

"Jamesina!" my mother replied.

"Oh, Marian! I am so sorry!" my aunt consoled, presenting my mother with the customary grievance gift—a pair of gloves. My mother smiled and handed me the gloves, which I stuffed into my coat pocket to join the other five pair.

Jamesina reached out and took hold of my mother's hands. I had never really noticed it before; but as I gazed at my aunt I could see the attentive eyes and the reassuring smile of my father. With long blonde hair flowing beneath her bonnet and a slim, shapely figure, my aunt was a beautiful woman physically, and blessed with an inner beauty that shown within her pleasant disposition and her incessant kindness.

The interlocking of hands between my mother and aunt extended into a hug as both women began to weep and it proved difficult to see both of them in tears, for I had always only witnessed their strength.

My uncle, Edward Brown, had snuck up beside me and laid his hand upon my shoulder. "I offer my condolences, Benjamin."

"Thank you, uncle."

The women remained locked in a tearful embrace.

"My, how you have grown," my uncle admired. "Look Jamey how Benjamin has grown since last we saw him."

My aunt pulled herself from my mother and wiped the tears from her cheeks with a handkerchief. "Why, yes," she said, glancing at me with a forced smile. "Quite a fine young man."

"How kind of you to make the journey from Lynn in such foul weather," my mother remarked.

"Good heavens!" Jamesina replied. "Nothing would have kept me from saying goodbye to my brother!"

"Why of course...I didn't mean..."

"Hush," Jamesina interrupted with a smile. "I know what you meant. It is difficult for both of us." My aunt turned toward me. "How old are you, Benjamin?"

"Thirteen," I replied.

"And a handsome thirteen at that," she added.

"How is Caleb getting along?" my mother asked, regaining her composure.

"Splendid, thank you," Jamesina replied. "He recently completed his theological studies at Yale and has been ordained the junior colleague to a minister in Connecticut. I expected him in Lynn last evening, but he must have been delayed by the weather. I left word we would be at the funeral this morning."

"Where has he been assigned?"

"The town of Simsbury," she responded proudly.

"Well, it will be good to see him."

My mother turned away to take one more look upon the gravesite. With a sigh and a whimper she turned back around and lifted her bloodshot eyes in the direction of my aunt and uncle. "It is so cold," she said with a shiver.

"Marian, I realize this is neither the time nor place to discuss such matters," Edward expressed, "but what are your future plans?"

My mother hesitated. "I...I don't know," she responded with an empty stare. "I suppose I could sell the tannery and make candlesticks. My mother once sold them and learned me the craft."

"These are difficult times for a widow and a schoolboy," Edward stressed. Standing shorter than Jamesina, my uncle tugged on the lapels of his jacket before circling his hand about a round midsection that sagged over the waistline of his breeches. "The king continues to send more redcoats to the colonies and their immoral behavior has been called into question. And now that the Townshend Acts have gone into effect, dissent has begun to run high, particularly with the publication of Dickinson's *Letters From a Farmer in Pennsylvania...*"

"I do not read the political literature of disgruntled farmers," my mother interrupted with sarcasm.

"What Edward means..." Jamesina interjected with a glance towards me and a soft whisper, "...is that a woman needs a man about the house."

Insulted that my aunt thought less of my manliness, I lowered my head and gently kicked the snow.

"Margaret Winters claims to have been violated by a young British soldier," Jamesina added. "It is not safe for a woman to be alone."

"Well, I do have a cousin who lives north in Falmouth and we could stay with her," my mother replied.

"And Benjamin?" Jamesina asked. "What is he to do? Come spring he will have finished with secondary school."

"He will accompany me, of course."

"Marian, the shoemaking business is booming in Lynn," Edward offered. "The need for apprentices is growing every day. I, myself, employ two journeymen at present and have no need for an extra hand; but I do know of a man who trains apprentices to become journeymen for manufacturers looking to hire. It might be prudent for Benjamin to take advantage of such a teacher and develop a useful skill he shall use the rest of his days."

I was attracted to the idea. "Yes, mother! It would be a great experience!"

"I don't know," my mother deliberated. "At this point my fingers and toes have frozen. It might be best to continue this discussion aside a warm hearth."

"Yes, Marian. I agree," Edward replied. "Come let us walk you to your chaise."

As the three adults stepped in front of me, I hesitated and lingered behind, deciding to explore the area where I had seen the dark apparition.

I plodded half-way across the snow-blanketed cemetery, winding in between staggered headstones until reaching the location where I was certain the stranger had stood. After a few moments of probing the newly fallen snow, I was astounded to find the absence of a single footprint, with the exception of my own. With a confused expression, I stood motionless for a few moments listening to the faint howl of the wind.

"Benjamin?" a voice called out from behind me. Its suddenness startled me so much that I tumbled face down into the snow.

Quickly I rolled over and brushed the cold snow from my cheeks and forehead as the gentleman who stood above me reached down and offered me his hand.

"Benjamin? Are you all right?"

I sighed with relief. "Caleb," I acknowledged embarrassingly. "I slipped."

Caleb helped me to my feet. "It has been awhile, cousin," he said. "I'm sorry to hear of your father's death."

"It is hard," I replied, brushing the snow from my coat.

Six years older than I, Caleb had already completed two years of university study in New Haven and so it surprised no-one when Jamesina announced his new assignment as a minister in Connecticut —it was expected. Friends and companions at an early age—my cousin, my brother and myself, were inseparable as youths; but time and circumstance had changed all of that. As far as I could remember, my cousin's presence acted as a constant reminder that no matter how good I was at something, he was always better than me. An over-achiever, he excelled at all he attempted. Bright, handsome, and charming, Caleb's qualities invoked the family's pride and gave encour-agement to my parents that my brother and I would follow the trail of his success; but that was yesterday and the events of life had altered such plans.

"Where's your mother?" Caleb asked as he removed his braid trimmed tricorn to shake the snow from it, revealing his light brown hair fashioned with one roll over the ears and pulled back to a plait tied with several ribbons.

"She's at the carriage."

"Come," he insisted with a warm smile. "Let's replace the somber images of today's events with fond memories of the past."

I returned the smile—glad that Caleb was here. I believed I wept as we crossed the graveyard...the first tears I had shed since my father's death.

THE GLOW OF THE FIREPLACE AND THE COMPANY OF LOVED ONES thawed my mother's body and warmed her disposition. Soon she became convinced that Edward's idea for my future was the best. I would go to Lynn to study the shoemaking trade as a journeyman and my mother was bound for Falmouth to spend time with her cousin.

CHAPTER 5

S pring arrived with much anticipation. The bright chorus of birds welcomed the return of emerald forests spotted with rainbow blossoms and heralded the first blush of longer days accented by fiery sunsets. This metamorphosis of seasons coincided with the transformation of my family. My mother rented out the tannery in Salem and on a sunny, breezy morning in May I bid farewell to her and we parted—she north to Falmouth and I south to Lynn.

The journey from Salem to Lynn is five miles and can be made by horse-drawn cart in just under an hour—providing it is done in fair weather. Nestled on the northern shore of Massachusetts Bay, the small town sets perched on an elevated seaboard tempered with craggy cliffs rising up from the ocean breakers. The rocky shore extends for six miles and is interspersed with cliffs, coves, beaches, and numerous bays. From the rugged coastline, Lynn spreads out westward some five miles into the woods. A dense coastal forest also forms the northern boundary of Lynn before a series of high, rocky hills spring up aligned like a fortress protecting the southern portion of the town. It is here on the long, narrow plain of southern Lynn that a network of streets cut through rows of white houses with green trees.

In addition to woods, Lynn is surrounded by a great quantity of water. A number of small lakes puncture the forest to its north; the Atlantic Ocean lies to the southeast; the river Saugus to its west; and a harbor to the south. A small peninsula, dominated by two rocky promontories known as Great and Little Nahant, leap out into the ocean from the southern side of the harbor, which is spacious but shoal, depriving Lynn of a port agreeable to large vessels. Nine miles to the south is Boston—sandwiching Lynn in between New England's two most productive ports. Seemingly situated in an unprofitable location, the town might have dabbled in obscurity if not for a flourishing iron and shoemaking industry.

As our cart entered the coastal town, we were greeted by the sentinel of Lynn—a gray moss-covered meeting-house with lofty wooden steeple surrounded by hemlock and fir trees. Rows of headstones sprung up from out of the earth behind the meeting-house, and a wooden pillory—its holes free of human limbs upon our arrival —stood firmly on the front lawn, exemplifying to what lengths one might go to achieve piety. From this building New England's main artery—Boston Street—stretched out before us, forming the backbone of Lynn as it branched off into side streets along its route through the town. Familiar proprietaries, such as blacksmith, miller, tailor, and grocer, could be found positioned in between saltbox-structured dwellings of wood with gambrel-roofs and low stone fences that predominated along the narrow street. Positioned behind these homes, a number of little wooden outbuildings—smaller than barns— stood close by every second or third dwelling. These workshops of the shoe industry were called ten-footers and numbered nearly fifty.

Half-way down a side street known as Park Street, the cart stopped in front of my uncle's modest two-story home with its own outbuilding in the rear. It was an older home with its gambrel roof sweeping down at the rear, nearly to the ground. A room was positioned on each side of the entrance and a chimney protruded from out of the center of the roof. The shingles were unbroken for any purposes of light or ventilation and the frame was of hewn oak covered with one thickness of weatherboards. The structure bespoke of warmth and once inside I felt right at home. Instantly the Browns accepted me with the same enthusiasm they displayed with their own son and I was even offered Caleb's old room—a small room set in the front of the house with a window facing the street. The room was crowded with a chair, bed, wooden desk, and a chest of drawers, leaving very little to imply that it had once belonged to Caleb with the exception of a stack of academic books gathering dust on the corner of the desk. These were piled high beneath a single wall-hanging of a map which I could not recognize.

I spent the better part of the next several days at becoming acquainted with the shoemaking industry by accompanying my uncle to work in his "manufactory"—as he would call it. Anyone nearing six feet in height needed to lower his head when climbing through the narrow doorway into the cramped quarters of the outbuilding. The daily work scene appeared routine—usually two men straddled low benches serving as worktables while my uncle supervised the operation and kept a record of orders and charges. The two journeymen worked at cutting out pieces of leather that formed the upper portion of the shoe and would tack the uppers and soles to a wooden lasting block shaped like a human foot, where they would be sewn together. Each man carried his own kit of awls, broadfaced hammers and half-moon shaped sole knives, and were very possessive about their tools, cleaning and fondling them at the end of each day as a woman caresses and clings to her jewelry.

Light proved a necessity for a shoemaker and thus the inside of the ten-footer was very bright—the result of a great number of windows set in all four walls of the outbuilding; but the hastily constructed shanty could not keep out the ferocious winds of a nor'easter. Such storms proved a nuisance in any season, and the tiny, box-shaped metal stoves of the ten-footer were little match for the frigid gale of December, January, and February. Work for a shoemaker in these bitter wintry months proved to be quite unpleasant at times. Often the chattering of teeth muffled the tapping of our hammers.

The slow, meticulous art of shoemaking could grow tiresome were it not for the gift of gab. A man who could labor all day without conversing with his fellow workers proved poor company. Thus ten-footers rivaled inns as forums for the latest colonial news ranging from local gossip on who was courting whom to heated debates over politics. It was not uncommon to find several men from off the street jammed into a ten-footer testing their ideas with the manufacturer and journeymen. The source of such information did not discriminate and hailed from men of all professions; but the most reliable source proved to be the post rider who would arrive in Lynn once a week with mail and news from beyond Lynn.

Before long, my uncle introduced me to Lynn's most famous shoe-maker, John Adam Dagyr, a Welsh immigrant who employed and trained journeymen. His shoemaking improvisation changed the craft and had put Lynn on the map. For the outbuilding, or ten-footer as many referred to it—replicated throughout Lynn—was his creation, and he had several on his property. The work inside each individual ten-footer consisted of only a single job in the preparation of the shoe —the task of a journeyman in one outbuilding might be restricted to cutting leather, while in another the job would be to puncture holes into the leather. In this way an apprentice could be exposed to all facets of shoemaking by spending time in each outbuilding. Finan-cially, Dagyr's operation was a modest one; but his unique approach at making shoes encouraged many shoemakers to take up residence in Lynn. Soon the small Massachusetts town became synonymous with shoes. With a smile and a handshake I became Dagyr's newest apprentice.

On my second day of training under the tutelage of Dagyr, my uncle provided me with a shoemaker's kit as a gift. I was a proud young man as I entered the ten-footer that morning with my own set of awls, knives and hammers—exhilarated by the new plateau that lay before me. It was as though a door had been thrust open to a new and promising chapter of my life.

On the very same day came word of the arrival of the British frigate *Romney* and suddenly mine was not the only new era springing into existence. Armed with fifty guns, the vessel's menacing presence in Boston Harbor proved to be an ominous sign of things to come as colonial hostility toward taxation began to swell throughout the colonies.

CHAPTER 6

ynn, Massachusetts – 1769

L I had grown from a boy to a young man with the passing of a year. On the outside my voice deepened, facial hair began to appear, my height reached another inch or two, and Jamesina's cooking added bulk to my frame. On the inside, my apprenticeship with John Dagyr had instilled confidence and responsibility within me. Toiling twelve hours a day, six days a week was hard work; but this experience fostered an appreciation for the power of industry—and above all, it was not long before I became a capable journeyman. My father would have been proud.

Those of us who now had acquired the skills to work for a shoe manufacturer waited for an individual—attracted by Lynn's shoemaking growth—to build a home and a manufactory and then advertise for the services of a journeyman. Some of the more impatient lads packed up their kits and wandered off to other colonial cities in search of employment. Others became cat whippers—shoemakers who moved about the countryside resoling shoes from door to door. Since I had a room and a roof over my head, I was in a much better position to bide my time and continue to work for and learn from Dagyr. The Welshman's industry expanded at a rapid pace and often I was given the task of bringing shoes to market. Thrice a month I loaded a cart with orders of new shoes bound south to Boston or north to Salem to peddle the footwear. Within these port cities, eager merchants gobbled up the shoes, unloading them to local buyers as well as sailors for market across the Atlantic.

As for my mother, we corresponded by letter each month and she visited me in Lynn twice during the year over the religious holidays. Her new home in Falmouth seemed to be very agreeable to her as she lost weight and rekindled a blithesome spirit I had not seen in years. I was saddened with each goodbye.

Despite having resided in Lynn for over a year, preoccupation with my training as a journeyman did not afford much of a social life beyond the outbuilding. I became friends of those with whom I shared the confined quarters of the workshop; but it was strictly a working relationship. Aside from recognizing a face at the Sunday service, I knew few names in the small town.

I soon discovered that accompanying my growth spurt was a new-found interest in the opposite sex. This proved to be a bothersome development since my brief contact with the females of Lynn came during the Sunday service. Often I could hardly concentrate on the three hour sermons with the young lasses seated to my left and right clad in their best Sunday dresses of colorful hooped-petticoats and long white kerchiefs. The warm spring weather persuaded some of the rather daring young ladies to arrange the triangular kerchief, draped around the neck and tied with a bright bow at the chest, so that it would reveal the cleavage of their breasts. The more I gawked at the lasses, the more I prayed; but to no avail. I do believe I even prayed for a colder summer that year.

Of all the young ladies at the Sunday service, there were two, comparable in age with my own, who seemed to hold my attention each week. With face and hands the color of ivory and long brown hair that rested softly upon her shoulders, the first young lady I speak of intrigued me not so much for her beauty, but for her character. For the poor soul was without the use of her legs; yet she appeared undaunted by her handicap as her cheery disposition remained constant. Week after week she arrived at the meeting-house with a middle-aged man dressed in the finest waistcoats and buff breeches. He would follow close behind her as she dragged her flaccid limbs down the aisle with the help of wooden crutches. In turn they were accompanied by a plump Negro woman who appeared to be the property of this man. Routinely each Sunday, the woman assisted the girl into the square-backed pew before retreating to the rear of the meeting-house. From there she would climb the steps to the loft in the gallery to take her seat in the section set aside for Negroes and Indians.

In spite of the girl's crippling condition she beamed with a perpetual smile and every hymn burst from her lungs with joyous exuberance. Watching the girl proved contagious and one could not help but smile along with her. I likened the sweet thing to a young robin with its wings clipped, chirping as if every day were the first of spring.

The other lass displayed a firm, slender and budding figure with a face of some color that indicated she spent several hours of the day in the sun unprotected. The vanity of most females would not allow for such a look, but she seemed to approach her femininity with indifference. The glow to her face was accented by freckles, and when tucked up underneath a bonnet, her shoulder-length auburn hair exposed a sleek neck of porcelain skin. I studied her calm, apathetic temperament during the Sunday services and imagined her as defiant and independent—quite a daring combination for a woman, let alone a young lady. She rarely smiled and approached the prayers and hymns with a lackluster effort. Yet I found her presence stirred excitement within me.

As fate would have it, the *three* of us would come to form an enduring triangle that would remain steadfast in a time when a sinister presence moved to expose the dark side of a town numb with naivety.

CHAPTER 7

M*ay, 1769*
Late one Saturday afternoon I had returned to Lynn from a day's work delivering shoes in Boston. Hurriedly I unhitched the horse from Dagyr's cart and fastened the reins to the horseblock before beginning a sprint through the network of streets until I arrived at the front door of Edward and Jamesina's home. My urgency had its roots in my stomach since, being that it was Saturday, I was very much looking forward to cod for dinner.

Upon throwing open the front door I was immediately engulfed by a variety of sweet aromas that had found their way from the kitchen into the small entry hall. Removing my tricorn, I tossed it over the baluster of a stairway rising three runs from the hallway and entered the doorway to my left that opened into the great room with its kitchen and dining area. A grand fireplace was positioned in the center of the room where a large iron kettle hung from a trammel above a small fire. Jamesina stood in front of a brick oven set to the left of the hearth with its iron door open and glanced over her shoulder as I entered the room. She gave me a smile and then reached inside the glowing oven with a long-handled wooden peel retrieving a steaming loaf of rye bread, and set it down in the center of an oaken table before shutting the oven door.

"In time for dinner, I see," she acknowledged, resting the peel against the wall, before wiping her hands on a white linen apron she had slung around her neck and tied at the waist.

"It smells delicious."

"Well go round back and wash up. Dinner will be served soon," Jamesina instructed, lifting the kettle's lid to inspect its contents.

"Yes, ma'am."

"Oh, I nearly forgot!" she blurted, stopping me in my tracks. "There was a gentleman stopped here this morning inquiring about thee. He was certainly well-mannered and well dressed. He seemed to be someone of importance; but I don't think he was from around these parts. His skin...it was dark—lighter than a Negro mind you—more the glow of an Indian; but he was much too dignified for a savage. And his eyes...he was blessed with the most astonishing eyes. He mentioned making your acquaintance in Salem and took it upon himself to return a cask you had lost."

"A cask?" I repeated with a disconcerting twang. I followed Jamesina's eyes and found it resting in a corner.

I stepped slowly toward the barrel as if it were some demonic object and knelt upon one knee to explore its staves. Most noticeable was the hickory binding that had been broken at one end and I stared at the damaged cask in disbelief before my stomach began to churn as images of falling to the forest floor raced through my mind. Slowly I traced my fingers over the carved initials B.P. at the cask's end. "Cyrus Eblis!" I gasped.

"Cyrus who?" Jamesina asked.

I staggered to my feet.

"Good heavens! Benjamin, you're as a white as a ghost!" Jamesina described. "Are you ill?"

"He's followed me here!" I mumbled.

"Is something the matter, Benjamin?"

Ignoring the question, I picked up the cask—still heavy from the molasses inside, and carried it through the great room and out the rear door to the back of the house.

Outside in the fading afternoon sunlight I set the container down and retrieved a wooden basin resting on top of a birchen bench and followed a narrow stone path that wound through Jamesina's small colorful garden of crown-imperials, pansies, and daffodils, stopping at a circular stone well. A wooden pail with handle attached to a long rope rested beside the well and I lifted the bucket and lowered it down into the dark hole.

The songs of chirping birds filled the air around the well; however the pleasant sound could not lift my spirits as the reappearance of the cask and the memory of Cyrus Eblis had startled me. I leaned on the edge of the well for a few moments and tried to make sense of it all; but I had no explanation.

Suddenly, when I stooped over the side of the well to retrieve the pail I heard a faint voice and pulled my head up and out of the opening to see if someone was there in the garden; but there was no-one. I leaned over the circular stone wall again and heard it once more —the voice of a boy. Only then did I realize that the voice ascended from the well and peered down into the darkness of the circular structure, although I could distinguish nothing in the black hole. And then the boy cried out my name with a frightening wail that fell away as if he were falling to the depths of the well. Awe-struck, I remained frozen for a moment, before hurriedly gathering in the bucket and sloppily filling the basin. I dashed back to the rear door of the house spilling water along the path.

Upon reaching the backdoor, I set the basin—now only half full— on top of the bench. Cupping my trembling hands, I dipped them into the bowl, scooped a handful of the cool water and splashed my perspired face. After drying my face with linen, I glanced back down into the basin and was horrified to see that the reflection looking back up at me was not my own; but I recognized it as my deceased brother Jordan's with eyes closed and hair and forehead stained with blood. My heart raced and I knocked the basin from the bench, stepping back from the spilled water as if it were diseased.

"Benjamin?!"

I spun around to find my uncle stepping from the house.

"What troubles thee?!"

Still numb with terror, my lips would not move.

"What is it son?!"

I took a breath. "I...I was...frightened!"

My uncle scanned the area. "Frightened of what?"

I hesitated and then responded with the first thing that came to mind. "A dragonfly," I lied.

"A dragonfly?" my uncle scoffed with disbelief. "The *devil's darning needle.* I think such a creature would surely be a poor match for a young man of your size," he mocked. "Come, we have a special dinner guest this evening."

"A special guest?" I replied, unable to hide the suspicion in my voice. "Is he local?"

My uncle glared back with a curious smirk. "Of what size was that dragonfly?"

I found myself at a loss for words.

"Pay no mind," he said stepping toward me and placing his arm around my shoulder. "If I were to tell you the identity of our guest, I would ruin his surprise," he added as he led me inside the house.

When we entered the great room I stopped—unnerved by the presence of a man standing with his back toward me. The stranger, who was busy assisting Jamesina in setting the table, wore a cuffless pea-green waistcoat fashioned with rounded front corners. I said nothing and waited for the guest to reveal himself much to the bewilderment of my aunt and uncle.

"Benjamin, are you feeling better?" Jamesina inquired, disclosing my presence.

The man quickly turned around in my direction. It was Caleb. A rush of relief and excitement filled my soul as I quickly paced toward my cousin and we embraced. Standing at least an inch taller than me, Caleb released his grip, placed his hands on my shoulders and stepped back within arm's reach, grinning at me. "Well cousin, it appears as though my mother's cooking has done thee well," he remarked.

"Yes, she is too good to me," I acknowledged turning toward Jamesina with a smile.

My aunt returned the compliment with a modest smirk as she set a huge smoking hotchpot filled with savory fish chowder down on a table-board. "Come boys and eat before the food grows cold. Then you may feast on one another's flattery while feasting at my table."

Our mouths watered as our eyes danced across a table cluttered with an array of delectable items—baked apple pie, homemade apple butter, oven-baked rye bread, pumpkin stewed whole in its shell, and the thick chowder mixed with corn, beans, pieces of cod, and chunks of potatoes. Each place-setting was set with pewter plates, bowls, spoons, knives, and drinking-mugs, while a large silver flagon rested beside a salt-cellar serving as the centerpiece for the table.

"Mother, would you desire us to be seated below the salt-cellar?" Caleb asked throwing me a sarcastic glance from his position across the table.

"You're all grown-up now, Caleb, but if it pleases thee," Jamesina countered.

Caleb chuckled. "What a foolish old rule—to seat the children at one end of the table below the cellar. Do you not agree, Ben?"

Before I could respond, Jamesina rebutted. "Tradition runs strong in this household, my son. Strong family bonds are built around old customs..." she continued and then glanced up at the middle timber beam that ran from end to end of the ceiling, "...like the summer-piece that supports the frame of this house."

"I remember as children how my brother and I were required to stand at the table during meals, forbidden to speak until the meal was ended," I contributed as I sat down at the table. A rush of adrenalin enveloped me as the terrified vision of my brother in the water basin filled my thoughts again.

"It doesn't surprise me, Benjamin. Your father and I were raised in a very strict household," Jamesina said, her gentle voice erasing the ghastly images from my mind. "The fruit of such discipline is witnessed by the quality of our children," she added as she worked at dipping a ladle in and out of the hotchpot, filling our bowls with the fish chowder.

When she had at last filled her own bowl, Jamesina sat down and turned toward her husband, seated at the head of the table. "Father, shall we allow our young clergyman to say grace?"

My uncle nodded and gestured toward Caleb. We bowed our heads and with an eloquent style straight from the church lectern, Caleb offered a brief thanksgiving for food and family.

After echoing Caleb's amen, my uncle, armed with a long-handled pewter spoon, helped himself to the stewed pumpkin before passing it to me.

"Caleb, what brings you to Lynn so suddenly?" I asked as I dug out a great spoonful of the steaming vegetable.

"I am passing through on my way to Salem where I am to attend a meeting," Caleb answered quickly—never lifting his eyes from the table.

"It is a religious meeting?" Edward asked.

Caleb slowly looked up and shook his head. "No."

Edward set his knife and fork down and sat back with a sigh. "Caleb, you are a gifted young man," my uncle began. "Your hard-work has been rewarded with a college degree and a congregation. I had never the opportunity to be learned in a college and thus your success has kindled a youthful fire in my bosom. Your mother and I are very proud. I am not one to question your business, for I am confident in your wisdom..."

"However...?" Caleb interjected with a smile.

"However, like I know myself, I know your passion. When discovering a cause for which to fight you are relentless in its pursuit. These are dangerous times and suspicions run high. Thus when word has it that you have been seen in the company of Samuel Adams, it is only proper that I question your judgment."

Caleb leaned across the table toward me. "Ben, have you been tutored in the shoemaker's second fine art—that of gossip?" he asked with a grin.

Edward produced a frown. "You are old enough to make your own decisions, thus I speak not as father to son, but as man to man," he offered sternly.

"Eat your chowder before it gets cold!" Jamesina scolded. "I paid two pence for a pound of cod in Salem and it would be a sin to see it go to waste over such silly bickering!"

Caleb gave his mother a smile and then glanced over at his father. "Forgive me, Father. For I mean no disrespect."

Edward found enough comfort in Caleb's apology to begin eating his chowder.

"But Father," Caleb quickly continued. "I fail to see the crime in associating with Sam Adams—a respected member of this state's legislative assembly. He is a brilliant man with bright new ideas."

"He is a member of the *Sons of Liberty*!" Edward retorted, tearing a piece of rye bread from the loaf. "They are a band of restless renegades with their fate resting at the end of the redcoat's rope!"

I stirred with excitement at Edward's mentioning of the *Sons of Liberty*, who were rapidly acquiring legendary status throughout New England. Behind the closed doors of the ten-footers, covert tidings described the dubious feats of this colonial group of activists;

although never had my uncle made mention of the rebels under the roof of his own house.

"Adams may be connected with the *Sons of Liberty*," Caleb professed. "But one man's rebel is another man's freedom fighter. We have become unwilling financiers of King George's war machine—paying taxes so he may keep his barbaric troops well-fed and well-armed to do their plundering about the globe!"

Edward bit down hard on the rye bread.

"In the eyes of King George, the American colonies exist only to serve the King," Caleb continued. "American goods are produced so that England can sell them abroad and profit from them; yet the King's greed remains unfulfilled and thus the colonies are burdened heavier with taxation!"

"I do not support taxation," Edward revealed, scratching his head nervously. "Nor do I condone the trail of depravity left by English soldiers in America; but England is the strongest empire in the world! Surely she could snuff out the slightest flicker of rebellion!"

"David prevailed over the Philistine with a sling and with a stone!" Caleb countered.

"Caleb, what is wrong with our lifestyle?" Jamesina interjected. "We have a roof over our heads; plenty to eat; and the good Lord to look after us."

Caleb reached for the flagon and poured steaming hot tea into his cup. Lifting the cup to his lips, he took a sip and then grimaced. "Mother, how long has it been since your flagons have been filled with English tea?"

Jamesina raised her brow and threw a coy glance toward Edward.

"Although it has not yet been put to vote, many of the retailers in Lynn have decided to stop purchasing tea while the Crown insists we pay the duty of three pence on a pound," Edward explained. "It would seem the Townshend duties have stirred much discontent. Recently your mother has been making tea from raspberry leaves."

"Raspberry tea?" Caleb frowned. "Mother you've answered your own question."

"But Caleb, we've become quite fond of the raspberry tea. Your father seems to enjoy it very much."

Edward acknowledged Jamesina's claim with an indecisive shrug of the shoulders. "As long as I have my ale I can get along without English tea," he explained. "Caleb, you are a man of the cloth. Religion and politics is the *devil's* recipe—mix the two and all *hell* can break loose," my uncle added smugly, handing his empty bowl to Jamesina. Quickly she replenished the bowl with a refill of the chowder.

Caleb threw both arms into the air. "Father, I could not agree more! Why then does King George profess this God-given right to meddle in the affairs of his subjects?! In doing so he has indeed unleashed all *hell* upon the colonies! It was John Locke who believed that effective government obtains power from the people it governs! The colonies lack effective government because the people are absent from the process!"

"What you speak is treason," Edward said callously, retrieving his bowl from my aunt.

Suddenly a lull appeared in the conversation and I felt the tension in the room. I saw this as my opportunity to jump in. After all, I was riddled with guilt for having begun the war of words with my inquiry into Caleb's sudden presence in Lynn.

"Caleb, who is John Locke?" I asked suddenly.

Caleb smiled at me with interest and washed down a mouthful of food with a swig of tea. "He was an English philosopher, Ben, who lived around the turn of the eighteenth century. A brilliant man was he. Dissatisfied with the English Crown as a governing body, Locke believed that all men should possess the right to choose their leaders," he said with excitement before quickly dabbing the corners of his mouth with a piece of linen. "Locke lived in an age when the rapid advances of science challenged the Christian doctrine. Most people of his day accepted one or the other as the truth. Locke, however, proposed a bold alternative—combining the two, arguing that religion and science could both be successfully applied to analyzing the problems of his day."

I was impressed with Caleb's description of Locke; but unprepared. If I would have had a response for him, I would have surely used it. As it was, I lacked my cousin's educational background and equated philosophy with boredom. Instead of continuing the conversation, I glanced over at Edward whose abrupt silence spoke loudly as his wounded ego wrestled over the previous conversation with his son.

Caleb followed my eyes and, as I knew he would, attempted to indulge the sullen patriarch.

"Father, there is nothing that gratifies me more than a healthy debate with thee," Caleb began, perking his father's interest. "And although our opinions may differ, such verbal engagements always serve to sow a seed of wisdom from which to call upon in my travels."

Caleb was splendid—a true artist at work. Watching him brought to mind the work of a craftsman, such as a shoemaker—using the talent within his hands to fashion a shoe. His words were sincere, for his gift was one of charm and integrity—using such personal attributes to mold and sway the opinions and attitudes of ordinary people.

"I realize that the Crown is not entirely fond of the *Sons of Liberty*," Caleb continued. "Rest assured, father, I have no immediate intentions of becoming an outlaw."

Edward acknowledged Caleb's mending words with a nonchalant nod of the head and some indistinguishable jargon—mumbled after placing a large piece of apple pie in his mouth. After taking a gulp of tea, my uncle turned toward me. "Benjamin, I have good news."

I was surprised.

"Emery Kerstland, a friend, has need of a journeyman in his manufactory. He is a respected member of this community whose parents were some of Lynn's first inhabitants, and, might I add, first shoemakers. In fact his is the original shop opened by the first Kerstland in America. It is located at the southern end of Lynn and holds more comforts than a ten-footer."

"And...?" I pressed with great anticipation.

"And he expects you tomorrow at dawn. The wages are fifteen shillings a week."

"This is wonderful!" I exclaimed.

"I've already spoken to Dagyr and he wishes you good fortune," my uncle added.

"Thank you, Uncle Brown!"

"Don't thank me, Benjamin," Edward responded. "Your hard work for Dagyr has not gone unnoticed by many townsfolk. Your employment is well-deserved."

It was not uncommon for an apprenticeship to last four or five years. So uncle's announcement of my new employment with Emery Kerstland proved to be an exciting revelation. Nothing, it seemed, could spoil the moment…and then came the wind. A powerful gust of wind blew open the front door and burst into the dining area from the entry hall, nearly pulling the second door from its hinges. The blast of air rattled Jamesina's decorative collection of silver porringers from their hooks on the edge of a shelf and sent them crashing to the floor.

"What in *blazes*?!" Jamesina cried out.

The wind bounced from wall to wall like a caged animal before the cold rush of air passed through us, sweeping across the dinner table and displacing a number of items in its wake. It whirled about the center of the room directly overhead for a second or two before being drawn to the fireplace. Inside the hearth it extinguished the small fire and was pulled up the chimney with a high shrill.

"That would be the strangest…!" Edward began.

"Father…" Caleb interrupted, rising slowly from the chair with his eyes transfixed to the open dining room door, "…we have a visitor."

Standing in the entry hall the faint light of dusk revealed the silhouette of a tall figure in a round hat.

"Who goes there?!" Edward demanded.

The room grew silent.

"Pardon my intrusion," the stranger remarked, standing faceless in the shadows. "I intended for to knock; however the sudden burst of wind threw open the door and invited me in."

"What can we do for you?" Edward asked.

Slowly the stranger removed his wide brimmed hat. "I've recently acquired a place of residence in this charming little town of yours. As it so happens that I manufacture *soles*, I am in need of a journeyman. It has come to my attention that your boarder, Benjamin Pratt, might have an interest in such employment."

I didn't need a face to recognize the stranger and neither did Jamesina.

"I believe it is Benjamin's friend!" my aunt blurted. "Come and share some dinner and tea," she offered.

"No!" I exclaimed, jumping up quickly, startling my aunt and uncle. "I mean…I have found work, sir…I mean…!"

"How soon we forget, Benjamin. The name is Cyrus Eblis," the stranger interjected, still faceless in the shadows.

"Good friend, thy timing is somewhat unfortunate," my uncle

explained. "Benjamin was offered employment only this afternoon, and has accepted."

Initially the stranger said nothing. The silence probably lasted only a few seconds but it seemed like hours.

"Very well then," Eblis uttered slowly. "I thank you Mrs. Brown for the tempting offer of tea. Perhaps at a later date we can share pleasantries. Benjamin," he added harshly as he returned the hat to his head. "It pleases me so to see you again. My offer for your services is always open."

I could feel Eblis' icy smile cut right through me. Just then the dining room door swung shut of its own power obstructing our view of the dark stranger. Caleb leaped from the table and rushed to the entry hall to be sure the front door had also closed, while Jamesina pranced over to the window.

"How odd," Jamesina mumbled still peering out the window as Caleb re-entered the great room and returned to his seat at the table. "He has left the entry hall has he not, Caleb?"

"Yes. He's gone. I didn't see him."

"Nor did I. Surely I would have seen him leave by way of the front gate?" Jamesina surmised still peering out the window. "It's as if he vanished into thin air."

"Benjamin, I found your behavior unbecoming!" Edward denounced. "The gentleman came to offer you employment and you rejected him with the least semblance of appreciation! And yet you are an acquaintance of this man? Be it known, guests are treated with respect under this roof!"

"I apologize, Uncle."

"Now Father, let's not be so hasty in scolding Ben," Caleb defended. "Am I not the only one who detected fear in Ben's response to this Cyrus fellow? Fear is hardly a quality from which friendships are forged."

"I am not afraid of him," I lied.

"What is your explanation, Benjamin?" Jamesina asked, now on her knees at the opposite end of the room busily gathering her fallen porringers. "And what of this cask?"

"What cask?" Edward inquired.

I felt cornered. "Caleb is right...Master Eblis...that is what he calls himself...is hardly a friend." I thought it best to be reserved lest my sanity be called into question. "A short time before my father's death I met him one afternoon in Salem. He helped me..." I paused to choose my words carefully, remembering that I had stolen the container, "... retrieve a cask of molasses which, in my hurry, I left behind. Eblis returned it this morning."

The blank stares of my aunt and uncle indicated they were unconvinced.

"He helped you retrieve a cask of molasses...and returned the lost item to you this morning?" my uncle repeated. "Your father has been dead some time now. What is so important about a cask of molasses that a man would hold onto it for over a year before returning it to you?"

"I don't know," I grumbled. "I cannot help but feel that there is something evil about this man."

"Evil?" Edward repeated sardonically. "Eblis might be an eccentric fellow, I'll give you that, but evil?" my uncle questioned as he rose from his chair and stepped over to the fireplace. Reaching up onto the mantle, which was set just high enough from the floor that he could touch it while standing on his toes, my uncle ran his hand across the smooth wooden mantel-shelf until locating the circular tinder-box. With the fire extinguished and the shadows of dusk descending upon the room, he realized the need for light and brought the object over to the table, removing the flint, steel, and scorched linen from inside the box. He set a candle down in front of him and began the arduous task of catching a spark struck by the clash of flint and steel.

"Benjamin, has Master Eblis done you harm?" Jamesina asked.

"No...I...I just don't trust him," I stammered and then looked across the table at Caleb for help.

"Mother, please pass me some of that delicious apple pie," my cousin requested. "We all have our suspicions," he added. "Some of us even tend to suspect prominent colonial legislative members of involvement in revolutionary groups. Is that not right, Father?"

My uncle looked up with an irritating frown.

Caleb continued. "I will say this, Master Eblis' entrance was certainly eerie."

"Caleb, have you forgotten the temperament of the North wind?" Edward challenged, preoccupied with the flint and steel.

"Then let me say, it is the timing of Master Eblis' entrance that I find to be certainly eerie," Caleb corrected.

"Well, whatever it may be that has my young nephew spooked by our new neighbor, I'm certain time will change his opinion," Jamesina punctuated with a warm smile as she replaced the last porringer. "Besides, Benjamin begins his new job tomorrow and needs to keep his mind clear."

"Tell me, Benjamin," Edward began, still engaged in catching a spark. "Had there been no offer for employment from Emery Kerstland, would you have accepted the offer from Cyrus Eblis?"

"I would have not."

A few moments later my uncle ignited the linen and passed the flame to the candlewick. The remainder of the meal was finished in silence.

CHAPTER 8

Later that evening after Edward and Jamesina had retired upstairs for the night, I found myself stretched out on the wooden floor in front of the hearth and its dying fire. The spring night had grown considerably cooler and so Caleb tossed another log onto the flames which enhanced the rosy glow of the room. Propping my head up against one of Jamesina's hand woven quilts, I whittled a piece of wood with my Jack-knife as the crackling flames threw dancing shadows off the walls. Caleb gave my crossed feet a playful kick as he strode past me and stepped over to a rocking chair.

"I've heard of the *Sons of Liberty*," I acknowledged. "They are talked about around the shop."

Caleb offered a coy grin as he sat down. "And what is said?"

"Oh, some like your father believe them to be criminals and restless youth, while others believe they have good cause."

"It will be difficult to unite all of the people."

"Unite them in what way?"

Caleb sighed and looked to the ceiling, maintaining a rhythmic rocking motion in the chair. "There is a great storm brewing, Ben. Colonial dissent is mounting like a great thunderhead and the King has turned a deaf ear to the thunder."

"I hear talk of battle. Do you really believe men would die for taxes?"

"It's not just taxes, Ben. It's freedom. Yes, men would die for freedom."

"You told your father you do not belong to the *Sons of Liberty?*"

Caleb ceased rocking and shifted his weight to the edge of the rocker, drawing my attention. "Shhh.." he cautioned, holding his index finger over his lips. "I would hate to burden my father with more than he needs to know; but I have not lied, Ben."

"But the meeting you are to attend?"

"It does not involve the *Sons of Liberty*. It is a general meeting of concerned New England citizens who are actively following this growing storm I speak of," Caleb enlightened, continuing to whisper. "Nevertheless, it remains dangerous since the Crown has pledged to silence the voices of dissent. The speaker at the meeting is John Hancock—the man whose ship, *Liberty*, was seized by the redcoats this year last. My mother and father do not understand such matters so it is best not to worry them. Much is happening beyond the streets of Lynn. Sometimes I wonder if Lynn is not suspended in time—a village of shoemakers whose sole contact with the world outside is, well...it's soles!"

"Clever," I acknowledged.

"For example, are you aware that only recently the royal governor of Virginia dissolved the House of Burgesses? In doing so the governor has denied Virginians active participation in their own government! It was punishment because Virginia has joined other American colonies in their refusal to purchase imported English goods until the repeal of the Townshend Acts. These are serious crimes by the Crown and warrant serious actions!"

"Lest a local need reminded of the Townshend Acts, there is Ian McMahon who hasn't stopped complaining since *Newhall's Tavern* ceased serving his favorite brand of Scotch whiskey," I countered.

"And my mother's tasteless raspberry tea," Caleb added as he bounced up from the rocking chair. He paced toward the hearth and stopped, peering into its flames. "A new dawn awaits this continent!" he said impassionedly. "God help us if war is in His plans! And if it must be war, we can only pray that out of the raging fires of conflict there will emerge a new government—a Christian government of the people. John Locke wrote that the chief goal of man is to enjoy happiness in this world and in the next. A government removed from the tyrannical grasp of the King and placed in the hands of the people will be a great leap toward such goals! It will be exciting, and I want very much to have a role in such a government."

"As a politician?"

"No. Simply as a Christian. My role as a minister not only affords me the opportunity to profess the word of the Lord, but is also one of influence," Caleb said spinning away from the fire and toward me. "Many prominent colonial statesmen and outspoken critics of the King are active Christians. My position has given me the opportunity to build relationships with such men."

"Like Samuel Adams," I responded quickly.

"Yes...like Samuel Adams." Caleb turned back toward the fire. "There are many minds and souls that can be reached from the lectern. The ministry can be a powerful and inspirational instrument in such troubled times as these."

A man's voice from out in the street interrupted us. It was the bell-man and we paused to listen to his familiar tidings. "Ten o'clock and all's well!" he called out.

Caleb turned away from the fire and made his way back to the rocking chair. Always in control of his emotions, my cousin's fiery analysis of the current political climate seemed so out of character. His nature was one of subtle persistence in the quest of matters that interested him, not the quick, opinionated defender that preached to the hearth and dominated the dinner conversation earlier in the evening. It was a side to my cousin that I had not seen before—a side that disturbed me and so I decided to change the subject.

"Hanging from a wall in your room, where I am staying, is a map. I do not recognize it," I inquired.

Caleb thought for a moment and then smiled. "It is a map of ancient Persia."

"Persia?" I was unsure. "I've heard of it, but..."

"At one time it was a great empire located in the Middle East. Today it separates the Ottoman Empire from India," Caleb informed —his voice now much more sedate. "I came across the map as a young lad while in Boston. My mother and I had gone to market when I happened upon a sailor asleep in an alley. The man laid across the hard cobblestone with his flat cocked hat pulled down over his eyes and his head resting on a large burlap sack. Unaccustomed to seeing a man asleep in the busy city streets, I believed him to be dead. To test my assumption, I dropped an apple on his chest." Caleb grinned and fell back in the chair. "Well the man jumped up half scared to death! When he realized what had happened, he gave me such a foul tongue lashing that I cried. As it turned out the sailor's ship was ready to pull out to sea and he would have missed the boat had I not awakened him. In an effort to silence my crying and as a gesture of thanks, the sailor handed me a rolled piece of faded parchment and disappeared. It was the map.

"Although I found the map unrecognizable at first, I became fascinated by the intricate detail of its lines and intrigued by the names of distant lands. Throughout my schooling I became obsessed with the knowledge of Persia and continued to study the ancient land in my days at Yale. As a result, I could spend hours boring thee with tales of Darius, Xerxes, and the wonders of Babylon. It has become a hobby of mine."

"It is a strange hobby for a minister," I countered.

"Speaking of strange, your story of the cask at dinner this evening certainly fits the description."

I set the Jack-knife and stick down at my side, folding my arms behind my head. "Caleb, do you believe in the devil?"

Caleb laughed. "My good cousin, if there were no devil there would exist no ministry."

"But I mean really believe!" I emphasized, sitting up. "There is a girl that I watch at the service each Sunday who I would not consider to be religious. She does not partake in the prayers and seems to be burdened by being there; but, even so, she takes her seat in the meeting-house each Sunday since it is what she is supposed to do. A minister is supposed to preach the word of God and condemn the devil. Do you really believe Satan exists?" I persisted.

"Yes...I believe the devil to exist," Caleb replied convincingly. "Ben, surely you do not believe this Eblis fellow to be the devil?"

"He is evil. I am convinced of this."

"Ben, times have changed and people have more sense than they did one hundred years before. But if such an accusation reaches the wrong ears there may be those—even in this day and age—willing to try you as a witch and hang you from the great oak in Salem!"

"That is where he took me! The hanging tree in Salem!" I blared, rising to a position on my knees. "He said he had been there before and enjoys celebrating the anniversary of the witch hangings!"

Caleb sat back. "That is certainly strange. Just how did you come to meet this Eblis?"

"A few months before father's death, I took a cask of molasses from the back of the grocer Wrigglenecke's cart and ran off into the woods..."

"Benjamin Pratt! You stole a cask of molasses?!" Caleb interrupted with raised eyebrows and a large grin. "I would never have pictured you the boy thief."

"It was wrong of me," I admitted.

"Don't let it trouble you," Caleb advised calmly. "Romans says: '*For all have sinned, and come short of the glory of God.*'"

I reached for my Jack-knife again and turned it nervously within my hand. "Well, I took the cask and stumbled into Eblis in the middle of the forest. After he persuaded me to carve my initials into the cask, I was led to the hanging tree. There he frightened me with talk of madness and then vanished! He even produced a fire in the palm of his hand!"

"A magician?"

"I tell you Caleb, I watched him vanish into thin air! I turned my head for a moment and when I turned back around, all that remained was a sudden gust of wind!"

"Like this evening?"

"Yes. I was so frightened that I left the cask in the forest and ran home!"

"Did you see him again?"

"Yes, at my father's funeral. He was alone in the distance."

"Did you confront him?"

"He vanished!" I replied, watching Caleb's face remain expressionless. "I didn't see him again until this evening. And this afternoon, after two years, he returned the cask!"

"Where is it?"

"It rests out back. I'm tempted to toss it in the ocean!"

Caleb sighed, rubbing his fingers over his chin. "It is an eerie tale, I'll give it that, but I wouldn't go about calling him the devil just yet," he cautioned. "There are worse sins committed every day that might warrant a visit from Satan, but not the theft of molasses."

"I agree! Why then does he continue to haunt me so?!" I exclaimed, picking up the whittled stick and tossing it into the fire. "And, stranger still," I added, turning back toward Caleb, "I believe I heard Jordan at the well this afternoon and I am certain it was his reflection I saw in the water basin!"

"Jordan? Your deceased brother?" Caleb asked, now with a tone of disbelief.

I nodded. "Do you think the souls of my father and brother are suffering in Hades?"

"Ben, your father was a good man and your brother was too young to encounter the sins of the world," Caleb reassured. "They are with the Lord."

"Then, am I mad?!" I asked, rising to my feet.

Caleb hesitated. "No, my good cousin. You are not mad. I believe you are over-worked; guilt-ridden by thoughts of taking that cask; concerned about your mother; and plagued by your father's sudden death."

Disheartened by my cousin's quick diagnosis, I sighed.

Caleb rose from the chair and placed his arm around my shoulder as I stared into the burning hearth. "Ben, for now do your best to avoid Eblis. If your troubles with him persist, then write me in Simsbury," he advised with a smile. *'The Lord shall preserve thee from all evil: he shall preserve thy soul.'"*

Outside the bell-man passed again. "Half past the hour and all's well!"

CHAPTER 9

U nlike the outbuildings of Dagyr's operation or those on the grounds of my uncle's property, there were shoemakers about Lynn whose work was conducted within a small one-room shop with its front door opening into the main street. Such shops were easily recognizable by the large wooden boot that hung outside above the entrance. These were operated by the descendants of Lynn's original shoemakers and some of their establishments were a century or more old. The work force of such shoemakers usually consisted of family, and they lived under the master's roof with the living quarters located on the second floor and to the back of the shop.

Emery Kerstland's shop fell into such a category and as my uncle had explained to me, his work place contained more comforts than the outbuildings. A large hearth warmed the shop in the winter and the nectarous aroma of cooked food emerging from the kitchen—located to the back of the work place—proved a pleasant substitute for the lingering odor of wet leather. It was here that I found myself on the following morning at dawn, standing quietly as my new employer clad in a leather apron, explored the contents of my wooden journeyman's kit.

"Clean tools," Kerstland muttered. "One can tell much of a person by the appearance of his tools."

A man of average height with a strong build, Kerstland scratched the bald spot on the top of his head and peered at me through a pair of round spectacles. "So you are the nephew of Edward Brown?" he remarked. "Good stock in that Brown family. Caleb is a fine young man."

Kerstland stepped before the shop window and the rays of the morning sun produced a silvery sheen on the hair at the side and back of his head. Stopping near the wall, the shoemaker reached up and waved his hand at a large black cat resting on a wooden shelf. The cat hissed and leapt from its position landing daintily upon a nearby table.

"That's Angel," Kerstland introduced, reaching up and retrieving a smoking pipe and a tobacco pouch from the shelf. "She belongs to my daughter, but I don't mind her company. She clears the shop of mice." He gathered a pinch of tobacco from out of the pouch and pressed it into the bowl of the pipe. "Do you speak?" he asked sarcastically.

I was unprepared. "Yes...Master Kerstland."

"Good. I was beginning to wonder," he joked as he reached for the iron pipe-tongs hanging from a nail in the wall. "This shop is a might bit different from those ten-footers, is it not?"

"Yes. Quite different."

"Kerstlands have been shoemakers here in Lynn since the year sixteen forty-six. Now I don't claim that my operation is more successful than others in Lynn, such as Dagyr and your uncle— because it's not. With only one journeyman in my employ at present, I cannot compete with the numbers of shoes that they produce. And as the colonies continue to grow, so will the shoe industry in Lynn," Kerstland explained, pacing over to the fireplace where a small fire burned. Using the pipe-tongs, the shoemaker pulled a glowing coal from the fire. He placed the pipe stem in his mouth, held the coal to the tobacco within the pipe bowl and puffed on the stem several times before he was certain the tobacco caught fire.

"The success of my business lies with tradition," Kerstland continued. "As a man relies upon his own tailor for the proper fit in coats and breeches, Kerstland shoes have been in the same families for generations. It is these same families that look for the Kerstland quality in shoemaking—a quality that ye father's father sought many years before."

Kerstland took a seat on a work bench as the air of the shop filled with the sweet scent of cherry tobacco. "I mentioned I employ a journeyman," the shoemaker explained, removing the pipe out from in between his lips and blowing a ring of smoke into the air. "The lad's been called home to Salem due to the sudden death of his mother."

"This is tragic," I offered.

"Yes...however one man's misfortune is another man's gain," Kerstland countered massaging the back of his neck. "I have only a few rules, Benjamin. Yet a violation of any one rule may affect your employment within this shop. Is this understood?"

"Yes, Master Kerstland."

The shoemaker replaced the pipe in between clenched teeth. "You must be punctual; of good moral-standing; and provide regular attendance at the Sunday service," he said.

"Yes, Master Kerstland."

"Good. Then welcome," Kerstland added with a smile and a handshake. "Well, there's work to be done. There's a cart loaded with casks of leather outside in the alley. You can get started by assisting Sam in unloading the cart."

I stepped outside and turned into the alley that ran adjacent to Kerstland's shop where I found a two-wheeled cart loaded with a dozen casks. Standing on top of the cart was a thin boy clad in breeches and a vest that appeared two-sizes too large—even his tricorn drooped low covering the tips of his ears, resting just above the eyebrows. With the sleeves of his white shirt rolled up to his elbows, the boy worked at sliding a cask over to the edge of the cart.

"Sam?" I asked. The boy stopped, turned toward me and pressed the sagging tricorn up from out of his eyes. "I'm Benjamin Pratt, the new..."

"Journeyman," he finished with a scowl. "Well don't just stand there! Lend me a hand, journeyman!" he said mockingly with a high pitched voice.

Sam continued to slide the casks to the edge of the cart where I began the process of hoisting a container of leather upon my shoulder and carrying it into the shop. As we worked at clearing the cart, we spoke not a word to one another, and finding this to be very awkward, I decided to spark a little conversation.

"In what capacity are you employed by Master Kerstland?" I pried.

"Journeyman, save your words for interested ears," Sam replied sharply without looking up. "The more labor of the tongue, the less labor gets done."

Angered by this remark, I stopped working and placed my hands at my hips. "You're not very pleasant, are you?" I growled.

Sam smirked and then shoved a cask off the cart forcing me to react in catching it to prevent it from dropping to the ground. "Only seven more to go, journeyman!" he barked. "And then you are rid of me."

I clenched my teeth and turned away from the cart.

Several casks later, I waited at the edge of the cart, but Sam had stopped and so I looked up to learn the reason for the delay. "Come on!" I exclaimed, realizing that my partner seemed to be preoccupied with a man crossing the street. Wearing a tattered and dusty black coat and a black tricorn, the slouching man hobbled across the cobblestone, and as he glanced back over his shoulder in our direction, I noticed a black patch covered his left eye. He sneered at us before turning away and entered another shoemaker's shop.

"Come on!" I repeated and reached up, grabbing Sam's ankle. He responded by stomping on my hand, forcing me to cry out and release my grip on him. I groaned and placed both hands on the cart in an attempt to hoist myself up onto it; but Sam countered my attack by rolling another cask at me, blocking my ascent. I made a second attempt but was stopped this time by a girl's laughter. Spinning around, my eyes beheld a pretty blond haired girl, who I assumed was at least my age or older, dressed in a bright blue bonnet and matching colored dress, standing in the street having a good laugh at my expense. I could feel my face warm with embarrassment and politely tipped my tricorn in her direction. She responded with a slight wave of her hand, but as I began to respond with a wave of my own, I realized that she was waving to Sam and not me. She shook her head and continued walking as I stood frozen, with my eyes on the young lass, until she disappeared from sight.

"You have made me appear the fool!" I yelled, turning toward Sam.

"You didn't need me to look the fool!" Sam replied. "Don't be alarmed...it's only Master Kerstland's daughter!"

"Kerstland's daughter?!" I was mortified. Turning around, again I worked at climbing the cart and this time I tossed aside a cask Sam had moved in front of me as I mounted the vehicle. "Now I shall teach you a lesson in respect!" I boasted.

Sam ducked and tried to slip by me but I reached out and wrapped my left arm around his neck, knocking the tricorn from his head. Just as I prepared to deliver a blow with my fist to his stomach, I noticed the considerable length of Sam's hair that now hung down without the aid of the tricorn to conceal it and I grabbed a section of the auburn locks with my fingers, finding it to be soft and fine. Releasing my hold of Sam's neck, I pulled my partner into an upright position and stepped back to examine him. Gazing into hazel eyes accented by a freckled face, I was surprised to discover that Sam was not a he, but a she. And not just any she; but the girl I had grown accustomed to gloating over during the Sunday service.

"You're...you're...a girl!"

"Brilliant deduction!" she remarked cynically as she reached down and retrieved her tricorn. Quickly she placed the hat back upon her head and tucked her hair up underneath it.

"I'm sorry...I didn't know...I mean, how could I've known...?!" I stammered.

"Never mind. We best finish unloading this cart before my father begins to wonder what is taking so long."

"Your father? Your father is Master Kerstland?!"

"Yes. Now come on, let's finish!" she appealed, reaching down to slide another cask across the cart.

"Wait!" I cautioned, now full of questions. "What is your name and why do you dress as a boy?"

She sighed. "Journeyman, we must finish!" she persisted.

"The name is Benjamin," I corrected. "And I refuse to unload any more of these casks until you've told me the truth."

"And risk the security of your employment?"

"As much a risk as you take," I shot back. "What a grand story to be told around the shops of Lynn of Master Kerstland's daughter who desires to dress as a boy."

The girl produced a look of contempt and placed her hands on her hips. "My name is Samantha Kerstland."

"Samantha," I repeated with a grin. "And why the boy's clothing?"

She glowered. "To look as a boy, of course! For seven years I have worked in my father's shop."

"You've worn a disguise for seven years?"

"No. Only recently and only when I work outdoors."

"Why?"

"Because it is no place for a girl! Everyone in this town has their roles defined for them. If you're something you're not supposed to be —people talk."

"And you're afraid of what people may think?"

"Of course not," she replied indignantly. "It is my father's reputation that I worry about—his business. There has been many a young journeyman, such as you, seeking employment over the last seven years. Had they known there was no job opportunity available in the Kerstland shop because a girl was doing a man's work, it may have angered a few and hurt my father's business."

"There are girls who sew in the shoemaker's shop," I pressed.

"Yes, but sewing is a woman's responsibility. You would not find my mother or sister out here unloading this cart or beating leather soles with a hammer. Spinning and reeling; weaving and cooking; candle and cheese making," she rattled off with disgust, "such is woman's work. I have little interest in such duties. I enjoy working outdoors in the sunshine with the tools of a shoemaker; a carpenter; a cooper—but I speak of man's work.

"So I've masqueraded as a journeyman to help my father; but now he insists that I assume the role that God has blessed me with," she said with disdain. "For I can no longer play the part of a young boy," she explained, now blushing.

"And your departure is my gain?"

"Yes...Benjamin."

"And the lass you referred to as Master Kerstland's daughter?"

"It is my older sister, Muriel. Do you think she's pretty?"

"Yes...I mean," I hesitated, choosing my words carefully. "I don't know...maybe."

Samantha scoffed. "Let's get back to work," she encouraged and reached down to move a cask.

"Now be careful, Samantha. The casks are heavy..."

Samantha snarled and pushed me from the cart.

"What have I done now?!"

"Don't patronize me, Benjamin Pratt!" she exclaimed, shaking a finger at me.

"Forgive me," I apologized. "I promise it shan't happen again...Sam."

I returned to assisting Samantha with the cask removal, energized now by her presence and preoccupied with her femininity, when suddenly I was distracted by the clicking of horseshoes against cobblestone. I stopped my chore and turned to view the horse and its rider, sensing both had drawn near to me. With delight I recognized Caleb saddled atop a black steed.

"My cousin the journeyman," Caleb acknowledged with a smile and looked up at Sam. "Good morning," he greeted.

Samantha smiled slightly and nodded.

"Caleb Brown, this is Saman...Sam," I introduced. "*He* is another of Master Kerstland's employees."

Caleb tipped his hat in the direction of Samantha and leaned over his horse, extending his hand which I shook. "Well, I'm bound for Salem, Ben. Here, I have something for you," he said reaching inside of his waistcoat and withdrawing a small book. He handed me the work with black leather cover and I quickly flipped through the pages, recognizing it as a Bible. "Remember to write me in Simsbury regarding last evening's conversation. And when your pen fails you, I suggest Psalm ninety-one. I have folded the page as a marker."

"Thank you," I said.

"I bid you farewell," Caleb added as he righted himself upon the horse and addressed Sam. "It's been a pleasure, Sam. I am certain my cousin will be exceptional company."

Sam forced a smile.

"Caleb, take care and Godspeed," I said, slipping the Good Book into the back pocket of my breeches.

Caleb pulled on the horse's reins and guided the mare out into the main street where it broke into a steady trot as it headed south out of town.

"Thank you for not saying anything," Sam remarked. "I wasn't very nice to you earlier, and I deserved less."

"Don't mention it," Ben said with a smile.

Sam returned the smile and then looked beyond me. Suddenly the warm glow of her face faded as she became preoccupied with events across the street once again.

I followed her vexation and turned to find the man with the eye patch now exiting the shoemaker's shop. The stranger shuffled across the street and was moving in our direction, clutching the end of a sack that had been thrown over his left shoulder.

"Oh, no..." Samantha uttered under her breath and quickly turned to slide another cask across the cart.

"What is it, Sam?"

"Never mind. Pay no attention to him," she mumbled.

When I turned back around the man was on top of me. "Good day lads," he acknowledged with a scratchy delivery that erupted into a wretched laughter.

"Good day, "I replied apprehensively, peering at the severe looking man. He was plagued with a crooked nose and a large scar that originated from underneath the eye patch, running the length of his cheek.

Sam did not respond nor did she look in the man's direction.

The man dropped his sack to the ground and pounded the side of the cart with his right fist. "Where's your manners, lad?!" he hollered at Sam. "I said good day!"

She never lifted her head but acknowledged his presence with a soft, "Good day."

The man broke into his annoying laughter once again with a breath that produced such a foul stench that I thought surely it could make a horse whine. He scratched strands of white hair jutting out from underneath his tricorn and flakes of dried skin fell upon the shoulders of his dark coat. Sneering, he looked me over with his good eye, bulging and bloodshot.

"Pratt," he addressed, running his tongue over parched lips and surprising me with knowledge of my identity. "My employer bids thee greetings."

I hesitated. "Who...is your employer?"

The man grinned and belched out the name, "Cyrus Eblis."

I was startled and the horrid little man sensed it.

"Yes, yes! That's right! Cyrus Eblis!" The man raised his hand and turned, pointing across the street. "Yonder lies his shop!" he yapped and lowered his arm, resting it upon my shoulder. I held my breath.

"Don't be a stranger, now," he whispered. "It wouldn't be polite."

Lifting his arm from my shoulder, the man turned away before throwing one final scowl in the direction of Sam, and hoisted the sack back up and over his shoulder. With a disgusting belch that seemed to set his legs in motion, he moved away from the cart and proceeded down the alley disappearing around the corner.

CHAPTER 10

It was said that the smile returned to Adrian Lyttleton's face when the pine box containing the corpse of his wife had been lowered into her final resting place. For the meek, somber-faced English immigrant, life in America proved terribly bitter wrought from an unhappy marriage perpetuated by a nagging wife. Large in stature, overbearing in character, and immensely obstinate, Adrian's better half was anything but. Her domineering presence about the Lyttleton shop had reduced her husband's vocabulary to little more than a servile, "Yes, dear."

Chained by a marriage vow to a life of torment, the apothecary of Lynn had no-one to blame but himself. For Adrian's spouse hailed from a wealthy English family and so his greed supplanted the compatibility of matrimony. Throughout the early days of their marriage, Adrian learned to tolerate his discordant wife with the realization that each passing day brought his wealthy in-laws—declining in health—closer to eternal rest and the Lyttleton's closer to their inheritance.

When Adrian's in-laws expired only hours apart, it was then that the submissive husband realized that his luck was bad. To his and his wife's utter astonishment, they discovered that their anticipated benefactors had splurged their fortune and died nearly penniless. Instead of leaping into financial security, the inauspicious Lyttletons plummeted into a position of poverty, receiving little more in the way of inheritance than just enough to make a fresh start of it in America.

Shortly after the end of Britain's war with the French and Indians on the

American continent, the Lyttleton's set sail for colonial Massachusetts. Lacking trade skills, Adrian had dabbled a little at preparing medicines while in England and upon settling in the town of Lynn, he decided to draw upon his meager experience and open a store where he could prepare, prescribe, and peddle medicines to the ailing. He deemed himself an apothecary, which was not uncommon at this time, since no candidate needed to be licensed. With an English text of patented medicines at his side, Lyttleton might combine Scotch Pills and Godfrey's British Oil with Native American roots and herbs such as mayapple, sassafrass, and slippery elm, to concoct a medicine that, with a little luck, could cure an ailing woodsman.

Initially, Lyttleton's new-found career afforded him and his wife enough money to make a comfortable living in Lynn. Then the arrival of a more credible physician a year later coaxed business away from Adrian and the comfort he had known seemed to vanish overnight. Making matters worse was that the nagging continued. There were no more dreams of quick wealth to muffle his squabbling wife. Day after day her bickering resounded inside his head like the relentless explosion of cannon.

Then suddenly one chilly wintry morning Adrian's spouse approached the apothecary with a headache of her own, compounded by fever and chills. Adrian knew just what to prescribe—a soothing syrup known as elixir paregoricum, which was a complex mixture of opium, honey, licorice, benzoic acid, camphor, oil of anise, potassium carbonate, and alcohol. As he worked behind the wooden counter of his shop measuring, weighing, and finally mixing the ingredients with stone mortar and pestle, his wife complained with a jangling voice. She complained of her headache; of the weather; of the appearance of the shop; and of the speed at which he worked; but when she regretted their marriage with an acidic tongue, the final cannon burst. At that point Adrian reached beneath the counter and retrieved a small unmarked bottle. He had prepared the poison hemlock for such a moment but had yet to find the courage to use it. Pulling the cork from the bottle, he poured the powdery contents into the stone mortar and continued his mixing. Sweat began to form on his brow and anxiety accelerated his breathing. He glanced up at his barking wife who seemed so engrossed with her bellicosity that she suspected nothing.

Adrian's heart pounded as he dumped the syrup into a cup of cider and handed it to his wife. She snatched the cup from his trembling hand with the swiftness of a striking serpent and quickly drank the cider.

Adrian remained motionless as he watched her slam the empty cup down on the counter. Quickly the apothecary rushed toward the door and bolted it before drawing the wooden blinds of the store windows. When he turned around, his wife glared at him with a thankless look—one he had seen a thousand times before and he chuckled inside thinking how at last it seemed such an appropriate look. Suddenly she gasped, clutching her throat with both hands as her face altered colors like the skin of a reptile. Bulging eyes rolled back inside of her head and she shook violently before crashing to the floor.

Adrian stepped slowly over to the body that lay motionless. Reaching down he lifted her wrist, feeling for a pulse. The soothing syrup with hemlock had worked; for Adrian raised his head and listened to the silence of the room. Then he grinned.

DUSK FELL UPON THE TOWN OF LYNN AS THE REPULSIVE MAN WITH the eye patch arrived at the home of Adrian Lyttleton. The apothecary had just returned home from work at his store when he heard the knock on his door. Irritated by the thought of a visitor at the end of his work day, Lyttleton growled as he threw open the front door to find Patch standing at his doorstep with a wide grin and a burlap bag slung over his shoulder.

"And who might you be?" Adrian asked.

The revolting man snickered. "Call me Patch," he grinned.

Adrian did not find the nickname amusing. "Well man, then what is it that you want?" he asked annoyingly.

"Thy soles are ready," Patch replied, snickering again.

"Soles?"

"From the shoemaker, Cyrus Eblis."

"Ah, yes," Adrian remembered. "Come inside."

Adrian winced from a whiff of Patch's foul body odor as the grubby man shuffled past him and stepped inside. Making his way to the center of the small main room of the house, the odd delivery man dropped the burlap sack onto the wooden floor in front of the fireplace. He glanced about the room and slowly paced toward the cold hearth, drawn to the variety of iron pots hanging from trammels attached to a wooden back-bar extending across the fireplace beneath the opening in the chimney.

"It tis odd to set eyes upon a cold hearth at this hour of the day," Patch remarked. "Your woman must be away?"

"There is no woman," Adrian replied quickly.

"Hmm..." Patch remarked with surprise. "A man without a wife is like a captain without a compass—charting a blind course through lonely seas."

"My wife is dead," Adrian replied quickly and callously.

"So you are lost at sea," Patch countered with a smirk.

Adrian grew perturbed. "I have no time for this conversation..."

"What a grand old fireplace," Patch interrupted still staring at the hearth. "It has been a long time since I've seen a back-bar made of green wood," he added, bending over and reaching up inside the fireplace. He ran his hand against the charred green timber that rested on the projecting inner ledges of the stone fireplace, about eight feet from the floor.

"Yes. I need to replace it with an iron one. Now please, I'd like my shoes."

Patch continued to flaunt an insolent grin that made Adrian uncomfortable and walked back toward the burlap sack. Pulling its drawstring loose, he reached deep inside, fumbling around for a moment before retrieving a pair of low black calfskin shoes with buckles that sparkled in the fading sunlight streaming through the window.

Adrian was pleased. "Very nice," he remarked taking the shoes from Patch. "What is the price?"

Patch pulled tight on the drawstring and tossed the sack over his shoulder. "Master Eblis will collect the fee in good time."

"I insist on paying for them now."

"I am to take no money. Master Eblis will collect the fee later," Patch repeated turning for the door.

"Very well then," Adrian said with a frown. "I shall pay...later."

Patch swung open the door and could be heard laughing as he stepped from the house.

LATER THAT EVENING, ADRIAN SAT IN A WOODEN CHAIR IN FRONT of the burning hearth engrossed in his favorite pastime—reading the poetry of Shakespeare by the dim light of a small fire. He lowered the book for a moment and glanced down at the new pair of shoes on his feet, transfixed by the dancing flames of the fire that reflected in the clear buckles. At one point the burning wood crackled and he looked up and smiled, reveling in the silence that engulfed the room. "I should have done away with her a long time ago," he thought. He returned to his reading but soon found himself straining his eyes to distinguish the print, realizing the light from the fire was fading. Looking up at the fireplace he watched the flame mysteriously shrink and then with a poof, extinguish itself.

Adrian set his book down, rose from the chair and approached the hearth. Grasping an iron, he poked at the burning embers and tossed another log into the fireplace. Quickly it ignited, producing a flame, and Adrian set the iron beside the hearth before returning to his chair. When he reached for the book, the flame again began to shrink and with another poof, it was gone. "This is madness!" Adrian barked, lifting himself from the chair. He approached the fireplace a second time and decided that the fire might not be getting enough of a draft. Carefully maneuvering around the glowing embers, he lowered his head and stepped into the hearth, stooping underneath the back-bar to get a look up inside the chimney. He peered up into the blackness for a few seconds when suddenly there came a sharp splintering sound. Adrian could not move fast enough to avoid a large pot falling from above that struck him on the head. The blow rendered the apothecary unconscious as the back-bar of green wood broke in half and crashed down upon him.

Sometime later, Adrian opened his eyes and felt the thumping in his head, but it could not match the pain that streaked through both legs. Lying face down, he lifted his head and turned it to view the large piece of charred wood that clamped his legs to the stone floor of the hearth like a vice and grimaced in agony. "I've locked the door! No-one will find me here!" he lamented. Adrian glanced over at a dying ember in the far corner of the fireplace and realized the force of the collapsed back-bar had extinguished most of the other coals. "Thank God there is no fire!" he sighed and laid his head back down, shutting his eyes.

A few minutes had passed when the smell of smoke returned Adrian to the reality of his nightmare. Opening his eyes, he lifted his head and turned it toward the hearth scanning the area for fire; but he found none. Yet the scent of a burning flame continued to grow stronger. Adrian peered out into the darkness of the room and gasped when he distinguished the figure of a man seated cross-legged in his chair. The stranger's identity was concealed behind the cover of the works of Shakespeare which he held up with one hand in front of his face.

"Help me!" Adrian cried out. The stranger did not move. "My God, can't you see that I am in need of help! I'm right here in front of you!"

"Shhh," the stranger replied from behind the book. "I'm flattered but I am not the God to whom you plead. Kindly refrain from interrupting, for I've nearly finished this passage."

Adrian was stunned. His feeling of helplessness had now erupted into seething anger. "Damn you, man! I'm injured!"

"Shhh," was the reply.

Adrian began to weep and with exasperation rested his head back down upon the stone floor.

A few moments later the tormented apothecary heard the book close and lifted his head again. He now saw that the stranger enjoyed a smoking pipe, with its glow illuminating the features of his face. Adrian strained his eyes to make out the stranger's identity. It didn't take long. "You are the shoemaker—Eblis!"

Eblis removed the pipe from his mouth. "*...Angels are bright still, though the brightest fell. Though all things foul would wear the brows of grace, yet grace must still look so...*," Eblis recited in dramatic form. "*MacBeth*. How I do adore Shakespeare! What mastery of the tongue this poet did have! And it tis the tongue that gives man dominion in the animal kingdom."

Adrian glared back with shock and bewilderment. "Are you mad?!" he blared. "Can you not see my situation?!"

Eblis lowered his pipe and brought a finger to his lips. "Why, yes. It appears quite smashing," he replied with a grin.

Adrian dropped his head with dismay for a moment before lifting it again. "How did you get in here?!" he inquired and then wailed as pain shot through his lower body. "What do you want from me, shoemaker?! Does my predicament amuse thee?!" he grimaced. "I'm in pain, man! I believe the beam has broken both legs!"

"And who is it that bickers now?" Eblis replied coyly.

"What is the matter with you?! I have done nothing to you! Why do you torment me like this?!" Adrian wailed again from the pain.

"Dear gentleman, I have come to collect my fee."

"Thy fee?! Damn you, Eblis! This is no time to settle debts!"

"Ah, but it tis," Eblis retorted now holding up the index finger of his right hand. Placing the pipe back into his mouth, Eblis pressed the end of his finger into the burning bowl and puffed on the pipe stem until his finger had caught fire. Awe-stricken, Adrian watched with terror as Eblis removed the burning finger from the bowl and held it upright. Appearing unaffected by the fiery appendage, the shoemaker pointed his finger toward the fireplace. "It is my guess, Adrian, that you have not thanked thy God enough. It is a burning question, is it not?" Eblis inquired with a sinister laugh. Then a stream of fire protruded from the end of the burning finger, leaping across the room and igniting the collapsed beam that pinned Adrian to the floor.

"You are the devil!" Adrian cried out, wriggling desperately as the flames crawled across the beam.

"No, Adrian! I am the brightest angel!" Eblis replied, rising from the chair. Slowly he stepped closer to the trapped apothecary who worked frantically to free himself. "Before I forget, Adrian, there is someone who anxiously awaits thee." Eblis reached down and picked up an iron pot that lay on the floor and bent over to hold the pot close to Adrian's ear. "Do hear the voice that has guided me to thee," he instructed.

From out of the pot arose the shrieking scorn of a woman. "Adrian! Adrian! Where are you?!"

"Do you recognize her?!" Eblis asked with a sardonic cadence. "Why, my dear apothecary, it tis thy wife!"

Adrian screamed.

"She awaits your arrival for an eternity of togetherness!" Eblis roared with laughter drowning out Adrian's agonizing cries as the flames had now reached his breeches and raced across his clothing, quickly engulfing his whole body and igniting his flesh.

The demon stood before the fireplace with outstretched arms and bellowed grotesquely with an inhuman bark that seemed to arise from the bowels of hell. He repeated, "...*THE BRIGHTEST ANGEL FELL*..." over and over again with such fervor, that the repetition was followed by sudden combustions exploding randomly about the room until the entire house had been consumed by flames.

CHAPTER 11

The smell of smoke filled the streets of Lynn as the spectacular blaze illuminated the black night. The clanging of the bell-man's bells and cries of fire alerted nearly all the residents of Lynn to the calamity that had befallen the Lyttleton home at the intersection of Myrtle and Holyoke Streets.

Rushing into the street, the townsfolk assembled in front of the burning building with their fire-buckets, quickly forming a double line that ran from the burning building to the nearest well. From the water source, the filled buckets were passed quickly from hand to hand up one line of persons to the scene of the fire, where the water was then thrown upon the burning house. The empty buckets then returned to the water source by way of the second line of people.

Stationed in the dry line, I assisted in this effort for several hours until the fire was extinguished; although our attempt to save the structure proved futile when the black smoldering walls of the house caved in. The collapse of the scorched timber brought a halt to the operation and the two lines slowly broke up.

"Some fire, ey Benjamin?" a voice said from behind me.

I turned around to find Emery Kerstland.

"I believe it was the apothecary Lyttleton's home," Kerstland added. "Is your uncle about?"

"He was near the front of the line," I replied before noticing Sam standing behind her father. How different she appeared than when last I saw her with auburn hair, ruffled by sleep, hanging down and resting on the shoulders of a girl's laced jacket. She offered a quick glance before looking away with a simper.

"There he is," Kerstland said, looking beyond me. He turned toward his daughter. "Sam, I wish to have a word with Edward Brown..." and then turned back toward me, "...stay here and keep our young journeyman occupied. I understand you've made Samantha's acquaintance?"

"Yes, Master Kerstland," I replied.

Kerstland patted me on the shoulder as he walked by.

"Hello, Sam," I said.

"Hello," she responded, crossing her arms at her stomach.

I was at a loss for words and stood there helpless as the few seconds of silence seemed like hours.

"Again, I am sorry about this morning," Sam delivered.

"I'm not bothered," I offered shrugging my shoulders. "And I am sorry as well," I added before sinking my hands into the pockets of my jacket.

"I hope Master Lyttleton was not at home this evening?"

"Yes," I said turning briefly to glance back at the pile of smoldering wood. "I don't believe anyone could have survived such a fire."

"He lost his wife a few months ago," she informed, brushing the bangs from her eyes. "Her passing occurred around the same time that Master Hassett was thrown from his horse and killed."

"Who was this Hassett?"

"He was a shoemaker whose shop is positioned across the street from my father's. The shop is now occupied by Cyrus Eblis," Sam added.

"Eblis?" I loathed, drooping my head.

"How do you know Cyrus Eblis?"

"Know him?" I asked with a flinch, looking up.

"Yes. I heard that beast of a man, Patch, say to you this morning that Eblis bid thee hello."

I stammered. "I don't know him...I've only met him; but I don't *know* him."

Sam seemed unconvinced by my response. "Well, I have yet to meet him, and I am in no hurry to do so," she reflected, gathering her thoughts. "Something is not right in that shop."

I was curious now. "How do you mean?"

"Oh...pay no attention to me," Sam reconsidered. "It's silly."

"No, please, continue," I urged.

Sam hesitated for a moment and studied my face until convinced my interest was sincere. She leaned closer to me and lowered her voice. "Well...my room faces the street and I've seen lights and shadows of people...sometimes..." she paused. "Oh...you'll think I'm insane."

I reached out and grabbed hold of her left hand—an impulsive action to be sure, but it struck a chord. "Please, what do you see?"

Sam caught her breath before continuing. "Sometimes I've seen animals—horned beasts inside the shop at all hours of the evening," she added before gently pulling her hand from mine. She gave me a whimsical look as if waiting for me to burst into laughter.

"Go on," I persisted.

"These lights...they are odd. Usually they display a rainbow of colors. I believe the bell-man has seen them too, for when he passes the shop it is with hurried feet." Sam's delivery was rapid and the fear growing in her voice genuine. "And any manufacturer that can employ such an eerie man as Patch must be his equal. The one-eyed man is rumored to have the past of a pirate who was run out of Lynn years ago; but now it is as though the town has become blind to this man's returned presence."

"How was Eblis able to acquire Hassett's shop in such a short period of time?"

"The shop is still the property of Hassett's son, Daniel. Eblis first appeared in Lynn at the funeral of Master Hassett. Rumor has it that Eblis and Daniel made some sort of agreement. It's probably not true, though."

"Why not?"

"Daniel was born with a sickness of the mind. He is slow compared to others his age—a child's mind locked inside the body of a growing young man. He is very quiet and timid, but his look is empty and frightening. And he stares with far away eyes."

"What of Hassett's mother?"

"She died years ago—struck by lightning of all things. Some of the townsfolk say it was Daniel's curse. He is an only child and it seems that his mother could never come to terms with his mental state. It is said that she was very hard on him. And as far as anyone knows, Daniel has no other living relatives. Some believe that perhaps he and Eblis are related."

"How convenient for Eblis to appear just as Daniel's father dies."

"My father approaches," Sam warned. "It's best we end this subject."

I nodded my approval and turned away from Sam to view Emery Kerstland walking toward us clutching the handle of a fire-bucket in each hand.

"Here Benjamin," Kerstland said, handing me the leather bucket marked with Edward Brown's initials. "Your uncle asked me to give this to you. He would like you to inform your aunt that he has decided not to venture straight home just yet. There's still some cleanup to be done."

"Father, was anyone hurt in the fire?" Sam asked.

"Yes, darling. Unfortunately we found Adrian Lyttleton's body. At least that is who we believe it to be. Strangest thing," he continued, scratching his head. "Even though the body was burned beyond recognition, his shoes were nearly untouched by the blaze—yes...strangest thing I've ever seen."

CHAPTER 12

Perched precariously on the edge of the jagged cliff, I stood mesmerized by white capped breakers crashing against the multitude of rocks below. The blood red sky dominated the world around me, broken only by black clouds that rolled with great speed overhead, while the icy wind moaned and chilled my soul. Suddenly the earth beneath my feet began to give way as sections of rock splintered and tumbled down away from the cliff, disintegrating on impact with the boulders below. I managed to maintain my footing and quickly backed away from the cliff's edge as the rock and soil disappeared before me.

Escaping the toppling ledge, I ran toward the forest and into its sea of purple oak, coming to rest beside a lofty tree. Soon the wind ceased its bewailing, inviting an eerie silence that engulfed the woods as a thick milky mist crept in between the tree trunks, blanketing the forest floor and converting it into a world of black and white. Suddenly the distant sound of clopping hooves from a sprinting steed cut through the stillness. Breathless, I hugged the oak and listened as the nearing hooves replaced the rapid beating of my heart. Then without warning, the great oak flung its branches around my body with the speed of a cracking whip, fastening me to the trunk of the ghoulish tree. As I struggled to free myself, a multitude of acorns rained down from above, striking me in waves. It was then that I set eyes upon the black silhouette on horseback racing toward me with the fiery eyes of the steed and its rider shining through the mist like beacons, drawn to the oak and its prisoner. With every ounce of strength my adrenalin could muster up, I managed to pull the branches from *around my body and break free from the oak's grasp. I backed away from the tree and watched as the rider drew closer when suddenly the specter on horseback thrust his arm in my direction and a spinning object whistled past my ear, sinking into the bark of a nearby sapling with a violent thud. The object was a large knife with silver jagged blade and handle crafted of curly maple. I gazed, transfixed by the imbedded blade; but when I reached for it, the knife began to move and I watched in disbelief as it transformed into a red serpent coiled around the trunk. The snake hissed and lunged at me with exposed fangs forcing me to once again take flight with the rider still in pursuit.*

Panting furiously, I weaved my way around the many trees with swaying branches, dodging their monstrous limbs that lunged at me like a thousand arms. I could not see my feet as the mist obscured the forest floor concealing the large root that sprung from out of the earth and I tripped over it, falling face down to the ground. When I rolled over the rider was upon me. He pulled tight on the horse's reins and the beast stopped and whined, kicking high into the air with its front two legs. It was then that I noticed the noose at the end of a rope swinging from a tree limb high above. Quickly pulling myself into a sitting position, I began a backwards crawl but my escape stalled when my back collided with a cold, stone object. I spun around to discover a headstone with the inscription concealed behind a thick layer of dust. Frantically I worked at brushing away the dirt to reveal the name of...

The bells clanged.

I sat up in my bed, awakened from my nightmare in a cold sweat. As it was a warm September night I enjoyed an opened window in my bedroom and began to try to remember the details of my dream when the bells clanged again. Certain the hour was late, I thought to myself that the last time I had heard his bells deep into the night had been several months ago—the night of the Lyttleton fire. *Please not another fire.*

I rose from my bed and stepped to the window peering out into the moonlit night that cast a grey luster upon the dark houses of Park Street. I heard the bells again and then saw a small group of people running with the bell-man down Park Street before disappearing around the corner. The clanging faded in the distance, but I could not see smoke or a structure ablaze.

Preparing to step away from the window, I took one more glance down into the street below and was surprised to find a man standing directly beneath my room, wearing a rounded top hat. At first I assumed it to be my uncle—thinking he may also have been awakened by the bells—but as I wiped the sleep from my eyes and looked closer, the figure below stood much taller and thinner than Edward Brown. When he slowly lifted his head and glared back at me with an odious smile, the moonlight sculptured his features against the darkness revealing the face of Cyrus Eblis.

I pulled back away from the window and quickly remembered the Bible Caleb had given me. It rested on the desk. I retrieved it and returned to the window, fumbling through the book and using the gleaming moonlight to search for the marker my cousin had left me. Suddenly I came upon a page with its top corner folded over and followed my finger down the column until reaching five lines that Caleb had underlined. I eased my head back out of the opening and looked below to find Eblis remained steadfast, still staring up at the window.

My attention returned to the book and with a trembling voice I read aloud: "*I will say of the Lord, He is my refuge and my fortress: my God; in Him I will trust!*" I paused as though I had cast a magic spell and lifted my head out of the window again. Eblis still stared back at me, now flashing a sinister smile. He gloated as though daring me to hit him with more scripture. Desperate, I continued: "*Thou shalt not be afraid for the terror by night; nor for the arrow that flieth by day;...For He shall give his angels charge over thee, to keep thee in all thy ways!*" Again I looked down beneath the window. The shoemaker sneered, turning casually away from me before pacing from the house, moving with a deliberate, arrogant gait until he disappeared around the corner of the opposite street. I gazed back down at the book with dismay, unconvinced that the Biblical reading caused his disappearance, for I had anticipated the underlined passage would have produced a more dramatic reaction from Eblis.

I stepped away from the window and after setting the Bible down on the desk I returned to bed, but not to sleep. My heart continued to race as images and questions of the dark shoemaker clouded my mind. *Eblis is truly the devil. Am I the only one who senses evil within him?*

Strange as it seemed, the obscure shoemaker was rapidly acquiring one of the most respected reputations in town. His business lacked the numbers of customers that Kerstland and other shoemakers enjoyed; nevertheless, Eblis spent large sums of money in all the shops of Lynn, which did not go unnoticed by those affected by the status of wealth. The few who did claim to know him spoke highly of him; but this was mere gossip, for he remained aloof and a stranger to most of Lynn's residents. The only exception of this of course, being the repulsive Patch and Daniel Hassett, whose acquaintance I had yet to make. And perhaps a third exception might have been myself; for it was beginning to appear as though my encounter in the forest of Salem had forged an eerie relationship against my will. The reason for it I could not yet explain. I felt cursed. *What does he want of me?*

Then there was the metallic squeak. I recognized it right away as the doorknob to my bedroom. Slowly I pulled myself into a sitting position in bed and stared out at the knob from across the room. It turned slowly and stopped, then turned again and stopped. I held my breath. *The door is not locked.* I waited for the door to slowly swing open, but nothing. The knob turned again. Still the door remained shut. Suddenly the squeaking of wood could be heard and I watched in terror the wooden door begin to swell and bend inward as if someone on the other side was trying to force their way inside.

I turned toward the desk. *The Bible.* But before I could leave the bed to retrieve the Holy Book, it rose from the desk of its own power and fluttered weightlessly about the center of the room. I was petrified. The pages began to turn with considerable speed and with great force it flew across the room and crashed into the wall with a loud thud, before falling to the floor.

I stared at the book, now resting motionless upon the wooden floor when suddenly the door was thrown open. I gasped and prepared to leap from the bed when I recognized my uncle standing in the doorway.

"Ben, what was that sound?"

I swallowed hard and sighed with relief.

"Ben, are you all right?"

"Yes, uncle. Just a nightmare, that's all."

"What was that sound?"

"A book...the Bible. It fell off of the desk."

My uncle studied me with a look of skepticism. "All right...well, then goodnight."

"Goodnight," I replied as he slowly shut the door behind him.

CHAPTER 13

The night grew into morning and so with weary eyes I rose before dawn. Since the summer's heat had lingered into the beginning of autumn, I decided to wash outside by the light of the full moon, but noticed the moonlight begin to fade as dark clouds passed before it. A clap of thunder rumbled through the sky and instantly large droplets of rain began to fall. Hurrying to return inside, I was distracted by the pattering of water as it pelted against a large object resting beside the house. It was the cask of molasses with my initials, left outside to gather dust and cobwebs. *I must be rid of this cask today.*

The steady downpour materialized with the faint daylight and continued throughout the morning, converting the streets and alleys of Lynn into pools of murky water broken by islands of cobblestones where the street was raised. The rain clouds sifted the rays of sunlight, eclipsing the town in paleness, requiring a fire to cast the necessary light about Kerstland's shoemaking shop. Seated on a bench beside the burning hearth, I faced the window of the shop and watched sheets of rain beat against the panes of glass while I worked at punching holes into the leather soles with my awl. Master Kerstland and Wright, the other journeyman in Kerstland's employ, had rushed off to the second floor of the building to repair a sudden leak in the roof, leaving me alone in the shop.

My job with Master Kerstland progressed better than expected.

He seemed very pleased with my work, which bolstered my confidence and contributed to a relaxed work atmosphere. According to the shoemaker, the shop was the busiest it had been in years and we worked at a steady pace to fill all the orders. I enjoyed the environment of the shop, but throughout the hot summer months I had grown particularly fond of making shoe deliveries since the task took me outdoors.

My relationship with Samantha continued to be a work in progress as our friendship was cordial but distant; although I was delighted to see that her desire to masquerade as a boy had begun to wane. I usually saw her at least once a day during the work week as she would wander into the shop to fetch Angel, deliver a message to her father, or bring us some baked goods from the adjoining kitchen. I was truly disheartened on those rare days that our paths did not cross.

On this day, I especially hoped to run into her. The events of the following evening had terrified me and she seemed to be the only one in Lynn with whom I could trust with such matters. So it was with a warm "Hello," that I greeted Sam as she stepped gingerly through the doorway from the kitchen into the shop balancing a pewter plate of steaming muffins.

"Good morning, Benjamin," she replied with a smile before turning away from me to set the plate of muffins down upon a table in the center of the shop.

I gazed upon her sleek frame that complimented her white blouse and coarse woolen skirt, chuckling to myself on how much more feminine she appeared than when we first met. She turned around quickly and surprised me, catching me looking in her direction, which forced me to look away and down at the finished sole. I replaced it with another and reached down into my tool kit which was set beside my left leg and searched for my marking wheel; but it was not there. I then looked down on the floor around my right leg, but still could not locate the wheel and reluctantly glanced up at Sam with embarrassment. She slowly approached me with a sassy gleam and when near to me, she reached down behind the bench where I sat and retrieved the tool from the floor.

"I believe you are looking for this," she said with a smirk, handing me the wheel.

"You have read my mind," I replied.

"No. Remember, I know your profession," she countered boldly. "How I do miss working with my father's tools."

Angel quietly emerged from underneath her father's desk and scampered toward Sam. "There's my little kitty," Sam cooed, lifting the black cat up from off the floor. "Do you enjoy keeping Benjamin company?"

"I hardly know when she is here," I responded.

The cat purred and Sam set the animal down. She returned to the table, lifted the plate of muffins and carried them toward me. "I thought you might be hungry for a muffin?" she offered extending the plate toward me.

"Yes. That sounds good," I said selecting one of the steaming cakes.

She handed me the pewter plate and then pulled down on the skirt hanging below the apron. "Be careful, they are right from the oven," she cautioned as I sunk my teeth into the warm, moist muffin.

"Delicious," I acknowledged.

Samantha smiled and glanced out of the window. "What a miserable day," she observed.

"Yes. It hasn't stopped raining all morning."

"I had hoped to go riding this afternoon."

"Riding?" I asked before stuffing the final muffin morsel into my mouth.

"My grandfather has a farm with stables out near Cedar Pond, and my horse, *Savior,* is there," she said, straightening the kerchief tied about her neck. "Do you ride...for sport, that is?"

I hesitated. "Of...course," I stammered.

Sam giggled with disbelief. "Then maybe one day we can go riding," she said with sarcasm as she paced over to the large shop window facing the street.

"Sam. Did you hear anything last evening?"

Sam glanced at me from over her shoulder and then turned back toward the street. "What do you mean?"

I lowered my voice. "I was awakened by the bell-man and saw a man standing beneath my window. It was Cyrus Eblis—I'm certain. You spoke of the strange goings-on across the street. I thought perhaps you might have seen something last night?"

Sam did not turn around and stood silently for a moment. "It was warm," she began. "I had my window opened. Across the street I heard noises and saw what I spoke of before."

"The lights and animals?"

"Yes."

"Did you see Eblis?"

Sam spun around with a troubled expression. "No. Tell me Benjamin, why does Eblis trouble thee so?"

I wanted to tell her at that moment; but I delayed and suddenly the door to the kitchen swung open and in burst Master Kerstland. "I need some nails," he blared, pacing over to a desk and pulling open one of its drawers. He rummaged through the drawer for a few seconds, grabbing a handful of nails. "Well, hello Sam," he said, slamming the drawer shut.

"Good morning, father."

"Hardly. I'm sorry you cannot go riding today."

"So am I."

Kerstland walked over toward his daughter and gave her a soft kiss on the forehead.

Suddenly the front door to the shop blew open. The noisy crackling of rain striking the cobblestone street filled the shop as an old woman crept in from outside. Hunched over, she turned to shut the door of the shop behind her and propped a dark walking cane against the wall. Ignoring our presence, she began brushing the rain from her black hooded cape while her rumpled dress dripped water until a puddle had formed beneath her feet. Finally she spun around, pulling the hood down and exposing a head of gray hair tucked up beneath a black calash. A long nose called attention to her triangular face that came to a point at the chin and she was marked with a large brown birthmark on her left cheek.

I was repulsed by her haggard appearance and taken back when Angel hissed and darted past the woman, reflecting our impressions.

"Bad luck," the woman remarked with a sharp, grating Irish brogue.

"Why...why Miss Darcie," Master Kerstland clumsily divulged. "What a pleasant surprise."

"Liar!" she rebutted with a nasty tone. "You're appalled and confused by my sudden presence!"

Stunned, Kerstland was at a loss for words.

The woman smiled, contorting lines of age that traversed the wilted skin of her face. "Now don't cha be flatterin' yaself Master Kerstland," she cautioned, rubbing her hands—one over the other—like a rodent cleansing its paws before eating. "I am not here to purchase shoes. I have stumbled into your humble shop only for relief from the rain."

"It is such a dreary day," Kerstland replied, maintaining his good nature.

"On the contrary, it tis the rain that brings me outside into the streets. When the clap of thunder woke me this mornin' I could hardly contain my excitement!" she shrieked. "I donned my best dress so that I may celebrate and revel in the presence of nymphs and undines—gift of Neckna and the essence of plant life!"

I thought the woman mad and turned slightly toward Sam whose expression spoke the same.

The woman squealed with laughter once again. "Of course I speak of water. Precious rain water that nurtures my Basil, Laurel, Myrtle, Jezebel, and Iris," she continued annunciating each herb with reverence. "So I welcome the gift of Neckna; but tis this clothing—the product of Eve's folly—that troubles me on such a glorious day. I must pace my activity lest I drown in my garments." She continued to rub her hands as though she drew strength from the two large silver rings that she wore. Suddenly her head turned slowly toward me as if she were responding to a command. When our eyes met, she stood motionless for a few moments, studying me with great curiosity. Slowly she paced toward me never lifting her eyes from mine.

"What is thy name?" she asked of me.

I hesitated for a moment. I didn't want my silence interpreted as fear, so I spoke up boldly. "Benjamin," I said. "Benjamin Pratt."

She scratched the side of her face with a long bony finger. "Tis his doing that has guided me here this morning," she spoke, deliberately with a softer tone. "I'm convinced of it now. Master Eblis has spoken of thee," she revealed.

I was dumbfounded and looked helplessly at Kerstland and Sam who both appeared as confused as I.

The woman laughed again, exposing crooked stained teeth. "All in good time. All in good time," she predicted turning away from me.

"You speak of Cyrus Eblis?" Kerstland asked. "How is he?"

"He is...busy," she replied with laughter. "Lynn is a town of many tattered *soles*."

"You are referring to shoes?" Kerstland inquired.

The woman squealed with laughter once more. "Master Eblis is a fine, fine manufacturer," she replied coyly pulling her hood back over the calash. "I have taken up much of your precious time. And one should not waste time listenin' to the babblin' of an old woman. Besides," she added waving her arm at us, "your politeness sickens me!"

"Yes Miss Darcie, but..." Kerstland began.

"Enough!" the woman blared, snatching her walking stick. "I must go," she added reaching for the door handle. She stopped and turned around once more, glaring in my direction. "But I must say it twas certainly a pleasure stumblin' upon your shop today. And Master Kerstland, I do wish ya luck in maintain' the quality of your *soles*," she concluded with a grin before turning away. She stepped back out into the downpour pulling the door shut behind her.

Kerstland watched as she hobbled past the store window. "Is that good or bad luck, Miss Darcie?" he mumbled.

"What a strange old woman," I described.

Kerstland turned toward Sam and me. "She did seem fascinated with you, Benjamin. So you are friends with this Eblis fellow?"

"No...I hardly know the man!" I exclaimed. "I've only met him once!"

"She speaks highly of Eblis, as do others. He must manufacture a very good shoe?" Kerstland concluded. "And you certainly must have made an impression on him, Ben?"

I didn't want to plead my innocence any longer and looked to Sam for help.

"I think Miss Darce is a witch!" Sam interjected.

"Samantha! Hold your tongue!" Kerstland scolded. "She's a bit frightening, I agree; but the term witch stirs up trouble! Besides it is not proper for a young lady to cast such judgment!"

"I'm sorry, father."

"Who is she?" I asked.

"A chandler," Kerstland replied. "Her candles are popular, but she's something of a recluse."

"Recluse?"

"Yes. The old spinster's a hermit—rarely seen. She spends most of her days indoors," Kerstland explained.

"*Like sheep tied to the land...*" I mumbled, remembering my first conversation with Eblis.

"She makes potions and casts spells," Sam added.

"Samantha?!" Kerstland berated.

"She does!" Sam persisted. "Lizzie Ballard told me that Mary Burrill so longed for a husband that she sought the help of Miss Darcie. The old woman told her that when an apple is peeled before a candlelit mirror at the eleventh hour on the last day of October, the image of one's future spouse will appear. Mary Burrill did as she instructed and she saw the face of James Axey!"

"What happened?" I asked.

"James and Mary Axey have been married for two years now!"

"Sam, be careful with such stories," Kerstland warned.

The front door to the shop swung open again and in bounced a large, portly man with puffed cheeks that supported the monocle in his right eye.

"Constable Dixey," Kerstland greeted. "What brings thee out in such foul weather?"

"Good day Emery," he said as he removed his tricorn exposing a powdered wig with puffs at the side. Tucking the tricorn underneath his left armpit, he reached for a muffin with his right arm. "May I?"

"By all means," Kerstland replied.

The large man devoured the muffin with two bites and then reached into the pocket of his red waistcoat, blotched by the rain, to retrieve a handkerchief. "Rain and heat—each a discomforting product of nature that when combined, can be truly wretched," he complained while wiping the saturation from his brow with the handkerchief. "But it is fitting weather for the news I bear." The constable paused and turned toward Sam. "Why Samantha, you grow prettier with each day."

Sam acknowledged the compliment with a forced smile.

The constable adjusted the sagging belt around his waist that supported a leather sheath carrying a long sword. Instinctively the lawman brought his left hand to the hardwood grip of the sword and grasped the black leather that wrapped the handle. "Emery, the news I bring hardly befits the ears of such a fine young lady as your daughter."

"Sam, join your mother and sister in the kitchen," Kerstland commanded.

Sam frowned. "Yes, father."

"And Benjamin, why don't you..." Kerstland began.

"No. The lad can stay," the constable interjected. He waited until Sam had left the room. "There was a lass disappeared in Lynn last evening and I believe there to be unfairness in regard to her disappearance."

Kerstland gasped. "My word, who?!"

"Josiah Hood's daughter, Anna," the constable replied.

"Oh, poor Josiah!" Kerstland lamented, slowly retreating into a chair. "How did it happen?"

The constable set his tricorn down on a table and pulled the monocle from his eye. He breathed on the eyepiece, fogging the glass and then wiped it with his handkerchief. "Well, it seems that Anna was returning home from enjoying a late dinner at the Basker's home."

"Yes. Basker's daughter is Alice. She and Anna are inseparable," Kerstland interjected.

"That was yesterday," Dixey offered stoicly, peering into the monocle before fitting it over his eye. "She had made the trip a hundred times before at such an hour; however, last night someone was waiting for her. She never made it home."

"How can you be sure she hasn't just run off...strange as it may sound?"

The constable cleared his throat. "An article of clothing was found —a cotton shawl. The Hoods have identified it as belonging to Anna. It is bloodstained."

"How could something like this happen in Lynn?! It is such a peaceful town of friends among friends. Who could do such a terrible thing?!"

"I wish I knew. If Anna was indeed a victim of foul play, nothing of its equal has occurred in my years as a constable. In fact, one need to go back to the year twenty-four to find mention of violence among men in Lynn, when Indians commenced an attack on a sloop on the banks of the Saugus River—damn savages," Dixey recounted strolling over to the bench where I was seated. "My first inclination was to attribute this horrid act to the red man, but it does not bear the markings of tomahawk butchery. I need to solve her disappearance before the governor learns of this. The last thing Lynn needs is a unit of excitable young redcoats patrolling the streets with loaded muskets."

"Have you any suspects?"

The constable ignored Kerstland's question and looked down at me instead. "And what is your name?"

"Benjamin Pratt," I replied nervously. "I am the journeyman in this shop."

"Edward Brown's nephew," Kerstland added.

"Edward Brown—the shoemaker?"

"The same."

"So many shoemakers," the constable remarked as he reached down and picked up a pointed iron tool that rested on the lasting jack. "Is this your tool?" he asked, tapping the sharpened end of the instrument.

"It is. It's an awl," I replied.

"What is the purpose of such a tool?"

"It is for punching holes in leather so that the soles may be stitched together," I described.

The constable turned toward Kerstland. "I suppose you own an awl as well?"

"That I do," Kerstland informed. "It is a standard tool among all shoemakers and journeymen."

"All shoemakers and journeymen," the constable repeated with a sigh. "There were several tiny holes found in Anna's shawl that appear to have been made by a thin, pointed instrument. I believe it was an awl," he surmised setting the awl back down upon the jack. "But the shoemaker's in Lynn number nearly fifty, and each has a handful of journeymen in his employ. As you have indicated, all would seem to own an awl. And then one must not overlook the blacksmiths. That is easily a hundred suspects." The constable wiped his brow again. "Where to begin?"

"Perhaps Anna was seen with someone prior to her disappearance?"

"Yes, perhaps." The constable sighed again. "Emery, we go back a long time and I wish not to insult an old friend; but you must understand it is my duty that I ask every shoemaker to account for his whereabouts last evening between the hours of nine and ten."

"I understand. I had just heard the bell-man announce the hour of nine o'clock before falling off to sleep with my wife at my side."

"Did you hear or see anything strange before falling to sleep?"

"No."

"May I see your hands?"

"I'm sorry?"

"Your hands please."

Kerstland complied and held out his hands turning the palms upward. The constable examined them closely. "Thank you," he said and then turned toward me. "And you—where were you last evening?"

"I too was in bed."

"Did you hear or see anything odd?"

I hesitated.

"Well?" the constable persisted with a suspicious glare.

"I heard the bell-man."

"At nine o'clock?"

"No...much later. He was ringing his bells to sound the alarm. I thought it might be a fire again."

"It was the bell-man who found Anna's shawl. Show me your hands," he instructed. I did as he asked.

"May I ask the purpose of examining our hands?" Kerstland inquired.

The constable studied my palms and looked up at Kerstland. "I found purple stains on the girl's shawl as well. I believe them to be berry stains."

"Mulberry?"

"I believe so," Dixey replied giving Kerstland a quizzical look. "Emery, why would you assume they would be mulberry?"

"There are a number of shoemakers in Lynn who grow mulberry trees," Kerstland revealed. "The mulberry tree leaf is a favorite diet for silk worms."

"Silk worms?"

"Yes. It can be very cost-effective to produce one's own silk as opposed to importing the fabric," Kerstland explained. "Silk is used for the ribbons on dress shoes."

"I see."

"The Hassett residence has mulberry trees growing behind the shop and ten-footers," Kerstland divulged.

"Thomas Hassett? He's deceased isn't he?"

"Yes. The shop is now occupied by the shoemaker Eblis. He has moved in with Hassett's son."

"Eblis?" the constable repeated with surprise glancing down at his own boots.

Kerstland sensed betrayal. "Are they new boots?"

Dixey looked up at Kerstland. "I'm sorry Emery. A journeyman in the employ of this Eblis fellow just happened to arrive at my front door the other day and by chance he had a brand new pair of boots for sale. He saved me a trip into town as I was in need of a new pair. I know that I have purchased shoes from you for years, but..."

"Think nothing of it," Kerstland interrupted saving the stammering lawman from greater embarrassment. "I'll just have to charge you double the next time."

The constable produced a laugh and Kerstland an insincere grin.

"In any event," the constable began with a serious tone once again, "I believe I should pay this Eblis and Daniel Hassett a visit. The fact that there are mulberry trees on the Hassett property is somewhat troubling considering the evidence found on Anna's shawl."

"Is Benjamin your only journeyman?"

"I have another one. Wright is at present upstairs tending to a leak."

"Wretched weather," the constable cursed and then reached for his tricorn which he placed back upon his head. "Well, then, Emery, I think I will call upon Cyrus Eblis," he said pacing toward the door. "I shall be around later to speak to this man, Wright," he added as he reached for the door handle.

"Constable," I called out, for I could hold my tongue no longer.

"Yes?"

"I saw him last evening. I looked out of my window to see the bellman running down the street and saw Eblis beneath my window!"

The constable released his grip on the door handle. "How can you be sure the person beneath your window was Eblis? It was dark, was it not?"

"There was a full moon and I recognized his face. He looked up at me."

"You must know him well?" the constable asked with raised brow.

"I know him."

The constable surveyed my expression for a second or two, searching for emotion that my words did not reveal. "Are you afraid of this man?"

I took a deep breath. "I am."

"I see. Was he alone?"

"Yes."

"Hmmm," the constable mumbled, scratching his chin. "Odd for a stranger to be out alone that late at night. Well, thank you, Benjamin," he acknowledged pulling open the front door.

"Constable," I called, interrupting his departure again. "Be careful."

The constable cracked a sardonic grin. "Do not worry now, lad. I'll be careful," he assured turning with a quizzical wink for Kerstland before exiting the shop.

Within seconds of the constable's departure Sam burst into the room from out of the kitchen. "A killing?!"

"Samantha! What have you been told about eavesdropping?!" Kerstland reprimanded. "A body has yet to be discovered. Let's pray the lass will be found unharmed," he added.

"I could not help but overhear!" she exclaimed pulling me by the arm. "You told him of Eblis!"

Kerstland thrust his hands in the air. "You are sharing secrets now?!" He turned away and stepped to the window peering out into the street. "Purple stains?" he mumbled, shaking his head.

Sam hurried across the room to join her father at the window. "Look! The constable has reached the front door!"

CHAPTER 14

The constable stepped up to the wooden door with a sigh, pulling the collar of his jacket tight around his neck as a light rain continued to fall. With a deep breath he pounded, and after a few short series of knocks he stepped to the right of the door, placing his face against the foggy glass window. The inside of the shop was dark and quiet, so Dixey pounded again. A crack of thunder split the heavens startling the constable for an instant and he backed away from the door to get a better view of the entire shop. As he did the sound of creaking hinges returned his attention to the door and he watched it slowly open.

Dixey cautiously approached the opening door and caught a glimpse of the young man standing behind it.

"Daniel?" the constable called out through the rain.

There was no response, just a dazed expression peering back from out of the shadows.

The constable stepped closer to the open door and pored over the young man, who was clad in a wrinkled white morning gown that appeared two sizes too big. "Daniel? I am the constable."

The young man stared back with wild and piercing bloodshot eyes, highlighted by dark circles against a pale face. Running his hand nervously through ruffled, oily hair, Daniel proclaimed quickly, "I am the watchman!"

"The watchman?"

"It is raining," the boy deduced, biting his lower lip.

"Yes it is raining. May I come inside?" the constable asked, aware that he needed to tread delicately with Daniel's troubled mind.

Daniel extended an open hand beyond the shelter of the shop and collected rain water in his palm. He brought his hand to his parched lips and lapped the water from it like an animal.

"Daniel, will you invite me inside?" the constable repeated.

"Do you have an appointment?"

"No. I..."

"One must have an appointment to see the prince!" Daniel interrupted.

"Do you speak of Cyrus Eblis?"

"One must have an appointment to see the prince!" Daniel shouted one more time and slammed the door shut.

The constable was exasperated. He paused for a moment before knocking again. Quickly the door swung open.

"I am the watchman," said the scrawny emaciated young man. "Do you have an appointment?"

The constable played along. "Yes. I have an appointment with the prince."

Daniel slowly smiled. "Then he awaits thee in the middle ten-footer," he replied before shutting the door.

The constable sighed and shook his head. He stepped away from the door, before proceeding to the side of the shop and down a narrow alley flooded with the runoff of rain water from the rooftops. A short distance from the street the alley opened into a small soggy field where three wooden outbuildings stood. On either side of the ten-footers, a dozen or so carefully aligned trees sprung up in a row, positioned one in front of the other, shrouding the workplaces with leafy canopies. The constable took a moment to examine the branches of one of the trees and found it littered with clusters of dark berries. "Mulberry!" he described aloud with excitement before sloshing eagerly across the damp lawn. He stepped up cautiously to a small window set on the side of the first ten-footer and peered inside; but he could not discern much as the outbuilding was dark and appeared unoccupied. Dixey threw open the door to the wooden shanty and dipped his head to step inside. Like the Hassett shoemaker's shop, the small building was dimly lit by what little daylight filtered in through the glass windows on such a dreary day. The ceiling of the outbuilding echoed with life from the surging and diminishing raindrops altered by a shifting wind, and the stationary shadows of sedentary tools indicated that his was the lone presence inside the ten-footer. Two long work benches extended the length of the room upon which several buckets and tools were set, and the constable swatted his way through a maze of large cobwebs extending from the ceiling as he approached one of the work benches. He stopped to run his fingers across the dust covered surface of a lasting jack, glancing suspiciously about the shelving running the length of one side of the outbuilding that supported dozens of shoes. "Strange," he mumbled. "This building looks as though it has not been used in years?"

Hurriedly the constable exited the outbuilding and proceeded toward the ten-footer positioned directly behind it—the middle outbuilding. Again he found the door unlocked and cautiously stepped inside, shutting the door behind him. As Dixey stood quietly inside the doorway adjusting his eyes to the faint surroundings, the pounding rain ceased.

Realizing he was alone again, the constable began a slow pace down the center of the outbuilding. Unlike the previous ten-footer, long tables dominated the inside of this building, arranged in two rows and each supported a great many deep wooden trays. Dixey noticed a soft crunching sound like the crackling of a fire that drew him to one of the trays which revealed a multitude of tiny black silkworms busy devouring a bed of mulberry leaves.

The constable turned and walked to the rear of the outbuilding where he explored another table with trays, only these were full of white cocoons. He picked up one of the round objects and delicately traced his finger across the silk.

Suddenly a gush of wind blew open the front door and Dixey turned to see the figure of a man pass through the doorway. As the stranger entered the outbuilding, the door closed behind him of its own power and the dark figure stepped over to a pewter lamp that hung from a hook on the wall. As the intruder lifted the lamp the candle inside illuminated causing the constable to gasp at the display which was accomplished without the use of steel or flint.

The figure held the lamp up in front of his face and emitted a sinister smile. "Hello, constable," he called out.

The constable dropped the cocoon back inside the tray and clumsily emerged from out of the shadows at the rear of the building. "Master Eblis?" he inquired.

"Tell me constable, does your title allow you the privilege of snooping about the property of another?"

"I am investigating a young girl's disappearance and found the door to this outbuilding open."

Eblis did not reply. He just gazed upon the constable with a fiendish grin. Dixey found the silence unnerving and began to feel perspiration bead up upon his brow.

"Thy shoes," Eblis remarked. "Does thee approve?"

The constable took a breath and glanced down at his boots. "Yes. They are fine." Dixey returned his eyes to Eblis and studied the shoemaker's thin frame that was clad in black from his wide-brimmed circular hat to his boots. Ironically, he sensed something familiar about the shoemaker. "Have we met before?"

"Perhaps," Eblis teased with a stilted grin. "But today it is Daniel that has brought thee to me."

"Oh...yes. Daniel. What is your relationship with the young man?"

"He is as a son." Eblis paused. "Now what of this disappearance you speak of and how does it involve me?"

The constable cleared his throat and pulled tight on his jacket. "The young girl is Anna Hood and she did not return home last evening. I believe she may have met with foul play."

"Death?" Eblis asked with interest.

"I cannot be certain; however I do believe that she is at least in need of medical attention."

Eblis smirked. "Death itself is universally accepted. It is the manner by which that causes such affliction." He paused, adding, "And you believe that I am responsible for her...disappearance?"

Eblis had surprised the constable by alluding to his implication in the matter. "I believe that someone may have attacked her with a shoemaker's awl, so I am making inquiries of all the shoemakers of Lynn," Dixey explained with growing confidence. "I can see that you produce your own silk?"

"You can see very well," Eblis countered setting the lamp down upon a bench and strolling slowly past the constable.

Eblis' procession to the rear of the shop afforded the constable a moment to examine the burning lamp.

"It is a crime to raise silkworms?" Eblis asked sarcastically as he lifted a cocoon from the tray.

"No, of course not." The constable could find nothing odd about the lamp. "You can account for your movements last evening between the hours of nine and ten?"

Eblis returned the cocoon to the tray and turned toward the constable. He slowly removed his hat, running his hand slowly through his thick black hair that was pulled to the back and tied with a ribbon. "I enjoy a walk each evening. Last night was no exception."

"Were you alone?"

Eblis continued to smile as if playing with the constable. "I was."

"Did you hear or see anyone?"

"I saw the boy."

"The boy?"

"Benjamin Pratt. Come now, constable, is he not the reason why you are here badgering me?"

The constable removed his tricorn and wiped the sweat from his brow with a handkerchief. "Did you hear a girl scream?"

"I did."

The constable was surprised. "What did you do?"

"Nothing. It was a warm night. Windows were open. I assumed it was the widow Pierson and Johnathin Poole the bell-man."

"How do you mean?"

"How do I mean?!" Eblis repeated with a sinister laugh. "That fine, upstanding citizen; devoted husband; and father of six children, Johnathin Poole has been engaged in an irreverent relationship of the biblical nature with the humble widow for some time now! She's definitely a screamer, you know!"

The constable was aghast. "I do say!"

"All the while, the unsuspecting Mrs. Poole tucks the children into bed and faithfully awaits the return of her hard-working husband." Eblis snickered and began a slow pace toward the constable from the back of the ten-footer. "We all have our secrets, do we not, Constable Dixey?"

The constable grew unnerved again, but remained steadfast.

"You have come to me on the accusation from a tormented boy

with a wild imagination," Eblis continued, stopping directly in front of the constable. He delicately traced his finger across the official's white neckcloth. "What if I admitted to having knowledge of this girl's disappearance?" he asked with a whisper.

"Do you?" the constable uttered.

Eblis drew a wicked smile.

The constable trembled but summoned the courage to speak. "A witness saw you outside in the streets of Lynn last evening at the time of the girl's disappearance!" the constable stammered intrepidly. "And upon inspection of an article of clothing belonging to Anna, I found berry stains that may have been on the hands of her attacker! The red mulberry tree produces such berries! The same red mulberry that you now grow behind this ten-footer as a source of food for your silk-worms! What do you have to say in your defense?!"

"Surely there are other shoemakers in this village that have mulberry trees on their property," Eblis challenged with a wide grin. "Are you going to arrest me, constable? Or rather should I inquire on how it is you plan to arrest me? For goodness sakes man, you've come here unarmed!"

As if on cue, the constable gripped the handle of the sword that dangled from around his waist with his right hand and pulled the blade from its sheath. He held the weapon out before him in the direction of Eblis, but suddenly the steady wooden sword handle became cold and slimy and Dixey watched in disbelief as the sword itself fell limp and dropped away. It was at that moment that the constable realized he no longer held a sword but now clutched the end of a three foot serpent that wriggled and hissed, dangling above the floor. The constable screamed and dropped the serpent. "What is this black magic?!" he cried out as the serpent slithered away and disappeared into the shadows.

Eblis reached out and snatched the constable's neckcloth. "You try my patience!" he bellowed releasing his grip. The petrified constable looked down upon his neckcloth and saw the berry-stained imprint of Eblis' palm on the white fabric.

Eblis howled with laughter as the constable stared back with a frightened glare.

"How dare thee!" Eblis growled. "You have invaded my sanctuary with a probing tongue spewing justice while masquerading your own corruption behind an unsightly periwig; a nonsensical title; and a theatrical performance that has cozened the imbecilic population of this vile town! Immune from justice and above the law—you play the part well!"

Eblis threw both of his arms toward the ceiling. Simultaneously an unseen force propelled the constable into the air and threw him back against the wall of the outbuilding and crashing to the floor. The constable groaned as pain shot through his body and he opened his eyes to find the colors of the spectrum had vanished from the room, which was now dominated by a hazy reddish glow exploding outwards from Eblis' position in the center. The wooden walls of the ten-footer began to pulsate like the chambers of the heart, creaking with each intermittent swell and the constable shook violently with fright as Eblis began a slow pace toward him.

"It tis time to collect thy fee!" Eblis growled.

Seated in an upright position, the constable frantically backed his way against the wall with Eblis' approach. The sinister shoemaker came to a stop a few feet from the constable and noticed Dixey's monocle resting on the floor. Eblis stomped on the eyepiece, turning his foot to crush the glass. "Justice is blind!" he exclaimed slowly bending over the constable, placing a hand on each knee. "Tell me, Constable Dixey, have you become so engrossed in this preposterous masquerade as a lawman that you've forgotten the young Indian squaw? You do remember her—the one whose skull you shattered with the butt of your musket?!"

The constable rolled his tongue over parched and trembling lips and uttered a response. "How do you know of this...?!"

Eblis' grin widened. "Confess thy guilt! It's been a long, long time hasn't it constable?! Time tends to heal old wounds and the wisdom of age spawns repentance and a desire for forgiveness! I have called upon you at this time for I fear you are moving in that direction...you are weakening! So it is time to be reminded!"

"I was justified!" the constable defended. "It occurred during the Indian War! She was the enemy—an ally of the French!"

Eblis' grin vanished from his face as he reached down with his right hand and gripped the constable by the neck. He pulled Dixey into a standing position and pressed his back to the wall. Eblis growled. "You might be able to deceive the sinful townsfolk of

Lynn..." he bellowed in a gruff voice, "but...DO...
NOT...DECEIVE....ME!!"

Dixey found himself staring into Eblis' eyes with their rapidly
rotating iris' that grew in size, drawing the helpless constable into a
state of hypnosis. When the evil shoemaker tightened the grip around
the constable's throat, the trance was broken and Eblis had been
transformed into a large, bronze-skinned Indian warrior with shoulder-length black hair. He wore only the skin of a deer around his waist
and his embittered face and muscular body displayed streaks of a
colorful war paint. Still gripping Dixey's throat, the Redman lifted the
lawman several feet above the floor. Suspended in mid-air, the
constable gasped for air, kicking his dangling feet wildly, while the
Indian snarled and produced an infernal growl. "CONFESS!!" he
hissed.

The constable spouted, "She...she was...enemy...!"

"SHE WAS WAMPANOAG!" the Indian challenged.

"No! Enemy...!" the constable persisted.

"WAMPANOAG—ALLY OF THE COLONIES!"

The constable's face had now turned a shade of purple. His eyelids
grew heavy and he could feel himself losing consciousness. "Wan-
panoag...yes she was Wampanoag... and I killed her! I raped her...and I
killed her...!" he gasped.

The Indian released his grip and the constable crashed to the floor
panting. Towering above Dixey, the warrior pounded on his chest with
his fists and emitted a harsh cry.

Still gasping, Dixey lifted his head. Despite his frightening situation, he gathered up enough courage to hurl a final insult. "She
deserved to die! Filthy savages—all of you!" The constable's voice
began to fade as he lowered his head with shame and gazed down at
the wooden floor.

When the constable lifted his eyes again, he noticed that the
warrior now clutched a hatchet within the palm of his right hand.
With his left hand, the Indian reached down and plucked the wig
from atop Dixey's head, tossing it aside. Before the constable could
react, the savage reached back down and grabbed hold of a patch of
the law man's thinning hair, holding his head steady, slowly raising the
right arm that held the hatchet high above the constable.

Dixey gripped the Indian's powerful left arm and begged for mercy as tears streaked down both cheeks. The Indian belted out a high shrill and swung the hatchet at the constable's head. Dixey closed his eyes and cried out.

When he realized he had felt nothing after anticipating the explosion of the hatchet against his skull, the constable slowly opened his eyes. With probing fingers he cautiously ran his fingers across the top of his head and looked up to find the Indian had been replaced by Eblis, who stood above him with an accusatory scowl and arms folded across his chest. "By masking your prejudice behind the guise of war, you have secured your fate! The Indian...well, he was a glimpse of your destiny, my good constable! For this scene will be played out for all eternity!

"One hundred years before, the sentence for such a crime as rape and murder was to be hanged by the neck in a manner that kept the criminal barely alive! Next the bowels were cut out and set ablaze before the criminal's own eyes, and finally the head was lopped off and the body quartered! But such a sentence bestows more punishment upon the witnesses who are faced with the grim task of mentally preserving the scene! For the accused it is but a few minutes of pain! Thy greatest mistake, Constable Dixey, was that the circumstances of life did not afford thee the luxury of an earthly sentence...as it is, I am left as your accuser! And make no mistake," he growled, "There exists NO repentance in my kingdom!"

The constable sank his head into his hands and wept.

"The stench of your cowardice pollutes this building! LEAVE ME NOW!" Eblis commanded and pointed toward the door. Instantly the door swung open of its own power.

The shattered constable pulled himself to his feet, picking up the wig. He gazed submissively at Eblis as he placed the hair piece upon his head. Suddenly he felt a bristly sensation against his scalp. Reaching up to his head, Dixey placed his hand upon the wig and retrieved a small, slimy object. Quickly he brought his hand back down and opened his palm to find a live silkworm. The constable shuddered and tossed the worm to the ground and quickly yanked the wig from his head. Eblis roared with a sinister laughter as the constable glared with horror upon the white hair piece blanketed by hundreds of the busy silkworms that he held within his hands. Dixey flung the wig to the floor and bolted from the outbuilding.

. . .

FROM THE WINDOW OF OUR SHOP, WE WATCHED THE CONSTABLE emerge from out of the alley on a *dead* run and as he made the turn onto the main street, he slipped on the wet cobblestone, falling face down into a large puddle. Hastily he picked himself up from out of the water and continued his dash down the center of the street.

"Why does he run?!" Kerstland asked aloud as he exited the shop.

We followed Sam's father outside into the rain to get a better glimpse of the fleeting constable when suddenly a vein of lightning streaked down from out of the sky. With a blue flash of light, the bolt of electricity impaled the constable, dropping him to the cobblestone as a tremendous explosion of thunder rattled the shops along the street. The terrifying incident stopped us in our tracks for a moment and then we rushed to the aid of the unfortunate lawman lying face up against the wet cobblestone. Dixey's eyelids remained opened and his lips apart—frozen in a final breath of death, while a wisp of smoke emerged from out of a large black hole that had been bored into the chest of his vest.

Sickened by the sight, I grimaced and looked away as Kerstland attempted to shield his daughter from the horrifying display.

Soon a small crowd gathered around the constable and as someone began to inquire about the events preceding Dixey's flight down the street, eyes followed eyes until the bystanders had all turned their heads to the rear. Strolling slowly down the center of the cobblestone street with a haughty stride that commanded the respect of the townsfolk as if he were the king himself was Cyrus Eblis, clutching a red tricorn and a white periwig. The crowd parted and Eblis stepped through the group. He acknowledged me with a wily glance before gazing down stoically upon the constable's body. "Unlucky soul," he began. "He had set his wig and tricorn down upon one of my trays for to dry, when some of my silkworms found their way into the powdered hair. When the constable placed the hair piece back upon his head, the silkworms seemed to terrify him into such a frenzied state that he ran from my outbuilding with not so much as a farewell." Eblis reached down and placed the tricorn and periwig upon the constable's chest. "Farewell Constable Dixey," he offered, with a devious grin.

CHAPTER 15

By noon the rain had ceased and the sun reappeared; although the day's transformation could do little to lift our dampened spirits after having beheld the Constable's violent death. Business went on as usual as the brightening of the day encouraged Kerstland to fulfill his promise of a shoe delivery to a notable lawyer. The affluent gentleman, Albert Goode, resided in a large house just north of the fishing village of Swampscott in the northeastern section of Lynn. Kerstland asked me to make the delivery and so I hitched the horse to the shoemaker's two-wheeled cart, grabbed the burlap sack containing a pair of jackboots, and climbed atop the perch of the wooden vehicle. With a "giddy-up" and a slap of the reins, I guided the horse-drawn cart down the street toward my uncle's home; for I saw this as a perfect opportunity to finally be rid of the cask of molasses that Eblis had burdened me with. And so my first stop was at the Brown residence to retrieve the wooden barrel.

Once I had procured the cask, I climbed back into the cart and headed east through the streets of Lynn. After only a few blocks the row of white houses ended and the narrow, muddy road carved a route through a forest of white and pitch pine interspersed with white and red cedar. My horse clopped along, splashing mud and pulling the cart through several inches of mire at various places along the road that required an extra snap of the reins to free the vehicle when the wheels would become stuck in the mud. Before long I emerged from the forest, continuing along the route that was now raised, winding through and a few feet above a red bog of cranberry shrubs spreading out on either side of the road. After a few minutes the road narrowed and gradually ascended upwards away from the bog as it carved a circuitous route around the larger stones of a rocky hill. A huge boulder dominated the peak of this rising ground composing the summit of a fifty foot high rock formation known as *Black Will's Cliff*, made popular in a local story that claimed an Indian named *Poquanum*, who the early colonists called *Duke William*, once inhabited the hill.

The eastern face of the rock was sheared exposing the height of the cliff that dropped away abruptly, and the road, which now began a descent, proved more hazardous. Beneath the rocky formation the profusion of cranberry shrubs returned to dominate the geography until disappearing as the fringe of the tiny fishing village of Swampscott. I stopped the cart for a moment to gaze upon the stunning view from *Black Will's Cliff*. Beyond the pointed arched roofs of the fishing village towered the masts of fisherman's boats standing at attention from their positions moored to the docks in the harbor. Soaring gulls squawked and circled the masts, gliding effortlessly with a steady breeze that pushed the dark rain clouds of the morning out in the direction of the horizon. A crack of thunder could be heard faintly in the distance, competing with the rhythmic splash of rushing water against a shoreline of shining gray sand.

The horse began to pull the cart down the hillside in the direction of the shoreline north of the fishing village, when I came upon another cliff appropriately called *Dread Ledge* for the dangerous shelf of rocks that extended out above the raging surf below. Pulling on the reins of the horse, I brought the cart to a stop, removed my tricorn and climbed down from the perch. At the rear of the cart, I hoisted the cask of molasses upon my shoulder and carried it over to the ledge.

I paused to gaze down into the churning surf spewing the foamy water over the coarse-grained greenstone and the view left my stomach churning as well—a symptom of my fear of heights acquired years before as a result of my brother's accident. Yet I realized that to be rid of the cask completely, I would need to overcome my fear and climb farther down the ledge to prevent the barrel from becoming snagged on a group of rocks. *The cask needed to be destroyed.* I took a deep breath and began the dreadful task of descending the cliff.

I tried not to look down as the spray of cold saltwater saturated my face with each wave that crashed against the ledge, and carefully maneuvered my way down the shelf, planting one foot at a time on the slippery rocks. When I felt certain I was far enough down the cliff to heave the cask out into the surf, I tossed the heavy object away and watched it explode against the rocks. The barrel splintered into a thousand pieces of wood, momentarily contaminating the white surf with the dark syrup; but before I could revel over the cask's destruction, the rock supporting my left foot broke free and toppled down the cliff, disappearing beneath the swirling water. I managed to shift my weight to my right foot—my arms outstretched at my side as if I were balancing on a high wire—and slowly brought my dangling left foot back in and rested it on a stable rock, leaning back against the cliff wall. I stood there motionless for a moment, gathering my courage before slowly turning over so that my stomach pressed against the wall hugging the rocks. The thoughts of falling into the surf petrified me and I became frozen to the ledge.

Suddenly a burst of ocean spray saturated my back, rescuing me from my trance. I began grappling the slimy rocks with both hands and managed to slither up the shelf like a serpent. As I neared the crest of the ledge, I reached up to grab a large stone from which to pull myself over the top, but at that instant the rock beneath my right foot gave way and I felt myself sliding back downward. Quickly I snatched another protruding rock in an effort to halt my slide and glanced menacingly at the surf below.

"Benjamin!" called a voice from above.

I looked up and to my horror saw the gloating face of Cyrus Eblis staring down at me.

"It would seem that cask has been more trouble than it's worth!" he called out with a smile, seeming to delight in my predicament. Clad in his customary grey frock and wide-brimmed circular hat, the sinister shoemaker knelt on the ground and extended his upper body out over the shelf as a gargoyle is fixed to the lofty ledge of a church. I don't recall what I feared more—the raging surf below or the devilish grin of Eblis above.

"Are you frightened?" Eblis teased. "I wonder Benjamin, if your brother Jordan felt as you do now before falling to the base of that cliff?"

How does he know of Jordan? "Leave me alone!" I cried out.

"And what hand did you play in your brother's tragic end? Why it was your hand that pushed him! Was it not, Benjamin?!"

Eblis had opened an old wound and I was quickly on the defensive. "It wasn't my doing!" I yelled. "He slipped...he slipped! It was an accident!"

"My, my. Poor Benjamin. Again I find you in a vulnerable situation. Yet I fail to understand why you have gone to so much trouble to be rid of a cask of molasses—a symbol of our friendship...of our union?!"

"Union?!" I yelled with anger, glancing down at the surf and then back up at Eblis who now offered assistance extending his right hand toward me.

"Here my young friend, give me your hand!"

I hesitated. "Why have you followed me to Lynn?!"

"Do you not trust me, Benjamin?! Your hand!" he persisted.

"No!" I called back defiantly. "I'll take my chances!"

Eblis sneered. "I detect hostility in your voice, Benjamin! I shall say you are hardly in the position to bear malice toward anyone, let alone a friend!"

"You are not my friend!" I yelled. "What do you want of me?!"

The smile ran away from Eblis' face. He withdrew his hand and rose to a standing position at the edge of the cliff. The hat he wore was set in flight and his cape unfurled with the wind. He cast a vengeful stare and pointed down at me. "You are fortunate this day, Benjamin! For I am in no hurry to acquire that which I desire; but the time draws near!"

I trembled and looked down at the raging surf once again and then looked up; but as suddenly as he had appeared, the sinister shoemaker was gone.

I found a burst of energy and pulled myself over top of the ledge on all fours before stumbling to my feet. Eblis had truly vanished. There was no-one in sight; although an unsettling calm permeated the air elevating my fear. Quickly climbing onto the perch of the cart, I placed the tricorn on my head, and brushed the mud from my soiled clothing. With a hurried snap of the reins I turned the cart around, proceeding away from *Dread Ledge* and back toward *Black Will's Cliff* wrestling with those threatening words of Eblis. *What did I have that he desired?* The words teased and tormented me.

The horse began to pull the vehicle up the hill when my attention was suddenly drawn to the craggy face of *Black Will's Cliff*, stunned at the sight of a boy clinging to the rocks with his back toward me. He looked to be in trouble but made no sound. Pulling on the reins, I stopped the cart and gazed up with amazement, unsure of what course of action to take. Without warning, the boy lost his grip and fell away from the cliff; although from my vantage point I could not see where he landed. Quickly I jumped from the cart and ran through the marshy soil and its sea of cranberry shrubs until reaching a spot where I could see the base of the cliff littered with rocks and open with sparse vegetation; but no boy lay amidst the rubble. *Was it real? Did I see a boy fall from the cliff? Is this the work of Eblis?* My mind was laden with questions and with frightened feet I hurried back to the cart.

Climbing onto the seat of the vehicle, I guided the horse and cart forebodingly past the rocky summit of *Black Will's Cliff* and down the slight grade through the cranberry bog. Turning my head, I surveyed the vast hillside of stemmed plants speckled with its red fruit, looking for someone or something I did not understand, when off to the right the boy reappeared. He stood statuesquely waist-high in cranberry shrubs at a distance that made it impossible for me to distinguish his face. My mind filled with terrifying images of my brother's final moments and I felt glad I could not identify the specter—certain now I was being haunted.

The horse pulled the cart up to a fork in the road and so I steered the vehicle off to the right, bound now in a northerly direction and away from the woods. Still the specter loomed in the distance and I snapped the reins to quicken the horse's pace while keeping a steady eye on the ghostly presence; but my concentration was shattered when the wheel of the cart struck a large rock in the road jarring the vehicle. I directed my attention away from the cranberry bog to check the condition of the cart wheel before glancing back in the direction of the specter—but it was gone. Unnerved, I brought the cart to a stop and scanned the bog. The eerie stillness was broken by a steady breeze that rustled the cranberries, carrying the faint sibilance of breaking waves. I cringed and rubbed my sweaty palms against the leather reins. "Giddy-up!" I commanded, snapping the straps; but the horse would not move. "Giddy-up!" I persisted, to no avail. "What is the matter?! Giddy-up!" I shouted again, but the horse maintained its frozen pose with not so much as a glance back at me. I was dumb-founded.

Suddenly, at a distance of nearly ten rods from the cart, the specter materialized in the middle of the road ahead of me. I could not believe my eyes. Where there was once dirt, the physique of the boy incarnated from out of thin air, convincing me that a solid figure of flesh and blood blocked my path.

I do not recall how or why I climbed down from the cart; never-theless, at one point I was standing beside the horse staring at the ghost, which remained motionless. Still I could not see the boy's face and suddenly, as though I were in a trance, I began a slow march toward him. Each step seemed to carry me further from the world I knew into a realm of the supernatural, for I could no longer feel the breeze or hear the ocean and the cranberry bog disappeared within a milky fog. Even the road before me vanished; although my feet continued to touch solid ground. Yet the apparition of the boy grew clearer. I remembered his suit of blue silk with buttonholes of silver thread, the sandy blond hair that appeared perpetually ruffled by the wind, and the wily curvature of his smile, bespeaking of a calculated wit that I had emulated a thousand times. *Jordan...It is my brother!*

"Hey there!" The two words stopped my advance and I turned around. As I did, my world reappeared like the departure of dew at daybreak. A rider on horseback called to me, "Do you need assistance?!"

I turned back toward the specter; but it was gone.

"I say there, do you need assistance?!" the gentleman called again as he drew near.

"No!" I replied and hurriedly returned to the cart.

The rider slowly passed me by, studying me with a curious look before directing his horse into a gallop. As the stranger disappeared ahead of me, I climbed aboard the vehicle and snapped the reins, sending the horse back into motion pulling the cart. I would not see the specter again that afternoon.

A SHORT TIME LATER THE CRANBERRY BOG GAVE WAY TO A SERIES OF grassy knolls highlighted by patches of samphire. Occasional groves of pine and birch, spared from the Indian's hatchet and the white man's axe, broke the colorful pattern of green grass and white flowers, providing sanctuary for the melodic whippoorwill. The change of scenery helped to clear my mind of the macabre encounters at the ledge and in the cranberry bog.

Emerging from one such grove, I came upon a wooden gate attached to a low stone wall. A long dirt road, beginning inside the gate, linked the highway to the front door of a grand white house and I guided the horse and cart inside the open gate and up the road, admiring the green terraces staggered with pine and oak trees that surrounded the road on either side. As I approached the front door, I noticed a girl positioned off to the right, many rods from the house in the direction of the ocean. Seated on a wooden chair equipped with two large wheels at the sides and a smaller wheel set in the front, she appeared to be painting on a piece of canvas that rested on an easel set in front of her. She acknowledged my presence with a wave of the hand and continued painting.

Pulling on the reins, I stopped the horse and cart before the front door and gazed upon the house. The seven-gabled Turner house in Salem was the largest home I had ever seen; although this three-story house rivaled its immense size and stunning architecture. I looked up and marveled at the great number of windows in the house. Glass was expensive in the colonies, but this home featured twelve windows on the façade and those located on the first floor were equipped with eighteen panes each.

I jumped from the cart grabbing the burlap bag and reached inside pulling out the shiny pair of black jackboots. Tossing the bag back onto the cart, I proceeded to climb four stone steps that led to a small porch situated between two columns that supported a flat square roof with a white balustrade. Off to one side of the stone steps were positioned several wooden planks nailed together to form a narrow ramp which I assumed was used to accommodate the wheelchair. Even the polished brass door knuckle bespoke of wealth and I used it to call upon the occupants of the home after viewing my disheveled reflection in the ornament.

A few minutes passed before the door opened and I was met by a chubby Negro woman in a white muslin cap tied underneath the chin. She studied my soiled shoes and breeches with a suspicious glare.

"Good day," I greeted.

"What is it?" she asked brushing her hands on an apron splashed with baking powder.

"I have jackboots for Master Goode," I explained holding the shoes up for her to see.

"At least they is cleaner than ya own."

I was embarrassed. "I've had an accident."

The woman nodded. "Is ya hurt?"

I shook my head.

"Hmmm. Master Goode is away on business."

"The shoes are paid for. I have only come to deliver them," I said presenting her the jackboots.

She took the pair of jackboots from my hand and bid me good day.

I smiled and tipped my tricorn before descending the steps as the door closed behind me. Preparing to hoist myself onto the cart, I was once again distracted by the girl in the wheelchair and I paused to watch her hand swish the brush across the canvas. At that moment a stiff wind whipped across the yard, lifting the girl's fawn-colored hat from her head. As the big brimmed hat tumbled lazily across the yard, I decided to make a gallant dash to retrieve it; but my chivalry quickly turned to foolery, for upon reaching the fluttering object I slipped on the wet grass and fell back on the seat of my breeches, losing my own hat in the process. Embarrassingly I glanced over at the damsel who was bent over with laughter and pulled myself from off the ground, plucking both hats from the grass. I began stepping in the direction of the girl who ceased giggling with my approach, regaining her composure behind a pleasant smile. It was a smile I had seen before, and I recognized her as the handicapped girl who I watched in attendance every Sunday at the meeting-house.

"I seem to have embarrassed myself," I said handing her the hat.

"Thank you and please forgive my laughter," she responded pleasantly. "It's just that...when you slipped..." she erupted into laughter again and I too found myself chuckling over the incident.

She held out her hand. "I'm Rachel Goode."

"And I am Benjamin Pratt," I responded shaking her hand.

"You have brought something for my father?"

"Shoes. I am a journeyman under the employ of Emery Kerstland."

"My father has known Master Kerstland for years. I presume you live in Lynn?"

"Yes. I live with my uncle and aunt—Edward and Jamesina Brown. My mother lives in Falmouth," I explained and stepped closer to get a look at the painting. The incomplete portrait was of the seascape to the east of the house. I glanced beyond the easel at the blue line of the ocean's horizon appearing just above the edge of the cliff. "It is very good. You are an artist."

"It is a perfect hobby for someone like myself—confined to this chair. It is my escape," she explained. Playfully she placed the hat over her light brown hair that was creped, with two rolls at each side. She adjusted the hat, making sure its small crown was placed in the center of her head and then produced a curious smirk when she caught a glimpse of my soiled breeches and shoes. "I didn't realize the price you paid to rescue my hat?"

I looked down at my breeches and then up at Rachel. "Oh, I did this earlier...an accident on my way to your house."

"How terrible. Are you all right?"

"Yes. It was nothing."

Rachel smiled and turned away from me. I took a moment to admire her delicate features complimented by a slender build beneath her quilted, white cotton, Holland gown. Not wanting to appear too obvious in my circumspection, I resumed the conversation. "Your painting—it is a striking likeness of the cliff and horizon, but I notice one error. It is the birch tree. The one you have painted is blossomed with its branches full of green leaves; however the one I see before me is dead. Its limbs are scarred and its branches barren."

Rachel sighed and sat back with a look of contentment. "I like to imagine the tree as it was. Benjamin, look closely at the largest limb on the tree. What do you see?"

I looked up from the easel and out at the tree on the edge of the cliff. "It looks to be a nest."

"Yes. Even that which is deformed by nature has a purpose," she enlightened with a quizzical smile.

I didn't know what to say. Rachel lifted the brush she held in her right hand and dabbed at the blotches of paint arranged in a circle on a wooden palette. She inserted her left thumb inside the palette hole and lifted it from her lap, exposing a small Bible. She began lapping the colors against the canvass.

"The Good Book," I observed.

Rachel looked down at the book in her lap and then up at me with an angelic grin. "It gives me peace."

Our conversation was interrupted by the Negro woman who called to Rachel.

"It's all right, Dinah!" Rachel replied and then turned toward me. "She looks after me. It's not often that a stranger comes to pass the time."

"Is she a slave?"

Rachel giggled. "In name only. We are more civilized under the roof of our house. Dinah is treated as one of the family."

"I don't know many of her kind—Negroes I say."

"If you know one good person with a heart as big as a kettle, then you know Dinah. How many girls of my kind do you know?"

"How do you mean?"

Rachel paused from her painting. "Confined to a chair with wheels," she retorted. "My father had it made special."

"Only thee."

"Yet, your conversation with me has been longer than the one you had with Dinah."

"It is different...I've returned your hat," I stammered.

"But you have allowed her color to impede your cordiality."

"I have not. I had nothing to say to her. My only motive for our conversation—yours and mine--was to retrieve your hat. I would have done the same for the Negro," I explained. "Besides, your servant is much older and..." I paused to carefully select my words, "...much heavier than you."

Rachel chuckled.

I placed my tricorn back upon my head. "I best be on my way."

"Oh, Benjamin. How rude of me. I didn't mean to appear hostile. Sometimes I can be so judgmental—I know."

"No, it is nothing. I understand. It's just that I really must be returning to Lynn."

"Well, if you must go," she offered, holding out her hand which I accepted. "I have really enjoyed talking with you. Please come by and see me again."

CHAPTER 16

C hristmas, 1769

I remember the evening well. The joyous celebration of this holiday began as a pious one, arriving with much anticipation as the residents of Lynn were eager to distance their memories from a year marred by three strange occurrences—Adrian Lyttleton's fiery demise; the violent death of Constable Dixey; and the unsolved disappearance of Anna Hood—the latter which continued to have the townsfolk on edge after nightfall.

Earlier in the day the religious gathering lasted well over six hours. The energized atmosphere was charged by an uplifting sermon and the wooden frame of the meeting-house rattled from the soul-stirring chorus of hymns and prayers. Later, Jamesina assembled a luscious feast centered on a savory turkey that left our stomach's splitting from gluttony. As the day progressed she continued to labor over the hearth, preparing a variety of tasty appetizers for the evening's Christmas party, for, like many of Lynn's shoemakers, Edward Brown had enjoyed a successful fiscal year and decided it was as good a year as any to host a holiday party. The event brought scores of friends into the Brown's home for a night of true merriment—compliments of my aunt and uncle. When my mother arrived from Falmouth, the holiday season seemed complete; although I found myself wrestling with a bout of depression. No matter how hard I tried to forget it, Christmas conjured up memories of my father's death and this grim recollection, coupled with my concern of the ongoing nightmares of Jordan, left me immune to the jocularity surrounding me.

The roaring fireplace burned bright as the large room of the Brown's home filled quickly with invited guests—many of with whom I was familiar, such as the Kerstlands. Dressed in their best suits and gowns, the colorful crowd dined on Jamesina's appetizers, plum pudding, and mince meat pies—filled with bear's meat, dried pumpkins, and sweetened with maple sugar—while gulping from mugs of cider, ale, or rum. Some even braved my aunt's rancid raspberry tea, which made a political appearance at the party. The duty of three pence on a pound of English tea remained a fiery issue in Lynn and Jamesina desired to advertise her cooperation in the call to discountenance the use of foreign tea.

As I twisted and turned through the crowd I caught bits and pieces of conversations ranging from tea and disgust over the Townshend Acts to the establishment of Dartmouth College. There was a man glorifying the recent assassination of an Indian Chief called Pontiac, and another who bragged of the exploits of a frontiersman with the name of Daniel Boone who had ventured into new territory west of the colonies called Kentucky. By the time I reached the table where the flagon of cider rested, my head was spinning from a surplus of information.

After filling my mug, I turned back toward the crowd and noticed Samantha busily maneuvering her way around bodies as she moved toward me. How beautiful she looked. I was unaccustomed to seeing her dressed so lavishly, clad in a long waist, short-sleeved green gown with an immense frill at the elbow. On top of her head she wore a calash bonnet of green silk that fell back in folds exposing ringlets of auburn hair that bounced against her shoulders.

Sam smiled upon reaching me and extended her mug. "Would you pour me some cider?"

There were one hundred compliments I could have given to describe her appearance at that instant—and I believe any one of them would have taken our friendship to a more intimate level; however, I found humor in how the large hoop, quilted into the hem of the gown, produced an enormous display of the lower person. Before I could make light of it, Sam interjected, "And not a word about my gown!"

"It looks...nice," I described.

"Many have told me so; but my feet are aching and I'm afraid to pass near to a table of food lest I clear it with this gargantuan object I have surrounding my waist!" she described as I began filling her cup from the flagon. As I poured, from out of the corner of my eye I caught a glimpse of Sam's sister Muriel, gliding across the room with a dignified step. Her well-proportioned figure called attention to her costume—a crimson brocade over a petticoat of white satin embroidered with a colorful design. The striking young lass appeared quite confident and very forward in eliciting conversation as she meandered her way through the sea of guests.

"Yonder is your sister."

"How could you miss her?" Sam replied in a repugnant tone. "She's very good at it, don't you think?"

"Good at what?"

"Flirting. Watch how she baits the hungry wolves with a giggle and a soft whisper with each word she speaks. Words so soft that a gentleman need lean his face close enough for to hear...so close that he can feel her warm breath against his skin and suffocate from the scent of perfume that envelops her!"

I found the description exciting. "Perhaps I shall go speak with her," I said with a coy grin.

The comment brought a scolding glare to Sam's face. "Why don't you?!" she dared.

I laughed. "I'm having fun with you."

"Well, if those with whom she speaks were to hear her whining at the top of her grating voice—*Sam, where are my shoes?!...Sam, where is my bonnet?!*—it would be enough to set the teeth of the hungry wolves on edge and send them running for the hills!"

"I gather you have a dislike for your sister—jealousy perhaps?"

Samantha's face flushed with anger. "Perhaps not!" she responded quickly. "It is her attitude. She is well-equipped to capture the lust of any man, but she is very cavalier about brandishing her attributes. It is like the King's soldier in Massachusetts who does as he pleases because he wears a red coat and carries a musket."

"Don't look now, but her attributes are pointed in our direction," I warned as Muriel moved toward us. Her arrogant smile grew larger as she approached, gently swinging the perforated box containing perfumes that hung from her waist.

When Muriel stopped before us, the teenage beauty cast a spell over me that left me tongue-tied and warm with fever.

"Well, what a lovely couple," she said mockingly.

Sam clenched her teeth and forced a smile. "Muriel, I would like you to meet Benjamin Pratt—a journeyman in father's shop."

I nodded. "Hello, Miss Muriel."

"Charmed, I'm sure," she greeted, turning up her chin and batting eyelashes as though she were the Duchess of York. "I know who you are, Benjamin. My little sister speaks of you quite often," Muriel divulged with a coy glance at Sam.

"He is a good friend," Samantha defended quickly, "and that is the manner in which I speak of him."

"Today a friend, tomorrow a..." Muriel paused and paraded her eyes up and down my physique. "Tomorrow a better friend," she added quickly.

I didn't know how to take the comment, but the incensed look upon Sam's face implied that I was better off not knowing. Although they were sisters, I found it interesting how very different their personalities.

Suddenly chilled by a cold draft, all three of us immediately turned toward the entry hall door where my uncle greeted a man wearing a waistcoat of bright red cloth with silver buttons and close fitting breeches. When the guest removed his white scarf and black tricorn I saw that it was Caleb. He stepped into the room from the entry hall and before he could adjust his vest, my cousin became flocked by a great many admirers.

"Is that not Caleb Brown?" Muriel asked with piqued interest. "He is as handsome as they say. I must make his acquaintance."

Sam and I looked at one another whimsically as Muriel disappeared into the crowd.

"Well, what did you think of my sister?"

"You are very different than she."

"I'm not certain how I should take such a comment?"

"It's a compliment—from one...friend...to another."

Sam took a sip from her mug. "Caleb is very popular. The guests are drawn to him as though he were the governor himself."

"Yes. He certainly has found the right profession."

"I, myself fail to see the attraction to a religious man."

"It is not religion that draws these people to my cousin; but rather, I am convinced it is his nature. He is very charming and intelligent." I paused, staring across the room at Caleb. "There are men born into this world to lead and those born to follow. Caleb's been given a wonderful gift—the ability to lead and influence people."

"And what about you?" Sam quickly countered with a quizzical smile. "You are of the same blood? Were you born to lead or to follow?"

I turned toward Sam. "There is only one Caleb in our family. I am happy as a journeyman."

"Do I sense jealousy in your voice?" she pried.

"I admire Caleb...I always have. His reputation speaks for itself."

Sam drained the last ounce of cider from her mug, set it softly down upon the table and gazed at me with a grin. "The leader is a reflection of his followers. For without those that follow there would be no-one to lead," she said before turning away.

I pondered her statement for some time, standing there in front of the table like a piece of furniture. As Caleb inched his way across the room, with his jaws moving faster than his feet, I stood alone, immaterial as though I had disappeared. *Perhaps Samantha is right—maybe I am jealous. For I have not the charm, wit, looks, or brains of my cousin. Yet, how could I compete? Why should I compete?* A feeling of emptiness set in upon me, so I slipped through the crowd and exited the back door.

Stepping out onto the snow-covered cobblestone at the rear of the house, I found the air to be chilly but crisp and the full moon loomed just above the roof tops like a curious friend. I sunk my hands into the pockets of my breeches and with the toe of my right boot began to trace the name *Jordan* in the snow. When I had finished, I leaned over and scooped a handful of wet snow from off the ground, molded a solid ball and tossed it with surprising accuracy at the branch of a neighbor's tree. "Good shot," a voice acknowledged from behind me. I turned around to find Caleb stepping through the back door.

"Do you remember as boys how we skimmed stones across Spring Pond?" Caleb recalled, his breath appearing in the cool evening air. "Of the three of us, yours was always the best arm."

"You can't make a living skimming stones," I replied.

Caleb grinned. "Thank goodness for my sake."

"And I remember how Jordan would forever try to persuade us to throw in an easterly direction claiming we were throwing with the wind," I continued, recalling the pleasant memories with a smile. "But it didn't take long to realize that we were throwing into the sun and unable to see the extra skip Jordan claimed each one of his stones would take." Indiscreetly I brushed Jordan's name from the snow with the sole of my boot.

Caleb produced a smirk. "No handshake my good cousin?"

I stepped toward Caleb and shook his hand which extended into a firm hug.

"Now what brings you out here? The party's inside?" Caleb asked, gently pushing me away.

"I needed some air."

"And I the same. It seems as though all of Lynn is present this evening."

"You are certainly popular."

Caleb chuckled. "It's not that I'm popular, Ben. It's that I hail from somewhere else. For many of the guests, places like Boston and Simsbury are a far cry from Lynn. And so I bring news. People are hungry for news—news of the latest in fashion; news of colonial response to British taxation; news of important people such as Samuel Adams and Benjamin Franklin; news of..."

"News of the Sons of Liberty," I interrupted.

Caleb laughed, "Yes, even news of the Sons of Liberty."

"So what news do you bring?"

"Let me think," Caleb said, pausing for a moment. "Well, in Philadelphia the use of umbrellas as a protection from the sun suddenly became very popular this summer last and thank goodness powdered wigs have gone out of favor. It is now fashionable throughout the colonies to wear the natural hair, which I have done for years; although some men of the law profession still desire the wig."

"And what of British taxation?" I pursued eagerly.

Caleb grinned, amused by my desire for information. "I can tell you that all thirteen colonies are united in their boycott of the Townshend Acts," Caleb informed with excitement. He set his hand upon my shoulder. "Ben, I came outside to escape such questions. Every time I turned around, someone was asking my opinion of taxation. It was all quite taxing." He laughed at himself. "Although...I was approached by a beautiful young lass with the boldness to inquire of my marital status."

"Muriel Kerstland," I offered.

"Kerstland? The shoemaker's daughter?"

"The same."

"She is very attractive; but I found her somewhat presumptuous. Would you not agree?" Caleb described with a smile.

"Oh, yes. You are too kind with your description."

Caleb laughed. "Which reminds me, Ben, how is the journeyman life?"

"Work is steady and I enjoy it very much."

Caleb bent over and scooped a handful of snow from off the ground, packing it into a ball. "And what of that eerie stranger who so frightened thee? What was his name?"

"Eblis. Cyrus Eblis."

"Yes, yes. That's him. Eblis—I can't help but think I've heard the name before," Caleb said as he threw the ball of snow at the neighbor's tree, missing the target. "I did not receive a letter from you so I assumed you had resolved your fears," he added, brushing the remnants of wet snow from his hands.

I did not answer.

"Well?" Caleb asked, turning toward me.

I sighed. "I have not seen him in months. He must be away."

"And your suspicions?"

I took a deep breath. "They have not changed. I believe he is responsible for at least two eerie incidents that have occurred in Lynn this year—the death of Constable Dixey and maybe even the disappearance of Anna Hood."

"Yes, I know. My aunt wrote me of these tragic events. To have a young girl disappear and possibly killed on the streets of Lynn is simply shocking," he said shaking his head with disgust. "The constable's death was an act of God—lightning or something?"

"It was lightning, but I question the divinity of the act."

"I see," Caleb scoffed, rubbing his fingers against his chin. "Who is the new constable?"

"Captain Toomey, and very reluctantly, I might add—especially with Anna Hood's disappearance still unsolved."

"I can imagine. Ben, you mentioned that you believe Eblis to be responsible for these events? That is quite a bold accusation, so what proof do you have that the shoemaker is involved?"

"I saw Eblis out the night of Anna's disappearance and he was with the constable shortly before he died. Eblis was the last to see both alive—I'm sure of it."

Caleb glared at me unconvincingly.

"And then on the cliff..." I continued before being interrupted when the back door suddenly swung open, revealing Jamesina who stood holding it ajar. "Here you are! What are you doing out in the cold?"

"Fresh air, mother," Caleb replied.

"Son, there are a great many guests asking for thee. Why don't you come inside now and oblige them?"

"Yes, mother," Caleb acknowledged. "More questions of taxation," he said to me with a sarcastic glance. "We'll talk later, Ben."

Caleb turned and walked toward the backdoor, disappearing inside. As the door began to swing shut my mother appeared, delicately maneuvering the immense hoop of her black satin dress through the narrow doorway. She stepped outside clasping the dress on either side so as to lift the material in an attempt to prevent the hem from dragging in the snow.

"Hello, mother," I greeted.

"Benjamin, the day has been so busy that we've had little opportunity to speak."

I brushed the snow from the bench and sat down.

"It's very cold out here," she said, crossing her arms at her stomach. "My, how you have grown Benjamin. You have become a very handsome young man."

I dropped my head, somewhat embarrassed.

"I met Emery Kerstland this evening and he's told me what fine journeyman skills you've acquired. Your uncle was right in bringing you to Lynn. Your father would have been very pleased."

I looked up, stirred by the mention of my father. "Do you miss father?"

My mother smiled and approached me. "Not a day goes by that I do not think of him," she revealed, resting her hand upon my shoulder. "And although he is in our thoughts every day, we must come to the realization that he is gone and move forward with our lives. Your father forged the life that we now lead and he has given us pleasurable memories from which to draw upon; but we still possess needs. Memories are wonderful and something that no-one can take away from you." She paused, "However it becomes necessary to summon the living for the fulfillment of one's needs."

"I remember our home in Salem," I replied.

My mother released her hand from my shoulder. "Your home is now here, in Lynn," she said, still smiling.

"When do you plan to return to the house?"

The smile ran away from her face as she bowed her head. "I have no plans to return, Benjamin. In fact I've recently sold the property."

I was surprised. "Then you are moving to Lynn?"

She looked up. "No, Benjamin. I'm staying in Falmouth. I've met someone." She hesitated, carefully choosing her words. "No-one could ever replace your father and the love we shared; but I am still a young woman and Aidan—that is his name—has become an important part of my life. His companionship and support over the last twelve months has helped fill the emptiness within my heart." She paused and eagerly awaited my response.

I didn't know how to respond. There was no anger; no regret; no jealousy; no excitement—I was numb. "I'm happy for you mother," was the best I could do.

She hugged me. "I was concerned on how you might react. But I should have known better—for you have grown up. Aidan is anxious to meet thee. In fact, he was to journey here with me but his work has kept him at home."

"What work is this?"

"He is a joiner and is currently overrun by a great many orders for the construction of coffins."

"Coffins?"

"Yes. Strangely, in the past month alone six people have met their death."

"That is strange. Lynn has recently lost Adrian Lyttleton and Constable Dixey. And Anna Hood remains missing."

"Yes, it is very sad. The deaths in Falmouth have all been accidental; but have come in bunches. This week last, a neighbor—God bless her—was crushed to death by the hooves a frightened mare while she walked to the Sunday service. Tragic thing. She was such a friendly soul. Only the day before we were discussing her new shoes—a bright pair of clogs crafted from the skillful hands of a cat-whipper."

"A cat-whipper?" I repeated with much curiosity in my voice.

"Why, yes. In fact I believe she told me that the cat-whipper hailed from Lynn."

My heart began to race. "What was his name?" I asked slowly rising to my feet.

"I don't believe she told me his name," my mother said before chuckling.

"What is it, mother?" I pressed.

"Oh, nothing...It's silly, really. Actually quite morose in the wake of her untimely death."

"What are you talking about?"

"It seems that Molly—that was my neighbor's name—had become attracted to this cat-whipper. She mentioned that he had the strangest eyes. As I remember it, she said that one eye was blue and the other brown."

My heart stopped and my jaw dropped. *It can't be? Is Eblis in Falmouth?*

"Benjamin?! The color has faded from your face! What is the matter?!" my mother inquired. "Have you taken ill?!"

Suddenly the clopping of horse's hooves against the cobblestone broke me from my trance and I turned away from my mother and in the direction of the horse. I took two steps to my right and peered around the side of the house to get a view of Park Street. On the opposite side of the street was positioned a closed black chaise with its horse at rest, while a portly Negro woman, who I recognized as Dinah, stepped from out of the carriage at curbside. She was followed by a man who moved past her and proceeded up a walk where he was admitted into a neighboring home. Dinah waited until he had entered before climbing back inside the chaise.

I stepped back over to where my mother stood and placed both my hands on her shoulders. "Mother, I see an old friend. In that it grows colder why don't you return to the party and I shall follow you momentarily," I advised.

"Well, all right. Don't be long."

"And mother...," I continued, still with a hold of her shoulders, "...

promise me you will avoid contact with this cat-whipper—the man with one eye blue and the other brown."

"But Ben...?"

"Promise me," I interrupted with conviction. "I know this man," I explained, now with a whisper. "His name is Cyrus Eblis. He is not a good man."

"Ben, surely you do not believe that this man is responsible for Molly's death? It was a horse...a horse without a rider that trampled her," she scoffed.

I smiled and lifted my hands from her shoulders. "I...I just worry about you. Please promise me?"

"It is a very strange request, Benjamin, but if it will make you feel more at ease..."

"It will!"

"Then you have my word."

I kissed her on the cheek. "Now I must say hello to my friend."

"We shall speak later," she said. I watched her until she re-entered the house before turning away and beginning a stroll across the snow-covered yard and in between the horseblocks that staggered parked carriages and tied horses belonging to my aunt and uncle's guests. When I began crossing the street toward the chaise, Rachel Goode popped her head out from behind the collapsible hood of the carriage and pulled back her loose hooded cloak trimmed with fur. "Merry Christmas, Benjamin Pratt!" she called out with a large smile and a wave of her hand.

Her quick and friendly recognition of me produced a smile of my own. "And to you the same!" I replied stepping up to the chaise.

"Why it be that young man with them soiled breeches," Dinah described poking her head from the chaise as well.

"They're much cleaner this evening," Rachel acknowledged play-fully. "He's obviously the guest of a party."

"This is my home," I said, pointing across the street toward the house.

"So you're the host?" Rachel inquired.

"Not exactly. It's my aunt and uncle's party," I informed and then noticed the string of gold beads fastened around her neck. "You too are dressed for a party."

"Yes, we are bound for Saugus."

"Saugus?" I was curious. "That is quite a journey from Swampscott. It must be a special host?"

"The host is a client of my father. My father happens to be a respected lawyer with wealthy clients and the governor will be in attendance."

"The governor? So you'll be drinking English tea this evening?" I said impudently.

Rachel frowned. "I don't enjoy politics. My father's profession practically requires his attendance at such events. Frankly, I find it all quite boring."

"Why have you stopped here?" I asked, gazing upon the house in which Rachel's father had just entered. "Is that not Duff Kennedy's home—the hatter?"

"Yes. My father is picking up an order—gifts for our host's wife and for the governor's wife," Rachel replied. She extended her head forward and tilted it toward the sky capturing the reflection of the moon in her eyes. "What a glorious evening! The Lord has provided calm weather and the light of a full moon to celebrate the birth of His son! If only every day were as Christmas!"

I cleared my throat and looked away.

Rachel detected my lack of enthusiasm for the holiday. "Benjamin, what troubles thee?"

I sighed. "I lost my father on Christmas Day."

"I'm sorry."

"I often wonder why the Lord chose Christmas to take him?"

"Does ya think the Almighty has a calendar up there in heaven with Him?" Dinah interjected.

"It is a terrible thing to lose someone close to you at this time of year," Rachel sympathized.

The squeaking hinges of a door grabbed my attention and I looked beyond the chaise to see two men conversing at the front door of Kennedy's home.

"Benjamin, you did mention that you read the Bible?" Rachel asked.

"Yes...yes, that's right," I lied. Despite my cousin's belief in the power of the Lord's prayers, I had not looked at the book since it had failed to ward off the demon shoemaker on the night of Anna Hood's disappearance.

"I set aside one hour every evening to read the Holy Book. It brings me peace. Maybe you could join me some evening?" she asked.

"Yes...maybe I could," I replied with little enthusiasm.

At that moment, Rachel's father stepped up to the chaise clutching a hat box underneath each arm. Dressed in a long gray coat and wearing a red tricorn atop a white powdered bag wig, the gentleman gave me a stern look. "Good evening, young man," he greeted.

"Father, this is Benjamin Pratt," Rachel introduced, placing the hood of her cloak over her head. "He is a journeyman in Master Kerstland's employ."

"Please convey to your employer my satisfaction with the boots," he said as he climbed up onto the perch of the chaise. He set the hat boxes aside, quickly grabbed hold of the reins and snapped them, setting the horse in motion.

"Goodbye, Benjamin!" Rachel called out as the chaise rolled past me and down the street. I watched until it rounded a corner, disappearing from view.

"A female admirer?" a voice called out inquisitively.

I turned around to see Sam. "Just a friend."

I walked toward her.

"She is the daughter of the lawyer from Swampscott, isn't she?"

"How could you tell?"

"The chaise and the slave. Not too many of Lynn's residents have such luxuries. I have seen her at the Sunday service."

I looked down the empty street. The moon cast long shadows against the white-blanketed cobblestone and patches of snow sparkled beneath the glow of staggered street lanterns, like diamonds set against the blackness of a cavern. "Will you walk with me?"

"Just a little ways. It is December, you know," she replied with sarcasm.

Side by side we began a stroll down the street in a southerly direction.

"She walks with crutches, doesn't she—the lawyer's daughter?" Sam asked.

"Rachel Goode? Yes, she is a cripple."

"That is a pity. I don't know how I would react if suddenly I lost the use of my limbs."

"She reads the Bible. It gives her peace of mind."

"But it can't help her mount a horse."

I turned toward Sam with a scolding glance and she just shrugged her shoulders.

"She's asked me to join in her Bible reading," I continued. "Although I didn't have the heart to tell her that I am not the avid Holy Book reader that she may think I am. Nor am I a strong believer."

"You don't believe in God?"

"Of course I do. I just don't believe in the power of the Book."

"Power of the Book? Are you suggesting the Bible has some sort of magical power?" Sam scoffed.

"No...I don't know," I replied, now confused. "Caleb suggests certain readings for certain situations and he talks of them as if they are to be used like magic spells or something."

"It's all about faith, Ben. Not magic spells. Rachel's a cripple. She needs her faith."

"There are times when we are all in need of faith."

"You are speaking of your concern with Master Eblis?"

I nodded.

"I don't believe Cyrus Eblis has been in town for some time?" Sam deduced.

"He's not. I believe he's in Falmouth where six people have died in a month. The latest was a woman who purchased a pair of shoes from a cat-whipper from Lynn. I suspect he may have been the cat-whipper."

"It has been quiet in his absence," Rachel commented. "Maybe he won't be back?"

"No. He'll return."

"Look," she said stopping. Grabbing hold of my arm she directed my attention across the street where a young man teetered along pacing in a manner which left a zigzag pattern in the snow. "It is Daniel Hassett."

"The same Hassett that rents out the shoemaker's shop to Eblis?"

Sam gave an affirmative nod of her head.

"*Well speak of the devil.* I've been anxious to meet this Daniel. I wonder what he can tell us about his boarder?"

"Why don't we wish our neighbor a Merry Christmas?" Sam decided with an incriminating glare.

"Yes, why not?" I agreed, excited by Sam's thirst for adventure.

Cautiously, Sam and I crossed the street and proceeded toward the young man who suddenly froze with our approach.

"Merry Christmas, Daniel," Sam greeted as we stopped a few rods before him.

The young man gazed at us from underneath a soiled hat that was slightly turned up. His face matched the color of the snow and patches of gray lurked beneath each eye. "What do you want?" he snarled with a parched, quivering voice.

"Well...we haven't seen Master Eblis about recently, and were wondering where he might be this day," I replied.

Daniel pulled at the waist of his black and white striped breeches while shifting his eyes back and forth from Sam to me. He breathed heavily and rolled his tongue over dry lips. "He is away," he mumbled and then fixed his eyes on Samantha. "You are the girl from across the street," he hissed with widening eyes.

I sensed Sam was beginning to grow uncomfortable in his presence. "Is your master in Falmouth?" I asked.

Daniel did not acknowledge my question but remained entranced with Sam. "I watch you," he whispered taking a step closer to her. "You have hair like fire!"

I stepped in between Daniel and Sam and repeated, "I say there Daniel, is your master in Falmouth?"

My advance broke Daniel's wild-eyed stare and his facial features contorted as the young man retreated several steps as an animal does when sensing fear. He began to breathe heavily, filling the frosty air before him with a misty vapor from rapid exhalations like a bull snorting before its charge.

"Daniel?" Sam called out stepping into his view once again. Daniel shifted his gaze to her. "We are interested in ordering soles from Master Eblis," she baited. "When is he to return?"

Daniel slid his fingers slowly along the lapel of his long grey coat. He swallowed hard and blinked in rapid succession. "My master is not here. I am to keep the book of orders. It is an important task," he described with excitement. "Give me your name, pretty girl."

Sam hesitated. "We shall come around later in the week," she explained with a gentle cadence. "Then we may speak with your uncle in person."

"Uncle?" Daniel looked confused.

"Master Eblis," Sam explained.

"Master Eblis is my prince!" Daniel stepped closer to Sam and slowly reached out to stroke her hair. Samantha remained motionless and allowed the crazed young man to play with a lock of it. He twirled a few auburn strands in his fingers and doted over it with a delight that frightened both Sam and I. "My mother's hair was as yours," he whispered with heavy breathing. "She beat me," he added calmly as if the painful memory had been relived so many times it could only numb him. "There is a fire that burns within you! The fire hurts! It cries out and makes you hurt others!" At that moment, Daniel tightened his grip on the lock of Sam's hair and pulled hard, jolting her head before releasing his hold. She screamed and I quickly stepped in and shoved the strange young man to the ground.

Daniel glared up at me with a vindictive scowl and began barking like a wild animal. I grabbed Sam's hand and we stepped briskly away from him, crossing the street.

From the opposite side of the street we watched Daniel slowly pull himself to his feet, ceasing his yowling. He stood motionless staring at us as his glower shifted into a childlike grin, and then suddenly began retreating with backward steps before turning and dashing off down an alley with a gurgled cry.

"Are you all right?" I asked Sam.

"Yes," she replied rubbing the side of her head. "I was only frightened, that's all."

"He is certainly one odd fellow," I described.

"Yet, I feel sorry for him," Sam lamented. "He's a troubled child trapped inside the body of a growing man."

"And the ward of a prince," I added. "Only, a prince of what?"

CHAPTER 17

Daniel's prince did return much to our dismay. And if the renewed presence of Cyrus Eblis were not enough to dishearten our new year hopes for peace and harmony, word of the arrest of Alexander McDougall—one of the leaders of the Sons of Liberty—by British soldiers in New York, compounded our worries.

Not long after the first of the year, my mother returned to Aidan in Falmouth and Caleb rejoined his congregation in Simsbury. As for our promise to Daniel about purchasing shoes from his prince, Sam and I decided evasion to be the wisest course.

March, 1770

A HEAVY SNOWFALL DURING THE FIRST WEEK OF MARCH ENCASED the geography of Lynn in white. Gambrel-roofed houses draped by snow provided dimension to the melded landscape, while the tranquility of the surrounding forest was measured by barren branches trimmed in white.

To the west of the town of Lynn flows the river Saugus, having its source in Reading Pond, ten miles from the sea. The term river is a generous one in that its shallow depth and narrow width make it barely sufficient for a mill stream; but now the bite of winter had reduced the crooked river to a sliver of running water that fought the encroachment of ice and snow expanding its banks.

The popular Anchor Tavern is set on the west bank of the river—a stone's throw from a wooden bridge of about two hundred feet in length that crosses the river and links the Boston Road. Located at the midpoint between Boston and Salem, the Anchor became one of the most celebrated taverns in the county.

Dusk had fallen on this particular evening and the darkness along Boston Road near the bridge was broken only by the glimmer of light from a square tavern window.

Beneath the swinging sign-board that depicted the Anchor's emblem, Patch pulled opened the creaking heavy wooden tavern door, emitting the hearty laughter of men's voices cutting through the stillness of the night. Patch wiped the drool from his lips with his sleeve and followed the sprightly sound inside, exchanging glares with the half dozen men scattered about the smoky, raftered ceiling tap-room, before locating the object of his interest. Tall, buxom, with long fiery red hair, the woman with the name of Tirzah stood leaning against the bar's counter.

As a member of the world's oldest profession, Tirzah's unwholesome reputation made her a popular addition to Massachusetts' taverns. It was said that the pleasures she provided were such that some of the colony's most notable figures were rumored to seek out her services—the most preposterous involved Reverend Sparston and his taste for the impious fruit of this woman. The beginning of a stage chaise route between Boston and Salem afforded Tirzah the opportunity to peddle her wares in both port cities and established her as a regular at the Anchor.

Pacing over to the cage-like bar with swinging gate, Patch stopped beside the woman. She stood standing with her back turned toward the spooky little man, as she conversed with another patron.

"Tirzah?" Patch called out boldly.

The woman turned and glared down at the smaller Patch with a condescending smirk.

The large burly man with whom Tirzah conversed was not amused by the interruption and stepped back away from the bar where he could get a look at Patch. "It twas I who was talking to the lass!" he blurted. "Now be off with ya!"

Tirzah reached for a foaming tankard of ale that rested on the bar and brought it to her lips. "I'm busy," she said to Patch before taking a swig from the tankard and turning away from him.

Patch reached inside of his long black coat and retrieved a bulging sack which he dropped on the counter. The impact of the sack against the wooden surface created the unmistakable sound of clinking coins and immediately Tirzah spun back around.

Patch grinned. "My employer desires your services for this evening," the eerie man baited.

Tirzah set her tankard down on the counter. "Just like that, ey? Where is he?"

The burly man to her left stepped away from the bar once again and now positioned himself in between Tirzah and Patch. "How about I toss you outside, ya one-eyed badger!" he exclaimed as he reached for Patch.

Tirzah grabbed his arms and pushed him away. "Richard! Leave him alone!" she intervened and lessened her grip with a playful stroke of his arm. "Thanks for the drink sweetie, but perhaps another time!"

"Tirzah, what is this?!" the man exclaimed, confused. "I thought you said you were done with this dirty profession of yours?!"

"I am done!" Tirzah snapped back and then slid her arm around Patch's shoulder. "I'm only curious as to whom it is that is willing to throw so many coins at me."

Richard hissed under his breath, giving Patch a final infuriating stare, and reluctantly walked across the room and over to the coat rack. Quickly he grabbed his coat, turned with a look of vengeance and exited the tavern.

"I lost a potential customer," Tirzah explained. "This will cost your employer."

Patch grinned. "Name your price."

Tirzah was impressed. "Who is this man?"

Patch cautiously looked about making certain no-one was within hearing distance. "Master Eblis," he whispered.

Tirzah took another swig from the tankard and turned away from the eerie little man. "I'm not so sure tonight laddy...I mean I'm trying to turn a new leaf ya know—clean myself up."

Patch said nothing.

"I've grown tired of being the village whore!" she said before downing another large gulp of ale.

Still maintaining a silent stare, Patch slid the pouch of coins in front of the woman. She slammed the now empty tankard down upon the bar and began caressing the bag of coins with her fingers. "Well maybe just this one more time," she said with a gleam in her eye. "But this'll be the last, I tell ya!" she promised and then turned toward Patch. "Well, let's not keep your Master waiting."

"I have a chaise outside," Patch replied quickly.

The woman stepped from the bar and over to the coat rack retrieving her cloak. Pulling her hood over her hair, Tirzah stood statuesque-like for a moment to clear her head of the several pints of ale she had indulged. Patch adjusted the tricorn that had never left his head and held open the door. With uneasy steps Tirzah proceeded through the doorway of the tavern and out into the night.

Patch had just finished assisting Tirzah into the closed chaise when out of the shadows appeared the burly gentleman who had left the tavern moments earlier embarrassed and enraged that Tirzah had abandoned him at the request of the eerie little man.

Tirzah spied him first. "Richard!" she cried out, alerting Patch.

Patch turned just as the man grabbed the shoulder of his coat. "Quiet, bitch!" the angry man called out to Tirzah. "You were mine tonight! You lied to me! I will not be made the fool!" With his other hand, the man seized hold of Patch's neck. "I'm gonna tear your other eye out...ya freak!"

Suddenly Patch pulled his right arm out from inside his jacket and in his hand he clutched a large knife which he pressed against his attacker's stomach. Taken by surprise, the man quickly released his grip on Patch's shoulder and neck.

Patch grinned and backed Richard against the carriage still pressing the blade of the knife hard against his stomach.

"I don't want no trouble!" the defenseless man now plead with hands raised. "You can have the whore and I'll be on my way!"

Patch stood motionless for a moment, transfixed by the power he held within his hand. The burly man had been reduced to a frightened animal and Patch realized that with one quick thrust he could cut him open.

"Let him go!" Tirzah exclaimed. "He's a fool! He's had too much to drink!"

Patch agreed. More importantly his master would be very upset if he didn't return soon with Tirzah, so the one-eyed shoemaker's helper slowly pulled his knife away from the man and stepped backwards. Richard saw this as an opportunity to dart away within safe distance of the knife-wielding Patch, who climbed up onto the perch of the chaise and grabbed the reins.

"I better never see the likes of ya back here again, ya crazy bastard!" Richard yelled as the horse pulled the chaise onto the road moving in a direction away from the tavern and into the blackness of night.

THIRTY MINUTES HAD PASSED BEFORE THE CHAISE STOPPED IN FRONT of the Hassett residence. After stepping from the carriage, Patch assisted the woman from the vehicle, and the two proceeded around the side of the house, arm-in-arm plodding through the snow. When they reached the first ten-footer behind the house, Patch handed her the sack of coins and pushed open the door to the wooden outbuilding. "I will see you soon," he said with a sinister smile.

Tirzah slowly stepped inside as Patch shut the door behind her, and she removed her hood while glancing around the dimly lit ten-footer. The faint candlelight of a pewter lantern attached to a hook hanging from the center beam of the outbuilding threw shadows about the room; but it was the sudden movement of the long shadow to the rear of the ten-footer that startled the woman.

"Good evening, Miss Tirzah," the shadow greeted moving closer toward the light at the center of the room. "So good of you to come on such short notice."

The shadow's feature materialized underneath the lantern and Tirzah felt relieved to see the handsome, clean-shaven face and well-groomed raven black hair of Cyrus Eblis.

"It pleases me to see your appearance is very much different from that of the frightening messenger who has brought me to you. He nearly killed a man tonight!" Tirzah proclaimed as she undid the string of the cloak tied around her neck. "This is certainly an eerie arrangement—meeting in the cold and darkness of a...what is this place—a shoemaker's shop? It is so cold in here," Tirzah grumbled with a shiver tossing the cloak upon a bench.

Eblis said nothing.

Tirzah held up the sack of coins. "This will cost ya another one of these," she added shaking the sack. "I did not think shoemaking to be such a profitable enterprise," she commented as she began to browse about the ten-footer. "Why, look at all the strings," Tirzah remarked as she grabbed a handful of waxed linen lying in three foot lengths across a table. Positioned beside the strings was a smooth, curved iron that quickly drew her fascination and Tirzah set the strings back down, reaching for the tool. "This is certainly a curious instrument," she described, lifting it off the table. She turned toward Eblis. "Darling, you are certainly a quiet one."

"The iron is used to burnish the sole," Eblis replied stoically.

Tirzah set the iron down and turned once again to the shoemaker. "How is it that I cannot see thy breath, yet mine is as thick as fog in this frigid room?"

"Come beneath the lantern and feel its warmth," Eblis commanded.

"Surely the light from a lantern cannot provide heat for more than a few inches beyond its pewter?"

"Come hither," Eblis repeated.

Tirzah placed the sack of coins down upon a table and paced slowly toward the center of the room stopping directly beneath the lantern and only inches from the shoemaker. She gazed into the eyes of Eblis. "It must be the light in here," she remarked studying his eyes. "No they are different. The color of your eyes, they're different." She turned her attention back to the lamp and instantly an expression of astonishment filled her face. "It really is warm! How can it be?"

"You are comfortable?"

"Yes. Strangely, I am." Tirzah placed both hands on the back of her neck and dipped her head. She pushed the long red hair from off her neck and removed her hands, allowing the hair to fall neatly behind the ears with a shake of her head. She lifted her eyes and gave Eblis a playful smirk. "You are a very handsome man, Master Eblis. Have you a wife?"

"There are many who desire me—a betrothal of souls," Eblis confessed. He raised his head, placing both hands underneath the white neck-cloth he wore and ruffled it gently. "Marriage only works to suppress man's animalistic desires. The wedding vow is as a leash is to a domesticated animal. It is women, such as yourself, who exist as a disruption—coaxing the husband from the leash—and reminding us all that man cannot escape his innate desires."

"I have certainly had my share of animals," she remarked with disdain and glared with curiosity upon Eblis. "You don't appear to be an ordinary shoemaker. You speak with an educated tongue and with such passion," Tirzah expressed, her playful smirk now transformed into a look of desire.

"I am passion...and all the feelings you now possess."

Tirzah began to breathe heavily. She undid the hooks at the back of her gown and slipped one arm at a time from its sleeves. "I have never done it in a shop such as this," she said, kicking the shoes from her feet and allowing the gown to fall to the floor. "But once I did perform the dirty deed with a miller inside a small post mill. I remember lying on that hard wooden floor with the miller mounted on top of me, exhausting himself at my expense, and all I could concentrate on was the bloody banging of the turning vanes," she recalled, stepping from the gown that lie around her ankles.

"Lovemaking for you has lost its pleasure?" Eblis pried.

"It has become routine," she admitted unfastening the petticoat from around her waist. "But there are times when I am still moved." Tirzah accented the statement with a sensual glance toward Eblis as she folded the petticoat neatly and tossed it over a bench. "It is fortunate that you have sought me out tonight."

"I agree."

"I mean that I've found religion and had decided to abandon this sinful profession."

"Then why are you here?"

"I don't know. I told myself I would not be enticed this evening and had successfully resisted the advances of Richard," she described now clad only in underwear of cotton cloth and a vest-like bodice. "Then your strange little friend wandered into the tavern and my will power weakened. At first it was the lure of all that money, but now it's something different that calls me." Tirzah teased her client by gently brushing her hands across her breasts. She grinned, "You must be the *devil* himself..." She moved to undo the string that laced the front of her bodice as Eblis began to move in a circular pattern slowly around the undressing woman.

"Thy body is luscious!" Eblis exclaimed. "I can see how it has enticed many men to the sins of the flesh."

Tirzah removed the lace from the last hole and pulled the bodice opened, exposing her supple breasts as Eblis continued to circle her.

"Well, are you going to just pace around me like some wild animal, or are you going to take me? I was serious about finding religion you know...I might just change my mind."

Eblis stopped. "Tell me Tirzah, what is it like to be an object of desire...to be passed around like a tankard full of ale? Are you at peace with yourself?"

"I'm standing here nearly naked, and you are asking me questions? Time is money, Master Eblis."

Eblis brought his finger to the side of his nose. "Money! Thou has exchanged thy morality for wealth. Are you a wealthy person, Miss Tirzah?"

"No...or else I wouldn't be standing here naked in the middle of some bloody shoemaker's shop!" she exclaimed, growing incensed.

"Surely hundreds of men have paid for thy sexual talents. Where then has all the money gone?" Eblis moved closer to the woman. "Alcohol, Miss Tirzah, and opium. They are your vices, are they not?"

Tirzah could not respond, mesmerized now by the rapid rotation of the iris' of Eblis' eyes.

Eblis brushed the back of his hand against her cheek. "Such soft flesh. It is so refreshing to know that man's innocence can be warped by beauty." Eblis looked away, breaking the trance.

Tirzah's eyelids fluttered and her face grew flush.

"So you say you've found religion?" Eblis derided. "Pity though, that thy religion did not find you."

Tirzah gripped the bodice and pulled it tightly, now hiding her breasts. "I feel very strange, Master Eblis," Tirzah said with trepidation. "Maybe this is not a good idea?"

Eblis extended his arm toward the woman. In his hand he clutched a pewter mug filled with ale that he pulled from nowhere. "Here, drink."

Tirzah shook her head in refusal.

Eblis raised his voice. "Drink!" he commanded.

Tirzah, now overcome by a sense of fear, reluctantly took the mug from Eblis' hand. She clutched the object with both hands and took a large mouthful of the ale. Pulling her mouth from the cup, she slowly traced her tongue over her moist lips as though they harbored droplets of water amid the desert sun.

Then Eblis extended his other arm toward the woman. In it he held a pair of woman's clogs. "Place them on!"

Tirzah took the shoes from his hand with a dumbfounded expression.

"It tis your new *soul*, of which you, yourself, have helped create!" Eblis explained.

"I don't understand?! This is all very strange!"

"Place them on," he ordered.

Tirzah bent over and slipped into the new soles.

Eblis reached out and placed both of his arms inside the bodice and around her waist. Gently he slid his hands up to her shoulders and slid the bodice down her arms until it fell to the floor. Tirzah's momentary fear had now been replaced by a sudden surge of passion, and she closed her eyes, releasing a soft sigh as Eblis rolled his tongue over her neck and slowly lifted her arms above her head. With his left hand behind her back, Eblis pointed toward the table covered with strings. The waxed linen stirred and suddenly sprang to life, rising to a vertical position on the table. With a slight movement of the fingers, Eblis willed the three foot strands to fly, and the talismanic strings danced gracefully through the air in the direction of Tirzah. They hovered beside the raised arms of the unsuspecting woman for a moment, and with the speed of a striking serpent, the pieces of linen flung themselves around the woman's wrists, tying them together with a knot.

Tirzah opened her eyes. "What is happening?!" she demanded. She lowered her arms and saw that her wrists had been bound together. "I did not agree to this!" she exclaimed. "Untie me at once!"

Eblis reached up and pointed at the lantern hanging from the hook attached to the center beam above their heads. Tirzah followed the direction of his arm and watched in amazement as the lantern left the hook of its own power and fluttered down coming to rest on a bench.

"What sorcery is this?!" Tirzah screamed.

Eblis flung both hands upward and instantaneously Tirzah's arms were thrown up over her head as she began to levitate from the floor. She continued to scream and began to weep as her bound hands came to rest around the hook in the ceiling. "Please let me go!" she cried out, suspended from the center beam of the ten-footer, kicking wildly. Immediately several other strings left the table, soaring through the air and upon reaching Tirzah, flung themselves around the woman's ankles securing her legs.

Eblis turned and pointed toward the door of the ten-footer and it swung open violently. Through the doorway stepped Patch.

"Miss Tirzah, there comes a time when I need to reward thy faithful servants. This is such a time."

"No!! Please, no!!" she wailed.

"Patch rather prefers young girls to women. For it twas a woman who put out his eye with a poker."

Patch grinned and picked up the curved iron resting on the table. He carried the object across the room and over to where Eblis stood beneath the woman.

"What are you going to do to me?!!" Tirzah cried out.

"Why, Miss Tirzah...," Eblis replied. "...Patch is going to burnish your *soul.*"

Patch pulled a bench alongside the hanging woman and set the burning lantern on top of it, stepping aside as Eblis positioned himself behind the lantern. The demon shoemaker waved his open palms over the lamp and instantly its light and heat intensified tenfold. The demon turned away from the hanging woman and waved his arm in the direction of a table littered with a half dozen hammers. The tools came to life and ascended a few inches above the table with their heads facing downward, suspended in mid-air as if being held by spirits. Suddenly the hammers began striking the wooden table, creating a loud pounding that deafened the woman's cries for help.

Tirzah watched with terror as Patch held the smooth end of the curved iron over the raging lantern. Eblis had stepped away from the two of them and she viewed his shadow crawl against the stationary objects within the ten-footer as he made his way toward the door; but to her horror it was not the shadow of a man, but that of a hunched horned beast with pointed tail. She screamed again as Patch turned to her with beads of sweat running down his hideous face, for he clutched the iron—now red-hot—and with a look of satisfaction stepped toward the helpless woman. Slowly lifting his head, he flashed a diabolic grin as the woman shook violently and screamed with terror. Wearing a sadistic gaze he applied the scorching iron to the skin of Tirzah's leg.

Patch returned the iron to the fire and then reapplied it to another section of the woman's skin. The trauma of being burned repeatedly arrested Tirzah's heart long before Patch had completed the gruesome task. When he finished, every inch of the woman's body was blackened with burns.

Tirzah's sudden disappearance from the tavern nightlife of Massachusetts brought a suspicious frown to the many faces of her innumerable clientele; although there was little one could do. For the slightest inquiry into her whereabouts might call into question the reputation of the probing gentleman. There were those like Richard and the proprietor of the Anchor who believed the strange circumstances surrounding Tirzah's meeting with the eerie one-eyed man resulted in foul play; but no body was ever found. And then there were others who felt perhaps that Tirzah did finally find religion.

CHAPTER 18

A combination of events led me to the Goode residence for scripture reading a little more than two months after Rachel's first invitation. I had experienced several successive nightmares focused on Jordan and by chance I encountered Rachel in town one afternoon in early March. Untroubled in her presence, a surge of courage enlightened my soul, enhanced by her own lofty self-esteem and heartiness. So when she again asked me to join her for scripture reading, I threw aside my skepticism of the Holy Book and decided to accept the invitation.

Upon completing my work in the manufactory that day, I borrowed my uncle's cart and journeyed north to Swampscott just as dusk painted the frigid horizon. Blanketed by snow, the cranberry bogs did not appear as menacing as when last I traveled this route and I made the trip in good time. Dinah invited me into the house with a warm smile and a lighthearted comment in reference to the cleanliness of my clothes, while leading me from the entry hall into the parlor where she offered me a seat before disappearing through another doorway. Seated on an upholstered chair, I glanced around at the elegantly paneled room which included a fine shell-carved corner cupboard and a desk of cherry wood. Through the open doorway I could see a long wooden table and a dozen chairs partially obstructing my view of a large central chimney with three stoves positioned at the far wall.

Suddenly Rachel appeared in the doorway seated in the wooden chair with wheels. "So good of you to come," she said with a smile as Dinah pushed the chair into the parlor.

Dinah adjusted the colorful quilt that covered Rachel's white embroidered muslin gown from the waist down. "Is there anything else you'll be a needin', Miss Rachel?" Dinah asked.

I watched as Rachel pulled a Bible out from underneath the quilt and set it on her lap. I, in turn, retrieved my book out from inside my jacket.

"No Dinah. That will be all for now. Thank you," she replied, adjusting a long, round cushion, covered with a black crape that set on the crown of her head over which her hair was combed back and fastened.

The Negro woman turned and exited the parlor closing the door to the kitchen behind her.

"Are the roads passable?" Rachel asked me.

"There is much snow, but I had little trouble with my cart."

"My father is late in returning from Boston. I thought it might be the result of the snow."

"You have a very nice home," I admired scanning the large room.

"Thank you; although I think it much too large for the three of us."

"How many fireplaces does it have?"

"Eight. It keeps Dinah very busy," she said before opening the Bible in her lap. "Benjamin, what passage brings you the most peace?"

"The most peace...?" I stuttered, caught off guard by the question. I fumbled through the book. "I...I don't know?"

"You do read the book?" Rachel asked with doubt in her voice.

"Yes...yes," I stammered as I came upon the page Caleb had marked. "Here it is!" I announced with relief. "Psalm ninety-one!"

"Will you read?"

I nodded reluctantly and cleared my throat. "*He that dwelleth in the secret place of the most High shall abide under the shadow of the Almighty. I will say of the Lord, He is my ref'...*" I stumbled.

"Refuge," Rachel assisted.

"*He is my refuge'...*" I continued, proceeding to fumble my way through the entire passage. I hardly believe that I managed to fool my reading companion into thinking I was familiar with the reading;

but if I hadn't, she never let on. Rachel continued to politely correct my pronunciation and listened ardently with a wistful expression.

When I had finished, I lifted my eyes slowly and peered up at Rachel from behind the pages of my book.

"What is it that you fear, Benjamin?"

"Fear? What makes you believe I am in fear of something?"

"The psalm you have read speaks of comfort in time of danger."

Nervously I traced my fingers across the pages of the Bible.

"Of course you need not tell me if it is your wish," Rachel added.

"It is the unknown," I blurted. "I fear the unknown."

"Then you must confront your fears. What do we truly know of the Lord beyond what is in our hearts and on these pages?" Rachel offered. "Yet the Bible tells us: *'The fear of the Lord is the beginning of knowledge: but fools despise wisdom and instruction',*" she recited from memory before adjusting her quilt and leaning closer toward me. "I once feared horse-drawn carts and the outdoors. Aren't you curious to know why I'm trapped in this chair?"

I frowned. "I've wondered."

"When I was a little girl, my mother and I were on our way to market. The horse that pulled our cart was frightened by a snake. He bucked and the cart was overturned, crushing my mother to death and breaking my spine. For the longest time I did not leave the house— full of anger, sadness, and self-pity. Fortunately I began reading the words of the Bible and found that for every troubling situation—no matter how perilous—there exists words of comfort. I began to find wisdom in these words and thus my life had new meaning. It is the power of faith."

I was moved by her words. "I admire your faith."

Rachel sat back in her chair and lifted the book from her lap. "Psalm 149," she said and began to read: *"Praise ye the Lord. Sing unto the Lord a new song, and his praise in the congregation of saints. Let Israel rejoice in him that made him: let the children of Zion be joyful in their King. Let them praise his name in the dance: let them sing praises unto him with the timbrel and harp. For the Lord taketh pleasure in his people: he will beautify the meek with salvation..."*

Suddenly the door to the parlor was thrust open and Rachel's father appeared.

"Father, I was worried!" Rachel acknowledged with excitement. "I thought the snow might be impassable."

"It is not the snow, dear," he said with disgust as he began pulling the leather gloves from each hand. "It is the bloody Bostonians! This afternoon a senseless mob confronted a British sentry in the streets. They provoked a violent response by the soldiers who fired their muskets into the crowd," he described brushing a dusting of snow from the shoulders of his cape. "Dinah!" he yelled. "Where is that bloody woman?! Dinah!"

"Were there any deaths, father?"

"Three Bostonians lay dead where they fell and there were others wounded," he replied untying the cape from around his neck and removing the tricorn. "Yet, rumors abound. Depending upon with whom you speak, the numbers vary. It's a bloody mess! The colonies will find opportunity with this incident!"

Dinah appeared and Master Goode threw his cape, gloves, tricorn, and a jacket into her arms.

"What will happen?" Rachel pried.

"If this colonial insurrection continues to mount, these lot may have invited a bloody war! I don't know how much longer the King can afford to look the other way!"

"The King has ignored the pleas..." I interjected abruptly and paused as Master Goode suddenly threw a stern glare in my direction.

"Father, you remember Benjamin Pratt?" Rachel spoke up. "I introduced you to him on Christmas."

"Yes...I remember. Kerstland's journeyman. You were saying, Benjamin?" he directed toward me.

I chose my response carefully. "I...was...only remarking...that the King has ignored the pleas of the colonies for some time now. Maybe that is the problem...?"

"You are in a position to argue this point?" Master Goode replied coyly.

"I'm sorry Master, I don't understand?"

The lawyer folded his hands behind his back and began a slow pace toward my chair. "What I mean is that you are educated in this matter? Is there some logic behind mob violence?"

"I hear much talk around the shop," I sighed. "Many have

expressed discontent over the King's reluctance to allow the colonies the right to conduct their own affairs."

"Talk around the shop?" Goode repeated with a grin. "It sounds to me as though this shop-talk is one-sided. The colonies owe much, if not everything, to Great Britain. She is their creator, guardian, and source of sustenance. Our language, traditions, heritage...they are all English. Great Britain is the most prosperous nation in the world! The living standards that exist on the British Isles and within her colonies are the highest on the globe! If the American colonies choose a destructive path and sever their ties with the Crown, then the colonies will surely bring about her own demise!"

Rachel's father tone grew more passionate. "Let me give you a history lesson, young man! Were it not for the throne of England the American colonies would be speaking and smelling of bloody French! Instead of transforming this wild continent into some semblance of civilization, we'd be trading and trapping with the Indian savage and marrying his squaw!" Goode glanced at his daughter, took a breath, and lowered his voice. "The problem with these bloody colonies is that we've forgotten our roots. Without the root, the tree dies."

I sensed that the lawyer had offered his closing argument so I placated him with a simple, "Yes, Master Goode."

Goode adjusted his vest and approached Rachel. "Sweetheart, the day's events have exhausted me, so I think I shall pay a visit to the kitchen and grab a morsel to eat before retiring for the evening."

"Goodnight, father," Rachel bid as she received a gentle kiss on the forehead from the lawyer.

Goode then turned toward me and with a slight nod in my direction, he exited the room.

"Benjamin, pay no mind to my father," Rachel advised with a whisper. "He is very strong-headed when speaking of politics. It is an angry subject with him."

I lifted the opened Bible from my lap and glanced down at a line that appeared to leap from the pages. I thought it appropriate and so I read it aloud: "*For we are consumed by thine anger, and by thy wrath are we troubled.*"

CHAPTER 19

ynn – May, 1770

It was Saturday—a wonderful spring afternoon. The sun burned warm and bright in a clear blue sky and the pleasant scent of flowered gardens circulated about the town. Seated atop my uncle's old gray mare, I absorbed the soothing rays of the sun as I guided the animal in the direction of Cedar Pond. Sam had invited me to her grandfather's farm to horseback ride and the agreeable weather heightened my anticipation--not necessarily to ride, but to see her.

The road upon which I traveled wound along the eastern bank of the Saugus River through a thick, overgrown forest of pine. At one point the serenity of the woods was broken by clinking hammers where curling smoke rose above the treetops. Its origin was the iron works whose furnace fires were reflected upon the surface of the river, and as I passed I could hear the gruff murmur of faceless voices whose livelihood depended upon the precious metal.

Not long after, I happened upon the placid waters of Cedar Pond —the dark surface of which I could distinguish intermittently, viewing it from in between rows of cedar trees that dominated the sloping landscape from the road to the bank of the pond. Riding adjacent to the small body of water, I followed a narrow path that had been neatly carved through the wood until it opened into a large clearing. A farmhouse and a red barn occupied the center of the clearing which was encircled by a fence made of timber.

I followed the path running alongside the fence until arriving at an opened gate and steered the mare inside the clearing. Immediately I noticed an individual dismounting a horse and quickly recognized the long, auburn hair of Samantha. She paced toward the fence and climbed it, surprising me with her athleticism as I recalled her masquerade as a boy, and the circumstances surrounding our first meeting. The memory brought a smile to my face and I continued to fix my eyes on her as she strolled across the clearing to meet me while I pulled on the reins to bring the cart to a stop.

"You've made it!" she greeted, stepping up to the cart wearing a blue vest thrown over a white shirt.

"Of course I made it," I replied. "Your directions were good."

She pulled down on the wide waist-seamed riding jacket with narrow straight collar and flashed a smile before bending forward to neatly tuck her buckskin tight fitting breeches into the long black boots that rose to a height just below the knees. Most women wore such breeches underneath a petticoat, but Sam was not like most women.

"Is this your horse?" she asked.

"No. I do not own my own horse. It belongs to my uncle."

"Well you can fasten the animal to the hitching post near the barn," she instructed brushing a strand of hair from her eyes. The lovely strand dangled about her forehead, independent from the rest of her glistening auburn locks which were pulled to the back and plaited.

I snapped the reins and the horse began its trot toward the barn while Sam turned and walked back toward her own horse.

A few minutes later, I found myself leaning against the timber fence admiring my friend who was once again saddled on the back of her bronzed horse. With its long, fine mane hanging almost to the knees and its bushy long tail swaggering behind it, the mare trotted in a circular pattern under Sam's guidance.

Sam looked over and smiled at me. "Take heed!" she called. "You may learn something!" Gripping the reins with both hands she turned her attention to the horse. "Walk. Ho!" she commanded with a high ringing voice. Immediately the horse responded by shifting into an accelerated trot. I was captivated by the ease and confidence she displayed maneuvering the large animal and I could see that a rush of exhilaration filled her face. Sam gathered the reins, "Gal-lo-o-o-op---," she directed and the horse raised its head. "Ho!" she signaled. Instantly the animal began a gallop toward the far side of the fenced-in area, and in the distance I noticed a wooden bucket resting on the ground with its handle upright. Sam bounced violently up and down on the saddle as the horse charged in the direction of the bucket. It was impressive to see her sitting atop the mare in such a manner—straddling the saddle—since most females rode only side saddle and not for sport. Leaning forward, she maintained her grip on the reins with her left hand and dropped her right arm at her side. With the reins still within her grasp she now gripped the mane of the horse with her left hand and reached down with her outstretched right hand dangling free of the animal. As the horse reached the bucket, Sam shifted her position from the center of the saddle to the right side of the mare. She stiffened her right arm and lunged toward the bucket in an effort to grab its handle as the animal passed; but she missed, nearly falling from the horse. She reached up, grabbed the horse's mane with her right hand and pulled herself squarely back onto the saddle. Sam sat upright and pulled lightly on the reins until the animal slowed to a trot and turning the horse around, she guided the mare back in my direction.

I waited until she was near to me. "That was exciting," I acknowledged as she brought the horse to a halt.

"I missed the bucket!" she exclaimed, out of breath. She reached down and patted the horse on the neck as it stopped near the fence.

"It looked dangerous," I offered attempting to deflect her disappointment.

Sam placed her right hand on the pommel of the saddle and swung her right boot over the croup of the horse. She brought her right foot down alongside the left—still in the stirrup—and leapt from the animal. "Yes," she replied. "I was showing off. I should have known better," she divulged, bending over to press the wrinkles from her breeches with both hands.

Sam stood up straight and pulled down on her vest. "Now it's your turn."

I scoffed. "I must admit, I wasn't entirely honest with you when we first spoke of riding," I disclosed apprehensively.

Sam stepped beside her horse with a smirk. "I thought so," she said stroking the mare.

"I can certainly ride a horse; but not for sport," I revealed, somewhat embarrassed. "To be honest, I had intended on passing myself off as a rider; but after watching you, I don't think it to be wise."

Sam paused from stroking her mare and turned toward me. "Why are you here, Benjamin?" she inquired with a raised eyebrow and a quizzical smirk.

I hesitated momentarily, thinking of how I could bend the truth, which was that I found her exciting and beautiful. "I...I wanted to see you...I wanted to see you ride."

Sam smiled, obviously satisfied with my attempt to dance around the question. "Well, I'm glad you came."

We looked away from one another with an uneasy silence replacing our conversation. I could feel my face red with embarrassment. "How long have you been here at the farm?" I asked in an effort to fill the void. It was a feeble attempt.

Sam smirked. "Now isn't that just like a man to change the subject?" she questioned. "I spent the night here. It is always a pleasure to see my grandparents."

"Then you've not heard the news?"

"What news?"

"Last evening at the meeting-house the town voted to discontinue the use of foreign tea."

"So? We have been avoiding English tea for some time now. Not a week goes by that you do not complain of your aunt's raspberry tea," Sam reminded me as she reached up with her right hand and grabbed the reins of her horse. She began a slow pace leading the horse in a walk.

I pursued her. "But not everyone has been so bold as my aunt. The vote passed last night. It is now law."

"That'll show the King. He probably has never heard of Lynn."

"Are you not afraid of war?"

Sam stopped. "War? There are rebels about, this I know; but I can't believe there would be enough fools among the colonists to think they can mount an army against the King? Besides," she added with a grin, "war is a man's game." She patted her horse. "Come Ben,

I'll show you how to ride for sport. It's invigorating. And who knows? You may find yourself in the cavalry one day."

I approached the horse on its left side as Sam held onto the bit to keep it steady. "What's its name?"

"Her name is *Savior*."

I patted Savior on her side and looked up into the bright sun, shielding my eyes with the palm of my hands.

Sam was puzzled. "What are you doing?"

"The other night I was reading in one of Caleb's school books how Alexander the Great broke a wild horse. It seems the horse was afraid of its own shadow so that when Alexander turned the animal toward the sun, the horse was calmed by the fact it could no longer see its shadow, allowing Alexander to mount it."

Sam chuckled. "Savior is not a wild horse. Believe me, I've been riding her for three years and I can assure you she does not fear her own shadow," she said, amused.

Facing the rear of the horse, I took the reins from Sam with my left hand and brought my left foot up and placed it in the stirrup. Then I reached up and grabbed the saddle with my right hand and pulled myself up on top of the horse.

"Very nice, *Alexander*," she mocked as I adjusted myself in the saddle. "Now be certain your right foot is in the stirrup?" I nodded that it was secure. "Good. Now pull gently on the reins to get her attention and squeeze your thighs and lower legs." I did, and the horse began moving forward.

I pulled gently on the left rein and guided the mare in a circular trot around Sam. "Walk. Ho!" I commanded and soon the horse was moving at a faster pace as I expanded the size of the circle with control of the reins. I had ridden smaller, older horses before, but only at a trotting pace, so I found myself excited to guide the great mare.

"Are you ready to let her out?" Sam asked with a grin.

I nodded.

"Good. The command is gallop...ho. And remember to use your legs too, Ben! Keep your left leg on the girth—the saddle strap—and bring your right leg back and give a kick!"

I looked down to my left and located the saddle strap, making sure my left leg was on it. When I pulled hard on the left rein, the horse—still in a trot— resisted and braced its neck against my pull. I continued to pull on the left rein and then kicked the animal with my left foot. The horse never broke stride but suddenly turned sharply causing me to slide off the saddle and onto the ground. The fact that I was no longer in the saddle caused the horse to stop suddenly. "Stupid horse," I mumbled, staring up at the animal. The horse responded by lowering its great head and snorting.

Laughing, Sam came to my aid and pulled me to my feet. "You kicked with the wrong foot. I told you to kick with the right."

"Oh, it was my fault was it?" I responded sarcastically with a smile.

"Maybe next time I will teach you how to dismount."

"I did it wrong?"

Sam laughed some more and grabbed the reins of the horse. "Let's go and sit awhile. I think you could use the rest."

Leading the horse, Sam led me to the timber fence and I hopped up and perched myself on the beam. Sam tied the reins to the timber before dropping into a sitting positon on the grass, gazing up at me with a smile.

"What is wrong?" I asked, as her extended smile piqued my curiosity.

"You're funny," she acknowledged. "I don't get a chance to see you like this."

"I'm embarrassed. I deceived you about my riding skills and fell from your horse."

Sam giggled. "I think it's nice to show your weaknesses," she said pulling a tall blade of grass from the ground and inserting one end in between her teeth.

"I don't think I've seen your weaknesses yet," I countered.

"Of course not," she replied. "I have none."

I laughed. "You enjoy riding?"

"Yes, Ben. I enjoy it very much. It is my escape," she revealed closing her eyes with a soft smile as she enjoyed brushing the end of the blade of grass against her face. "And what about you?" she asked with eyes now open.

"Me?"

"Yes, Ben. What is your escape? Where do you go on the days you are not working in my father's shop?"

"Well, I am usually at my aunt and uncle's home helping with chores."

Sam smirked and I realized she found my answer boring.

"But..." I continued. "There are days where I go to the beach," I revealed.

Sam's smirked evolved into a pleasant smile. "The beach, that's nice."

"I find the sound of the ocean breaking against the shores to be very peaceful," I added.

"I enjoy the beach as well," Sam revealed. "I adore riding Savior up the beach and the feel of the salty air blowing against my face and through my hair as I ride. It is very liberating."

I gazed upon the horse as it lowered its head to devour a clump of grass. "Savior...you certainly have strange names for your pets."

"Strange?"

"Yes. Your cat is Angel and your horse is Savior. Yet I hardly think of you as a religious person."

"Oh? And just how do you think of me?"

"What I mean is that you're not very enthused by the Sunday services."

"So now you're spying on me during the Sunday service?" she implied with a smile.

I sighed.

"Never mind. I watch you as well," she added, with an inviting grin. "So, should I be enthused?"

"Do you not believe in God?"

Sam scoffed. "I believe in God. Look around at the beauty of this place," she offered turning her head about. "How could one argue that God did not have a hand in its creation?"

"I'm confused," I sighed again.

"It's the Sunday service; the town preacher; the rules and regulations—they're all so...so unnatural...like a game," she described. "I'm sure God has no rules and regulations for where the trees grow or the rivers run."

"Perhaps, but humans need guidance. How can one account for so many being drawn to the meeting-house or to a preacher for faith?"

"I suppose not everyone can easily find God," Sam surmised pointing toward the far end of the fence. "Look at that beautiful bird!"

I turned and watched a cardinal settle on the timber. It ruffled its bright red feathers for a moment, jerked its tiny head about, and then in an instant took flight.

"On the subject of religion Ben, how is the lawyer's daughter?"

"Rachel? She is well."

"You've seen much of her in the last several months, have you not?" Sam pried throwing a coy glance in my direction. "The Bible is certainly a lengthy book."

"What are you implying?" I asked, now on the defensive.

"I think she likes you."

I sensed jealousy in her tone. "Well, we are only friends."

"Really? All that time spent alone together...perhaps she feels romantic toward you?"

I blushed. "We read the Good Book together. That is all."

Sam produced a whimsical grin and flung herself backwards onto the grass.

"You don't know what you say. Rachel is a good friend...and this is all," I repeated.

Sam crossed her hands behind her head and gazed up into the blue sky. "I saw Daniel the other day. He glares at me with desirable eyes."

"He's mad."

"Thanks," she said with exasperation.

"You know what I mean."

"What does Rachel say of Master Eblis?"

"I haven't told her."

Sam sat up, supported by her arms on the ground at her sides. "You haven't told your Bible-reading soul mate of the reason why you read—that you fear the dark shoemaker who lurks across the street?" she asked with a teasing cadence.

"I've had no reason to tell her. Eblis is my problem," I added. "At first I did begin reading the Bible because of my fear of Eblis, but now that is not the reason. I find peace in my time with Rachel—and peace only," I clarified. "She is innocent and truly sincere."

Sam frowned. "You sound as if you are infatuated by her?"

I hopped down from the fence and stood above Sam. "I would very much like you to meet her."

"I am not interested in your Bible reading sessions," Sam blurted with a scowl.

"No. I don't mean that. This coming Friday night a group of

Negroes—both slave and free—plan to gather in the forest to pay tribute to another of their kind—an African king. It's an annual celebration for them of which Rachel's Dinah is a participant. It's restricted to the Negro, but Rachel knows of the location, and assures me that we can watch it from a safe distance undetected."

"The little angel sounds as if she's got some adventure in her."

"I think you would like her," I added. "Naturally, because of her condition—crippled and all—she needs someone to accompany her."

"Naturally. And you've agreed to be that someone?"

"Yes. Maybe you would consider joining us?"

"Sneaking through the forest at night to spy on a group of slaves seems out of character for this Rachel."

"I think you're jealous." I blurted boldly.

Sam's eyes widened. "Jealous?! Of her, come now, Benjamin. You flatter yourself!"

I smiled, realizing I had struck a chord. "She says it is a harmless meeting and not far from her home," I replied. "Will you join us?"

Sam pulled another blade of grass from the ground, brushing it gently against her freckled cheek. "I shall consider it."

"Good," I smiled and looked off in the distance to where the bucket rested. "The bucket—have you ever succeeded in grabbing it from the back of a galloping horse?"

Sam grinned. "No." She paused and with confidence added, "But there will be a first time."

CHAPTER 20

After a week of deliberation, Sam surprised me when she accepted my invitation to seek out the African celebration in the forest. Not only was I excited that my two female friends would finally meet, but I welcomed Sam's presence in my uncle's cart as we journeyed through the cranberry bogs on route to Swampscott. Although the apparition failed to reappear on the successive trips I had taken up the coastline, the memory of my brother's ghost continued to trouble me.

Dusk had nearly fallen when we arrived at the steps leading to the front door of the Goode residence.

"It's so big," Sam admired, gazing up at the white house. "Her father's a lawyer, is he not?"

"She's not like her father," I said attempting to dispel any preconceived notions Sam might be harboring toward the law profession. "You'll like her, I promise," I added jumping from the cart perch.

"Ben, why are you so concerned about my feelings toward this girl?" Sam asked as she followed my movements around the front of the cart.

"Because you are my friend...," I replied, extending my hands upwards toward her to help her from the perch, "...and so is she."

Sam pushed my hands away and leapt from the vehicle without my help just as the door to the house swung open where Rachel appeared in a standing position, supported by crutches underneath each armpit. "Hello!" she greeted.

"Hello, Rachel," I replied. "Rachel Goode this is Samantha Kerstland," I introduced swinging my hand toward Sam.

The two girls smiled at one another. Sam studied Rachel's gown of buff glazed chintz with a critical eye and I sensed that the shoemaker's daughter was slightly embarrassed of her own drab calico with skirt of coarse wool. I wanted to assure Sam that she needn't worry about such things with Rachel, but I dared not speak at the risk of her scorn.

"We haven't much time. The sun will be lost soon," Rachel warned. "Dinah is already gone and my father has left for Boston on business." She hobbled through the doorway. "Ben, would you mind pulling the door shut behind me?"

I jogged up the wooden ramp meeting Rachel at the door, and closed it. "Shall we take my cart?" I asked.

"No. We will travel the Indian path through the forest. The path is not wide enough for a cart," Rachel revealed. "We shall take my pony. Ben, if you would be so kind to go around back to the stable and fetch her. Inside the stable you will also find a lantern and tinderbox, which we will need when the sun goes down. I shall travel on horseback."

"Don't forget the bridle and saddle," Sam directed toward me, teasingly.

"I'll be back shortly," I assured and climbed back on top of my uncle's cart.

"Ben, I wouldn't attempt to ride the pony," Sam joked.

I grinned and tossed Sam her short hooded cape that rested on the seat of the cart. Snapping the reins I steered the cart off toward the rear of the house.

"I'VE BROUGHT ALONG MY CAPE AS WELL," RACHEL REMARKED. "I'M sure it will be cold in the forest at night."

Sam politely smiled and threw the cape around her shoulders. "You're not frightened about going into the forest after dark?" she asked.

"I am, a little...but it is exciting. I don't get to experience much excitement," Rachel revealed. "And Dinah, our Negro, has done this before without incident."

Sam approached Rachel.

"So finally we meet," Rachel continued, adjusting her wide-brimmed riding hat. "Ben has told me much about you."

"He has?" Sam pried with interest, tying the string of the cape around her neck.

"Yes. Did you know he's enamored with your hair?"

Sam nervously pulled at a lock of her hair that flowed free and rested on the back of her neck and shoulders. "My hair?" she asked and then both girls erupted in laughter. "It's so funny. The first time Ben and I met I hid my hair underneath an oversized tricorn. Your hat...it's very pretty," Sam complimented.

"Oh, please try it on," Rachel offered, balancing the crutches under her armpits to remove the hat from her head. She handed the hat to Samantha who gently fitted the powdered blue hat over her hair.

"You look pretty," Rachel complimented.

Samantha bit her lower lip and moved her head about.

"The window at the house...take a look at yourself," Rachel advised.

Sam stepped quickly over to the window and admired her reflection in it.

"Ben's also told me you ride a horse very well, and he speaks highly of your skills around the shoemaker's shop. In fact had I not seen how pretty you are with my own eyes, I would have been certain that Ben's Sam was a boy."

Sam smiled and stepped back over to Rachel. "And he's told me of you," she said removing the hat. "He admires your inner strength."

"And not my hair?" Rachel was quick to respond, sparking a round of laughter again. "I'm not certain who should be more flattered?"

"He's cute, isn't he?" Sam pried.

"Very," Rachel agreed. "Sam, I've seen you at the meeting-house; yet how odd it is that we are brought together by the same boy. We are the wings upon which he glides," Rachel suggested.

Sam looked askance. "I hadn't thought of it that way."

"With your skills and persistence..." Rachel began.

"And don't forget my hair!" Sam added.

Rachel chuckled. "Of course, and your hair...I can see that you provide Ben with strength in the human spirit."

Sam leaned over and placed the bonnet back atop Rachel's head. "And you...the Holy Spirit," she countered.

Rachel rolled her eyes up at Sam. "How can he go wrong?" she asked with a smile.

I RETURNED DELIGHTED TO SEE MY TWO FRIENDS CONVERSING; although at the sight of me they burst into laughter and I realized that I was the subject of their giddiness. I didn't mind, grateful that their two worlds had come together so amicably.

I tossed the saddle onto the back of the black pony and handed Sam the tin lantern and tinderbox before gently bending over and sliding my left arm underneath the back of Rachel's legs and wrapping my right arm about her back. She leaned her crutches against the side of the house and I lifted her as both girls again began to giggle. I brushed off the silliness and placed Rachel sidesaddle on the back of the pony.

With Rachel guiding us from atop the pony, we proceeded down the front yard and out the gate onto the main road. Sam and I stepped along with the trotting animal—she stood out in front of the pony pulling its reins, while I positioned myself on its right side now carrying the lantern and tinderbox. We proceeded westward along the main road for nearly a quarter of an hour until we came to a great oak tree on the northern side of the road. Rachel instructed us to leave the main road and take the forested path appearing just before the oak.

"What is it that the Negroes do out here in the forest?" Sam asked as she guided the pony from off the main road and onto the path.

"They remember their homeland," Rachel replied. "One of them— I believe he is the property of Thomas Mansfield—was actually an African king before he was sold into slavery. Dinah calls him Pompey."

"How horrible it must have been to have gone from being a king to a slave," I wondered aloud.

"Yes. This is their opportunity to relive the happy days of their former lives in the land near the river Gambia."

"Gambia?" I asked.

"Dinah has told me that many of the slaves in these parts have their roots in the area of the river Gambia in West Africa," Rachel enlightened. "Here in the woods of Massachusetts the women gather flowers to crown their king and the men tell stories of African life."

"It sounds all so...so sad," Sam concluded.

After traveling for an additional quarter of an hour, the dense green forest that hemmed us in on either side of the path gave way to a field of grave markers. Here tree trunks were replaced by gray headstones casting long shadows that moved slowly across the grass in the waning hours of twilight.

Sam and I stopped and I looked up at Rachel. "The path ends," I said, unable to disguise the unsteadiness in my voice.

"Yes. We must proceed across the graveyard," Rachel replied calmly. "This is the final resting place for former residents of Swampscott."

I turned toward Sam who gave me a quizzical look. "What is wrong, Ben? Are you frightened?" she teased.

"Of course not! I just wanted to be certain the trail was correct." The truth was that I had certainly had my fair share of specters and Eblis since my arrival to Lynn, and suddenly finding myself in an old graveyard proved to be quite unsettling.

"Fear not, Ben," Rachel consoled. "My mother will watch over us. She is buried here."

I didn't know how to respond to Rachel's comment; although I failed to find comfort in her words. Nevertheless, I took a deep breath and we started across the graveyard moving solemnly past the thin slates of stone with rounded ends exposed to the heavens. The positioning of the headstones resembled the symmetry of an apple orchard and we proceeded with delicate steps fearing to awaken the dead. Each stone, having been engraved with fancy markings bespeaking of the identities of those who lay silent beneath our feet, protruded upwards from out of the ground in various shapes and sizes. And although some of the older oblique markers had begun to fade, most were in good condition. The exception that caught my eye stood alone within the shadows of the long branches of a mammoth oak with the limbs of the arboreal sentry towering above us. It was easy to understand why the founders of this colonial resting place spared the magnificent tree from their axes, and beneath its foliage stood the deformed marker with its top half broken away, partially buried under a large fallen branch that rested beside the tombstone.

Rachel had sensed my curiosity with the broken marker. "There lies the buccaneer," she described. I turned and looked up at her. "He's been buried there for some time now," she continued. "It looks as though the fallen branch has scarred his marker."

"Lightning must have brought that limb down," I guessed. "I'd like to take a closer look," I said, leaving the girls and stepping toward the headstone. When I had reached the marker, I bent forward and parted the tall grass that hid the inscription. The epitaph was separated by the damage to the headstone; but I restructured the wording by observing both halves. It read:

BURIED WITH CUTLASS, HERE LYETH YE BODY OF CAP DADE
MAY HE FIND PEACE WITH HIS MAKER AS HE FINDS HERE IN THE
SHADE

NO MAN BE HIS EQUAL WHENCE HE HELD YE BLADE

TOOK A BALL FROM A MUSKET AND NOW HERE HE BE LAID

"Hurry, Ben!" Sam called.

I righted myself, returning to my friends, and together we continued our procession until arriving at the center of the graveyard, where Rachel located her mother's headstone. We stopped as our handicapped friend closed her eyes in prayer. I removed my tricorn out of respect and I found those few moments of solitude to be timorous and sensed the same from Sam. No sooner had Rachel's eyelids opened did I return the hat to my head and we began a brisk movement across the remainder of the graveyard.

On the other side of the cemetery, the forest reappeared and we followed another path that had been neatly carved through the thick vegetation until it wound down to the banks of a large pond. At the sight of this calm body of water, we beheld an interesting structure— that of a long, narrow bridge that did not cross over the pond, but floated on top of the smooth, glasslike surface. The wooden bridge, which I estimated to be some four hundred feet in length, was held fast by two ropes that were tied to the trunks of two large trees on either side of the pond.

"Caleb told me of this floating bridge when I was younger!" I remembered with excitement.

"This is Floating Bridge Pond," Rachel described.

"It is aptly named," Sam added. "I've heard of this place as well."

Carefully we stepped onto the buoyant bridge that wobbled underneath our weight, producing ripples in the water that distorted our mirror-like reflection on the surface of the pond. We had fun crossing the unique structure, laughing and carrying on just as Caleb had described doing many times as a boy; although Rachel's pony seemed very anxious with each step taken on the unsteady surface. We did our best to calm the animal and when we stepped off the bridge onto the opposite shoreline, we picked up another path and proceeded due west.

The path ran alongside an alluvium commencing from the shores of the pond. This tract of rich, black soil had been transformed into an open meadow of peat moss that extended for over one hundred rods until disappearing within a forest of black spruce. We stepped carefully across the soggy soil that captured the footprints of others who had recently preceded us along the same route. At one point we stopped to observe a pool ten feet in circumference that consisted of a dark, oily substance. I handed Samantha the lantern that I held in my right hand and grabbed a long stick from off the ground. I poked one end of the broken branch into the viscid matter and when pulling the stick out, the clammy black liquid coated the end of the branch. "Tar," I described tossing the stick aside. "Be careful where you tread."

The sun had nearly set, painting the horizon a bright orange, as the path emerged from a dense clump of forest to the sight of a huge boulder. It was here that the path split into two, like the branches of a divining road. To the right side of the rock the trail continued in a northwesterly direction and to its left the path veered southwest. Rachel looked confused.

"Well, which path do we take?" I asked.

"I'm...I'm not sure?" Rachel revealed. "Dinah did not mention any forks."

"Is your Dinah expecting us?" Sam inquired.

"Oh, no. The ritual is for Negroes. I had only hoped we could observe it, undetected...from a distance."

"If she doesn't expect you, how is it that you've come by directions to this ritual?" Sam persisted.

"Dinah has spoken many times of this event. So often that she has revealed its location without notice."

"Except for the fork?" I added.

"Oh, I feel such the fool! For I am not certain of which path to take?!"

Sam sat down upon the boulder. "Maybe we should go back," she advised. "Maybe we would be violating something that is sacred... something not for our eyes?"

"Oh, no! I don't think so! It's nothing like that, I'm sure," Rachel informed us. "The only reason we go uninvited is that the Negro believes the whites to be uninterested in such tribal customs. Dinah has told me this. She has never taken me herself because I feel it might embarrass her. Sometimes it is hard to expose who you really are to those who have always seen you as something else."

"Well, I say we should take the south fork," I decided.

Sam rose from the boulder. "How can you be so sure?"

"Well, I'm not sure," I replied, "but look at how much the north fork is overgrown with low branches. The south fork appears more traveled."

Sam studied the topography but seemed unconvinced. "What if you're wrong and we become lost in the woods after dark?"

I pointed to the lantern that Sam still held in her possession. "We have light for when the sun sets and tonight we shall have a full moon," I said now pointing upwards into the dark blue sky of dusk where part of the moon appeared just above the treetops sharing the heavens with a setting sun. I looked up at Rachel. "Do you have an objection to the south fork?"

Rachel shrugged her shoulders. "I feel so badly about this."

"Don't feel bad," I consoled. "We'll take the south fork and if we don't come upon the slaves in due time, we shall turn around." Sam rose from the boulder and I stepped toward her with a confident smile, gently removing the lantern from her hands. I took the lead down the southern path while Sam grabbed the reins of the pony and followed me along the route.

A short time had passed before the sunlight had disappeared from the forest. The full moon sat high in the sky now and its brilliance transformed the woods into an eerie world of shadows set against a silvery sheen.

"Ben, the moon is bright, but in this forest I think I would feel better with some additional light," Sam offered with a tone of discomfort in her voice.

I agreed and stopped. "Hold this," I said handing the lantern to Samantha. I opened the tinderbox and pulled the flint, steel, and cloth out from inside the box. Striking the flint against the steel several times, I tried to catch a spark before being startled by the hoot of an owl that interrupted the stillness of the forest. I looked up and followed the successive hoots to a nearby tree limb where the moonlight cast a silver glow upon the hooked and feathered talons of the nocturnal creature. With wide eyes set in the front of its face above a short, hooked beak, the bird watched our intrusion with swift mechanical movements of its large head.

"Hurry!" Sam hastened as I resumed my effort to catch a spark.

Moments later the cloth caught fire and I quickly ignited the candlewick inside the lantern. Sam sighed with relief. "Maybe we should go back now?" she questioned.

I realized she was probably right in her desire to leave the forest; however my youthful bravado ignored such logic. "Just a little farther," I insisted. And a little farther is all we traveled before coming upon a thicket of thorn and elder trees; although it was a haunting din that suddenly brought us to a halt. The sound seemed to have its origins behind a nearby hill of stones. The hill ran north and south and there appeared to be no immediate path around the stone structure.

"Do you hear that?" I asked of the others.

"It sounds like...chanting?" Sam acknowledged.

"Perhaps we have found the meeting place?" Rachel wished aloud.

I removed my jacket and threw it over the lantern to dim the light and conceal our presence. "We must proceed south along the path. I'm certain it shall lead us around the hill and then we'll be able to see what lies on the other side," I explained.

"Why not climb the hill?" Sam asked. "It doesn't appear very treacherous. I'll remain here with Rachel. I think we should be certain that it is the voices of Negroes we hear and not..." Sam paused.

"And not what?" I pressed.

"Indians?"

"And there may be only one entrance into the area on the other side of the hill," Rachel added. "I don't want to walk uninvited into the middle of the ceremony where everyone can see us."

Outvoted two to one, I sighed. "Stay here," I advised with a lack of enthusiasm.

Reluctantly I pushed my way through the shrubs until I stood at the base of the hill that ascended like the black walls of a fortress rising to a height of about fifteen feet above the forest floor. With a deep breath I mounted the first rocks and began my climb. The large rocks that sculptured this rising ground were stable and staggered in their ascent, enabling me to scale them with the ease of climbing stairs; although I was certain not to look down.

As I neared the top, the discordant voices grew louder and the air was noticeably warmer than below. I set the burning lantern, concealed by my jacket, down upon the ground and slowly lifted my head above the boulders at the top of the hill. A floor of stone and dirt stretched across a small valley below me for some twenty rods in width until ascending again as another hill. There were people in the center of the cove moving in the direction of a large flat surfaced stone—but I realized immediately that this was not a celebration of slaves; for there were thirteen dark figures, whose identities were concealed underneath the hoods of their long, black capes. One of the figures traced a circle in the dirt around the stone with the handle of a broomstick, and the other twelve joined this figure in forming a human circle around the stone paying homage to the slab of sandstone as if it were an altar. In unison they began to cry out..."*Beelzebub!*"

I shuddered at the sight of this, lowered my head behind the boulder and turned, slowly beginning a descent of the hill before stopping half-way. "Sam!" I called out in a whisper. She looked up at me and I motioned for her to join me with a wave of my hand.

Sam mumbled something to Rachel, seated sidesaddle on the pony, and tied the reins of the animal to the trunk of a small tree before moving through the brush and arriving at the base of the hill. I watched as she began her ascent up the rocks and I returned to the top of the prominence, crawling over to the boulders, careful to keep my head down behind the stone.

"What is it?" Samantha asked, approaching me in an upright position.

I motioned for her to get down on her knees behind the rocks. "Keep quiet," I warned with a whisper. "I don't think we've come upon Negroes or Indians. Look."

We lifted our heads and peered down at the bottom of the cove. The thirteen figures continued to chant and now were dancing in a circle around the stone altar.

"Witches?!" Sam deduced. "It's a witch's coven!"

The collision of warm air against the cold surface of the cove added to the macabre atmosphere by producing a layer of fog that crept across the valley floor. This blanket of mist shrouded the ankles and feet of the witches and gave the unearthly appearance that each was gliding upon air. The daughters of black magic seemed to be delighted by the sudden arrival of the fog and the tempo of their dance increased in fervor. With each successive circle of the stone altar the chanting grew louder, bouncing around the valley walls with such fury as to suggest the number of witches had increased ten-fold.

"Let's leave here, now!" Sam pleaded.

"No, wait! Something's happening?!"

Suddenly amid or perhaps brought on by the intense activity within the cove, there appeared a blue-silver light in the form of a sphere hovering in mid-air above the center of the altar. The mysterious light's brilliance began to grow brighter at an astonishing rate. At the sight of this, the witches ceased their dancing and chanting, and flung themselves face-down to the floor of the cove in prostration.

I wanted to be sure that I was actually witnessing such a phenomenon and not hallucinating, so I turned toward Sam. "Do you see that?!"

Sam shook her head in acknowledgement. "It's sorcery!"

And then the light exploded. The cove illuminated with a bluish glow for an instant before the light was rapidly drawn back into the center of the altar. The light swirled in a clockwise direction with the fury of a cyclone before expanding vertically until the rapid revolutions had produced a narrow column of spinning blue flames.

The cries of Beelzebub erupted once more, only now with more intensity. Suddenly a dark figure stepped from out of the column of blue flames. Silhouetted against the fire's light was a hideous frame composed of human arms, hands, and legs, with wings, cloven-feet and a horned head. With bowed posture and a short, thin tail protruding from its lower back, the beast towered above its coven of witches, straddling the altar as a king sits upon his throne. The sight of such a monster sent a rush of ice water through my veins.

"Ben!!...it's the *devil*!!" Sam exclaimed.

One of the witches rose slowly from off of the ground, turned, placed her back towards the monster and began a sluggish, backwards march in the direction of the beast. She stopped before the altar and spun around, pulling the hood from her head.

"Miss Darcie!" Sam identified.

The witch reached inside of her robe and retrieved a black candle which she held in her right hand, and a silver pendant of an inverted pentacle which she gathered with her left hand. She raised the pendant toward the creature and held out the candle. The beast spit on the candle and instantly the wick produced a flame. She turned away from the monster and began circling the coven of witches who were now retrieving black candles of their own from inside their robes. One by one they illuminated their wicks from Darcie's burning candle.

When the last of the candles had been lit, the thirteen daughters of black magic formed a line in front of the altar and disrobed—all the time with their backs to the monster. Then the beast turned its back towards their nudity.

"Can you name any of the others?!" I asked.

"I can't see their faces! Wait...I believe I recognize Charity Price! She is the blonde with shoulder-length hair!"

"Who is she?"

"The wife of Lynn's wheelwright!" she described. "Ben, what are they doing?!"

Beginning with Darcie, each witch, standing naked in the moonlight before the beast, approached the altar walking backwards while clutching a burning candle. When her skin touched the cold stone of the altar, she would whirl around and promptly kiss the buttocks of the beast.

"Ben, I'm scared! Let's leave this evil place!" Sam blurted with a trembling voice.

"I agree! I've seen enough!" I exclaimed turning away from the coven. In my haste to start down the hill, I dislodged a stone with my foot and the rock tumbled to the base of the mound, rattling the brush below. The sudden movement of the thorny bushes startled Rachel's pony and the animal began to whine.

Sam cringed. "The pony!"

I turned and lifted my head above the boulder once again. The dark ritual had come to an abrupt halt and the witches were scurrying to gather their clothing. And then I saw Darcie. The old woman stood before the altar and pointed upwards at me and as if on command, the beast turned its head in my direction.

I dropped down on my knees behind the boulder. "It's seen me!"

"Let's go!" Sam exclaimed, tugging at my shirt sleeve.

"You go first! I'm right behind you!" I yelled, grabbing my jacket; but in my haste, left the lantern behind.

Sliding and jumping from rock to rock, Sam raced to the bottom of the hill. My fear of heights forced me to make a hurried, but more cautious descent.

"What's wrong?!" Rachel inquired, surprised by Sam's rushed approach.

"Ben! Hurry!" Sam called.

"Go on!" I called back. "There's only room enough for two on the back of the pony!"

Sam quickly hoisted herself up on the back of the animal, positioning herself bareback in front of Rachel. "Hold on to me!" she instructed, before looking back at me. "Ben! The bridge...we'll meet at the bridge!"

"Go on!" I called back.

With a swift kick and a snap of the reins Sam forced the pony into a quick trot just as I reached the base of the hill.

I removed my tricorn and shoved it underneath my right arm with my jacket and began sprinting along the path. The distance between me and the girls continued to grow and behind me I heard the violent trampling of the forest vegetation, imagining an army of witches to be in pursuit. My heart raced and I willed my legs to move faster before a tree branch snagged my shirt, bringing my flight to a sudden stop. Breathing heavily, I turned to mark the progress of my pursuers and saw the forest illuminated by the blue light. It was the beast, not the witches that pursued me and I was losing ground.

"Ben!" Rachel called from ahead of me in the distance. "Ben, Keep up!" she cried out; but I could no longer see the girls.

FROM HER POSITION ON THE BACK OF THE PONY CLUTCHING Samantha, Rachel turned to look back at Ben. As she did the Bible slipped out from underneath her cape and fell to the ground. "My book!" she called out. "I've dropped my book!"

Sam pulled on the reins of the pony to slow the animal, but in doing so, she realized their situation was too dire to risk recovering a book—even the Bible. "We've got to keep going!" she exclaimed and snapped the reins again returning the animal to a quick pace.

I THRUST MY ARM AWAY FROM THE BRANCH TEARING MY SHIRT sleeve, but gained my release, and continued to run as the blue light grew closer. As I struggled to maneuver my way around trees and branches along the forest path I found myself nearly tripping over an object which I thought at first to be a large stone. Breathing heavily I stopped, looked downward, surprised to see a book on the path and reached down to retrieve it—a Bible. In lifting the book from off of the ground, I heard the owl hoot once again and raised my eyes to see the bird perched on a branch just above me. Suddenly the silver light of the moon against the bird's talon gave way to a bluish glow and the bird hooted one more time as it took to flight. Slowly I turned around and beheld the source of the blue light standing some twenty rods from me. The beast was huge, towering above me like a huge oak even with stooped posture. Unclothed and hairless with genitalia exposed, the Herculean body of the creature pulsated with a network of bulging veins traversing its blue skin that glowed like star sapphire. Its face was hideous, resembling that of a wild boar, with large, pointed ears and two menacing fangs that sprung up from the lower jaw.

Although I wanted to resume my flight, I could not move—my legs frozen in terror. The beast stared at me with eyes of coal black and slowly lifted its left arm, pointing at me with long, crooked fingers. "BEN...JA...MIN!!" it bellowed.

A feeling of doom enveloped me in the shadow of this behemoth, when suddenly I remembered the book. *Of course, the Bible!* Shaking violently I opened the book and fumbled through the pages. With trembling voice, I began reading a passage aloud. I don't even recall what reading I had selected, I just read. When the beast growled, I knew I had struck a nerve and began to raise my voice, still reading. Then out of the corner of my eye I caught movement and looked up to see the monster suddenly fling his right arm toward me, hurling an object that rotated rapidly in the air, spinning in its approach. Instinctively, in a moment of self-defense, I held the Bible up to shield my face and the object struck the book with such force that it sent me falling backwards to the forest floor.

Quickly I pulled myself into a sitting position expecting the beast to be on top of me; but the blue light had suddenly vanished and the monster along with it. The moon glow and the stillness of night dominated the forest once again and I looked to my left, finding the Bible on the ground and trembled at the sight of the large knife imbedded in the book. The blade had passed through both covers of the Bible and I pulled the knife from out of the book, studying its markings and recognized the handle crafted of curly maple and the wavy pattern of its steel blade. *How could I forget?* For it was identical to the knife belonging to Cyrus Eblis—the one I had used to carve my initials in the cask...and the knife in my nightmare. I picked myself up off of the ground, along with my jacket and tricorn, and placed the blade within the pocket of my jacket. The air was colder now and so I slid my arms through the sleeves of the jacket, pulling it snug over my chest, and placed the tricorn back atop my head. Clutching the Bible, I resumed my flight through the silvery wood.

It wasn't long before I came upon the boulder. Here I located the long stick for which I used to guide my way through the peat meadow and its pools of tar, emerging a short while later at Floating Bridge Pond; but the large body of water and its namesake were hidden under a thick blanket of fog. I found no-one at the beginning of the bridge and hoped that Sam and Rachel awaited me on the other side. The full moon had disappeared now behind threatening rain clouds and a steady wind began to moan.

Slowly I stepped onto the bridge and started across the structure, unable to see more than a rod before me. Within the dense fog, my ears had become my beacon and I listened as the bridge creaked with each footstep causing water to slosh against the underside of the structure.

In my estimation I had ventured nearly half way across the bridge when the sounds of my movements appeared to be growing louder; yet I had not increased my pace. I stopped, and as I feared, the bridge continued to reflect movement. Realizing now that I was not alone on the structure, my heart began to pound once again and the rhythm of my heavy breathing replaced the vibration of the bridge. I moved again, quickening my steps and when halting a second time, surprisingly all was calm. I turned to see what lie behind me but the thickness of the fog impeded my vision, and suddenly from out of the mist a hand lunged forward, grabbing hold of my arm. Terrified, I was speechless as the figure of the witch came into full view—it was Darcie.

"What say you, young Benjamin?!" she squealed. "Would it be genuine courage or the foolhardiness of a young man that brings thee to the forest after dark?! I gather it be the latter!" She laughed and released her grip of my arm.

"Leave me!" I demanded. "You're an old woman! I can toss you from this bridge!"

She remained steadfast. "Few outside the circle of darkness have been witness to the powers thee beheld this night at the cove; but it was as he wished!"

"As who wished?!"

"And so was thy escape!" she exclaimed lifting her arm and pointing her finger at me. "Make no mistake, young Benjamin, had he wished to take thy life back in the woods, he would have!" Her jangled voice grew more hostile. "And pay heed! Thy tongue is to remain silent about the events this night! Reveal nothing of the sabbat! If so much as one word is breathed from thy lips or from the lips of she with hair of fire, then the lamb shall serve as sacrifice to the prince!"

"The lamb?!" I questioned. "Be gone with you, witch!" I exclaimed.

She bellowed with a raucous laughter. "The lamb—thou knows of whom I speak! She with the chair of wheels—the cripple!" Darcie maintained her sinister laugh as she stepped backwards, disappearing within the fog bank with her laughter quickly fading, and then there was silence.

I set my feet into motion and when I heard Sam calling my name, I hurried my pace in the direction of her voice, until stepping safely from the bridge.

"Sam?!" I called out, straining my eyes to see through the fog and darkness.

"Ben?! Over here!" she replied. I followed the sound of her voice up a slight grade and soon found Sam standing beside Rachel still seated on the pony. At the sight of me, Sam rushed and gave me such a strong hug that she nearly knocked me to the ground. "I was so frightened for you!" she divulged. "When we lost sight of you, we feared the worst!"

"Ben?! Are you all right?!" Rachel called out.

I looked over at Rachel. "I am fine," I called back as Sam released her embrace. "Sam, did anyone step from the bridge before me?"

"I could not see...the fog is too thick. I did hear voices on the bridge. Was there another?"

"Darcie."

"Oh! That horrid woman!"

I turned away from Rachel and walked a few paces with Sam. "Lower your voice," I cautioned. "What have you told Rachel?"

"I told her there were witches."

"Say nothing more. Darcie warned me that if we speak to anyone about tonight, Rachel's life would be in danger. And although we could identify Darcie and Charity Parker, there were others. There seems to be none in Lynn with whom we can trust with such a story."

"What are we to do?"

Rachel called out. "Ben? Samantha?"

"Come. She grows suspicious. I shall write my cousin. Until that time we will reveal nothing of tonight. Agreed?"

Sam nodded and quickly we returned to Rachel.

"Benjamin, I prayed for you!" Rachel expressed.

"I am grateful," I replied stepping toward the pony and held up the torn Bible.

"My book!" Rachel exclaimed with delight. "I had dropped it back in the woods!"

I reached up and handed Rachel the Bible. "I'm sorry...I'm afraid your book has been damaged."

Rachel studied the Bible. "No bother. Forgive me, though," she said looking up. "I am bewildered by all of this tonight. What did Rachel mean when she said you saw witches?"

I hesitated. "I cannot be certain...but it was not the Negro ritual," I replied. "It is better that we say no more of this and pay heed to our safe departure from these dark woods."

Suddenly a bolt of lightning illuminated the forest and an explosion of thunder followed, rattling the woods and announcing the commencement of a steady rainfall. Quickly we started off along the path.

By the time we had reached the graveyard, the ground had become mire and our garments were laden from water. The thunder and lightning activity grew more intense and seemed to be bursting all around us, forcing Sam and Rachel to throw their capes over their heads, while the water from the heavens collected in my tricorn.

It wasn't long before the cold rain began to spill over the sides of my hat and run down into my eyes, compounding the blindness of nightfall, while the wind howled and bursts of lightning illuminated the headstones. The terrifying events of the night dominated all of our thoughts and we did not speak to one another as we started to move past the stone markers of the dead. At one point, I looked to my left as though some unseen force was guiding me in that direction and I set eyes upon the great oak tree, which at that instant became illuminated with a lightning burst. To my horror the flash revealed the presence of a man clutching a large sword as he stood beneath the oak. "Sam!" I cried out. "Did you see that?! Over there by the tree?!" I exclaimed pointing. Sam turned and followed the direction in which I pointed. A second flash lit up the tree again, but this time there was only the broken grave marker. Sam looked at me strangely.

Captain Dade? Did I just see him? I reached into the pocket and pulled out the knife that the beast had flung at me. *Why does this knife continue to find me?*

We completed the journey with weary and frightened footsteps; for we were as three children who were suddenly stripped of our innocence.

CHAPTER 21

As I had promised Sam, I wrote to Caleb in the days following our encounter with the coven of witches; but weeks and months went by with no reply before learning from my aunt that my cousin had journeyed to Europe—an invitation to lecture at his ministry's counterpart in England. From there he was to holiday for a short spell in London and Paris.

LYNN, SEPTEMBER, 1770

The summer grew long and time worked to erase the urgency of my desired correspondence with Caleb. The more we distanced ourselves from that diabolical spring evening, the more it seemed but a bad dream; however, I found that Sam's stubbornness would not allow the incident in the woods to fade from memory, and from time to time she continued to query me on the events of that strange night. Her persistence encouraged me to seek out more knowledge about the eerie knife in my possession and so when my uncle instructed me to obtain a new shoe for his horse, I carried the blade with me, arriving at the blacksmith shop of Nicholas Potter at the end of a long work day. I was sure to wear a leather sheath about my waist in the hope that the village smithy would call attention to my knife.

Clad in a leather apron, the busy blacksmith said little as he stood over the square fire hole set in the center of a stone forge. He held an iron horseshoe over white-hot coals with a pair of forge tongs, clutching them within his right hand, and with his left hand reached up and pulled down on a chain that was connected to a huge bellows. The bellows blew his furnace and the flames rose from out of the grate as a dragon spewing its fiery venom. With muscular arms that appeared to ooze with oil—a blend of sweat and black soot—the blacksmith turned towards me and with not so much as a glance, placed the glowing horseshoe against the flat top of his anvil. He lifted a nearby hammer and began pounding the shoe with swift, powerful blows, and when he had finished, stepped over to the patient horse that stood quietly beside the forge. Facing in the opposite direction of the animal, the smithy bent over and lifted the horse's right hind leg, placing it in between his own legs. Still clutching the shoe with his forge tongs, Potter pressed the scalding iron against the horny wall of the hoof. Smoke set up from the animal's hoof, but the horse felt nothing, and the blacksmith proceeded to nail the shoe to the hoof. When finished, he nipped off the end of the shoe with a pair of nippers, lowered the horse's leg and stood upright, stepping to the animal's side. "Thar ya go, young gal," he said patting the horse. "Now ya be able to run with the best of them." He turned toward me. "She's ready to go."

I made certain Potter was looking at me when I opened my jacket to retrieve the bag of shillings that I had brought along for payment and purposely held open the jacket for a few seconds so the knife might catch his eye.

"That be a mighty big knife for a lad," the smithy noted, much to my delight.

"Would you like to see my blade, Master?" I asked, slowly pulling the knife from the sheath.

When I held the blade up for Potter to see, his eyes grew as wide as the coals of his fire. "A Damascus blade!" he gasped. "Why I haven't seen the likes of it for some time now! Where did ya come by such a fine blade?"

"It is a gift."

"And quite a fine gift at that!"

"What did you call it?" I asked.

"A Damascus blade. Named for the city of its origin."

"I know of no city by that name."

"It is a far off place to the east...the land of camels and women with veils to hide their faces."

"Is it in Persia?"

The blacksmith looked confused as he scratched his head. "I know there's pretty women to the south in Boston and bottled whiskey to the southwest in Salem. There lies a frontier to the west from whence I get my coal and wood, and a great ocean to the east from whence I get my fish. What exists beyond those four points is for school masters, kings, and sailors to haggle over, and not the fancy of a black-smith from Lynn," Potter explained with a smile. "Now, may I hold that blade of yours?"

I handed him the knife.

Potter appeared mesmerized by the dazzling blade, slowly turning it within his calloused palms with the care one might bestow upon a sacred object. "It is a fine blade," he approved.

"Have you ever made such a blade?"

"Many years ago," he replied with a satisfying smirk, still staring at the knife. "Working every day from dawn to dusk, I could only make... maybe five such blades in one year's time. It is very difficult to produce a Damascus blade," he continued, handing the knife back to me. "One can forge an ordinary blade with but five pounds of coal. But a Damascus blade—well ya need at least your weight in high-grade coal."

"Why?"

"Well, look at the wavy pattern in the blade, lad. The grain is worked into the metal by the heat of the forge—it tis a combination of layers of welded steel and iron. Ya need a *devil* of a fire to produce such heat."

If only he knew. I thanked the blacksmith and placed the blade back within my sheath. After paying him for the horseshoe, I grabbed hold of the horse's reins and began to lead it from the shop.

"Lad!" the blacksmith called. I stopped and turned around. "Ya must have done a mighty fine deed to have been given such a gift."

THE FOLLOWING DAY WAS SATURDAY. MASTER KERSTLAND DECIDED to close the shop to celebrate his wedding anniversary and spend the day in Boston with his wife; although I think he would much rather have preferred to be at work. "One of the little compromises required of marriage," he would mumble—safely out of earshot of Mrs. Kerstland of course.

Realizing I was to have the day to myself, I rose with the dawn and journeyed by foot to the seashore. The tales of sunken shipwrecks and pirate's gold intrigued me as a young lad and I took the opportunity to comb the beach to retrieve whatever the sea desired to give up that morning. Shoeless and stockingless I paced south along the smooth and polished solid gray surface of sand as the cool saltwater of low tide broke against my feet; however the stingy sea had deposited only a multitude of broken shells and slimy seaweed in my path. At one point I paused to gaze at the bright orange sun ascending at the horizon where it appeared to rise from out of the sea. The morning rays produced a luster after the tide had receded, transforming the hardened sand into an extended mirror from which I could see the reflection of clouds passing overhead.

After scouring the beach for nearly two miles I came upon Nahant peninsula. This picturesque topography, which derives its name from the Indian term *Nahanteau*—meaning twins—is dominated by two highlands composed of a variety of rocks and cliffs separated by a beach more than a half mile in length. The geography here is quite extraordinary, characterized by a great many cliffs, caverns, and fissures. Great Nahant is connected to the mainland by Lynn beach and Little Nahant is positioned at the end of the peninsula.

My walk led me to the rocky cliffs on the northern side of Great Nahant and I was drawn to *Swallows' Cave*—a large passage beneath a high cliff. A flock of swallows soared above the entrance to the cave which was high enough for a grown man to pass through without having to stoop and seemed to be as wide as an average doorway. The sandy beach and sea water extended into the opening and at low tide the water's depth was but a few inches and easily passable, while inside, the cave expands its width and height, creating a perfect environment for the great number of swallows' nests that staggered about the diverse rock formations. At the center it becomes narrower and at a distance of about fifteen rods it opens to the sea on the opposite side of the peninsula.

I was nearly halfway through the cavern when I came upon a piece of broken coral half buried in the sand, which I retrieved. About the size of my hand, the reddish orange object was as hard as rock and I rolled it over in my palm, feeling its weight, when suddenly I heard my name being called from a point whence I came. I turned around and watched a brown horse galloping along the sand toward me. Upon its back the rider bounced with long red hair flowing with the rush of wind—it was Sam. I retraced my footsteps through the passage and emerged from out of the cave as my friend slowed the horse's gallop to a trot.

"Good morning," I greeted.

"It's happened again!" she exclaimed, out of breath. "Another girl disappeared last evening...Abigail Becker!"

I was stunned. "Do they suspect anyone?"

Sam hesitated. "No. Unlike the disappearance of Anna Hood, there is no evidence of foul play!"

I cringed. "Has the constable approached Eblis?"

"My father says Eblis has not been seen around Lynn for weeks."

Puzzled, I looked down at the coral in my hand.

"It's beautiful," Sam remarked.

I looked back up at her.

"The coral..it is beautiful. May I?" she asked leaning forward from her position in the saddle and extending her hand to me.

I placed the coral within Sam's open palm. "You may keep it," I offered.

"Thank you. I collect them," she revealed.

"I am saddened about the disappearance of Abigail Becker," I lamented, returning to the grim subject at hand.

"It's Eblis, isn't it Ben?"

"You have just told me Eblis is out of town?"

"But you suspect something evil of him, you always have!"

I sighed. "I can't explain it." I looked away from Sam and out at the blue ocean. "I don't know why I am connected to him. He haunts me..."

"Then you do believe Eblis to be behind these disappearances?" Sam pried.

I dropped my eyes from the horizon and gazed down upon the gentle surf rushing around my feet. "Yes..."

Sam dismounted and stepped toward me. I gazed into her eyes and decided not to hold back any longer. "He's the devil, Sam! Beelzebub,

Lucifer...whatever you desire to call it—Eblis is evil and he practices his sorcery across the street from your father's shop!"

Sam looked astounded. "The devil...?" she repeated with dissent. "I too witnessed the horned beast with you that night we came upon the witches; but how can you be certain that the monster and Eblis are one and the same?"

I reached for the sheath bound about my waist and withdrew the knife. "This blade! Eblis showed me this blade when we first met! And now he has succeeded in having the knife find its way back into my hands!"

"How do you know it's the same knife?" Sam asked.

"Because I showed it to the Smithy Potter and he explained how the blade is very rare and difficult to forge! The devil's a shoemaker in the shoemaking town of Lynn! Do you know what he told me the first time I met him?!" Without pausing for her response, I continued. "I asked what he did for his craft and he replied how he manufactured *soles*! At the time I thought he was referring to shoes! He meant *souls*, Sam—souls of the living!"

"Ben, it's all so unbelievable!"

I scoffed. "I didn't expect you to believe me. Caleb thinks I'm crazy as well!"

Sam reached out and took hold of my hand. "Ben, I believe you. I was with you at the coven of witches, remember? I too saw the beast. Before that night I would have thought you to be mad. Now, all I know is that I am very frightened. Abigail last night. Who is to be next? I've struggled since the night of the witches to look another woman of Lynn in the eyes, for I know not whom to trust. What other women of this town join Darcie in the black coven of witches? And many a night I've stared across the street at the strange goings-on inside the shoemaker's shop of Cyrus Eblis. Yes, Ben—I believe you!"

At that moment I felt such relief. "Thank you," I replied.

Sam released her hold of my hand. "Ben, we must do something about it! We must tell someone!" Sam pressed.

"And what of the threat to Rachel?" I asked, returning the blade to my sheath.

Sam sighed. "Then we must warn Rachel as well!"

"The witch said harm will come to Rachel if we reveal what we saw of the coven!" I reminded.

"But we must do something with our knowledge of this wickedness! When does your cousin return from Europe?"

"I am certain he is back; but I am not so sure that now is the time to seek his help. He is much too busy with politics in addition to his congregation, and there is much happening in the colonies at this moment. He's not about to run off and abandon his political goals for the purpose of chasing down a rumor of witches and demons!"

Sam sighed. "Well, how can you even be certain Caleb can help?"

I paused. "I'm not...but despite his political aspirations, I believe Caleb to be truly devoted to his religion. And if there is indeed a God, I think He would help my cousin. What other method can we use to fight the devil, if not God? However, I fear I have yet to convince my cousin that Eblis is what I say he is. My cousin doesn't have the time for my unfounded fears."

"And what of you, Ben? Eblis must be aware of your suspicion of him. Surely if you were a threat he would have hurt you by now. Yet he is slow to harm you?"

I hestitated. "He has harmed me...he has broken my sanity. I find it difficult to sleep after dark."

"My father is concerned. He has told me that you look tired," she interjected.

"I am plagued by the same nightmare, which I believe reveals my fate; although I am awakened before it ends. And the dream doesn't cease with daybreak. When I am awake..." I paused to stare out at the watery horizon, "...I am sometimes visited by my brother's...ghost." I turned and watched Sam shudder. "My brother fell to his death and I believe his spirit holds me responsible. We were playing, as young boys do, among the cliffs at the shore one afternoon. I played the part of a soldier defending the top of the cliff, and clutched a tree branch in my hand—it was my sword. Jordan, my brother, played the part of a pirate. He was always daring and thought himself invincible, so in an effort to capture the top of the cliff, he decided to scale the most treacherous side of the rocks knowing that I would never expect him to try such a feat; for we had been warned many times about the danger of climbing the rocks. I was standing with my back to the cliff when he appeared over the top of the ledge. He had not completely cleared himself from the edge of the cliff when he reached out and grabbed my shoulder. I became so surprised with fright that I spun around and instinctively shoved him away with the end of the branch. He laughed for an instant at my frightened reaction before a look of panic enveloped his face as he fell backwards! I shall never forget that look! He tried to maintain his balance, but disappeared over the ledge before I could react! It all happened so quickly!"

"Oh, how tragic!" Sam lamented. "I'm sorry for you Ben...but it was an accident! He surprised you before he had cleared the ledge! Your brother took a chance at climbing that wall of the cliff and it cost him his life! It was not your fault!"

I gazed at Sam. "Yes...maybe you're right; but I believe the soul of my brother has not found peace with his manner of death. His eternal unrest appears to be my burden in this world."

"How long has the haunting and nightmare tormented you?"

"Since my arrival to Lynn...no..." I corrected. "No, I believe the haunting and nightmare coincide with the arrival of Cyrus Eblis to this town!"

"Then it is Eblis who is the source of your problems!" Sam deduced.

I looked down once more upon the Damascus blade in its sheath. "You have reminded me of one such problem that I need to part with. First it was the cask and now the knife."

I paced over to the base of Great Nahant's promontory and found courage to climb the rocks to a height of about fifteen feet. Sam watched as I planted my unsteady footing onto the surface of a large solid rock, withdrew the blade from my sheath, and flung the knife out into the ocean. With a small splash the blade disappeared beneath the green waves as the water at high tide rushed through *Swallow's Cave* with great fury, producing a tremendous swishing sound that resembled the angry hissing of a monstrous serpent.

CHAPTER 22

ecember, 1770

    The two shadows embraced and shared a passionate kiss. She made reference to the cold night air and to the few inches of snow that blanketed the ground as he released his arms from around her waist and stepped gingerly from the house and down the path to the front gate. The door shut behind him and beyond the gate he proceeded with a wearisome stroll up Holyoke Street to the bend where it became Walnut. There he stopped and surveyed the area, finding the streets empty and silent. He set his bells down and rested his long black stave, tipped with brass, against a wooden fence, and quickly worked to light the candlewick of his pewter lantern. Once the beacon was lit, he pulled a silver-cased watch from his coat pocket and wound it with a key fastened to a small chain that hung from his breeches. "Three minutes to midnight," he mumbled. Turning back toward the small one-story house, which he could still see from Walnut, he watched as the light from a window gave way to blackness. The young, sultry widow Pierson had returned to bed with a large smile upon her face—satisfied once again with their illicit affair. With a sigh of relief, Jonathan Poole, the bell-man, retrieved his bells and tipstave and marched north on Walnut.

    Poole knew he would reach Federal Street just past midnight. Having just completed his sixth year as Lynn's bell-man, the thin, middle-aged watchman with the most recognizable gait in town, could have traveled his route blindfolded. The timing of his rounds had become routine. For even the occasional stop at the Pierson residence was strategically timed lest his affair be exposed.

At Federal Street, Poole paused and clanged his bells. "Past midnight, and all's well!" he called out before moving along. For the residents of Lynn the sound of his familiar delivery was reassuring—even in spite of the strange disappearances of Anna Hood and Abigail Becker. The disappearance of the second girl forced the constable to demand a lantern hung out on a pole from every seventh house in Lynn, and a second bell-man was also recruited; however he had taken ill this night and so Poole traversed the town by himself.

Poole had not been on duty during those evenings when the girls had vanished. He attributed his clean record to good fortune and trudged through the snowy streets of Lynn at a confident pace. But that confidence began to wane when the bell-man noticed the shadowy image of a tall man with a quick step appear from out of an alley onto Federal Street many rods before him. The dark figure wore a circular grey felt hat, while a black cape trailed him as he moved briskly with an undaunted stride. "What business has a man at this late hour?" Poole asked himself. The figure drew closer and the bell-man stopped.

"You there! I ask you to hold your position and identify yourself! I am the bell-man!" Poole commanded. The figure ignored Poole's request and continued his approach. "State your name!" Poole called out once again, now with trepidation in his voice. "I shall awaken the town with my bells!" Still the figure failed to heed Poole's warning and was now nearly upon him. Poole extended the arm that held the bells and shook his hand, but no clanging. Dumbfounded by the absence of sound, the bell-man continued to shake his arm feverishly, yet the bells remained silent forcing Poole to nervously examine the object, before looking up to find the man standing at arm's length before him. "Why...Master Eblis!" Poole recognized with surprise.

Eblis produced an icy stare and said nothing.

"Why did you not respond to my request, Master Eblis?"

Slowly Eblis' bottom lip turned upright producing a coy grin. "Your bells, they seem to have frozen?"

Poole looked back down at his bells. "That is certainly strange. The clappers are as stiff as my stave...though surely the air is not cold enough...," Poole paused and looked up at Eblis. "How is it that I can see my breath in the air, yet I cannot see yours?"

"Perhaps your eyes deceive thee?"

"Hmm..." Poole pondered. "Well, what is it that brings you out at the bewitching hour, as they say?"

Eblis hesitated before answering. "It seems I have lost my cat."

"Your cat?" Poole thought the response odd. "What color is she?"

"She is a he, and the color resembles the light brown of your scarf."

Poole glanced down at the scarf wrapped around his neck. "I have not seen such a cat."

Eblis brought his long index finger to his chin. "Now, if I'm not mistaken, the widow Pierson owns a cat. Perhaps my pet was drawn to hers—a female. The lure of sex is a powerful thing."

Poole said nothing.

"You saw nothing of my cat at the Pierson residence?"

"How's that...?" Poole interjected with brow raised.

"The widow Pierson," Eblis repeated calmly. "It occurred to me that you may have stumbled across my cat while rendezvousing with your partner in lust."

"I dear say Master Eblis! I do not know of what you speak!"

Eblis chuckled. "Oh come now, Poole. You cannot believe that your desire for fruit from the plentiful tree of this woman has remained a secret all this time?"

Poole was shocked. "I have a wife and three children!"

"Of course you do." Eblis reached up and patted the bell-man on the shoulder. "You are a sly one, Jonathan Poole."

Poole stammered with his mouth gaping so wide as to suggest one could shove his bells inside.

"Don't trouble thyself, good man," Eblis consoled sinisterly. He leaned in closer to Poole and spoke softly into his left ear. "There are only but three of us who are privy to this affair—the widow Pierson, yourself, and...I." Eblis smiled, backing away.

Poole looked at Eblis with a mopish stare. "I am embarrassed. It would please me Master Eblis if you did not repeat our conversation to anyone," he asked solemnly.

Eblis rested his chin in the palm of his hand, gently tapping his long fingernails against his bronze skin. "Hmmm...I cannot promise you anything, Johnathan Poole. For one cannot control the gossip circulating about a shoemaker's shop."

Deflated, Poole lowered his head. "Name your price."

Eblis' grin grew wide again and slowly he began to circling the dejected bell-man. Suddenly he stopped. "Yes, there is one thing!"

"I haven't much money!" Poole pleaded.

"Your soles!"

"I beg your pardon...?"

"Your shoes, bell-man! My lips shall remain sealed about this Pierson business if you agree to purchase soles from my shop."

Poole was surprised. "That is it? Shoes in exchange for your silence?"

"That is it," Eblis repeated, still grinning.

Poole sighed with relief. "I promise the first thing tomorrow morning..."

"Tonight," Eblis interrupted abruptly. "You will purchase new soles tonight."

"But it tis late? I must continue my rounds!"

"You shall continue thy rounds and upon reaching the meeting-house, you will know what to do," Eblis instructed.

"I'm confused?"

"What is the time?"

Poole glanced down at his watch. "Half past twelve."

"Then half past twelve and all is well," Eblis remarked and at that instant the bell-man's bells began to clang of their own power. Eblis grinned once more and suddenly a tremendous rush of wind lifted the snow into a blinding cyclone that encircled Poole. When the wind subsided, the shoemaker had disappeared. "Master Eblis?!" Poole called out. "Master Eblis?!" There was no reply.

Poole was shaken by the strange encounter with Cyrus Eblis but continued his march up Federal Street to the point where Federal intersects Boston Street. Here on the corner stood the meeting-house, and as Poole started across the street toward the building, he noticed a figure confined within the pillory. The man looked to be asleep with eyes shut as he stood hunched over behind the post. A dusting of snow had accumulated on the tricorn that set on his head, as well as on his hands which protruded through holes in the wooden framework that clamped shut around his limbs and neck.

Immediately Poole sensed something was not right. Although Lynn's justice proved swift and the punishment often harsh, it seemed odd to have a resident locked inside the pillory on such a horrid night. After all, the man could freeze to death and the pillory had not been designed as an execution device.

Poole quickly approached the prisoner and as he drew closer recognized him to be Jacob Bates, whose excessive passion for liquor made him a regular visitor to the pillory.

"Well what do we have here?" Poole inquired. "What be it this time, Jake? Too much to drink again?"

The man slowly lifted his head and opened his bloodshot eyes. His face was beet red from the cold and frost encircled his parched and broken lips. He opened his mouth to respond to the bell-man, but he could only utter a few indistinguishable sounds.

"Who was it that locked you up here, Jake?" Poole inquired, now feeling compassion for the prisoner.

Again Jake attempted to speak, but to no avail.

Poole grabbed the wooden pillory and attempted to pull the device apart, but it held fast with an iron padlock. "We need to get you out of here!" Poole remarked, now with deep concern. It was then that the bell-man glanced down upon the feet of Bates and noticed his shoes. For although the prisoner was clad in ragged and worn attire, his buckled shoes appeared clean and unscratched, glistening under the lantern's flame as if they were brand new.

"Jake, your shoes? Where did you get them?"

Bates swallowed hard and opened his mouth. He uttered a two syllable word that Poole could not make out. The bell-man lowered his right ear closer to Jake's mouth and Bates repeated the word, "Eb...lis..."

Poole raised his head. "Eblis?" he asked.

Bates slowly motioned his head up and down to acknowledge the bell-man.

Poole sighed with confusion. "I shall return, Jake! And I'll get you out of here!"

The bell-man turned and began a quick and steady pace toward the meetinghouse located across the street from the pillory. As he neared the building he began to slow his advance upon noticing a scraggly man seated upon the snowy steps. Poole stopped a safe distance from the man and noticed that he wore a patch over his left eye.

"Good evening, bell-man," Patch greeted with a disgusting belch.

Poole noticed the burlap sack resting next to the stranger.

"I have thy soles," Patch informed with a grin.

"What say you?"

Patch reached inside the burlap sack. "I am employed by Master Eblis," he explained as he pulled a pair of jackboots from out of the sack. "I believe these are yours," he said, rising to his feet and handing them to the bell-man.

Poole stepped closer, noticing how the smaller stranger stood with a slightly hunched back, and reluctantly accepted the boots. "Eblis' business certainly keeps odd hours? I only spoke to Master Eblis but a few moments ago. How could he have possibly gotten word to you about purchasing these boots on such short notice?"

Patch pulled the drawstring shut on the sack. "Put them on."

"Your daft dear sir! I do not intend to replace my boots out here in the streets of Lynn! I told Eblis I would purchase them tonight, but said nothing of wearing them!"

Patch reached out and grabbed the bell-man's arm. "Put them on —now!" he growled. "It tis his wish!"

"Who? Eblis? This was not part of the agreement! I shall not!" Poole exclaimed, pulling his arm out from within Patch's grasp.

Patch reached inside of his jacket, withdrew a large knife and wielded the blade at Poole.

"What is this?! Are you threatening me?!" Poole exclaimed. "There's a man freezing to death in the pillory and we are haggling about boots?!"

Patch grinned and shook the blade at the bell-man. "Put them on, bell-man! I shan't ask you again!"

Poole began to shake his bells, but once again they did not produce a sound. Frustrated, the bell-man turned his head briefly to glance back at the prisoner locked within the pillory and realized that confronting this strange ruffian over soles was secondary to Bate's dire situation. "All right! I shall put on the bloody boots!" Poole decided. He dropped his bells, stave, and lantern and sat down upon the steps. Quickly the bell-man exchanged his boots, all the time with a watchful eye on Patch. When Poole had fitted his foot into the second boot, Patch placed the knife back within his jacket. The one-eyed man then picked up the burlap sack and turned away from the bell-man. "This is madness!" Poole yelled out. "Tell your employer that terrorizing customers is no way to conduct business! I don't care what he knows of my situation! He'll be hearing from me!"

Patch never acknowledged the ramblings of the bell-man and soon the strange little man disappeared down an alley.

Poole scratched his head and gazed down upon the shiny boots. Suddenly the silence of the evening was broken by a loud beastly roar and the bell-man looked up with astonishment to see a large animal with a tawny coat creeping slowly on all fours behind Bates, who remained confined within the pillory. At first the bell-man thought it to be a dog, but when the animal hissed again, Poole could see its large fangs.

"My Lord—a mountain lion!"

By now Bates had sensed the presence of the lion approaching him from behind and began to wriggle and squirm in a futile attempt to free his head and arms from the pillory; but his sudden terrified movements only excited the ferocious animal.

Poole remained steadfast, fearing for his own safety. "My word! The poor soul's hung out there like a fresh piece of meat!" The bell-man turned toward the alley in search of Patch, but the strange man had vanished within the shadows of the buildings. He turned back to the pillory. "What to do?! I have no weapon!" he exclaimed aloud. Then the bell-man picked up his bells and began to shake them furiously; but they remained silent.

Bates finally managed to cry out with strained voice as the mountain lion roared. Poole retrieved the stave from off the steps and extended it outward as though he gripped a small sword, but before he could proceed with one step in the direction of Bates and the lion, he was interrupted by a voice from behind him. "Bell-man!" called the voice. Poole whirled around to find Eblis.

"Bell-man!" the sinister shoemaker repeated. "I see you've found my cat!"

"That beast is yours?!"

The mountain lion growled again and then pranced upon Bates from behind, swiping its claws at his backside. The razor-sharp nails shredded his breeches and drew streams of blood from each leg. The lion recoiled a few feet as Bates cried out in agony and the cat sprung upon the helpless man once more, clamping its powerful jaws around his hips.

"Do something, Eblis!" Poole pleaded.

"He's hungry," Eblis replied callously. "What is there to do?"

With its jaws locked about Bates' waist, the mountain lion shook its head violently and pulled with its teeth until it had ripped the lower half of the man's body away from the midsection. Bates fell silent as the beast ran off into the night with its game, leaving a ghastly sight as testament to its ferocious power. For the upper portion of Bates' body remained intact—his head and hands still confined within the pillory; however, all that remained of the man's lower half were pieces of shredded flesh and bone dangling above a dark pool of blood that stained the snow beneath the wooden apparatus.

Sickened by the site, Poole doubled-over and began spewing about the ground. He wiped his lips with the sleeve of his jacket, righted himself and seething with disgust and anger, he turned toward Eblis. "You bastard!" he blurted.

Eblis grinned and directed his right arm at Poole's feet, pointing with extended index finger. Suddenly the snow burst into flames and erupted into a circle of fire that surrounded the bell-man.

Poole, now filled with terror, dropped his bells and stave. Turning away from Eblis, he dashed through the flames and beyond the burning circle; although in his escape his breeches caught fire. He fell to the ground, frantically rubbing the wet snow over his burning breeches to extinguish the flames and looked up to view Eblis slowly stepping through the ring of fire, unscathed.

"It is time to collect my fee!" Eblis announced.

Poole quickly crawled to his feet and without looking back, began a mad sprint down the street. His home was located at the southern end of Lynn, far from his current location, so the nearest sanctuary proved to be the home of his lover—the widow Pierson. The bell-man reached the front door of her house and pounded furiously upon the door until it was pulled open just far enough for the startled widow to view the unexpected caller.

"Maggie! Let me in!" Poole pleaded.

The surprised widow swung open the door and Poole darted

inside. Panting from his flight, the bell-man quickly fastened the door behind him.

"John! What is going on?!"

"A madman follows me!" Poole revealed as he stepped to the window that set aside the door and peered out into the darkness.

She studied his scorched breeches. "Your breeches?! Have you been burned?!

Poole did not reply and continued gazing out the window.

"Is he there?" the widow asked.

"I do not see him; but he's a sorcerer! He may very well be concealed!"

The woman grew alarmed as she observed his frightened state. "Johnathan, you're scaring me!"

"I'm sorry, dear! But I have witnessed dark happenings this evening!"

"Well, this madman shan't find you here?"

Poole turned around. "He knows of us!"

"But how?!"

"Black magic!"

The widow gasped, taking hold of his hand. "Come. You shall remain here with me until it is safe," she advised. She pulled on his arm and guided him from the entry hall into the New England farm kitchen—a large room which served as the kitchen, dining room, and master bedroom. A grand hearth dominated the center of the back wall, but what gave the room its character was the "turn-up" bedstead attached to the side wall. The strong wooden frame was filled with a maze of rope fastened at the bed-head by hinges to the wall which remained hooked to the wall during the daytime concealed behind curtains. As it was evening, the bed was pulled down and the bottom half rested on two heavy legs.

Poole followed the widow into the room, gazing upon the long woolen night-dress that fell just above her ankles; but it was her shoes —satins slippers—that stopped him suddenly, causing the curious widow to turn toward him.

"What is this?" he asked.

"Whatever do you mean?" she replied, confused.

"Your slippers? Do you wear them to bed?"

"No, of course not. I couldn't sleep and I suddenly had this urge to try on my slippers. They're new. Why do you inquire of them now?"

"From whom were they purchased?"

The widow appeared puzzled by such questioning giving the circumstances of the evening; but she complied with his inquiry. "Well, if you must know, I'm to pay for them later. They were manufactured by the shoemaker who occupies the Hassett shop—Eblis or something. I find your interest in my slippers at this hour to be very strange?"

Poole's face turned white and he looked down upon his new jackboots. "These were made from the hands of Eblis as well! And so to were the shoes of Jacob Bates! Eblis is the madman who pursues me!"

Suddenly a loud banging upon the front door shook the room. Through the passageway that linked the farm kitchen with the entry hall they watched as the front door began to swell and bulge inward, nearly tearing its hinges from the frame as a powerful force seemed to be working at pressing down the door from the outside.

"He's found us!" Poole exclaimed.

"John! I'm frightened!" the widow cried out, falling into his arms.

The incessant pounding and swelling of the door continued for several minutes and then as suddenly as it had begun, it stopped.

"Is he gone?!" the widow inquired with distress.

Poole said nothing and listened to the eerie stillness.

And then the silence was broken once again. Only this time it resembled the harshness of splintering wood.

"What is that?!" the widow screamed.

"My God! The walls...they're moving!" Poole exclaimed as he watched with astonishment the destruction that befell the room. All four walls began to slide across the floor of their own power as a giant vice pressing inward toward the center, smashing objects as they moved.

"He's trying to kill us! The walls will crush us!"

The widow screamed again and buried her head into Poole's chest; but the bell-man threw her aside and rushed toward the door. Poole matched the door's inward movements with backward steps of his own as he worked frantically pulling at the doorknob. "It won't open!" he yelled. "Quickly—on the bed!" he exclaimed and the two hopped onto the mattress. They knelt facing one another and embraced.

The two lovers clutched each other ever so tightly and began to sob violently while objects broke and disintegrated around them as the room continued to shrink. Soon the bed was the last object to remain intact as the walls pressed in around all four sides of the bed. But to the astonishment of the terrified couple, suddenly the walls ceased their movement.

Johnathan and Maggie slowly lifted their heads with amazement and relief; but one tempered with caution.

"Is it ended?" Maggie dared to whisper. She held her breath sensing another presence near the couple and slowly turned her head to look behind her. There positioned above the two lovers resting in a sitting position on the headboard at the head of the bed sat Cyrus Eblis.

"No, Maggie. On the contrary, it's just begun!" the dark shoemaker bellowed.

The widow and the bell-man both screamed and the bed flew up backwards into its daytime position, sealing the two lovers between the wall and the mattress.

CHAPTER 23

Two days after the gruesome discovery of Jacob Bates' remains I was busy at work within the shop when Oliver Purvis, the locksmith of Lynn, stepped in from outside.

"Good timing," Master Kerstland acknowledged as he sat sewing the sole of a jackboot. "I've nearly finished your boots."

"Wonderful," Purvis replied stepping over to the raging fireplace. "It's a blasted cold one today," he declared rubbing his hands together over the hearth lifting his right hand to rub it through his thick brown hair that hung low just above his eyebrows. An average man in height and weight, Purvis' friendly disposition was incessant, inviting conversation and assuring him knowledge of everyone's business throughout Lynn.

"I would have had Ben run the jackboots over to your shop," Kerstland apologized.

"I had to be out in this wretched weather anyway," the locksmith countered. "Nathanial Henchman locked himself out of his bookbinding shop this morning. That's twice the old man's done that this month." Purvis removed his thick woolen coat and tossed it over a chair before focusing his attention on me. "How are you, Ben?" he asked taking a seat on a bench aside the fireplace.

"Very well, thank you," I replied as I punched holes into a piece of leather with my awl.

"That Kerstland's a slave driver," Purvis jested with a smirk.

"The boy's earning his keep," Kerstland countered.

"Did you feel the earthquake the other night?"

"Only slightly."

"Such a strange evening. An earthquake and a killer mountain lion all in one night. That must have been some large beast, ey Emery?"

Without lifting his head Kerstland rolled his eyes upward and peered out over top of the rim of his glasses. "You're speaking of the beast that mauled Jake?"

"Mauled...ripped in two is more like it! It was quite a bloody mess I've been told. It should be sometime before they confine a man in the pillory again; although you can't find one soul in this town who will admit that they were responsible for his confinement. Who would lock a man up in the pillory on such a frigid night? The constable denies any responsibility."

"Well someone did," Kerstland replied.

"It must have been some cat," the locksmith added. "Joseph Williams killed a large mountain lion two years ago just beyond the woods to the west of Lynn."

"I remember," Kerstland added. "Have they found the bell-man?"

"You haven't heard?"

Kerstland raised his head, pausing from his work.

"Oh, they found him, they did," Purvis revealed. "Dead in bed... with the widow Pierson."

"You don't say?"

"I do. She had a turn-up bedstead and while the two were in bed, the earthquake must have sent the bed flying back up into the wall crushing both their skulls."

"My...how horrible."

"The tragedy is how that fine woman, Mrs. Poole, is to deal with the revelation that her husband was an adulterer. They found them cuddled together; although it must have happened quickly; for they were still clothed. In fact they had shoes on—brand new shoes."

Kerstland turned toward me. "We didn't deliver any shoes...?"

I shook my head.

Then Kerstland glanced out the window to the shop across the street. I knew what he was thinking. I was thinking the same.

The locksmith followed Kerstland's stare. "Passed that Eblis fellow this morning. He looked to be on his way north out of town. I don't know what people see in that man, but he sure is popular. I think he's a scary one myself. Didn't so much as wave a hand or look in my direction this morning. Then again, he was movin' like the *Devil*."

Kerstland rose from his chair and held up the two shiny jackboots. "They're finished," he announced.

"Very good," Purvis commented. Rising to his feet, he picked his coat up from off the bench and withdrew several coins from inside the pocket. He handed them to Kerstland in exchange for the boots. "Thanks, Emery" he said as he pulled his arms through both coat sleeves. "Have a good day." Both men shook hands and the locksmith stepped through the doorway and out into the December cold.

"I am no longer surprised at what I hear happening about this town," Kerstland suddenly remarked, still staring out the shop window.

"Master?" I prodded.

"Although I wish ill upon no-one, I suspect Jonathan Poole and the widow Pierson got what was coming to them for breaking the Lord's commandments," Kerstland pronounced as he stepped toward the coat rack positioned in the corner of the shop and lifted his long waist great coat of blue camlet from one of the hooks. "I'm off to Richard Saddler's place in need of a new pair of eyeglasses," he said as he pulled on his coat. He deposited the coins from the locksmith into one of the coat's pockets, buttoned the garment, and reached for the wooden rack once again retrieving a blue tricorn that he placed on his head. "I shan't be long," Kerstland added leaving the shop.

I had resumed the task of punching holes into leather when after a few minutes I noticed an object from across the room lying underneath the bench positioned beneath the front window. I paused from my work and walked over to retrieve the narrow piece of metal that resembled a large fishing hook, and as I picked it up from off the floor I realized it to be a picklock. *It must have fallen from the breeches of the locksmith.*

My first reaction was to set it aside, for Master Purvis would surely find his way back to the shop as he retraced his footsteps in search of the lost instrument; but then I glanced up and out the window. Across the street the small wooden two-story Hassett shoe-making shop caught my eye, beckoning me with its large wooden boot swinging in the wind. I looked down at the picklock in my hand and up and across the street once again. My curiosity was piqued. *Shall I explore the ten-footer behind the shop? Purvis remarked how Eblis seemed to be on his way out of town and I have the means to gain entry?*

A few moments later, clad in a long coat and tricorn, I closed the door of the shop behind me and stepped down from the brick entry stairs onto the snow covered cobblestone as the cold morning air stung my face. Sinking my hands into the pockets of my coat, I began a brisk step to cross the street when I was startled to hear my name called out from behind me. I stopped and turned to my left where I watched Sam approach dressed warmly in a long stiff black stay draped with a purple cloak trimmed with fur.

I turned and paced slowly toward her, meeting before the door of Kerstland's shop.

"Good morning," she greeted pleasantly from beneath a black silk bonnet.

"Good morning, Sam."

"Did I smile for you?" she asked.

"What?" I was confused.

"Did I smile for you? I've had two persons this morning tell me that they've not seen me smile in some time now. Jeremiah Shepard has even inquired into my state of health. It seems I cannot hide my fear and suspicions. It's because of that night at the coven, Ben, for I know not whom to trust."

I sighed. "Yes, you smiled," I placated. "And yes I feel the same."

"Well...at least I can trust you," she said. "Have you heard from Caleb?"

"No," I replied disappointedly. "He must be very busy."

"Ben, we must do something! I do not know how much longer I can hold my tongue knowing that monster walks freely among the streets of Lynn!"

"Lower your voice," I cautioned, turning to look across the street at the Hassett shop. "I don't know whether our word in this matter will be good enough—even for Caleb." I turned back toward Sam. "We need some proof to support our claims."

"What type of proof?"

I did not want to involve my friend in my next course of action. "I'm not certain," I replied.

"Remember Ben, it is no longer just your problem," Sam said scrupulously. "Where are you bound?"

I hesitated pulling the picklock from the pocket of my jacket. "The locksmith left this behind this morning in your father's shop. I'm to return it."

"I've just passed Master Purvis. You're bound in the wrong direction?"

"Oh...thank you," I babbled, returning the instrument to my pocket.

"Ben, are you all right?" Sam asked suspiciously. "You seem preoccupied this morning?"

"Oh...just with returning the picklock," I quickly replied, forcing a smile. "Your father has gone for a pair of eyeglasses. Please be sure to tell him of my whereabouts."

She nodded.

"Good day," I said tipping my tricorn. I turned and began strolling in the direction from whence Sam had come, when after a few steps I turned slightly and waved to my curious friend who continued to mark my departure. A moment later, I turned again. Sam had now entered the shop so I stopped and proceeded across the street in the direction of the Eblis manufactory.

I approached the dark shop that was separated from the neighboring structures by a narrow alley running adjacent to either side of the building as the large wooden boot above the front door swung back and forth in the wind, squeaking as though it were welcoming or perhaps warning me. Shuffling down the long shadow of the alley in between the two walls of white clapboards, I entered the narrow passage that opened into a large backyard staggered with rows of winter-barren mulberry trees flanking three outbuildings. Plodding through the pristine snow, I turned several times to gaze uneasily upon the small second-story window at the rear of the house. And although behind its panes was blackness, I felt as if the window itself kept watch over my movements.

Upon reaching the door of the first outbuilding I turned the handle and pulled, but as I anticipated, the door was locked. *That would have been too easy.* Withdrawing the picklock from my pocket, I worked to insert the hooked end of the instrument into the keyhole, finding it difficult to keep my hand steady from the anxiety that enveloped me. I jiggled the picklock for a minute or two—which seemed an eternity—and then heard the click of the bolt. Grabbing the handle again, I pulled open the door and darted inside the ten-footer, pausing for a moment before quickly pulling the door shut behind me.

Rays of sunlight beamed through clouded windows providing the only light inside the ten-footer and at that point I realized the madness of wandering into the eerie building. I paced slowly toward the rear of the ten-footer, amazed to find dust and cobwebs covering the great many tools that were strewn about the work benches. Finding my way to the back of the ten-footer, I located a long book covered with black leather resting upon a shelf, and recognized it as the *book of orders,* which contained the record keeping of a shoemaker —his orders and sales. As I reached to open the cover, suddenly I was startled by the clicking of the door's bolt and I immediately dropped to my knees behind a workbench. The door creaked as it slowly swung open.

"Ben...?" called a voice.

I recognized it and stood upright. "Sam! What are you doing here?!" I asked with surprise.

"I thought I could trust you!" she scolded, closing the door behind her. "I suspected you were up to something, so I watched until you crossed the street and followed you in here."

"Did anyone see you?"

"I don't think so?"

I turned away and opened the black book.

"What did you find?" Sam asked, moving quickly to the back of the room.

"I need light," I uttered, lifting the book from off the shelf and pacing over to the window. Aided by the sun's rays I began reading down the list of names that occupied the first page of the book underneath the heading *Orders.* With each name I read, I grew more excited. "What do Constable Dixey and Jacob Bates both have in common?" I asked aloud.

"Well..." Sam thought. "They're both...dead."

"Yes! This book of orders reads like an obituary! Who was the man killed when his house caught fire this year last?"

"Lyttleton...Adrian Lyttleton."

I scanned the list. "He's here as well! The final two entries are Jonathan Poole and Margaret Pierson. Both were killed the other night during the earthquake!"

"What does it mean?"

"This is the *book of orders*! I suspect that everyone who orders a pair of shoes from Eblis has met death shortly thereafter!"

"I don't understand?"

"The two girls who disappeared—what were their names?"

"Anna Hood and Abby Becker."

I searched the list. "I cannot find any mention of either."

"Did they purchase shoes from Eblis as well?"

"I don't know. I just assumed..." I stammered and suddenly Sam screamed. Startled, I dropped the book and followed the direction of her eyes. She was looking at the window of the shop where the gloating face of Eblis' one-eyed assistant, Patch, returned the stare from outside. He grinned and quickly stepped from the view of the window. I turned toward Sam. "Did you fasten the door?!"

The door thrust open and I had my answer. Patch stood in the doorway for a moment, before stepping inside and pulling the door shut behind him. Terrified, I realized I needed a weapon and spied an awl resting on a workbench positioned to the left of where Patch stood. I lunged for the awl, but Patch moved quicker and he snared my right arm, pinning it to the bench. He held my arm steady with his left hand and gripped the back of my neck with his right. With my left hand free I reached up, pulled the tricorn from my head and held the hat over Patch's face, blinding his good eye. "Run!" I yelled to Sam. Immediately she darted past me and out the door.

Furious by my blinding maneuver, Patch snarled and shoved me to the ground on my back. Standing over me with a dastardly sneer, the one-eyed madman reached into his jacket and withdrew a large knife. At the sight of this I reached for the bench that was situated to my right and slid the wooden object in front of him, causing him to stumble over it as I sprang to my feet.

With a slow approach, Patch teased and terrified me by slicing the blade through the air, and I watched the blade's movements with careful eyes, backing my way around the room, until I found myself trapped in a corner. Patch's grin grew wider as he recognized my predicament. Desperate and frightened, I quickly surveyed the area around me and found a lasting jack within my reach. I pushed the elongated piece of wood in front of me to create a barrier between myself and the crazed knife-wielding Patch, and soon we were dancing about the jack as I dodged the evil man's jabbing. With each miss he would recoil and jab again. The more I dodged, the more frustrated he became, and then with one swift lunge, Patch had extended himself too far. I seized the opportunity to lift the jack from the floor and turned it sideways, thrusting it as a battering ram and shoved the base of the jack into his stomach, driving him backwards into the wall. The fiendish assistant crashed against the side of the building with a tremendous thud and fell limp to the floor groaning. I dropped the jack and ran from the outbuilding through the snow, across the street, and back into the safety of Kerstland's shop where I was reunited with a much relieved Sam.

I was thankful to be unharmed, but disappointed that Eblis' *book of orders* remained behind in the ten-footer. *I still lacked proof.*

CHAPTER 24

January, 1771

...He pulled tight on the horse's reins and the beast stopped and whined, kicking high into the air with its front two legs. It was then that I noticed the noose at the end of a rope swinging from a tree limb high above. Quickly pulling myself into a sitting position, I began a backwards crawl but my escape stalled when my back collided with a cold, stone object. I spun around to discover a headstone with the inscription concealed behind a thick layer of dust. Frantically I worked at brushing away the dirt to reveal the name of... I awoke in a pool of sweat on a winter night. The nightmare was always the same. Never would I be asleep long enough to discover the identity of the name on the headstone.

After illuminating a lantern that rested on a table positioned to the left of my bed, I stacked the pillows up against the headboard, propping myself into a sitting position. I feared to shut my eyes lest I return to sleep and to the frightening dream; for in spite of my curiosity to learn the name on the headstone, peace of mind was most important. With my waist and legs blanketed by a warm quilt, I decided to read one of the texts lying about Caleb's room. The book was a history of the Middle East and as I had hoped for some light reading, the text did not seem very appealing at first. I began leafing through the pages with little inspiration until I came upon a section that caught my eye. It described the story of a young Persian boy who grew up to lead a revolt against his grandfather and became a great king of Persia. The tale held my interest, but it was the king's name that excited me—for he was called *Cyrus.*

I became lost in the story before I noticed the room had become considerably cooler. With a shiver, I lifted my head from out of the pages and glanced over at the window to see if it might be ajar; but it was secure. Nevertheless the temperature inside the room continued to plummet and soon my breath materialized before me. Resting the book upon my lap, I stared out into the darkness as the lamp's flickering flame cast long shadows that wavered against the bedroom walls setting the imagination on edge. And then the bedroom door squeaked. As I watched the doorknob, it began to spin slowly. "Hello?" I called out with apprehension. There was no reply, yet the knob continued to turn. I trembled, recalling the eerie movement of the doorknob the night I viewed Eblis below my window and pulled the quilt from my legs, throwing my feet over the side of the bed. "Uncle Edward? Aunt Jamie?" I invoked suspiciously. Stepping from the bed I inched toward the door and placed my hand softly upon the doorknob —the turning stopped. With a deep breath, I grabbed hold of the knob and pulled open the door; but there was no-one on the other side. Suddenly a cold draft passed right through me, and I quivered turning toward the bed just as the door flew shut of its own power behind me. I turned back around and tried to pull open the door, but now it had locked as a milky white mist materialized in the room and hovered over my bed having no recognizable shape; yet its presence filled my heart with fear. Suddenly it seemed to drone until I could distinguish my name. "BEN...!" it proceeded to call out over and over again. I pitched my back up against the door and gaped at the specter, pressing the palms of my hands so hard against the wood that the nails of my fingers became embedded within the oak. With a tormented wail that raised the hair on the back of my neck, the specter cried out, "HELP ME! I'M FALLING...!"

"No, Jordan!!" I cried back.

Suddenly the apparition flitted about the room and I watched with horror as the books upon Caleb's desk crashed to the floor, one at a time as if being thrown by an invisible force. Only the Bible that my cousin had given me was spared this fate; although I watched as it levitated from the desk. The book became suspended in air for a moment before being thrust open and the pages turned in rapid succession until the covers slammed shut as it flew across the room at great speed striking the lantern and knocking it from the table onto the bed. Instantly the sheets burst into flames and the fire began to spread across the bed as black smoke filled the room. I wanted to move, but I could not—frozen against the door. The room began to shake violently and I heard pounding on the other side of the door; but in my terrified state didn't realize that my body blocked the entrance to the room, preventing my escape. My eyes began to burn and my lungs filled with smoke. I fell unconscious...

I AWOKE THE NEXT MORNING IN MY UNCLE'S BED. WHEN MY blurred vision had focused, I gazed up at familiar faces hovering over me with comforting smiles.

"Benjamin, how do you feel?" my aunt asked.

I could not answer but only coughed—my throat burned.

"We had another earthquake last night, Ben," my uncle explained. "It seems the force of the quake knocked the lantern onto your bed and the sheets caught fire. Fortunately, I was awakened by the quake and came to your room. I had a difficult time getting in though. You must have fallen trying to get out, blocking the door."

"Your uncle beat the fire out with a blanket," Jamesina continued. "It ruined the bed; but praise the Lord no-one was hurt!"

"You had better get some rest, Ben. I've told Emery Kerstland not to expect you into the shop today," Edward said as he patted the top of my head.

I nodded and looked down at my side. There, positioned next to me on the bed, rested Caleb's Bible—unscathed.

MY BRUSH WITH DEATH SHATTERED MY WILL TO CONTINUE AS A player in this evil game that shrouded Lynn. Eblis; the witches; the one-eyed man; my brother's ghost; and the beast of the forest had convinced me that the town was indeed cursed and that I could do nothing about it. As yet I did not understand my connection with the infestation of Lynn and so I decided to run and seek my own safety. The decision had been made. I would leave my aunt and uncle's place and move onto Boston.

A few days after the fire in my room, I celebrated my seventeenth birthday. It proved to be the perfect occasion for which to break the news to the Browns of my sudden desire to leave Lynn. In my explanation I spoke not of fear, but of a longing to reside independently and work in a city the size of Boston. Edward and Jamesina, although saddened, were easily convinced. I would write my mother and describe the same.

Never did I have any doubt that I could deceive my family about my reasons for leaving; however the difficult task would be explaining my departure to Sam. The awkward moment came the next morning as I was bidding farewell to Emery Kerstland while at work in his shoemaking shop. The shoemaker was thanking me for my work in his employ when Sam entered the room.

"Sam, Ben has some news for us this morning," Master Kerstland announced.

Sam looked at me with guarded anticipation.

I swallowed hard. "I'm...leaving."

Sam said nothing.

"He's bound for Boston," Kerstland interjected. "Pity to lose such a fine young man. Wouldn't you agree, Sam?"

Sam smirked. "Pity," she uttered. I could sense her anger.

Kerstland was puzzled by Sam's indifferent response. "Sam?"

Sam shook her head. "I'm sorry. I'm just surprised, that is all. We will all miss you very much, Ben," she rebuked and turned toward Kerstland. "Father, may I have a word with Ben...alone?"

Kerstland nodded, recognizing that Sam and I had developed a special bond. "Of course. I need to see the smithy anyway. I shall return soon," he explained as he retrieved his coat and tricorn before exiting the shop.

Sam waited until the door closed behind her father. "You're leaving?!" she inquired, now with much more passion. "Why?!"

"I long to work in a big city. The employ..."

"You're running away, aren't you?!" she interrupted.

I sighed. "It is time for me to move on, Sam. That is all."

"Do you think you can run away from your nightmares?!"

I turned away from Sam and stared out the window. "I hope so."

"Ben, it is only you and I who know of the evil secret behind Eblis' *book of orders* and the beast at the witch's coven! You just can't run off with the knowledge that Eblis' list of orders will surely grow?! You'll have the blood of Lynn on your hands!"

I turned back toward her. "My hands are already stained! There is nothing we can do here! Without the *book of orders* we have no proof and I dare not risk another encounter with that crazed Patch or the beast! Who will listen, Sam? Who in this town is innocent?!"

"I am innocent...as are you! And now you're going to give up—just like that?!"

"Perhaps I can fight this evil from afar?!" I offered carelessly in an effort to appease Sam. The reality was that I had no plan, for I had not thought that far ahead. "I fear if I stay here any longer I will be set ablaze in my bed while I sleep—just as the other night!"

"And what about me?! Do you not care for me?!"

Sam's remark stunned me as did the look of desperation upon her face.

"How do you mean?" I asked. It was the wrong response.

Sam dropped her head and began to sob. I believe it was the first time I had ever seen her cry. I didn't know what to say and probably because of my silence she gathered her composure, lifting her head in my direction. "You're a coward, Benjamin Pratt!" she bawled and burst from the room.

LATER IN THE DAY I WAS NORTHBOUND TO THE GOODE RESIDENCE to presumably hurt another friend. The weather was frigid and gray—reflecting my mood. During the entire trip I could not free my mind of thoughts of Sam and her final words to me. *How could I have been so insensitive? Will I ever see her again? How could I have allowed our friendship to be damaged by my fear?* I wanted so much to go back and tell her that I did care for her very much and that I had suddenly decided to remain in Lynn; but my dreadful state of mind, nurtured by the black magic of Cyrus Eblis, had rendered me spineless.

Soon I found myself seated inside the parlor of the Goode house. As I expected, Rachel exhibited her effervescent self, speaking favorably on each subject that we raised. I admired her virtuosity and craved her innocence for my knowledge of Lynn's dark side had become a heavy burden. As I had not seen her in several months, we caught up on lost time and she scolded me playfully for having abandoned our Bible sessions. She remarked about our first encounter when I had made a fool of myself in pursuit of her hat and we laughed. When my laugh had subsided I raised my head with sobering eyes and our smiles disappeared simultaneously.

"You have something to tell me?" she deduced.

I stood up and reached inside my jacket withdrawing a Bible. "First I want to give you something," I said. "For some time now I've wanted to replace your Bible that was damaged that night in the woods. I thought this might be an appropriate moment." I handed her the copy. "This is the book that my cousin Caleb had given me. His and my paths will cross again sometime soon and so I shall be sure to acquire another."

"Thank you," she acknowledged. "Where does he reside?"

"Connecticut," I replied sinking back into the chair. "I'm leaving. Bound for Boston."

"Will you be gone long?"

"It is permanent."

"Oh..." she gasped. "Then I shall miss you."

I dropped my head and stared at the tricorn that I now twirled in my hands.

"It's the unknown, isn't it?" Rachel asked softly.

I looked up, surprised by her remark; although I shouldn't have been. "Yes," I replied, ashamed.

"Tell me about your fear."

"The less people I involve, the fewer get hurt. I don't want to corrupt you."

"I'm your friend, Benjamin. You're leaving for Boston. The least you can do is to explain why?" she beseeched.

How precious she was. Her request melted my heart.

With a sigh I weakened. "I am plagued by an evil force that has come to Lynn," I divulged reluctantly. "I believe I am in need of a change of scenery before I go mad and before someone close to me is harmed."

Rachel's expression did not change. "What part do you play with this evil force?"

"I fear I am somehow responsible for its presence in Lynn. I believe it has followed me here and now all who are close to me are at risk."

"This is related to the night in the forest—is it not?"

I hesitated. "Yes."

"What do you think will happen when you've gone?" she continued. "Might this force follow you to Boston?"

"I cannot say."

"Have you confided in God?"

I rose from the chair into a standing position. Rachel's question had struck a nerve. "I have read the Bible directly to this force! It mocks the words of the Lord!" I proclaimed, running my hands nervously through my hair. "I tell you Rachel, I have called prayers out in the middle of the night to combat the forces of darkness! Still I am pursued by the Devil and haunted by..." I paused, not wanting to reveal too much information. "I am haunted by darkness," I concluded.

Rachel was surprised by my outburst. "Why have you not told me this before?"

"I was afraid you wouldn't believe me."

Rachel smiled. "Benjamin, I am your friend. Of course I would have believed you. And I understand if you need to go to Boston. But I'm not sure you will find peace of mind there?"

"Then where?" I asked.

Rachel lifted her arm, clutching the Bible in her hand. "In here, Benjamin. Here is your peace of mind."

I sighed.

"It is not the words that you read, Ben," Rachel explained. "It is the faith behind the reader. *But without faith it is impossible to please him; for he that cometh to God must believe that he is...*"

"I don't have your faith! And I don't know how to find your faith!" I exclaimed.

"It lies within. You will find it," she comforted.

I fell to my knees in front of her wheelchair and we embraced.

"I appreciate your candidness," Rachel offered. "It means a lot to our friendship."

I lifted my head. "Pray for me, sweet Rachel."

CHAPTER 25

Boston

Less than a week after I had bid farewell to my friends and family, I took the stage to Boston. It was familiar territory as my employment with Kerstland had brought me to the city on many occasions. Still I stirred with childlike anticipation each time I rode into the crescent-shaped coastal city that sloped gradually to the shores of the bay. For each visit to the Massachusetts capitol was as exciting as the first.

Boston is located only two hours south of Lynn by way of carriage; however travel between the two cities proved more difficult than it would seem. For the number of roads traversing Massachusetts numbered few and their poor condition proved unkind to wagons and horses. By far the greatest hindrance to traveling was opportunity. Rarely could one find the time to get away from his daily tasks to make such a journey. And then there is the want. In my case, Boston became my escape from the cursed town of Lynn.

Situated on a peninsula about four miles in circumference, Boston is truly a sailor's port, and one that is well-protected. The entrance to her fine harbor is defended by a strong castle where—as I was told upon my first visit—the Royal Navy mounted a hundred guns.

About two leagues distance from this fortress stands a light-house constructed on a large rock. This beacon of safety guided the many vessels that cruised in and out of the busy port on any given day--so many ships that within the harbor there is room for nearly five hundred ships to lie at anchor simultaneously. At the bottom of the bay a grand wharf has been constructed—about a half of a mile in length—appropriately called the Long Wharf and on the northern side of the wharf are built many warehouses for the storing of merchant's goods.

Boston is two miles in length and at its widest a mile and a half in breadth. Her buildings rise with an easy ascent westward for about one mile from the Long Wharf which lies east of the town. The city is composed of thousands of houses which are set along some sixty streets or more and some of the more splendid homes line several fine streets—the foremost of which is King's Street. The well-paved thoroughfare runs upon a line for about a quarter of a mile from the end of the Long Wharf, and at the upper end of King's Street stands the State House where the Governor meets the Council and House of Representatives. Several courts of justice are held there as well, along with many bookseller's shops, four or five printing-houses, and the Royal Exchange.

I found lodging in the garret of a house situated on the southwest side of the city. The owner was a middle-aged man named Davern who resided in the three-story structure with a wife and two small children. His manner was pleasant and trusting and his work took him to King's Street each morning as the proprietor of a printing shop. Because I lacked employment, I could sense Davern's disinterest in me as a boarder when first I came to inquire of the garret; however, over the course of our conversation I made mention of my cousin Caleb and to my good fortune Davern happened to know him. The garret was mine.

My new residence at the top of the house was a small room with two means of entry. One was located at the bottom of a narrow flight of stairs leading directly from the garret and provided access to the inside of the house. Naturally, Davern always kept this door locked. The other entry opened to the outside where there was situated a small wooden landing with a flight of stairs that descended two stories to the small backyard of the house.

The room itself had three windows that provided a view to the back, front, and northern side of the house and the southern wall supported the chimney that was positioned to that side of the dwelling where a small hearth had been notched out of the chimney from which I could draw warmth and light for the garret. The steeper pitch of the gambrel roof lay to the northern side of the house and thus the ceiling in my room sloped very low to the floor. The slope proved to be so pronounced that I found it difficult to stand on that side of the garret without slouching to avoid striking my head against the ceiling.

The garret window set to the front of the house offered a splendid view of the Mall. This strip on the lush green common extended for nearly a half mile and consisted of a fine foot path positioned in between two rows of young trees. I would quickly become accustomed to seeing young gentlemen and ladies on the Mall, fancying a stroll in their gay apparel just after tea time.

Soon after my arrival in Boston, I wrote to Caleb, Rachel, and my mother and would continue a regular correspondence with all three. My letters from Rachel were very important since I longed to learn more of the happenings in Lynn, particularly any mention of Sam or Eblis. I felt badly about not writing to Samantha, who I missed more than anyone, and on occasion I would begin writing a letter to her, only to discard it after a few lines. I knew in my heart that if anything could coax me back to Lynn, it would be an admission of affection from Sam; although my fear of Eblis stood in the way.

The art of shoemaking proved to be scarce in Boston and to my dismay, I quickly realized that I had to abandon my skills and seek employment within other fields of work. As I was a quick learner, it didn't take long and within six months in the capitol city, I held three different jobs. The first of these was that of a helper for a caulker who packed the seams of ships during their construction with hemp fibers from old ropes. My job was to pay the packed seams with hot pitch. This seemed to be a secure position with the great abundance of ship-building occurring within the port city, but the caulker with whom I assisted decided to relocate to Virginia and so before long I found myself seeking new employment. A few weeks after his departure I took a job in a paper mill where I was given the task of feeding pulp into the molding vats and stirring them with long-handled paddles. This proved to be grueling and monotonous work and so when Davern, seeing I was a hardworking and ambitious young man, offered me a position in his printing-house in the summer of 1771, I eagerly accepted. My responsibilities here consisted of running errands, sweeping floors, and absorbing ink. Ironically, my job title within the printing shop was known as *devil*.

It wasn't long before I discovered that Boston did not provide the refuge I sought from my macabre experiences in Lynn. For it was during this time that the real *devil* of my youth paid me unwelcomed visits on three separate occasions. I should also include that the nightmares which had forced me to leave Lynn returned, and as always I would awaken before the name etched into the tombstone was revealed.

September, 1771

My first of these three encounters with the demon occurred on a crisp, clear, pleasant evening filled with a magical ambiance that enticed many to remain outdoors well beyond sunset with the assistance of moonlight. After dining with the Daverns, I engaged in some merriment in the backyard with the children of my landlord, before the late hour forced me to bid all good night.

After climbing the long flight of exterior wooden stairs, I unlocked the entrance to the garret and threw open the door to a dark room broken only by symmetrical beams of pale moonlight cast by the window panes. Instinctively I reached for the flint that rested on a shelf just inside the entrance and closed the door behind me. Stepping over to the round table that was set in the center of the room I bent over the candle centerpiece and held the flint against the wick, but before I could strike the flint once, the wick produced a flame of its own power. At that instant I became startled by the silhouette of a man seated across the table from me, and in my surprise I dropped the flint and retreated several steps.

"Who are you?!" I demanded with a trembling voice.

The figure slowly leaned over the centerpiece and the candlelight illuminated his features. "Greetings, Benjamin," he said softly.

"Eblis!" I gasped, turning for the door and reaching it in a few steps as if gliding on air. Gripping the door handle I pulled but the door would not open.

"Why, Benjamin, surely you have not forgotten a good friend?" Eblis teased.

Realizing I was trapped, I slowly turned around to confront the evil shoemaker.

"What hospitality is this?" he continued. "Benjamin, I would have thought more of our friendship. We are bound to one another as fermented molasses and sugar cane are brought together in the production of rum. Did you actually believe you could run away from me?"

"What do you want?!" I snapped, barely able to produce the words.

"Why...I've missed you, Benjamin."

"Leave me alone!"

Suddenly a knock came against the door located at the bottom of the small stairway inside the garret. The voice behind it was Master Davern's. "Ben? Are you all right?"

I looked at Eblis, still seated undaunted at the table, and thought about yelling for help.

"Blood will be on thy hands, Benjamin," Eblis warned with an eerie calmness in his voice.

I stood silent, confused.

"Ben?!" Davern called again.

"I'm...I'm okay," I called back. "Just a bat is all," I lied. "It's gone."

"Goodnight then," Davern added.

"Goodnight," I replied and turned back toward Eblis. I stood motionless for a moment watching Eblis applaud my performance with a sinister smirk.

"What is your business with me?!" I inquired. "I am not a criminal nor do I bare malice toward anyone! Indeed I am a Christian and have not been party to your wicked ways!"

Eblis grinned, exhibiting an aura of arrogance. "I sit before thee real, not imagined. We have conversed and your fear of me is genuine. Would you not agree?"

"The town of Lynn is shrouded in death and deceit—all the result of your hand! Yes, you are real or I am mad!"

"Yet your abhorrence of me is rooted in...Christianity?" he questioned with a scowl and spat on the floor. "What proof have thee of the existence of the Christian God--this fisher of men? Have you seen Him? Touched Him? Spoken with Him?" Eblis leaned forward over the table while the reflection of the candle's flame danced within those strange different colored eyes of his. "Yet you do see me. How can you be certain that I am not the sole deity of this earth?"

"Because, there is good!"

"Every coin has two sides; yet it is still the same coin."

"I am not listening to you, devil! You cannot trick me into rejecting my God!"

Eblis slumped back into his chair. "Yes, the Good Book tells thee so—does it not? Where is thy crutch, anyway? I expected thee to quote some holy passage from the book to try and cast me from this room," he scoffed.

I trembled. "I…I think there's more to it than quoting scripture!"

Eblis chuckled sinisterly. "Benjamin, what if I were to tell you that the literature of your religion is an instrument of my missionary?" His deep voice grew with passion. "One needs only to look at the fragmentation of this religion of Christ…" he paused to growl like an animal at the mention of the Lord. "…and see the hatred and violence each denomination has for the other! Look at how the stories of the apostles have branded the Jews for eternity as killers of your savior—a Jew Himself!"

"I…I am not so well versed in such matters."

"Of course not! Those who claim to be Christians are such in name only! And I say to you Benjamin, *what's in a name?*"

I was confused.

Eblis lurched forward over the candlelight once more. "Because of my fondness with our relationship, I shall leave thee with this to ponder…this evening my prize shall be the one *sweet as honey*," he revealed and blew out the candle as his silhouette in the moonlight slumped back into the chair.

"What riddle is this? What do you mean *your prize?*"

There was no response from within the darkness.

"Eblis?!" I called out. Still no reply and I grew more frightened. I turned and grabbed the doorknob in an attempt to throw open the door once again, and found to my surprise that the door was now unlocked. I twisted back around and beheld the moonlight as it cast its beam inside the room revealing only the two chairs and a round table. Eblis had vanished.

. . .

THE STRANGE ENCOUNTER WITH EBLIS AND HIS RIDDLE TORMENTED me for many days and the riddle remained clueless to me for nearly a month. And then one afternoon in late October the weekly arrival of the post rider to the tavern situated on King's Street directly across from the printing shop, produced a customary flurry of activity. Like the scores of bustling men who swarmed upon the tavern, Davern and I were also drawn to the establishment in hope for some mail.

As we set out across the street pacing side by side, I gained an appreciation for my landlord's tall height and long gait. Although he was considerably older than I his thin frame and quick pace bespoke of a man much younger. Suddenly I became privy to another bit of insight into Davern's identity as a passerby offered a friendly greeting, calling out to my landlord by his full name. "Good day to you, Gideon Davern."

"And to you the same, Eli Knoch," Davern replied.

It was the first time I had really given thought to Davern's first name and it struck me as unique. "Master," I inquired, "Your Christian name, Gideon—do you know its meaning?"

"Feller of trees," he said without hesitation.

"How do you know this?"

"Nigel Higgins. He's an expert in such things. It's sort of a hobby, or rather an obsession with the man."

"Where would I find this man?"

Davern laughed. "Are you wondering about your name now? Well you may be in luck," he said as we reached the tavern. "For unfortunately Higgins' other area of expertise is rum. I wager we shall find him inside," he enlightened as he pulled open the tavern door.

Inside the crowded tavern we squeezed our way to the center of the room as the post rider called out the names on each envelope and parcel from behind the bar.

"By George, there he is!" Davern remarked. "Ben, if you look to your far left you'll find Nigel Higgins seated at a table in the corner. He's all alone."

The middle-aged man with ruffled salt and pepper hair sat with his back against the chair. He appeared clean shaven but wore a befuddled, glassy-eyed expression underneath a whimsical smile flanked by rosy cheeks and a bright red nose. Positioned on the table before him were a pewter mug and a bottle of rum.

"The man looks to have a jag on," I described.

"Of course he does. He's a boozer that one. I wouldn't say there's much of a career in just knowing the origins of names."

"How does he afford to drink?"

"That's the price for a name."

Suddenly the post rider called out my name and I made my way to the bar where he handed me a parcel. Retreating to the center of the room, I found a post to lean against as I worked at removing the wrapping from the package and discovered it to be a Bible from Caleb; for I had mentioned in my previous letter to my cousin of how I came to part with the Good Book just before leaving for Boston. However it wasn't the Bible that excited me as much as the letter that accompanied it. As he always did, Caleb began the letter with questions of me and news of he and his family; but near its end my cousin shocked me with the latest developments from Lynn. In late September another young girl by the name of Melissa Sheehan disappeared from off of the streets of Lynn. Immediately I thought of Sam and my stomach churned as I pondered her safety.

I returned the Bible and the letter to the package wrappings and turned to my right to observe Davern now preoccupied in deep conversation with several men. Turning to my left I located Higgins and decided to pace to the bar where I ordered a bottle of rum. The bartender seemed surprised by my choice of spirits, probably because of my age; but my quickness in producing payment dissuaded him from asking any questions. I then proceeded to the rear of the tavern where Higgins sat among the afternoon shadows, and as I stepped up to the table, the man's muddled expression sprang to life as though he had awakened from the dead.

"Good day, lad," he greeted with his eyes fixed on the bottle of spirits that I clutched in my right hand.

"I don't mean to bother you..." I began.

"They never do."

"...but I'm told you're rather good at the origins of many names?"

"And you would like to know the origin of your name, now, wouldn't you?"

"Well, I hadn't actually thought about my own, but I have several others that interest me."

Higgins lifted the rum bottle that set on the table before him and poured the last drops from it into his mug. "Several, ey?" he said before taking a swig from the cup.

I placed the bottle of rum down on the table. "How many names will this get me?"

Higgins smiled and lifted the bottle, slowly turning it and studying the dark liquor like a jeweler appraising a precious stone. "Three," he blurted.

"Three? Is that all?"

"Nothing comes cheap these days. What is thy name?"

"Benjamin Pratt."

"Well, Benjamin Pratt, what's it gonna be?"

"Three it is," I groaned.

"What's the first?"

"Melissa."

"Melissa? Now that's a pretty name. A love interest?"

"No," I replied quickly.

Higgins smiled. "Melissa. Well it's Greek and it means *honey-sweet one*."

I was speechless. *My prize will be the one as sweet as honey...Eblis! Bastard!*

"Are you all right, lad?" Higgins asked, witnessing the cross look that had contorted my face.

"Yes....yes," I stammered regaining my composure.

"The second?"

"Cyrus."

"Interesting name. It is Persian and means the sun." Higgins spelled it. "S...u...n. Sun."

I had expected darkness or evil, but not the sun. "Rachel is the third," I offered.

Higgins sat back and brought the neck of the bottle of rum that I had purchased to his lips. "Rachel is Hebrew. It means an ewe lamb."

"Lamb?" I repeated.

"Yes, that's right," Higgins replied pulling the cork from the bottle of rum with his teeth. He tipped the bottle in my direction in a display of thanks and poured a generous portion of the rum into his mug.

"Thank you," I said and began to turn away.

"Son of the right hand," Higgins mumbled with the cork still wedged in between his front teeth.

I stopped and turned back toward him. "What was that?"

Higgins peered up at me grinning. "Benjamin...your name. It's Hebrew for son of the right hand."

CHAPTER 26

The revelation of Melissa Sheehan's disappearance and Eblis' clue to her identity unnerved me greatly and gave rise to a genuine concern for Sam's well-being back in Lynn—so great of a concern that it inspired me to finally break down and write to her. My initial correspondence was brief and did not mention my recent encounter with Eblis; however I did express my concern for her safety in the wake of the Sheehan girl's disappearance and my desire to hear from her. To my delight, my letter set in motion a monthly correspondence with Sam that had me eagerly rushing off to the tavern with each arrival of the post-rider. Her bitterness toward my abrupt departure from Lynn appeared to fade with each ensuing letter and her words grew soft and comforting. In February, I found the courage to express my true feelings to my friend--how I missed her and longed to see her again.

MARCH, 1772

Time passed quickly and soon six months had gone by without any word of Eblis or any strange happenings in Lynn; but as my luck would have it, my sanity would be put to the test again.

One March evening just after dusk, I took a stroll along the Mall for the purpose of exercise and to retrieve fresh air, even though evidence of winter still blanketed the popular tree-lined footpath with intermittent piles of ice and snow. The air was cool and damp, cast over from a lengthy rain shower earlier in the day and a thick mist hung over the soggy path.

After walking back and forth along the Mall for nearly an hour, I decided to return home and was only a few blocks from Davern's house when overcome by an eerie feeling that I wasn't alone. I slowed my pace and came to a stop along the path, turning to my left to notice the figure of a man, dressed in a great coat with wide brimmed hat, leaning against a tree with his facial features concealed behind the fog. He was humming a tune—one I had heard only once before...*in the forest of Salem!*

"Who goes there?" I asked with a trembling voice.

"Hello, Benjamin."

Eblis! I turned and began to sprint in the opposite direction, running for nearly ten minutes before tiring and stopping to catch my breath. The fog was thicker now and I listened carefully for footsteps, although it was hard to hear anything over my heavy breathing.

"Benjamin," a voice called and I held my breath. I followed the direction from whence it came and found the dark figure leaning against a nearby tree. "You are surprised to see me?" the voice repeated.

I felt helpless realizing I could not outrun Eblis. "Go to hell!" I cried out.

Eblis laughed. "I've been there."

"Why do you torment me so?! Have you come with another clue?! I know you were responsible for the disappearance of Melissa—the one as sweet as honey! You monster!"

"Why have you not gone to the authorities with suspicions about me, Benjamin?"

"With what information?! You're the devil...you're not human! Why would anyone believe me?!"

"Tell me, Benjamin. In reference to our last conversation, have you seen thy Christ since then?" he asked, finishing the question with a beastly growl.

I showed no fear. "What do you think?!" I snapped back.

Eblis smiled. "I sense you are growing stronger. That is good."

"Stronger?! Tell me...Satan..."

"You do honor me."

"What relationship do you have to the beast I encountered in the forest?! The one that nearly took my life with the knife they call the Damascus blade?!"

Eblis snickered. "I am one and the same. And as the witch explained, had I wanted to take your life that day—it would have been done!"

I swallowed hard but found the courage to pry further. "Why the need to transform yourself into a monster for those witches that covet you?!"

"For that is what they expect to see, Benjamin. The secret of power is to control loyalty with fear. The daughters of witchcraft do not stray from the flock because they fear the beast—just as you now fear me."

"I fear you not!" I lied. "I have attended service in the meeting-house praising the Lord and have read the Bible! Those who fear God do not fear you!"

"Have you forgotten our last meeting? Benjamin, the Bible is the work of mere mortals! Man has not been created in the image of the Christian God, but rather it is the image and idea of God which has been forged by man!" Eblis growled again.

The puzzling statement, delivered with cold, callous dispassion, left me numb and speechless. My confidence waned and I began to run again in the opposite direction back toward Davern's house, covering only about twenty rods before stopping abruptly at the sight of a sudden break in the mist. As the fog parted, there before me materialized the evil shoemaker from out of thin air to block my path. He stood motionless with arms crossed at his chest with the sinister grin I had come to loathe splashed across his face.

"Did I say something wrong, Benjamin?"

My fear evolved into anger. "Who will you take tonight, you bastard?! What unfortunate lass shall become your next prize?! You are the coward Eblis! For you prey upon the defenseless! Come on... give me another clue! That's why your here now, isn't it?!"

"Are you challenging me, Benjamin?"

"I am no challenge for thee!"

"Then who is worthy? Caleb perhaps?"

I was taken aback by the mention of my cousin and found myself speechless again.

"Go home, Benjamin. Read thy psalms!" Eblis taunted as he filled the night air with his hideous laughter.

I found courage to speak. "No clue?!" I called out.

Eblis continued to bellow with a deep, sinister cackle, vanishing before my eyes just as a sudden cool breeze swept along the Mall rustling the bare tree branches.

ALTHOUGH I ANTICIPATED THE WORST, I WAS VERY SURPRISED AND relieved in the days that followed to hear of no new disappearances or deaths in Lynn.

Another six months came and went, the days bringing nothing new and little comfort to my tormented existence aside from my uninterrupted correspondence with Sam as well as Rachel. And from Falmouth I heard little news from my mother which I attributed to her budding relationship with Aidan. *Had she forgotten me?*

I continued to keep my latest encounters with Eblis a secret from everyone, especially Sam and as I suspected, every other letter of hers hinted of her desire to have me return to Lynn. The truth is that I would have returned to the Massachusetts city without hesitation, if I did not believe that Lynn was not the hub for Eblis' evil activities. And although I attempted to stand up to Eblis and profess I had no fear of him during our last encounter, I was very much afraid. *Sam was right about me being a coward.*

NOVEMBER, 1772

I don't remember Caleb entering the garret. When I opened my eyes he was standing over me, shaking me violently and calling out my name. I slumped back into the chair and rubbed both hands against my temples in an attempt to massage the thumping in my head.

"Ben, what happened here last evening?!" Caleb asked with concern.

I looked over at the window, squinting to see the sunlight shining through. "What time is it?"

"It's half past ten."

"In the morning?"

"Yes, the morning. Ben, what happened!?"

The table came into focus before me and I saw the Bible, an empty bottle of Madeira wine and the large knife.

Caleb picked up the knife and gazed at it. "A new blade?" Caleb asked with grave concern.

I thought for a moment. "Yes...I purchased it yesterday."

"For what purpose?"

I began to remember the events of the last night and tried to stand up but fell back into the chair. "I'm ashamed...."

"Ashamed?"

"Eblis...the damn shoemaker! The devil from Lynn! Caleb, he's driving me mad!"

"You were thinking of hurting yourself?" Caleb asked, very surprised.

"I don't know what I am thinking anymore!" I replied with head slumped in embarrassment. The thumping continued in my head as I reached for the Bible and slid it toward Caleb. "Open it to psalm ninety-one."

Caleb sat down in a chair and turned the Bible's pages until finding the psalm.

"What do you see?" I pressed.

"Three names...is this blood?"

"Yes. Written in blood. Read the names."

"Anna Hood...Abigail Becker...Melissa Sheehan. Who are they?"

"They are all victims of the same diabolical monster! He's the devil! The writing was done by his hand! He was here in this room last night as he has been every year since I have been in Boston, and as you can see for yourself, he has made known to me the names of his victims...his prizes as he calls them! It's a bloody game of his!"

"This is not your handwriting?"

"Of course not! He was here in this room!"

Caleb said nothing as he lifted the empty wine bottle. He turned it in his hand and looked back at me with disbelief.

"I've had enough of his tormenting!" I continued. "I am sickened to know the names of those poor innocent girls! I carry the burden of knowing their identities and the feeling of such helplessness because I couldn't help them! And the nightmares...I've had more than I can take! I cannot kill Eblis but I can end my own misery! Yet again I am the fool...gulping wine to give me the courage to perform the act and drinking so much of it that I fell unconscious before I could cut myself! Sam was right, I am a coward!"

Caleb grabbed my hand firmly. "'...*I take pleasure in infirmities, in reproaches, in necessities, in persecution, in distresses for Christ's sake: for when I am weak, then am I strong.*'"

I looked Caleb in the eye. "I feel as though God has abandoned us."

"I think you should rest now," Caleb replied in a calming voice. "Then when you awake and are in a better frame of mind we shall talk at length about this...this Eblis."

"It is fortunate that you are here," I recognized. "What has brought you to Boston?"

"God...for I have been asked to deliver the *Great and Thursday Lecture.*"

I stepped over to my bed and dropped down into it. Overcome by emotional exhaustion, I quickly fell off to sleep.

When I opened my eyes, I saw Caleb standing at the foot of my bed clutching a rod from a birch tree in his right hand. He stood with knees and arms bent, slashing the outstretched rod back and forth as though he were dueling with the air.

"What are you doing?" I asked, sitting up.

Caleb relaxed the arm that clutched the birch rod and turned to me emitting a comforting smile. "You're awake. How are you feeling?"

"I feel like someone hit me across the head with a broad axe. How long was I asleep?"

"A few hours."

"What were you doing a moment ago?"

"Practicing my fencing skills, my good drunken cousin."

"Fencing? I had no idea you fancied such a sport?"

"My journeys back and forth to Europe have introduced me to the sport."

"Such a skill is necessary for a man who delivers sermons?" I asked with sarcasm.

Caleb chuckled. "It is an excellent tonic for the body as well as the mind. One must be quick-witted and agile in mind and body to be successful in the challenging affairs of the world, as in the sport. Stand up. I will show you."

"Caleb, I assure you, I am in no condition for such exercise of body or mind."

"One must always be on guard in the duel that is life."

Reluctantly I agreed to appease my cousin and threw my heavy legs over the side of the bed and rested in a sitting position. "For what is it that brings you to Boston?"

"I am to deliver the *Great and Thursday Lecture* this evening."

"Yes. I thought that is what you had told me before I fell asleep. That is impressive, Caleb. Some of the most notable clergymen in the colonies have been invited to speak each week at the lecture."

"I am honored indeed," he said as he returned to slicing the air in coordinated movements with the birch rod. "Now get on your feet and I shall give you a lesson in fencing."

I groaned as I staggered to a standing position as Caleb tossed me a second birch rod which, to my surprise, I caught without difficulty. "Where did you find these?"

"The birch tree on the Mall," Caleb revealed yelling, "On guard!" He spread his legs apart, stiffened his core, and bent his knees while holding the rod out in front of him in his right hand.

I attempted to humor him by duplicating his pose.

"Strike at my head," he commanded.

"Your head?"

"It's right here," he mocked, pointing to his head with his left hand.

I grinned. "How? Shall I swing at your head?"

Caleb stepped toward me with his right foot and lunged forward with his right arm. Before I could blink, the end of the rod was pressed against my throat. "Just like that," Caleb instructed before retreating.

I took a deep breath and did as he asked, lunging my rod at his head. Needless to say, the birch never reached his throat. With a movement so swift that I could not immediately adjust to it, Caleb had defended against my lunge and the sequence ended an instant later with my cousin holding his rod horizontally to my stomach.

"I am dead," I deduced.

Caleb laughed. "Let me show you the move," he offered returning to the on guard position. "Lunge at my head again."

I did as I was instructed and slowly Caleb walked me through the steps of blocking the attack and cutting the opponent's wrist before spinning and ending up with the blade across the opponent's stomach. It was complicated at first and Caleb proved to be a patient instructor as we spent nearly an hour attempting to perfect the move.

Initially the purpose of the lesson was confusing to me, but throughout the session I felt rejuvenated. I had sunk to the depths of depravity during the previous night, nearly taking my life. Now Caleb had come to my rescue. His fencing lesson proved to be effective therapy as it worked to clear my thoughts and expel my fears, and it soon became apparent that my cousin's purpose was to ease me into a state of relaxation so that he might procure an untainted description of the malicious force that haunted me.

When we had at last finished our fencing lesson, Caleb and I sat down around the table. The Bible remained in its center, but the knife and the empty bottle of wine were gone—I assumed Caleb had discarded the bottle and secured the weapon.

My cousin positioned a quill, bottle of ink and a piece of parchment in front of him. "All right, Ben," he began. "As painful as this may be for you, I want you to tell me everything you can remember about this Eblis."

"So you believe me?" I asked eagerly.

"I do. How do you spell his name?"

"I've seen his book of orders and the spelling of his name was inside. It is E-B-L-I-S. Cyrus Eblis," I described as Caleb dipped the end of the quill into the ink bottle and wrote the name on the parchment.

"Eblis?" my cousin repeated, peering down at the name he had just inscribed. "Eblis...Eblis? Where have I heard that name?" Suddenly Caleb sprang to his feet. "My word! How ignorant of me! Of course!"

"What?! What is it?!"

"Eblis! It is the title given to the devil in Islamic mythology!" Caleb explained with enthusiasm.

"Islam? The religion of the Middle East?"

"Yes!" Caleb acknowledged, pacing the room with excitement.

"Damascus is a city in the Middle East, is it not?" I asked.

Caleb stopped his pacing and looked at me with curiosity. "Yes...why?"

"Eblis possessed a Damascus blade when first we met which I

eventually acquired. I came upon it after a hideous beast flung it at me in the forest!"

"What is a Damascus blade?"

"A brilliant knife with a splendid wavy pattern crafted in steel."

"Where is it?"

"I threw it into the ocean, eager to be gone with the evil ties to it."

"So we have two connections with the Middle East—Eblis and this Damascus blade you speak of."

"Three," I interjected. "Cyrus is a Persian name meaning sun."

"Son as in father and son?"

"No. Sun...s...u...n."

Caleb's eyes widened and I could tell he was impressed. "Very good, Ben! Yes, we have three," he agreed before returning to his seat at the table. "Continue your story."

I began with the story that was told to me years ago by Old Red that centered on the legend of the Beast of Cape Hatteras. Caleb stopped me half way through the tale and asked for the spelling of the ship's name—*Aeshma.*

I thought for a moment and then I remembered as if it were ingrained in my head as a nursery rhyme. "Aeshma? Ah, yes, I remember. A as in apple...E as in eye...S for the serpent slithering on by...H as in heaven...M as in man...A for the angel with the snake in his hand."

"Clever way of remembering it, Ben," Caleb remarked as he wrote the ship's name down on the parchment.

"It seems as though Old Red didn't want me to forget it. What does it mean?"

"Aeshma? I'm not quite sure. Some Middle Eastern connection, no doubt. Please continue."

I did. I recalled my encounters with Eblis and Patch; the names of the deceased within Eblis' book of orders; the witch's coven; the beast in the forest; Jordan's ghost; and my nightmare. It was a hellish walk through my recent memories and Caleb recorded it all, filling several pieces of parchment. When I had finished my recollection, we sat back in our chairs and gazed at one another.

"My dear cousin," Caleb began. "I am truly sorry that it has taken me this long to heed your cries. It seems that you have indeed looked the devil in the eye and endured much anguish. Despite the dogma of my ministry, I would have believed that such a meeting between mortal and supernatural was not possible. I now believe otherwise."

"What can we do? How can we rid Lynn of this evil presence? I mean someone has to do something and I think, for whatever reason, we have been given this mission."

Caleb studied me with intensity. "Mission?" he repeated. "Curious word, Ben, but I believe you're correct. We have both been drawn into this nightmare—me through my association with you." He ran his fingers up his forehead and through his raven black hair. "The legends of Eblis are derived from the tales of Solomon."

"King Solomon of the Bible?"

"Yes. The Solomon written of in the *Book of Kings*; however Solomon's dealings with Eblis are not found in the Christian holy book. Rather Eblis appears only in Arabic and Islamic folklore."

"But how can we fight the devil?! We have no powers that can equal his!" I pressed.

Caleb sighed and rose from the chair. "I have an associate in London—a man named Graeme Barnett. He's an expert in the occult. Granted, he's deemed by some as somewhat of a lunatic, but this is only because his field of expertise is misunderstood," he described stepping behind me and placing both hands on the back of my chair. "I'm not sure, but he may be able to help us." Caleb relinquished his grasp on the chair and stepped back away from it, reaching into the pocket of his blue jacket to remove a pocket watch and noticed the time. "I need to prepare myself for tonight's lecture. Ben, I must go. I shall write to Barnett and inform you immediately upon receiving his correspondence. God help us...."

CHAPTER 27

Lynn – December, 1773

      Although it was mid-afternoon, the dull gray winter sky hid the sun, darkening the inside of Edward and Jamesina Brown's home. A small fire burned in the hearth of the main room, throwing its warmth and light about the four corners, and the flickering flames brought to life the dancing shadows of furniture as Jamesina welcomed the temporary companionship while working her spinning wheel in front of the fireplace. Clad in a long blue dress and black bonnet, she hummed a children's tune while operating the apparatus with a foot pedal and collected the yarn on a loom. Over and under—over and under—went the task of weaving the yarn. The monotonous work, combined with the crackling flames of the hearth and soft whisper of the spinning wheel might have lulled Jamesina to sleep were it not for her penchant to carry a tune.

      Suddenly a loud knock exploded against the front door. The pounding startled Jamesina and she quickly jumped from her seat at the spinning wheel. "Now whom might be calling?" Jamesina asked herself aloud as she paced toward the door leading into the entry hall. She paused for a moment at the front window, but the angle did not permit her to identify the caller.

      Inside the entry hall Jamesina slowly pulled open the front door. A tall man dressed in a charcoal-grey frock with a dark circular wide-brimmed hat upon his head stood with his back to the door. He spun around and Jamesina gaped. "Why....Master Eblis!...Good day to you!"

"And to thee a good day as well, Mrs. Brown," Eblis replied cordially with a grin and a tip of his hat.

She felt a warm feeling rush through her body as she carefully studied the broad shoulders, tall height, and slim waistline of the dashing shoemaker. What *a perfect specimen*, she mumbled under her breath and then gasped slightly, hoping Eblis had not heard that.

"What can I do for you?" she asked.

"I was in the neighborhood delivering soles." His grin grew larger as he held up a small burlap sack. "I remembered interrupting your meal some years ago when I had called upon your nephew Benjamin, and I thought I just might stop by and say hello. I know it has been some time but something has drawn me to your home today. I apologize if this is a bad time? "

Jamesina did not know how to respond and before she could Eblis interjected, "May I say you look radiant today!"

Jamesina blushed. "Thank you...no this is not a bad time. Please come in out of the cold," she stammered, holding the door ajar while Eblis stepped inside. "Would you care for some tea?"

Eblis smiled. "Yes...that would be nice. Thank you."

The shoemaker removed his hat as he entered the main room ahead of Jamesina, and she paused to adjust her petticoat and half gown before straightening her black bonnet.

She followed Eblis as he paced over to the fireplace, stopping to gaze upon the spinning wheel, before setting down the sack he had carried inside with him. "A woman's life is very busy. So many tasks. So much responsibility," he said running his long fingers gently along the taut strands of yarn. "Every minute of the day is spent on chores."

"As they say, a women's work is never done," Jamesina commented as she reached up to retrieve a tea pot of boiling water that hung from the trammel over the fire.

"Yes," Eblis seemed to agree and added, "When do you find time to be with thy husband?"

Surprised by the question Jamesina nearly dropped the pot from her hands and turned back to look at the dashing shoemaker.

Eblis could see he had flustered the woman. "Come now, Jamesina...may I call you Jamesina?"

"Why yes...Jamey. Please call me Jamey."

"Jamey, you needn't be bashful. You are a beautiful and desirable woman. Your husband should relish the moments he has with thee."

"Please Master Eblis, you are embarrassing me," Jamesina uttered staring down upon the floor.

"Cyrus," Eblis revealed.

"I beg your pardon?"

"My name is Cyrus."

"Oh," was all Jamesina could reply. "I hope you don't mind raspberry tea—the tax on tea, you know."

"Anything from your delicate hands shall quench my thirst."

Jamesina lifted a pewter mug from the table and began to pour the tea from the pot into it. Her hands quivered slightly and she worked hard to mask her nerves in filling the mug. Eblis had stepped over beside her and she turned to hand the cup to him when her eyes met his. Instantly she was drawn into the variation in color between his two eyes as the shoemaker's suggestive smile quickened the beat of her heart, arousing an inward fire within her bosom.

"Thank you, Jamey," he said softly, taking the cup from her hand.

Jamesina quickly looked away and moved to return the pot to the trammel. "This is certainly a surprise having you call upon me today," she said, still with her back toward the shoemaker.

"I promised that one day we would share some tea," he replied.

Jamesina regained her composure and turned back around toward him. "But that was three years ago?"

"I never break a promise."

Jamesina stepped over to the large wooden table and sat down in a chair. "Please have a seat," she offered. Eblis accepted, retiring into a chair positioned opposite her.

"Tell me Jamey, how is your son?" he asked.

Jamesina was surprised by the question. "Caleb? He's doing quite well in his ministry." She sipped her tea. "Do you know him?"

Eblis grinned. "I know of him." The shoemaker leaned forward from his perch on the chair and looked deep into Jamesina's eyes. "Does he know?" he whispered.

"Does he know what?" Jamesina was confused by the question.

Eblis' face became expressionless. "Does he know...he is not your son?"

Stunned by the question, Jamesina dropped her mug, spilling tea over the floor. "How do you know this?!"

Eblis sat back in the chair, the grin returning to his face. "We all have our secrets...some are not so secure."

"How can you know this?!" she repeated with a tone of distress. "We have told no-one!"

Jamesina instinctively glanced over at the back door which was set off to her right.

"Your husband is at work out back...in the ten-footer, is he not?" Eblis asked picking up on her trepidation.

"We have never told anyone, not even our son! How do you know of this?!" she persisted.

"I do believe you when you say you have never told Caleb," Eblis began, "but a shoemaker's shop or ten-footer can be a house of gossip. I should know, for I manufacture *soles* myself."

Jamesina stood up and glared at Eblis with a scowl. The shoemaker did not return the look but continued to sip his tea. "Edward would never have told a soul!" she exclaimed. The visitor remained silent as she marched into the kitchen area to retrieve a piece of cloth.

In a few moments Jamesina had returned and was on her knees wiping up the spilled tea. She paused and looked up at Eblis still seated silently in the chair as tears welled up in her eyes. "I couldn't conceive...and suddenly like a gift from God he came to us. He was only an infant...a newborn in fact when Edward found him in a basket a few miles outside of Salem. He was left alone on the side of the road in the middle of nowhere. What type of person deserts a newborn infant and leaves the child alone in the wilderness? There was no-one around and we were new to Salem—having just arrived from Pennsylvania. We took the child in and gave him a home and love. We gave him a life. And then we waited for weeks thinking we might hear word of someone who had abandoned her child. But weeks turned into months and as we became more acquainted with the townsfolk, who acted as though the child was ours, we had become his parents. My brother and sister-in-law would not follow us to Salem for over a year after we arrived and with correspondence being slow, we were able to keep the truth from them as well."

Eblis set his mug down on the table and rose from the chair. He reached down and offered Jamesina his hand which she took, and helped her to her feet. She looked up at the shoemaker with doleful eyes. "My husband did not betray our secret..." she uttered trying to convince herself.

"Jamey, your secret is safe with me; but do you not agree that Caleb has a right to know the truth?"

Jamesina released her hold on Eblis and backed away from the shoemaker. "What business is this of yours?" she inquired, her tone growing angry now. "Have you come to bribe me?!"

"No my dear lady. In fact I have brought something for thee," he said walking over to the sack that rested on the floor near the spinning wheel.

"For me? Why? You have already brought me enough with your revelation!" she lamented.

Eblis lifted the sack from the floor and paced slowly toward his nervous host, stopping at Jamesina's side to set the bag down next to her. "Your black bonnet is like the layers of rock in a diamond mine," he described. "For when the dark outer layer is removed," he continued in a softer tone, bringing his hands up to her neck and undoing the string of her bonnet, "only then can one enjoy the true beauty of the stone," he finished, delicately pulling the bonnet from her head.

Jamesina tilted her head back and glared at Eblis with a skittish stare, infused by his passionate words. His sensual touch worked to instantly erase the feelings of anger, sadness, and confusion that had burdened her only minutes before.

Eblis bent over and reached into the sack. "And now, this is for thee."

"Shoes?"

Eblis smiled, pulled his hand from out of the sack and within his grasp he clutched a necklace of gold. Softly he laid the cold, dazzling jewelry around her porcelain neck and gently fastened it from behind.

Jamesina brought her hand to her neck and rubbed it against the necklace. "Master Eblis, I cannot accept this! I know very little of you!"

"It is a gesture of friendship—a beginning of sorts."

"But it is not right!" Jamesina exclaimed again, and with a rush of guilt turned to look at the back door.

"You are afraid of your husband?"

"I am a married woman!" she replied turning now to look into the face of Eblis. "I love Edward."

"Love and desire are two separate emotions. You strike me as a woman who lacks the latter. It is easy to love someone; but tis more complicated to desire. To deprive a woman of such an emotion is to smite her heart."

"Your words are wicked!" Jamesina gasped with coyness.

"Your husband is obsessed with his work. He is oblivious to you and the joys that your passion could bring him...as it used to be," Eblis persisted. "And what about your secret involving Caleb? He betrayed that secret...didn't he?" Jamesina was confused. Eblis brought his mouth close to her ear and lowered his voice to a whisper. "Do you not deny that you long for a man's gentle caress and desire nights of unbridled passion?" Jamesina closed her eyes, moved by his hot breath against her skin and she began breathing heavier, tantalized by the unmasking of her inner soul. "Jamesina Brown, you shall not be denied your fulfillment as a woman."

Eblis moved closer and pressed his face inches from her own. Jamesina opened her eyes and slowly leaned into the shoemaker as if drawn by a magnet, plunging her open lips into his. They pressed their mouths hard against one another's for several moments. The kiss energized Jamey, charging her with a vivacious rush that she had not felt in years. Slowly their lips parted. "Lord, help me," she blurted and at that instant Eblis pulled fast away from her as though he were suddenly struck by a sword. She opened her eyes to see Eblis' face gray and colorless. For an instant he appeared to Jamesina to be decades older.

"What did you say?!" Eblis gasped. "You're invoking thy God?!"

Stunned, Jamesina could not speak. "It was only a figure of speech..."

Eblis growled and retrieved his hat, placing it upon his head.

Jamesina dropped into a chair as reality set in. "What have I done? Edward...!"

Eblis quickly retrieved his bag and stepped through the entry hallway door and Jamesina watched as the front door swung open of its own power. Eblis moved to step outside before pausing in the open doorway and spun around toward Jamesina, flashing a smug grin.

"Now...you and I have a secret!" he called out. The door slammed shut of its own power again, blocking her view of the wily shoemaker.

Jamesina trembled and then remembered the necklace. She brought her right hand to her neck to feel the strangers gift, but to her surprise she no longer felt the weight of precious stones about her neck, but the soft fabric of cloth, for all that was fastened about her neck was a red woolen scarf. She gasped, "What black magic is this?!" and paced quickly over to the burning fire in the hearth. Frantically she worked to remove the scarf and trembled with disgust before tossing the scarf into the flames. As she watched the flames consume the woolen scarf, Jamesina's thoughts returned again to her son. "Caleb!" she mumbled. "How could he have known about Caleb...?"

CHAPTER 28

oston- December 16, 1773

B It was late Thursday evening and I had just extinguished the candles, tossed the day's final log upon the dying flames in the fireplace, and climbed into bed underneath a warm quilt when I was startled by a thud against the garret window. My visitations from Eblis had kept me on edge and so I trembled with each unexpected interruption.

I jumped out of bed and proceeded cautiously toward the frosted panes. Wiping the fog from the cold glass with my hand, I peered through the darkness and could distinguish the figure of a man on the frozen lawn below, bent over and packing the snow within his hands. I was somewhat relieved at the sight of this as I did not imagine Eblis would care to be engaged in such frivolity, so I threw open the window and stuck my head outside into the cold evening air. "I say there! What are you doing?!" I hollered.

The man righted himself and tossed a snowball in my direction that struck the clapboards to my left. "Hello, good cousin!" he replied.

"Caleb?! Is that you?!"

The man did not answer but turned and proceeded around the side of the house, trudging through the snow.

I pulled my head inside the window and shut it. Slipping into a pair of shoes to protect my bare feet from the cold floor, I crossed the room and threw open the garret door. The cold air stung my face as I leaned outside to look down the staircase at the man in a dark great coat who had climbed near to the top. When he lifted his head in my direction and delivered a familiar smile from underneath his blue tricorn, I could see it was indeed my cousin.

"At this height, I must say that you're close to heaven," Caleb puffed, out of breath from the climb. "I had forgotten how many steps."

"It hasn't deterred the devil," I countered.

"Yes. Don't remind me," he said before embracing me with a firm hug. He released his grip from around my shoulders and chuckled as he tugged at my white morning gown that fell just below my knees, exposing my legs. "I really must bring you some new clothing."

"Well it is after dark," I defended. "I was in bed."

"Is it that late?" he asked stepping past me and inside the doorway.

"What brings you here at this hour?" I asked as I closed the door behind him.

"Several reasons. I've just come from a meeting at the Old South Church," Caleb replied, removing his tricorn. "Samuel Adams led the meeting," he added stepping toward the hearth.

"His voice speaks very loudly these days. All eyes have been on the tea ships now in Boston Harbor," I added.

Caleb removed his heavy woolen great coat and tossed it over the back of a chair. "Governor Hutchinson will not allow the ships to leave Boston Harbor without payment of the duty on the tea," he explained crouching above the fire and rubbing his hands over the flames. "The storm grows near."

"What does Adams propose?"

"For the colonies to petition the Crown to remove Hutchinson as Governor of Massachusetts," Caleb said, spying two birch branches setting in a corner—the two branches he had brought with him during his last visit. He stood up and walked over to the corner where the branches were set leaning against the wall. He picked up one of the branches and tossed it to me. "Touche!" he called out as he assumed the on guard fencing position and began slicing his branch through the air. "Have you been practicing the move?"

"Why is one fencing move so important to you?"

"Because my good cousin, it is the one move that I have not yet mastered a defense against. It is the favorite move of my opponent across the Atlantic and has foiled me on more than one occasion. That is why it is important that you learn the move quickly. You are the key to my success."

"I see. So your sole purpose of interrupting my rest this evening is so you may perfect your fencing skills?"

Caleb grinned and tapped the end of the birch branch against the wooden floor. "Do you remember the move? I shall attempt to strike at your head..."

"Yes...yes. I remember it," I said with a lack of enthusiasm.

"Good. Then back to the fray," Caleb urged stepping toward me with his right foot thrusting the end of the stick at my face. I blocked his attack with my stick and pressed the branch on top of his wrist, forcing it down, before spinning completely around. I then attempted to swing it at his midsection, but Caleb jumped clear.

"Not bad," he said. "You only need quicken your reaction."

"By the time I have mastered this move, you and your opponent will have become too old to duel, I'm afraid."

Caleb laughed and placed his arm around my shoulder. "Thank you for the practice; but it is not the sole reason why I am here. How are you feeling? Anymore bouts of depression? Any visits from Eblis?"

"No. None. I feel good."

"Well, I have good news. Let's sit down."

Caleb sat down at the table while I gathered the candle and lit its wick with the flame from the fireplace. I hurried back to the table shielding the flickering flame with my hand and fixed the candle in the candleholder that set in the center of the table. Quickly I plopped myself down into a chair across from my cousin.

"I've recently received a letter from Yale," Caleb revealed. "I am being considered a candidate for the Board of Governors there."

"That is wonderful news! Congratulations! I would imagine you would be their youngest member?"

"Yes. Fortunately they have not considered my youth a deterrent to my potential selection...at least not at this juncture of the process."

"What have you done to get noticed by Yale?"

"My work in Simsbury for one, and my speech that I delivered at the *Great and Thursday Lecture* fell upon notable ears. But recently I have written several papers with Ezra Stiles, the president of Yale and another clergyman, Samuel Hopkins, promoting the idea of colonizing West Africa with free American Negroes."

"Interesting."

Caleb reached across the table and grabbed my arm. "Ben, I want this position very much," he expressed in earnest. "It is exactly what I have been preparing myself for!"

"Then you shall get it," I encouraged. "You have been successful at all you've attempted. Why should this be any different?"

Caleb smiled and released his grip on my arm. "Yes, you're right, good cousin. I will not be denied this opportunity."

"Let's celebrate. I have some cider," I said rising from the chair.

"Wait, Ben. I have other news that will interest you."

Slowly I slid back onto the wooden seat.

"I've heard from Graeme Barnett."

"Your friend in London?"

"Friend is a strong term," Caleb cautioned. "Let's say we have met and know of each other's work. In any event, he has revealed a great deal to me about Eblis and Solomon."

"Go on," I urged with great anticipation.

"Well the Christian Bible holds that God granted Solomon, the son of David, wisdom. *'And God gave Solomon wisdom and understanding exceeding such, and largeness of heart, even as the sand that is on the sea shore,'* he recited from memory. "However, Islamic folklore has it that Solomon obtained wisdom and riches with the help of an army of demons called djinn. These demons once roamed the barren land-scape and were believed to have the power to take on any shape and form—from insect to..."

"Shoemaker," I interjected.

Caleb nodded. "Yes, Ben...shoemaker."

"And perhaps the monstrous beast in the forest," I added.

"Perhaps. The intentions of the djinn are always evil," he continued. "There are supposedly five kinds of djinn with different degrees of power. The name Eblis was given to the most important and powerful of these. He is known as the prince of darkness."

"Prince?" I interrupted. "Daniel Hassett, the young man whose house and workshop has become the lair of the demon shoemaker of Lynn, refers to Eblis in this manner...as prince," I remembered. "Why would the demons help Solomon?"

"Solomon was indeed very wise. He was able to trick the demons into becoming his servants," Caleb described.

"How?"

"According to Barnett, Solomon had in his possession a magic ring which was set with a diamond. The stone had a living force of its own and protected him from evil."

I sighed with disappointment and sat back. "Where are we to find a magic ring?"

Caleb smiled auspiciously. "Ben, the magic ring doesn't exist. I believe it is symbolic."

"Then why are you telling me this if you don't believe the story?"

"Ben, I didn't say I don't believe the story," Caleb corrected leaning forward on his chair to make sure he had my attention. "If this Eblis character is truly something supernatural, then I believe he is a demon and not the devil, Satan, Lucifer, or whatever name you choose to describe the beast tossed out of heaven by God. The devil rules his evil domain with such powers that I am afraid only God can confront. No we are not dealing with the devil here; but rather a demon. Eblis is a demon who has come to Lynn to do Satan's bidding as did the djinn in the time of Solomon. It is as King George would certainly not stoop to sail across the Atlantic to personally direct the injustices in these colonies that are being performed at his command. The governors of these colonies, such as Hutchinson, are George's demons!"

"But how are we to fight this demon?"

"Solomon was able to tame the demons because they were attracted to his ring. If we could learn what it is that has attracted Eblis to Lynn, then we might use that as a way of entrapping him!" Caleb explained with zest as he rose from the chair, stepping over to a wall shelf to retrieve my Bible which he held up for me to see. "Solomon's story has proven the demon can be entrapped and defeated. And what demon or army of demons can defeat the clergyman with the Lord in his corner?" he proclaimed with confidence and opened the Bible. He flipped through the pages until he found what he was looking for and began to read: *"And the Lord said unto Solomon...if thou wilt walk before me, as David thy father walked, in integrity of heart, and in uprightness, to do according to all that I have commanded thee, and wilt keep my statutes and my judgments: Then I will establish the throne of thy kingdom upon Israel forever, as I promised to*

David thy father, saying, There shall not fail thee a man upon the throne of Israel.'"

Caleb's words were stirring but failed to convince me. "Just because our demon has chosen to disguise itself behind the name of Eblis does not mean we are dealing with the same djinn that Solomon tamed."

Caleb set the Bible back upon the shelf. He pressed both hands on the edge of the table and leaned forward over its center. "Benjamin, for reasons I do not yet understand, I believe you have been selected as a messenger for this demon. The descriptions you have given of the eerie events surrounding your stay in Lynn have begun to fit like the pieces of a puzzle. Eblis has supplied you with these pieces." Caleb lifted his arms from the table and swiftly swung himself back into the chair. "For example," he continued, now peering at me from the edge of the seat, "the ship *Aeshma* in the tale told to you by Old Red... Barnett wrote me that *Aeshma* is reference to one of the seven demons in Persian mythology. It is the demon of anger, jealousy, and revenge. Barnett even did some research into the records of the vessel's cargo. It left England in sixteen ninety bound for the Middle East with a scientist on board. When it set sail from Alexandria one year later, the cargo included a mysterious cylinder that had been unearthed somewhere in the sands of Persia. Witnesses in port before the ship set sail told how the crew was given strict instructions to stay clear of the cylinder, for it was an ancient artifact of some value."

"Yes...and I remember Old Red's tale of how the crew ignored those warnings," I recalled. "The ship was blown off course during a storm in the Atlantic east of the Azores."

"Ben, perhaps the djinn of Eblis had been concealed within that cylinder?" Caleb surmised.

I was intrigued. "What about the *Aeshma* that I saw in the port of Salem?"

Caleb shook his head. "I don't know Ben. Perhaps it was a sign from Eblis?"

"A ghost ship?"

"At this point, I would rule out nothing."

I rose slowly from the chair, rubbing my skin nervously just underneath the neckline of the morning gown. "It is you that can defeat Eblis! I will write my mother and tell her that I cannot be with her in

Falmouth this year for Christmas! Instead I will accompany you to Lynn and we shall spend the holiday with your parents! Then together we can confront the demon shoemaker!"

"Slow down, Ben!" Caleb cautioned. "I do not plan to go to Lynn this Christmas. With the prospect of being selected to the Board of Governors at Yale, I need to remain a while in Simsbury. I'm sorry."

I frowned. "But we must destroy Eblis before the next autumn!"

Caleb rose from the chair. "Ben, no matter what happens with the board selection, rest assured I will help bring this Eblis curse under control."

"Under control?! He needs to be destroyed!"

"One step at a time, good cousin. I promise I shall confront this diabolical shoemaker. You have my word."

I sighed. "I have your word...but I wish I had your faith."

CALEB STAYED THE NIGHT AND WHEN WE AWOKE THE NEXT morning we were not surprised to learn that while we slept a band of colonial activists disguised themselves as Indians and boarded the tea ships in Boston Harbor where they proceeded to dump three hundred forty-two casks of tea into the murky water.

Eblis was my personal nemesis, but soon it seemed that the whole of the colonies would have their own demons—some in redcoats... some called patriots.

CHAPTER 29

L*ynn*
    Alone within the ten-footer behind his home, Edward Brown leaned over a lasting jack and meticulously punctured holes into a leather sole with his awl, occasionally pausing to glance up at the dirty window pane or roll his head to give relief to a stiffened neck. Positioned in the rear of the outbuilding with his back to the door and facing the small stove that provided warmth on this cold day, the shoemaker suddenly felt a rush of cold air against the back of his neck. He turned and looked over his left shoulder and to his surprise found Jamesina stepping inside the ten-footer, closing the door behind her. She lifted the bottom of her long blue dress and stomped her boots on the wooden floor to discard the wet snow that had accumulated on the soles.

"Why this is certainly a pleasant surprise," Edward greeted with a smile. "Checking up on me, my dear?"

With a somber look, Jamesina remained silent as she untied the string to her bonnet and removed the black shawl that covered her head, neck, and shoulders.

Edward could detect that there was something wrong. His voice grew more serious. "What is it, Jamey?"

"Something has been bothering me for a few days now and I can no longer hold my tongue," Jamesina announced, resting the shawl on the back of a chair. "I need to know if you have told anyone about Caleb?"

"Caleb? Well...I brag of our son all the time..."

"No. That is not what I mean," Jamesina interrupted. "Have you ever revealed our secret to anyone?"

"Secret?" Edward thought for a moment before setting his awl down on a table. He leaned back in the chair, folded his arms at his chest and stared up at Jamesina. "I have never told a soul about how we found him in the forest. Is that what you mean?"

Jamesina nodded with a sigh.

"Why do you ask?"

"You are being honest with me, my husband?" Jamesina probed.

"Of course, my dear!" Edward's tone was growing angry now. "Where is all this suddenly coming from?!"

"The shoemaker, Master Eblis, came to see me three days ago inquiring if Caleb knew his origins."

"What?! Eblis?! But how..."

Jamesina moved quickly toward her husband and rested her hand upon his shoulder. "I don't know how he knows. How could he? You and I are the only ones who know. That is why I thought..."

"Thought what? That I betrayed our secret?" Edward finished.

"I'm sorry, Edward, but Eblis implied that perhaps you mentioned it to someone."

Edward stared ahead, deep in thought.

"Edward, there's more," Jamesina divulged bringing her husband back from his solitary query. "He gave me a diamond necklace."

Edward peered up at his wife. "Why?"

"As a gift."

"A gift? Why?"

"I don't know; but the necklace...the necklace of diamonds...it changed into a scarf!"

"What?" Edward was not sure he had heard her correctly.

"I swear to you, I felt the coldness and weight of the stones around my neck. It was real! But after he had left our home, the necklace, it... it was gone and replaced by a scarf!"

"He's a magician perhaps? Sleight of hand?"

"No, my husband! You don't understand! The necklace was fastened about my neck when it changed and his hands were nowhere near it! He had left our home! I was so frightened and sickened by the whole ordeal that I tossed the scarf into the fire!"

Edward rose to his feet and embraced his wife who began to sob. "Ben was right," she continued. "He is evil!"

"Does Caleb know of your encounter with Eblis?"

"No," Jamesina answered quickly. "But Edward, I fear Eblis may reveal our secret to him for he advised me to approach our son with the truth!"

"The truth is that he's our son!" Edward exclaimed. "No matter how Caleb had come to us, we have nurtured and raised him! He is our son!"

Jamesina sobbed again. "What are we to do?"

Edward took a deep breath. "I think I shall pay Master Eblis a visit."

The following evening...

Dusk had descended upon Lynn and a steady rain saturated the cobblestone streets. Inside the Newell Tavern, Edward Brown drained a second bottle of rum. He was not a regular customer at the tavern and so the usual patrons were surprised by the length of his presence and concerned with his excessive indulgence of spirits; but none intervened. Not even when he stumbled to his feet, tripping over chairs as he staggered to the door.

Outside of the tavern, Edward didn't seem to mind the cold air and the wet sleet that soaked his clothing, for his senses were numb. His thoughts were foggy from the alcohol and he stopped for a moment to remember why he was out in the streets of Lynn after dusk. "Eblis!" he mumbled as he reached inside his long coat and felt the iron barrel of the pistol he had concealed. Edward had no intention of harming Eblis, only to threaten him, but the persuasive quality of the pistol inspired him to bring the weapon along. He staggered a few steps outside of the tavern from the effect of rum, but if his consumption of alcohol had most impacted any one sense that evening, it was his blurred vision that would do him in; for he never saw the horse drawn chaise approaching from the south. Oblivious to the heavy street traffic, the intoxicated shoemaker took his last breath and stepped from the curb. Although the driver pulled hard on the reins, the wheels of the chaise continued to slide against the sleet covered cobblestone, crushing Edward Brown beneath them.

. . .

BOSTON – DECEMBER 24, 1773

Clad in a leather apron splashed with ink, Davern stood over a sturdy, wooden stand that supported the type case and picked out letters from the irregularly partitioned shallow tray. "Hutchinson is s... o...n?" he asked as he set the letters side by side lengthwise in a small three-sided tray. I answered his question with a nod.

"It's hard to believe tomorrow's Christmas, aye? Ben, you have no plans to see your mother this year?" Davern asked, as he slid the type carefully from the composing stick onto a page-sized tray.

"No, Master. Not this holiday. She is busy it seems."

"Well you're eating Christmas dinner with us then," he informed. "The galley's ready. Ben, let's pull a proof," he instructed as he inked the type with a brush.

I stepped up to the galley clutching a rawhide mallet while Davern set a piece of paper gently down over top of the type and I proceeded to hammer the paper. When I had finished, Davern lifted the paper, turned it over and set it down on a table. Meticulously he poured over the printed words, pleased with its appearance.

I stepped beside the printer and read aloud one line of the print that seemed to leap from the paper: "The Massachusetts assembly petitions the English Crown for the removal of royal Governor Thomas Hutchinson."

"Shocking, don't you say?" Davern inquired of me.

"But why? What has the governor done?"

"It appears as though the Crown has placed blame for the misbehavior of His Majesty's unruly Massachusetts Bay subjects on a lack of firm leadership by the governor. The colonists are now calling that whole tea episode the Boston Tea Party."

"The storm grows near," I mumbled, remembering Caleb's prophecy. And then, as if I had summoned him, my cousin stepped into the shop from out of the lively Boston thoroughfare. I was stunned. "Caleb!" I acknowledged with astonishment.

Caleb cracked a weak smile and removed the bright tricorn from his head. "Good morning, cousin."

"Master Davern, allow me to introduce my cousin, Caleb Brown," I announced with pride.

"Good day to you," Davern greeted walking toward Caleb with hand extended. "I don't expect you to recall, but we've met one time before," he enlightened while shaking Caleb's hand.

"Yes...Master Davern. It was in Malden, was it not? A few years ago?"

Davern was impressed. "Why, yes. You do remember."

"Caleb, what are you doing here? I didn't expect to see you again so soon?" I asked.

Caleb released his grip of Davern's hand and looked at me—his smile disappearing. "Ben, I am in the hope that you may procure a leave of absence for a short spell to accompany me to Lynn," he said with a sobering look.

"Lynn?" I was surprised. *Had my cousin suddenly changed his mind about confronting Eblis?*

Caleb glared back at me with glassy eyes. "My father is dead."

CHAPTER 30

ynn – January, 1774
  It was a cold, dreary winter morning—a morning appropriate for a funeral as a low layer of gray clouds blanketed the graveyard behind the meeting-house, while a frigid breeze struck in intervals stinging our exposed skin. A small gathering of family and friends stood ankle-deep in snow around an open grave to bid farewell to my uncle, Edward Brown. At my aunt's request, Caleb performed the service and remained very strong throughout—as I knew he would —unaffected by the deep sadness that marked so many faces and undaunted by his mother's constant weeping. It conjured up memories of my father's funeral.

I stood beside my mother and her Aidan. As I listened to Caleb's spiritual and solemn tribute to his father, my thoughts would drift to Aidan; for I could not see what my mother saw in the tall bearded joiner. Each time we met he seemed constantly preoccupied and aloof. Perhaps I was looking for my father.

Then there was Sam, standing in the distance behind me. Several times I glanced back over my shoulder to gaze upon her shoulder-length auburn hair that seemed but a memory dangling from beneath a black bonnet; although I was careful that her eyes did not catch mine.

Caleb finished the final prayer and two men began shoveling dirt atop my uncle's coffin. My aunt wept terribly, having had to be assisted by my mother as the gathering began to slowly break up, and I turned and watched Sam move with the crowd, head down, trying to negotiate her steps in the snow.

As the mourners began to scatter across the graveyard I felt a firm hand on my shoulder and turned slowly to find Caleb. "Well cousin, it is done," he remarked sadly.

"I'm so sorry," I replied. He dropped his head with a frown and I turned away from him for a moment in an attempt to relocate Sam.

Caleb followed my preoccupation and found its source. "It's the redhead," he deduced.

I turned back toward Caleb embarrassed. "I'm sorry, Caleb. You've just buried your father and my mind is elsewhere. It's just that I haven't laid eyes on her nor spoken with her in person for some time."

"*When I was a child, I spoke as a child, I understood as a child, I thought as a child; but when I became a man, I put away childish things,*" he quoted. "A child's indecisiveness might permit such an opportunity to slip from within his grasp. You are no longer a child, Ben, and neither is she. Go after her."

I turned and looked for her again and located the black bonnet at rest, for her departure from the cemetery had been delayed by a small group of familiar faces.

"Go, Ben. Opportunity will not wait," Caleb encouraged.

"Thank you," I acknowledged. "I will speak with thee later," I announced and started out in pursuit, plodding through the snow and meandering through the flock of stragglers who mingled about. My eyes remained fixated upon the black bonnet which had started to move again.

I closed in quickly with a frantic step that easily overcame her cautious pace. My heart was pounding and my thoughts raced with uncertainties, and as I came upon her, I reached out, gently resting my hand upon her shoulder. As I did she stopped and turned around.

"Benjamin!" she gasped.

"Sam, may I speak with you?"

"This is a surprise! You look well," she described with a soft smile.

I felt at home again gazing upon her freckled face and into her resolute and limpid emerald eyes. "And to you the same."

"I am sorry about your uncle," she frowned.

"Thank you."

"Ironic isn't it?" she suggested.

"How do you mean?"

"It was death that chased you from Lynn and it is death that brings you back."

Her sardonic wit cut deep; but I was glad she hadn't changed.

"I do regret leaving."

Sam scoffed. "How is life in Boston?"

"It is a storm front. More redcoats appear every day."

"We have our redcoats as well. In fact the constable was recently replaced by our new sheriff—supposedly handpicked by the Crown," she explained.

"I enjoy your letters. Thank you for corresponding," I said, changing the topic.

She looked deeply into my eyes. "I miss you."

I caught my breath, for her words moved me. "I've missed you too, Sam." My revelation had emboldened my courage. "And I am wrong to have left you so suddenly. And I have been wrong not to return. I am overcome with great guilt."

"Why have you not shared such thoughts in your letters?"

"My heart speaks louder these days."

"I remember a boy who was frightened...a boy who tried to run away from his fears. It was a selfish act, Ben," she admonished.

"I do admit that my heart cowered in the presence of the demon shoemaker. He haunted me...and he haunts me still."

Sam's tone soured. "Then you haven't changed?"

"Perhaps I've learned to deal with my fears; but Eblis is still here in this town! He is still delivering his soles! Look around Sam at the number of earth mounds and new headstones that litter this cemetery! They are new graves, many filled with his victims!"

"You are obsessed with him...still."

"And you are not?!" I countered, broaching a subject we had ignored in our recent correspondence. "Have you forgotten the beast in the forest and the witch's coven?!" I exclaimed.

Sam lifted her eyes and glanced around as though she were embarrassed by the tone of my voice and the subject of my words.

"Sam, you were with me in the forest!" I continued, hoping to elicit a response.

"I...I can't explain what I saw. I don't remember it all. I just want to forget it," she said, disappointing me.

"But Sam, you can't forget!" I plead. "You were the one that once pressed me for action! The mark of evil is all about this cursed town!" I continued. "A demonic shoemaker collects his souls while a witch and a one-eyed bastard do the devil's tidings!" My words were impassioned; although I worked to keep them at a whisper lest I call attention to our conversation. "And Lord help this new sheriff you speak of —redcoat or not! He now inherits the September disappearance or suspicious death of a young maiden in the sacrifice that seems to plague Lynn as if it were some village out of the dark ages! Surely you haven't forgotten that?!"

"We haven't had a death or disappearance in years," she countered.

"But those of the past remain unsolved and it can and probably will happen again!" I replied. "How do you sleep each night knowing there may be another victim?! For you are a young maiden as well!"

Those resolute eyes of hers had given way to a foreboding glare. "I must be going," she remarked quickly and callously. "In spite of your issues with Eblis I do miss you, Ben."

As she turned and began to walk away from me I reached out and gently grabbed her arm. She stopped, turned and glanced up at me.

"Sam, this town is blind to the evil that consumes it. Those who will remain will perish."

She said nothing for an instant, choosing her words carefully, before she uttered, "Then this town needs someone to open its eyes. If what you speak of is true, then Lynn needs a savior," she sighed. "Return to the safety of Boston, Ben," she finished, turning and walking away. I stood frozen, empty, sullen, watching the black bonnet shrink as it moved across the cemetery, finally disappearing within the confines of a chaise.

The wheels of her carriage were set in motion and I remained focused on the horse drawn chaise until I could no longer see it. I produced a deep sigh and began to walk away from my uncle's plot when I noticed Caleb standing alone staring down at a small field-stone. My cousin squatted and reached down appearing to brush a light covering of snow from the marker and I decided to join him.

As I approached him, Caleb remained squatting, oblivious to my presence.

"Caleb," I called out startling my cousin as he quickly rose to a standing position.

"Ben, I didn't know you were standing there."

I peered down at the small, naturally rounded fieldstone, marked with a brief engraving. It seemed out of place positioned among the oblong-carved sandstone with elaborate script engravings dominating the graveyard.

I read the name and date on the fieldstone out loud. "Bridget Campbell...born seventeen twenty-eight...died seventeen forty-eight. Who is she?"

"Ben, you have told me of your dreams and nightmares," Caleb said.

"Yes. I have a consistent nightmare that I am being chased by a dark rider in the forest who throws a knife at me. I believe the rider to be Cyrus Eblis," I recalled. "And I am always awakened just before the name on the headstone is revealed."

Caleb nodded. "Well I have not told anyone this, but I too have been besieged by a nightmare. It is the image of a young woman...a pretty woman with long dark hair and brown eyes. At one moment she is smiling at me and the next she is in agony—screaming horribly. And next I see a grave marker with an engraving on it. This is the marker!"

"Bridget Campbell?"

"Yes. I do not know the name nor have I ever seen it before," Caleb described. "Only a few moments ago I was walking away from my father's grave and I happened to look down and see this as though it were calling to me!"

"She died young—only twenty years of age," I stated.

"She doesn't seem to have been a woman of much influence or affluence by the appearance of her grave marker. It is but a fieldstone with just a name and date," Caleb added.

"You're sure you have never heard her name before?" I probed.

"Never. I have only seen it in my dreams."

"It is very strange," I concluded. "Come, Caleb. Let us go home to your house and get away from this cold place."

Caleb agreed and we strolled across the graveyard together.

. . .

AFTER LEAVING THE CEMETERY, I SPENT THE REMAINDER OF THE day at Jamesina's house where Caleb and my mother tried to console the mournful widow. It had been a depressing day and after a night of much consternation, I reluctantly heeded Sam's advice, for I had responsibilities in Boston and so I departed for the port city at sunrise.

CHAPTER 31

ynn – May, 1774

Lynn's most significant preacher, Reverend Richard Sparston, resided in a small two-story dwelling adjacent to the meeting-house where he preached. Recognizable by a thundering delivery that could rattle the rafters of the meeting-house with a sermon and by the Bible he carried everywhere tucked underneath his right arm as though it were an appendage, the Reverend's pious appearance ended there. His burly stature stood out in a crowd and resembled more of the physique of a longshoreman than that of a humble servant of the Lord. His face did not exude a warm comforting disposition, but rather was gruff and pocked-marked, bordered by long dark sideburns extending well below each ear. An avid religious soul might caution one not to be deceived by appearances, however the nature of Reverend Sparston only plummeted inward from the surface to the soul; for he was a crafty one, hiding his inequities behind the cloth.

On this warm late Spring evening, Sparston sat behind an oak wooden desk in his great room studying the sack of bulging coins that had just been set down on the desk before him. He rubbed the top of his unblemished bald head that was bordered by a perfect ring of hair circling the sides and back of his head from ear to ear, while a long plait of hair at the back of his head, tied with a bow, fell to his shoulders like the tail of an armadillo extending out from underneath its smooth shell.

The source of the bag of coins sat across from Sparston in the form of two British officers clad in red uniform jackets trimmed in gold and adorned with three dozen shiny brass buttons. They wore white gaiters below the waist and their powdered white hair extending outward beneath black tricorns, sported stiff curls that fell alongside their face at the sides, while a pigtail hung below the tricorns at the back.

Sparston glanced outside of the window set to the left of his desk and into the dark night. He had made his decision but wanted to be sure he had heard the offer correctly, while at the same time not trying to appear too eager, and with an indecisive look he brought his attention back to the officers who stood on the opposite side of the desk. "So our new governor, General Gage, has brought his army with him to Boston," the preacher deduced. "I knew it was only a matter of time before Hutchinson was removed." He leaned forward in his chair and gazed upon the bag of coins. "So tell me again, what is it that brings you all the way to Lynn and what is it that you need from me?"

"Information," replied one of the officers. "The Crown will pay for any information you can give us on the identity of rebels."

"Patriots?"

"Call them what you wish," the officer replied brusquely. "They're all criminals. Boston is certainly the hub for rebel activity, but we believe we have more friends among the colonists in the cities beyond Boston. Friends who know names."

Sparston sat back in his chair. "But why me? I am a man of the cloth?"

The other officer grabbed the candlestick that held a burning candle and moved it from its position set on the middle of the desk in between Sparston and the officers, resting it near the edge of the desk. He placed both hands on the smooth oak surface and leaned forward across it, staring directly into the eyes of the preacher. "Come now, Reverend. We know all about you. You're about as pious as Captain Nigel here," the officer scoffed, turning to the other officer with a laugh.

"And what he's trying to say is that I'm not very pious, Reverend," the officer clarified with a wicked grin.

Sparston looked surprised. "Why would I want to spy on my own congregation?"

"Because Reverend, they spy on you!"

"Spy on me?!"

"Reverend, we know how you've been pilfering the coffers of the meeting-house and of your addiction to rum," rattled off one officer.

"And we know of the various women you have taken to bed... married women, might I add. You have certainly gone to great lengths in your devotion to your flock, wouldn't you agree?" the other officer added sarcastically.

Sparston was red-faced and incensed. "This is blackmail!"

"Perhaps," said the officer who lifted his hands from the desk and returned to a standing position. "But you're getting paid, Reverend. All we need is information."

The preacher sighed.

"Come now, Reverend. It's not as if you're selling your soul to the *devil*," chimed in the other officer.

Sparston frowned. "I am in your service," he announced reluctantly.

"I knew you would be, Reverend," said the Captain grinning. "I knew you would be."

HOURS AFTER THE OFFICERS HAD DEPARTED THE SPARSTON residence, the Reverend sat on the edge of his bed muddling over the evening's events. As he relived the conversation with the officers, he looked down and noticed the new pair of low black calfskin shoes with large buckles. "Indeed that shoemaker Eblis does fine work," he mumbled to himself. The religious man then noticed how humid the night air had become and stepped over to the window, pulling it open. Placing both hands on the window ledge, he leaned forward, seeking a nonexistent breeze as he wiped the perspiration from his brow with a handkerchief. With a sigh he began to turn away from the window when he noticed a light illuminating from inside the meeting-house next door. "What in blazes?!" he exclaimed. He pulled away from the window, quickly tossing a shirt over his head and pulled his legs through a pair of breeches. Next he slipped his feet into the new pair of shoes, grabbed a ring of keys and rushed from the house.

"If this be one of those goddamn rebel groups meeting secretly in my meeting-house without my consent, there will be hell to pay!" Sparston snarled as he marched across the grass to the meeting-house, plotting a course to a side entrance. He raced up a few wooden steps positioned below a wooden door of the large, two shingled frame building with tall hipped roof.

The Reverend pulled on the door handle only to find the door locked, causing the religious man to pause with concern; but his rage supplanted any caution he may have thought about exercising, and hastily used a key to unlock it. Pulling the door open, he was surprised to find the inside of the building—normally dark at this hour—radiating with a reddish glow as does the horizon at dusk. Sparston's first thought was that the building must be on fire, but the absence of smoke laid that conclusion to rest.

The Reverend stood silently inside the doorway looking out into the large room supported by four large posts set in each corner. From his vantage point at the side he gazed directly at the rows of oak pews arranged symmetrically, positioned to face the lectern on a raised platform at the front of the building. What he viewed next startled him greatly; for there were individuals seated in every pew—the room was full. However none of the figures made a sound, remaining motionless—each clad in black hooded robes with their hoods pulled up concealing their identity, and all appearing to be fixated on the platform with its quiet lectern. Sparston's heart raced but he found the courage to begin a slow walk down the aisle adjacent to the pews watching carefully the stone-like figures, none of which paid heed to his presence. When he had reached the last pew he stopped slowly and turned toward the vacant lectern when a figure seated on the end of the pew reached out and grabbed his arm. The Reverend gasped and his heart pounded with such fury that it nearly exploded from inside his chest. The figure held tight to Sparston's arm and with his other hand pulled down the hood to his robe.

"I know you!" Sparston exclaimed. "You are the shoemaker —Eblis!"

"Indeed...indeed," Eblis replied with a sinister grin as he released hold of the Reverend's arm and rose from the pew.

"What is this?!" Sparston pressed. "What are you and these people doing here at this hour?!"

Eblis ignored the question and looked down at the Reverend's feet. "I see you are wearing your new *soles,*" he pointed out.

Sparston grew incensed. "Who are these people?! And why are they in my meeting-house?! It is nearly midnight! How did you get inside?!"

"I thought this to be God's house?" Eblis countered. "Is thee God?"

"I am the reverend of this house! God speaks through me!"

An explosion of thunder rattled the building, startling the Reverend.

"Why Reverend, it is your new congregation. You've been reassigned," Eblis revealed with an evil grin.

"I don't understand?! Who are you to tell me such things?!"

Eblis rose out of the pew and faced Sparston. "Come, Reverend. They await you," he said and began walking down the aisle toward the platform and lectern.

Sparston hesitated, causing Eblis to spin around.

"Reverend, you're among friends," Eblis assured with a large smile.

A second thunder clap rattled the meeting-house and set Sparston's legs in motion, slowly following Eblis down the aisle and up the steps of the platform. They stood side by side at the lectern gazing out into the congregation of hooded figures.

"Behold thy new congregation!" Eblis exclaimed extending an outstretched arm toward the faceless crowd. "A congregation of lost souls! They are sworn to follow you for eternity! For you, Reverend, are thy shepherd!"

At that moment the congregation responded eerily in unison as if on cue. They called out, "Salvum me fac!"

The frightened Reverend turned to Eblis. "It's Latin...what does it mean?!"

"Save me," Eblis revealed.

"This is madness! Who are they?!"

"I told you...they are your new congregation," Eblis repeated. "Are you prepared to tell them that you have not the power to save them, Reverend?! That you are about as loyal to your God, as is a colonial rebel to the English King?! I'm not certain how such a large group may react to hearing...the truth? You have made a career out of deception, why alter your approach now?"

Sparston turned to Eblis with a dreadful stare. "You're the spy!"

Eblis bellowed with laughter.

"Master Eblis, I have had enough of your little game! I am going now to seek out the sheriff and I swear if you and this mob of yours are not gone from this place of worship by the time we return, you will be arrested!" Sparston exclaimed as he stomped down the steps of the platform. At the bottom of the steps he turned around once more to confront Eblis who had remained at the lectern. "And you can tell your Redcoat cronies, the deal is off!"

"Oh Reverend, you are correct," Eblis replied. "This is indeed your meeting-house. For there are many who believe the god you claim to worship speaks through those with piety and honesty—two virtues that are unknown to thee! By your actions you have seen to it that there is no god present here! For this meeting-house is as hollow as a coffin!" Eblis turned once again back to the congregation and extended his arms to them. "BEHOLD THY ETERNAL CONGRE-GATION OF THE DEAD!" he barked.

Suddenly the congregation rose in unison and withdrew their hoods exposing human skulls and revealing an assembly of human skeletons concealed beneath the robes. The macabre congregation of the dead began to cry out, "Salvum me fac!" repeatedly and Sparston was terrified at the sight of skeletons that had been given a demonic breath of life. Suddenly the demonic congregation bolted from out of the pews and rushed the horrified preacher. The clicking and clat-tering of a thousand human bones filled the meeting-house and drowned out the Reverend's hysterical cries as the skeletal creatures descended upon him pulling at his hair, flesh and clothing with their bony fingers. Despite his fright, Sparston found the energy to fight them off, swinging his arms and fists furiously as he backed his way to the side door. Barreling into the door with his shoulder he quickly found himself outside and leaped from the steps onto the lawn in full stride, running off into the darkness screaming for help, as dozens of waves of skeletons poured out of the meeting-house in pursuit.

The clouds had opened by now and Sparston was beseeched by a heavy downpour as he raced across the small cemetery at the back of the meeting-house. Several times he slipped and fell on the rain soaked soil and would hurriedly climb back to his feet with the skele-tons on his heels; but the Reverend's next fall would be his last. As he turned to gage what distant now separated him from his supernatural pursuers, he paused to catch his breath and took a backward step, but his foot did not touch down on solid ground. Rather he plummeted backwards, his arms flailing at his sides as he tumbled six feet into an open grave that had been dug just before sunset for a morning funeral. He crashed to the muddy bottom of the pit with a hard thud, lying on his back. His head throbbed and he closed his eyelids as the cool rain poured down on his face before realizing his predicament; for when he opened his eyes he found himself staring up at the top of the pit and peering back down at him were a dozen or more ghastly skeletons. "Salvum me fac!" exclaimed one of the skeletons. Sparston cried out in terror and then one by one each skeleton leaped into the pit and atop the Reverend. As the number of skeletons increased within the hole, the tremendous weight that bore down upon the helpless preacher soon crushed his chest, suffocating him. His body was found alone in the pit the next day, buried beneath three feet of mud when the gravediggers attempted to clear out the open grave.

CHAPTER 32

une, 1774

J   Late in June I received a strange letter from Caleb who had remained in Lynn since his father's death to comfort his mother. The correspondence was short and vague, but requested my presence in Lynn with great urgency. I do recall one specific line of the letter, which read, "The time is now at hand."

I will admit at first I was less than thrilled to be returning to Lynn, especially since my last encounter with Sam had not ended so amicably, and my employer could not hide his dissatisfaction with my departure as well; but the more I poured over my cousin's words, the more excited I became about heeding Caleb's wishes. My cousin clearly needed me and although his letter mentioned nothing of Eblis, I could read in between the lines and sensed that the topic of the demon shoemaker had inspired Caleb to write. *Had Caleb finally decided to confront Eblis?*

After settling employment affairs and obligations with Master Davern, I headed north on horseback out of Boston, arriving in Lynn on a bright Sunday morning. At Davern's insistence I had purchased my first horse—a gray mare—and road the fine animal to Lynn without incident, guiding the horse through the empty main street; for as it was the Lord's Day most of Lynn's inhabitants were home at rest or at religious service. Occasionally I would stumble upon the sight of a few British soldiers patrolling the vacant streets—the result of rising tensions between the colonies and the King that had produced the unpopular Quartering Act, which provided for the stationing of British troops in occupied homes and inns throughout Massachusetts.

I stopped first at the Brown residence, finding none at home and concluded they would be in attendance at the meeting-house for the Sunday service. I secured my horse in the back of the house and traversed the familiar route on foot arriving at the building just as the service was to commence. After removing my tricorn, I stood in the rear and watched with surprise as Caleb climbed onto the platform and stood at the lectern. "Good morning," he greeted with his gentle, but commanding voice. "In the absence of a minister to replace the late Reverend Sparston, I have been asked to deliver today's sermon."

Only moments after Caleb had begun his lecture did I notice a stir in the middle of the congregation as a man suddenly rose from his sitting position in a pew and began climbing over people in a frantic manner—shoving, stepping, and falling over them before stumbling out into the aisle. Staggering to his feet, the man placed his hat back upon his head and shielded his face with a cloak that had been fastened around his neck. Doubled-over as though he were in pain, the man moved briskly toward the rear of the meeting-house. The congregation appeared startled by the strange actions and one concerned fellow who stepped from out of the pew in an effort to assist the fleeing man, was promptly shoved to the floor by him. Caleb too, seemed affected by the odd display, pausing from his sermon to observe the stranger in flight. I realized the man was moving in my direction so I stepped aside as he drew near, and when he passed me, he hesitated for an instant, lowered his cloak and hissed at me. It was Eblis. His face was the color of turquoise with his skin hanging down in folds as if it were melting wax, while the pupils of his eyes shone red as fire and he trembled as one might when inflicted with an illness. *What force could bring such discomfort to this demon?* Eblis quickly exited the building and I moved to follow him outside; but when I opened the doors, stepping into the sunlight, I could find no-one in all directions. Then I heard Caleb's voice resuming the sermon and I returned inside the meeting-house to view my cousin once again.

When the service had concluded, I rushed to the front of the meeting-house, moving against the flow of people who were exiting to the rear. I laid eyes upon Jamesina and Sam for an instant; although neither saw me so I refrained from approaching them, and I did look hard for Rachel but did not see her among the congregation.

When I came upon Caleb, he was surrounded by a small group of admirers who were busy sharing salutations and praising his sermon. My cousin politely ended a conversation with one individual when his eyes met mine, and he stepped from the small group and paced toward me. "Ben! So good of you to come!" he greeted with a firm handshake. "Give me a moment."

I dropped down in a nearby pew and waited as Caleb returned to the group and cordially resumed the pleasant superficial discourse. A short time elapsed before my cousin bid farewell to the last straggler in the meeting-house and when he was sure we were alone, paced over and sat down beside me in the pew.

"Did you recognize him this morning?" I asked with excitement.

"Yes...it was Eblis wasn't it?"

"Yes," I confirmed. "He seemed ill and weak. I think it was because of you, cousin! The demon was weakened in God's house before a preacher the likes of you!"

"Perhaps," Caleb agreed; although he did not share my excitement. "But I'm not so sure, Ben."

"You saw him leave the building! He looked like a wounded animal!"

"It could have been just an act?" Caleb wondered. "Perhaps he is laying a trap?"

"A trap?" I was confused. "For whom?"

"I'm not sure, Ben; but something tells me we may find out."

"Are you proposing that we confront this demon?"

Caleb nodded. "The time is now at hand."

"What has changed your mind?"

"Ben, my mother shared a secret with me recently," Caleb's tone grew even more serious and somber. "I am not the child of Edward and Jamesina Brown."

I was stunned! "What?! What are you talking about?!"

"Edward and Jamesina found me abandoned in the forest a few miles outside of Lynn when I was an infant."

I was shocked. "Do you believe this story?!"

"Yes...Ben, I believe it," Caleb sighed. "My mother was incredibly distraught in her revelation. I could feel her pain with each word."

"Caleb...I'm sorry."

"I'm not," my cousin said forcing a smile. "Edward and Jamesina saved my life. Everything I am, I owe to them."

"You are right," I replied. "But why would Jamesina reveal this secret to you now?"

"Eblis..." The smile ran away from Caleb's face as he spewed the demon's name. "Eblis knew of the secret. And Ben, I believe Eblis is responsible for my father's death!" My cousin's tone filled with vengeance. "My father had planned to confront Eblis the night he was killed! My father was not a violent man and apparently became so mortified by the knowledge that Eblis knew the secret and probably somewhat frightened to confront him, that he ended up drinking too much rum at the tavern. And thus he stepped out into the street intoxicated and never saw the chaise that crushed him!"

"Again, I am sorry, Caleb."

"No Benjamin. I am the one who is sorry that it has taken so long to heed your cries for confronting this demon. The time for lamenting has ended," Caleb announced. "It's now time for action!"

"Caleb, but what of his awesome powers? How do we fight him?"

"We won't fight him alone. We will have God on our side."

"And the magic ring?"

"Magic ring?" Caleb had forgotten.

"Remember the story you told me of Solomon and the djinn? Solomon controlled the demons with a magic ring," I recalled, my body heating up with passion. "If we are to believe what we witnessed this morning with the weakening of Eblis, then you, Caleb...you are the magic ring!"

To my surprise Caleb did not quickly dismiss my impassioned observation and seemed to revel in the moment, uttering, "Luke writes: *All things are possible.*"

CHAPTER 33

C aleb and I tried on two occasions over the next several days to gain an audience with Eblis—my cousin armed with only a Bible and I, having recalled the tussle with Patch, carried a pistol—the property of my late uncle that I had removed from a cabinet inside the Brown's home. However, each time we knocked upon the door of the old Hassett shoe shop we were turned away by the crazed Daniel who had grown more demented since last I saw him. Bereft of reason, he mumbled indistinguishable jargon constantly and staggered about with far away bloodshot eyes and wild, greasy, long hair that stood up in some places as does the needles of a porcupine. With a dirty, acne spotted face and wearing clothing always baggy and wrinkled, his physique had matured considerably since last I saw him. For he stood slightly taller than I with a lanky frame that sprouted large hands and feet, and when his shirt sleeves were rolled up to his elbows, it was hard not to notice visible veins traversing his skin, bespeaking of considerable strength. I thought it a mistake to still consider him a harmless boy.

We decided on our third attempt at gaining entrance into Eblis' shoemaking lair that we would force ourselves inside if Daniel again tried to turn us away.

DAWN HAD JUST BROKEN, SETTING THE HORIZON AGLOW WHEN WE

approached the door of the Hassett shop. I turned and looked over my shoulder and across the street at the Kerstland shoe shop which had not yet sprung to life at that hour, for my thoughts were of Sam at that moment, and I began recalling that Christmas night when she and I had encountered Daniel in the snowy streets. I turned to look at my cousin. "Caleb, this Daniel is just as much a victim of Eblis as those who have met with foul play upon crossing his path; for he knows not what evil has taken hold of him. Eblis is using the poor lad."

"*Servants, be obedient to them that are your masters according to the flesh, with fear and trembling,*" Caleb recited.

"Perhaps we should try to remove Daniel from the shoe shop," I suggested with sudden compassion.

"The boy is sick—even more so since he has been sheltered by the demon. Let's pray he does not stand in our way; but we cannot delay much longer and must strike at the root of the disease before we can cure this town. And the root is Eblis," Caleb concluded as we reached the door.

Caleb gave me a nod and I took a deep breath before pounding on the door. It took several minutes of continued knocking until the door was slowly pulled open. Behind it, Daniel squinted back at us, battling the new light of day that crept into the dark room.

"We demand to see Master Eblis," Caleb announced boldly.

Daniel rubbed his eyes. "My prince told me thee would come," he replied humbly.

Caleb was surprised. "Then your master is here?"

Daniel erupted into a raucous laughter.

"Daniel, your master, he is here?" Caleb repeated.

The laughter slowly faded as the crazed face behind the door took a deep breath and snarled, "My master awaits thee in the sanctuary."

"Sanctuary?" Caleb asked.

"Perhaps he means the ten-footer behind the shop?" I guessed.

Daniel shut his eyes for a moment. "It is his wish that I take you to him," he announced, and then his eyelids lifted.

The door swung open wide and Daniel emerged, barefoot and clad in a night shirt that extended to his knees. As we followed the strange man around the side of the shop he would turn and look back at us with every ten paces and giggle hysterically. I grew frightened and reached inside of my coat pocket to grip the pistol for comfort.

Daniel stepped up to the first of three ten-footers and I quickly moved in front of him blocking his reach for the door handle. "Caleb this is dangerous!" I warned, suddenly filled with second thoughts about our actions. "Eblis has the ability to destroy both of us with the wave of his hand! He possesses much power!"

Caleb did not flinch. "I know the power of God."

I sighed and reluctantly stepped aside as Daniel, breathing excitably, pulled open the door. With outstretched arms, Caleb held the Bible out ahead of him and marched through the opening of the ten-footer. I followed close behind, carefully watching Daniel as we passed him and stepped inside; but we found no sign of Eblis.

We waited with uneasiness in the quiet for a few minutes before Caleb addressed Daniel. "Where is your master?" he asked.

Daniel only laughed.

"Perhaps he awaits us in another outbuilding?" Caleb suggested.

"The *book of orders*!" I remembered, pacing quickly to the rear of the ten-footer. "Eblis keeps the book in this outbuilding! I had it within my grasp when last I was here but left it behind in my struggle with Patch!" I described, rummaging through the tools set upon a work bench.

"Benjamin!" Caleb screamed and I spun around to find Daniel racing toward me. He gripped the handle of a hammer, holding it up in the air and swung the claw side of the hammer down at me. I leapt to my right avoiding the tool which crashed upon the work bench embedding the claw into the wood. As Daniel struggled to free the hammer, I retrieved my pistol with my right hand and clubbed the madman on the side of the head with the handle of my weapon. Daniel moaned and dropped to the floor.

Caleb rushed to Daniel. "I didn't see him pick up the tool!" he exclaimed, bending over the motionless young man. He lifted his arm to check for a pulse.

"Did I kill him?!" I wondered, breathing heavily.

"No. He's unconscious," Caleb replied and stood erect. "You were lucky, Ben."

"And to think I wanted to rescue the poor soul!"

"Well, it doesn't appear that Eblis had any real desire to see us today," Caleb deduced, standing above the unconscious Daniel. "Perhaps we should search the other ten-footers?"

I sighed and looked to my left. "Wait," I cautioned as my eyes were drawn to an object resting on a work bench.

"Ben, what is it?"

I stepped over to the bench and reached down to touch a large knife with handle of curly maple. "It's the knife! His knife!" I described and lifted the blade with my fingers, gripping the handle in the palm of my hand. "Eblis forced me to carve my initials into the cask with an identical knife when we first met in the forest of Salem! And it is the same knife that the beast threw at me the night I was chased in Swampscott! The blade has found me again!"

Caleb appeared confused. "What is its significance?"

I continued to stare at the blade. "It is the object that binds us." At that moment I glanced back down upon the work bench and noticed three black candles. "Of course!" I spouted. "The chandler... Darcie! She can lead us to Eblis!"

"What do you mean?"

"She is a witch!"

"How do you know this?"

I hesitated, remembering Darcie's warning at Floating Bridge Pond and lifted one of the black candles. "Trust me Caleb. I know of what I speak."

"Then we shall seek her out."

As Daniel began to grumble from his positon on the floor, I tucked the large knife inside the waistband of my breeches and led Caleb from the outbuilding. After traversing six blocks of Lynn's main street, we arrived at the chandler shop, finding the shop door open and burst inside. The unsettling atmosphere that enveloped the shop was as I had imagined for a woman steeped in black magic; for every glance around the small room revealed hundreds of candles of all shapes and sizes—some black and some white. The wooden shutters were drawn and a dozen or so burning candles flickered, throwing eerie dancing shadows across the wooden walls. Strung up across the center of the small room from beam to beam were tin molds, swinging low enough that we needed to bow our heads to clear them as we passed underneath.

Caleb and I appeared to be alone in the shop and cautiously my cousin negotiated his way to a door set in the wall. "Do you smell that? It is lye," he whispered and leaned his head to press his right ear against the door.

My cousin slowly pushed against the door that opened into a dark, smoky room illuminated only by the light from a burning hearth. There we beheld Darcie standing in the shadows aside the fireplace hunched over a large black kettle set above the roaring flames. With her sleeves rolled up to her elbows, the scary old woman slowly stirred the boiling contents of the large pot with a wooden paddle. She glanced at us for a moment, unbothered by our sudden presence, before peering back down into the kettle. "Thou hast found me," she squealed.

"Woman, we need to speak!" Caleb demanded.

"Is thee blind? Does thou not see what it is that occupies me time? I am but a poor chandler who makes her living off the sale of candles and soap," she squealed, still stirring the cauldron with the paddle. "If I were to pause from my task to entertain thy question, or if I should happen to error and change the direction in which I stir this mixture of fat and lye, me soap would fail. And if me soap fails, then me stomach fails for I do not eat!"

"I am Caleb Brown," my cousin announced.

The old woman gasped and immediately ceased stirring. She rested the paddle against the inside of the kettle, slowly stepping around the large pot and walked toward Caleb, never taking her eyes off of him.

She stopped in front of my cousin and studied him from head to toe with an intense look of fascination as though she were trying to remember. Reaching up, she delicately touched Caleb's face with the long bony finger tips of her right hand. My cousin remained steadfast, gazing at her with caution. "Malik," she uttered.

"What did you call me?" Caleb asked.

The witch pulled her fingers from his face. "Yes...thou is Caleb Brown," she confirmed with a satisfying smile. "How you've grown."

"Grown? Woman, I have never met you before," Caleb answered quickly with a puzzled look.

The old woman continued to gaze upon Caleb. "Thou hast the same color of eyes."

"The same color of eyes as whom?!" Caleb demanded.

Darcie snickered, shut her eyes and sighed. After taking a few deep breaths she bowed her head, opened her eyes and shuffled back to her position at the side of the cauldron.

Caleb thought the woman mad. "I believe you know the question I've come to ask!" he called out.

Darcie grabbed hold of the wooden paddle and began stirring again. She grinned. "Aye."

"Then without interrupting your ritual, tell me where I may find Cyrus Eblis!"

She slowly raised her head and jeered. "Thy heart is filled with anger. The knight who is guided by vengeance shall hasten to lower his shield and find only destruction—his own. Are thou that knight, Caleb Brown?"

"I am unmoved by your riddles, old woman! I have interest in only one thing—tell me how I may find Eblis!"

"The black prince said you would be determined," she remarked with a sinister chuckle. "Very well. Thou shall find the dark one in the forest west of Swampscott where the daughters of the craft gather. Benjamin knows of this place," she scoffed, still stirring the bubbling kettle.

I was surprised that Darcie revealed my knowledge of the coven in front of Caleb, especially after she had warned me never to disclose it and threatened the life of Rachel if I did. "Do you think us fools, woman?!" I exclaimed and turned toward Caleb. "It's a trap! The place of which she speaks reeks of all that is dark and evil! We will be easy prey there!"

"It is apparent that Eblis feels the need to meet me on his terms," Caleb deduced. "Perhaps he finds strength in his lair of sin?"

I reached out and grabbed Caleb's arm to be certain I was making my point. "More the reason to stay clear!"

Caleb said nothing.

"Little boys," Darcie blurted out shaking her head from side to side. "Frightened little boys."

"Ben is right," Caleb declared. "It is a trap. I will let Eblis come to me. He cannot hide from me forever. Come Ben, she is of no use to us. Our business is done here," he added and turned away from Darcie, stepping toward the door.

"Wait!" Darcie called out, stopping Caleb in his tracks. My cousin turned around. "Thou hast an agenda with the dark prince and until thy agenda is fulfilled, Eblis will continue to collect his souls," she teased with a grin. "I will tell thee how to seek out Eblis. For it is his wish that I do this."

"We've no intention of conjuring up demons in the forest!" I exclaimed.

The witch laughed. "It is not thy decision to make. It has already been made for thee."

"Old woman, you may be impressed by the powers of the demon Eblis, for you have chosen a life removed from the dominion of the Lord, but I am not impressed," Caleb scolded. "I only pray that the Lord may forgive you."

Darcie spit into the kettle. "Ambition guides thee, Caleb Brown! For we all have our weaknesses!" she baited. "What does thy Lord tell thee of thy future?"

"I have placed my future in the hands of God by living His word! I do not need to gaze into a crystal ball to know of tomorrow!"

"Take an apple!" Darcie demanded.

"What?" Caleb replied, not sure he had heard her correctly.

"On the table to thy left rests a bowl of apples," Darcie explained. "Take one!"

Caleb found the wooden bowl and retrieved an apple.

"Rub the fruit within thy palms!"

Alarmed and concerned that Caleb was losing control of the situation, I blurted, "No Caleb! It's black magic!"

"Nonsense!" Caleb dismissed. "I will prove to her that she cannot trick a servant of the Lord!" Caleb rolled the apple within his palms.

"Good!" Darcie expressed with delight. "Benjamin possesses a knife. It tis the property of the dark prince. Use it to cut the apple crosswise in two!"

My cousin turned and looked at me. "Ben, the knife."

"Caleb, how could she have known I have the knife?! It is black magic, I say! You must stop this!"

"Go on! Do it!" she insisted.

"Ben, give me the knife!"

I sighed, withdrawing the knife from inside my breeches and handed it to Caleb.

He used it to cut the apple as she had instructed.

"Bring me half of the apple!"

Caleb handed the knife back to me and stepped toward the witch carrying the apple half within the palm of his right hand.

"Hold it up for me to see!" she commanded, ceasing her stirring.

Caleb held the apple before her.

"Closer!" she demanded.

My cousin obliged her and stepped closer. Darcie's eyes grew wide as she became transfixed on the apple core.

"Pentacle of Kore!" she gasped with a raspy voice. "Reveal what awaits he who clutches the core!" Darcie continued and grew silent for a few moments, never once lifting her eyes from the fruit. Caleb remained strong but I could sense him growing uneasy as we awaited Darcie's next move. Suddenly she snickered and slowly rolled her eyes up at Caleb. "In one week's time, thy ambition...thy future will be snatched from thee with the swiftness of a striking serpent!"

Caleb said nothing for a moment, then lifted the piece of apple to his mouth and defiantly took a large bite from it. "You've inhaled too much lye, old woman," he said, turning for the door.

Darcie quickly reached out and grabbed his arm. "Take heed, young minister!" she warned with a more serious tone. "Thou knows I speak of thy impending appointment to the board of Yale! The decision is in six days, is it not?"

She had Caleb's attention once again. "Go on," he said.

"Thou will be turned away by Yale's Board of Governors," Darcie revealed.

I could see the color leave Caleb's face.

"Listen carefully to what I say, for I shall say this but once." As she released her grip of Caleb's arm, the sardonic grin disappeared from her face and her voice became more direct. "Eblis has the power to resurrect thy glory and reverse the decision that shall be made by Yale's Board of Governors, but it requires that you seek out the dark prince." She took a deep breath, reached for the paddle in the cauldron and resumed stirring the bubbling brew. "At the first glimmer of light in the wee hours of the morning, thou must take the knife with handle of curly maple and cut a fork-shaped wand from the twig of a wild nut tree that has never borne fruit..."

"Caleb! She blinds you with trickery! Let us leave this place now!" I warned.

"We've come this far. I shall hear her out."

The witch snickered some more and stopped her stirring, moving from the cauldron over to the hearth. "Then thou must use the bloodstone," she continued.

"Bloodstone?" Caleb asked.

"Red coral," she described and reached overhead to retrieve three black candles from the mantle above the hearth. "These be consecrated candles," she described, approaching Caleb and handing him the candles. My cousin was reluctant, but took them from her anyway. "When the moon is full, with these three candles, the bloodstone and fork-shaped wand, journey to the place in the forest where the daughters of black magic assemble. There thou must draw a triangle in the dirt with the bloodstone. Set a burning candle in each point of the triangle and move to within its center. Standing upright, hold the wand out before thee and recite the name of Cyrus Eblis twice. When this has been done, the dark prince shall appear!"

Caleb slowly backed away from the witch and turned for the door. He moved briskly passed me without a word and I quickly followed him through the doorway.

"Fair thee well, young minister!" Darcie called out and then laughed with a creepy shrill.

Once outside of the chandler shop I turned toward Caleb. "You're not seriously considering conjuring up Eblis according to Darcie's instructions are you?! I mean, using black candles and standing inside of a triangle drawn in the dirt...it's all sorcery!" I attempted to reason. "I'm afraid for you!"

"'*I have not given you a spirit of fear,*'" Caleb replied.

I sighed. "Caleb, you were right about Eblis setting a trap! Think about it, we were destined to explore the demon's ten-footer and he knew I would find and take the knife with handle of curly maple—the very knife Darcie says you need to cut a wand from the wild nut tree! As that witch told us, it was all meant to be!"

"Perhaps," Caleb agreed. "But I see no other way, for Eblis is always one step ahead of us. Thus we must accept the demon's invitation and place our trust in God."

I dropped my head in exasperation, realizing nothing could change my cousin's mind.

"Ben, I need to journey to New Haven to be there when the Board of Governors makes their decision," Caleb explained. "So we must put all this Eblis business aside until my return."

I nodded.

"And Ben...I need the bloodstone—red coral," Caleb added. "Can you search the beach for it?"

"That won't be necessary. I know where we can find red coral here in Lynn."

CHAPTER 34

He pulled tight on the horse's reins and the beast stopped and
whined, kicking high into the air with its front two legs. It was
then that I noticed the noose at the end of a rope swinging from
a tree limb high above. Quickly pulling myself into a sitting position, I began a
backwards crawl but my escape stalled when my back collided with a cold,
stone object. I spun around to discover a headstone with the inscription
concealed behind a thick layer of dust. Frantically I worked at brushing away
the dirt to reveal the name of... I opened my eyes and sat up, breathing
heavily. The nightmare was as real and frightening as always; but as I
sat there in bed, watching the early morning rays of dawn slowly illuminate my room, I felt frustration and not so much the usual terror
that enveloped me as I awakened from the recurring dream. *Whose
name is on the headstone?* The question tormented me.

At mid-morning, hours after awakening from my nightmare, I
decided to pay a visit to Master Kerstland's shoemaking shop and was
delighted when my outing erupted into a pleasurable reception by my
former employer and his wife, producing nearly an hour of cordial
dialogue and reminiscing. It was wonderful to catch up with the
friendly couple who had been like family, and it produced a sense of
excitement for me as the inside of the shop—which had changed little
since my days of employment there—sparked a great number of fond
memories. Kerstland described his shoe business as still very busy, and
they inquired of my time in Boston as well as offering their condo-

lences on the sudden death of my uncle. As parents of two daughters, they shared their trepidation over the unsolved disappearances of Lynn's three girls and they lamented over the British Parliament's continued bullying of the Massachusetts colony. And I was very much surprised with the announcement of Muriel's recent engagement to Roman Eastgate, the son of a local sailmaker; although the absence of Samantha in the shop disheartened me, for seeing Sam had been the primary reason for my visit.

After exhausting my welcome and learning that Sam was riding at her grandparents that morning, I bid the Kerstland's a good day and set off on horseback to locate my good friend.

Saddled atop the trotting gray mare, I traversed the familiar route —knowing it by heart—riding along the eastern bank of the Saugus River, through a forest of pine, past the iron works and around Cedar Pond before arriving at the farm. I guided the horse over to the timber fence and was delighted to find Samantha outside riding Savior. Undetected, I observed with excitement as my beautiful friend, clad in her familiar riding jacket and tight fitting buckskin breeches with high boots, guided her horse in a circular gallop around the fenced-in area, and I realized she was focused on the bucket setting on the ground on the far side of the enclosure. *Come on Sam!* The horse moved at great speed and Samantha bounced violently in the saddle. As she grew closer to the bucket she leaned forward and shifted her position from the center of the saddle to the right side of the horse. She stiffened her right arm and lunged toward the bucket and grabbed its handle but as she began to raise it, the bucket slipped from her grasp. Reaching up, she grabbed the horse's mane with her right hand and pulled herself squarely back onto the saddle, positioning herself upright as she tugged lightly on the reins until the animal slowed to a trot. Turning the horse around, she looked in my direction, no doubt surprised to see a stranger watching her, and began leading the horse on a trot towards me. When she became close enough for me to see her face, I witnessed a large smile and she commanded the horse to gallop toward me.

As Sam drew near me, she brought Savior to a trot, emitting a flirtatious grin as she guided the horse through an open gate, bringing the animal to a halt next to my position seated atop the gray mare.

"Why, Benjamin Pratt!"

I applauded. "You almost had the bucket this time," I said.

Sam chuckled. "Funny, isn't it, how relentless we are in our pursuit of those things that continue to elude us."

"It is in our nature to conquer obstacles," I replied.

"Walk! Ho!" Sam commanded and her horse continued moving past me. I in turn, lifted the reins of my horse and gave it a gentle kick setting it in motion and quickly caught up with Sam and her mare.

"What obstacles are left for you to conquer, Ben?"

"I have a few."

Samantha gave a doubtful smirk. "I heard you had returned to Lynn, and was hoping you would find time to see me."

"I visited the shop this morning. Your mother and father appear to be well."

"Yes. I'm sure they were surprised to see you."

"I understand Muriel is to be wed. Eastgate is a fine man."

"I agree. I hope he knows what he's getting himself into," Sam said, turning toward me with a sarcastic grin.

At this point we had reached an open barn and after guiding our horses inside we dismounted. I hitched the reins of my mare to a wooden post inside the barn as Sam removed the saddle from her horse and pulled it into a stable. She brushed her hands together as if to remove any dirt from them and stepped over to me.

"You took the time to visit my parents this morning," she remarked. "I know how close you and my father..."

"I was there looking for you," I interrupted and without hesitation I reached out with both of my hands and placed them firmly on her waist. Quickly I pulled her into me and leaned my face into hers, planting a long kiss on her delicate lips, before pulling away, unsure of what inspired my impulsion to kiss her at the moment or unaware of how she may react. Samantha stared back at me with eyes wide open and her lips slightly parted, as if in shock, before suddenly reaching up and grabbing the center of my shirt. She pulled me back into her and we kissed again now with our arms flung around each other in a firm embrace, with eyes closed and mouths opened.

Sam pulled her head gently away from mine and we opened our eyes simultaneously. Her hands moved from my waist to both of my forearms and she slid her fingers down my arms until both our right and left hands embraced.

"Ben...that was a surprise," she said softly.

"Do you object?"

Sam smiled and shook her head slowly. "No. I've wanted to kiss you for some time. The truth is that I've missed you Ben."

I was delighted with her revelation but cautious in displaying my excitement. "Sam...with your sister preparing to be married, I need to ask you...have you...have you feelings for anyone?" I pried, my words stumbling over my sheepishness.

"I've had a few potential suitors over the years, Ben; although my heart beats strongly for one person," she admitted.

I sighed softly and dropped my head.

"That one person finally found the courage to kiss me this morning," she confessed, bringing a rush of adrenalin over my body.

I beamed and pulled her close to me again. We kissed some more —each successive kiss growing more impassioned, until after a few minutes our lips separated; although we remained clutching hands.

"Have you come back to Lynn to stay?" Sam asked with a look of excitement.

"Yes...I plan to find work soon."

Sam smiled and buried her head in my chest. I stroked her soft hair for a few seconds and then gently pushed her away, now with my arms clutching both of her shoulders.

"Sam we spoke of obstacles a few moments ago," I said gazing deeply into her green eyes. "I don't know how you will react to this, but the first obstacle I must address is Cyrus Eblis."

"How, Ben?" she asked, her smile disappearing.

I was encouraged that she did not immediately dismiss my objective. "With the help of my cousin."

"Ben, I'm frightened for you."

"I have confidence in Caleb," I reassured.

"What exactly do you have planned?"

"I believe the plan is to fight Eblis with the power of God," I explained with uncertainty in my voice.

"You've convinced Caleb that Eblis is the devil?"

"A demon and not the devil," I corrected.

Sam frowned but remained attentive. "What power of God?" she replied with doubt. "Have you seen such power? Ben, you must be careful. Maybe Caleb isn't all that you may want to believe he is?"

"How do you mean?"

"He is no different than you and me with the exception of a religious title."

Her underestimation of Caleb hit hard. "He has faith...strong faith."

Sam sighed. "Just be careful, Ben."

"Sam, I need something from you."

"What is it?"

"I need coral."

"Coral?" Sam looked puzzled. "Why?"

"I will explain later; but may I have a piece of coral from your collection? Preferably a piece that is the deepest red-orange you possess."

"This is all so strange? When do you need it?"

"Soon. I believe Caleb is to return from Connecticut next week."

Sam forced a soft smile and then leaned in to kiss me again.

CHAPTER 35

The following week, on a brutally hot mid-week July afternoon, Sam and I decided to venture to the beach as the town of Lynn baked under clear skies and relentless sunrays with little movement of air. We agreed the seashore might provide some relief from the sweltering heat, and both of us found commonality in our attraction to the coastline's picturesque and peaceful setting. I walked to the Kerstland shop where Sam met me with her horse, Savior, having brought the animal back to Lynn with her after visiting her grandfather's farm. We decided to take only one horse with us and my female friend permitted me—seated in the English saddle--to steer the animal while she positioned herself behind me. Resting side saddle on the back of the horse with her petticoat flopping over the left side of the brown mare, Sam grabbed my attention when she placed her hands firmly at my side in an effort to secure her position behind me. With the command, "Walk! Ho!" I set the horse in motion and we set off in pursuit of the coastline of Lynn.

A short time later, Savior was trotting along the edge of the seashore and we were savoring the cool ocean breeze that brought us relief from the hot sun. The repetitive sound of the rhythm of gentle waves breaking against the shoreline and the distant squawking of sea gulls with outstretched wings guiding effortlessly overhead with the breeze, filled the tranquil scene. At times the breeze became so strong that Sam had to release her left hand from my side to hold steady her chip hat, with the handkerchief that was fixed inside it blowing in the draft. Soon we arrived at an area of the shoreline that was positioned below a great many gray sand dunes spotted with clumps of tall sea grass bending in the direction of the wind.

"Stop! Ho!" Sam commanded to my surprise, since I controlled the reins. The horse recognized her voice, bringing our ride to a halt and before I could inquire of my friend why she had decided to stop at this location, Sam slid from the back of the horse and onto the sand in a standing position.

"Shall we go swimming, Ben?" she asked.

"Swimming?" I replied, bringing my hand to my tricorn and raising it above my sweaty brow.

"Yes...this looks to be a good spot. Just give me a minute," she said and proceeded to tackle the soft, shifting surface of the beach as she moved in the direction of the sand dunes, before disappearing behind one.

I dismounted the horse and began to stroke the head of the equine as I stood beside the large animal when Sam reappeared from over top of the sand dune barefoot pacing toward me, carefully shifting her weight as the sand beneath her was displaced with each step. In addition to discarding her shoes, my friend had removed her petticoat, corset, chip hat, and riding jacket—clad only in a woolen full-sleeved loose chemise-type gown that stretched to her ankles. When she had reached the hard sand near the water's edge, she became more confident with her footing, jogging past me and into the ocean with a playful smile. I watched as she waded out, negotiating breaking waves, until she became waist deep in the dark blue saltwater before turning toward me. "Ben, join me! The water is cool and so exhilarating on this hot day!" she called paddling the surface of the water with both hands.

"And what of Savior?!" I asked, unsure of what to do with her horse.

"Release the reins! It's all right!"

I dropped the reins and at that moment Sam let out a high shrill whistle. The horse took off and galloped out into the water in the direction of my friend until slowing when reaching a depth that reached up to its knees.

"Now you, Ben!" Samantha encouraged.

I removed my tricorn, tossed it on the beach and pulled my long sleeved shirt over my head, feeling somewhat strange exposing my bare chest to Sam; although I was not embarrassed of my physique.

"I will tell you Sam. When I swim, it is usually in the nude!" I called out in jest.

Sam laughed. "So do I!" she replied quick-wittedly, submerging completely beneath the ocean surface for a second before resurfacing. She looked stunning standing there waist-deep—her long auburn hair wet and pulled back from her forehead falling straight down upon her porcelain bare shoulders, and her shapely bosom accentuated by the wet chemise now clinging to her skin.

"Well, what are you waiting for?!" she shouted.

Hurriedly I removed my shoes and stockings and waded out into the water to join her, clad only in my breeches. I too submerged for a second upon reaching Sam, and when I surfaced, instinctively we embraced with a deep kiss—our wet bodies melting together. However, our passionate interlude was suddenly broken by a whine from Savior and we pulled apart giggling.

From our position in the surf Sam faced the beach and as I moved again to embrace her, her eyes looked beyond me. "Ben, look!" she called out halting my advance. I turned around to see a rider on horseback guiding his trotting steed up the beach in our direction. "Someone else looking to escape the heat?" she guessed.

As the rider drew near, I recognized his features. "It is Caleb!" I deduced turning away from Sam and wading toward the shoreline with excitement. Sam reached over, grabbed hold of Savior's reins and dropped down under the ocean surface to her neckline.

I stepped out of the surf just as my cousin's steed came to a stop on the beach to greet me. "Hello, Caleb!"

"Master Kerstland said I might find the two of you at the beach. Are you enjoying your swim, Ben?" Caleb said with raised eyebrow and a coy grin.

"Very much so," I replied with a grin of my own.

"I've no doubt," he acknowledged looking toward Sam with a large smile and a wave of his hand. Sam smiled and returned the gesture.

"Caleb, do you have news?"

Caleb looked down at me and his smile faded. "I've been rejected by the Board of Governors."

"Rejected?! I'm sorry, cousin."

"Apparently I lacked the experience of the man they selected over me."

"Caleb, do you know what this means?"

"Yes, Ben. I'm afraid I do..."

"Darcie was right! She prophesied that you would not be chosen by the board!"

Caleb pulled the tricorn from atop his head and wiped his sweaty brow with his shirt sleeve and gazed up into the bright blue sky. "Ben, there will be a full moon tonight, which means there will be another tomorrow night."

"Yes...I know."

"Will you join me in the forest?" he asked sedately, refocusing his attention from the sky to me. "I know the area of Floating Bridge Pond very well, but will need your help in locating the place where the witches meet."

"Yes...of course."

"I will need the fancy blade of yours before dawn tomorrow, for Darcie instructed that a fork-shaped wand needs to be cut from the twig of a wild nut tree that has not yet borne fruit at the crack of dawn," Caleb reminded. "I know of just a tree and will need to make the cut tomorrow."

"I will bring you the blade today."

"And tomorrow evening we will leave from home at dusk in search of the location of the witch's coven," Caleb added as he replaced the tricorn upon his head. "Oh...and we will need the coral. You do have the coral, don't you?"

I turned and looked out at Sam bobbing playfully up and down with the waves. "Yes...I have the coral."

CHAPTER 36

On the following day at dusk, Caleb and I started off together —each of us on separate horses—in search of the location of the witch's coven. My cousin had returned the fancy blade to me after procuring the fork-shaped wand at dawn and he carried the wand, a Bible, a tinderbox, and the three black candles Darcie had given him inside a small sack. I was a little more practical in arming myself as I carried the Damascus blade and my uncle's pistol —which I loaded—tucking both items inside the waist band of my breeches. The other object I carried with me was a small sack that contained the coral.

Our journey took us up the coastline from Lynn northeast to Swampscott and through a thick forest before arriving in the old cemetery. As we guided our trotting horses around the weathered headstones I kept my eye on the large oak tree that dominated the graveyard where I was certain I had witnessed the apparition of the pirate who lie buried there, and felt much relief when we passed through the burial ground without incident. To this point, most of our travel was completed without much conversation as I could sense that the anticipated encounter with Eblis and the ritual we were about to execute as the means of making contact with the demon shoemaker, weighed heavily upon my cousin's mind.

Our silence was broken when we arrived at Floating Bridge Pond and Caleb shared some of his childhood memories with me centered on the unique structure. As we slowly crossed the buoyant bridge, the day's sunlight all but faded, shrouding the surrounding forest in darkness and the large full moon peaked just over the treetops, casting a reflection in the rippled waters of the pond. On the other side of the bridge, our horses plodded along through the forest of back spruce and past the occasional pools of tar that pock marked this area of woods, before reaching the great boulder and the fork in the path.

"To your left," I instructed without slowing my horse and Caleb followed me along the southern fork of the path.

A short time later we came upon the thicket of thorn and elder trees that lined the base of a rocky hill.

"This is it!" I recognized. "The coven meets on the other side of these stones."

"Must we climb the rocks?" Caleb asked.

"We climbed them before but our situation required that we do so. I believe there has to be an easier way inside. Let's continue on this path," I advised.

We did as I had suggested and in a short time the path brought us to a natural opening in the rocky hillside extending from the forest floor to the peak of the hill, shaped in an oblique fashion, growing wider as it ascended. The top half of a large oak tree, which sprouted up from in between the rocks and had at one time towered over the stone, now lay horizontal across the opening some fifteen feet above the floor—a victim of a lightning strike—giving the appearance as though the triangular entranceway was framed on two sides by stone and at the top by oak.

The base of the opening was wide enough for a man to pass through on horseback and Caleb and I guided our horses across the flat dirt covered terrain and into the treeless narrow valley framed by the natural formation of a circular stone wall. Once inside the cove we dismounted our horses and fastened the reins to a large log. As it rose, the moon had grown in size since we crossed Floating Bridge Pond and hung high in the sky illuminating the cove with a silvery luster.

"Well Ben, this is the place?" Caleb asked as we paced about fifty rods from the entrance before stopping.

"It is," I acknowledged with some trepidation. "There," I said pointing in the direction of a large flat stone positioned on the ground in the center of the cove. "On that stone is where I first set eyes upon the beast!"

"Well according to Darcie we needn't deal with any stone so I would imagine right here where we stand is good enough to do what is necessary," Caleb decided.

My cousin reached into the small sack he carried with him and withdrew the tinderbox, candles, and fork-shaped wand dropping them at his feet. Then he pulled the Bible from out of the sack and held it in his left hand.

"Caleb, the Bible. Do you not think it might work against your ability to conjure the demon?" I asked. "Darcie said nothing about bringing it."

"Neither did she discourage its presence," Caleb replied. "I'm not sure what we are about to get ourselves into, Ben. So it is our protection. *'Put on the whole armor of God, that you may be able to stand against the wiles of the devil...'*"

I nodded in agreement, encouraged by my cousin's spiritual strength, and pulled the coral out of the sack, handing it to Caleb. My cousin bent over and with the rough edge of the coral, he carved a large triangle in the dirt. When finished with the design, he dropped the reddish-orange object, picked up the tinderbox and handed it to me. I quickly set to work using the friction of flint and steel to ignite a piece of cloth on fire while Caleb retrieved the candles and held the wick of each black candle to the flame. When all were lit, I extinguished the cloth fire as my cousin set one burning candle in each corner of the triangle.

Caleb next plucked the wand he had cut earlier in the day from off of the ground and stepped into the center of the triangle standing upright, facing the large flat stone set in the middle of the cove. Still clutching the Bible in his left hand, he extended his right hand out in front of him which held the wand and took a deep breath before turning toward me. "Whatever happens here tonight, Ben, keep your faith in God!" he offered.

I nodded, not having the courage to utter a reply and stood a few rods away from the triangle. I reached inside my jacket and placed my sweaty palm on the handle of the pistol that I had secured within the waist band of my breeches.

Caleb raised the extended wand to eye level and called out, "Cyrus

Eblis! Cyrus Eblis!" We held our breath and waited. The cove remained silent and after a few uneasy moments Caleb turned and gave me a quizzical look. "Have we missed a step?!" he asked.

Suddenly above the large flat stone there appeared a blue-silver light in the form of a sphere hovering in mid-air. *It was happening again just as I remembered.* The spherical light grew brighter and then exploded illuminating the cove with a blueish glow before being drawn back into the center, swirling clockwise before the rapid revolutions expanded vertically producing a narrow column of spinning blue flames.

"The demon is here!" I called out, trembling.

The silhouette of a person appeared standing upright inside the tall column of swirling blue light and when the figure stepped out of the light, to my surprise it was not the monstrous horned winged creature that I remembered from the witch's coven, but the physique of an ordinary man, wearing a long dark jacket and a circular wide brimmed hat. The man casually stepped from the flat stone onto the dirt floor of the cove and began a confident steady pace toward us. It did not take long for either of us to recognize the individual as Cyrus Eblis. *The witch's spell had worked!*

Eblis' approach ended a few rods from where Caleb stood inside the triangle as the swirling column of blue light behind him faded into the moonlight. He stared at us silently for a moment wearing a wicked smile—the same sinister grin I had seen a hundred times before in person and within my nightmares.

"Benjamin," he acknowledged, bringing his right hand up to the front of his wide brimmed hat and tipping it in my direction. "You expected to see the beast? I hope I have not disappointed thee?"

"I still see a beast!" I fired back passionately.

Eblis laughed, mocking my fury, and then directed his attention toward my cousin. "Malik...so after all this time we finally meet."

"Why do you call me this?! My name is Caleb!"

"As you wish," Eblis replied, still grinning.

Caleb dropped the wand and brought his left arm up in front of him and quickly opened the Bible that he clutched with his right hand. He breathed heavily and searched frantically before finding the passage he was seeking.

"And he seized the dragon, the ancient serpent, who is the devil and Satan,

and bound him for a thousand years, and threw him into the pit, and shut it and sealed it over him, so that he might not deceive the nations any longer, until the thousand years were ended...!" Caleb exclaimed at the top of his lungs.

Eblis never flinched but instead slowly brought his hands together and clapped, mocking my cousin's futile attempt to wound him with the words of the Lord.

Caleb became alarmed at this display and instantly rattled off another passage from memory. "'*Behold...says the Lord...I have given you authority to tread on serpents and scorpions, and over all the power of the enemy, and nothing shall hurt you!*'"

Eblis pointed his right hand in the direction of Caleb and instantly the Bible combusted into flames forcing my cousin to drop the burning book.

"Do you really believe that you can subdue me with words?!" Eblis bellowed.

I too was stunned by the sight of the Good Book bursting into flames but felt the need to cry out, "But demon I saw how weakened you were in the meeting-house when Caleb read from the scriptures!"

Eblis roared with laughter once more. "It twas but an act, Benjamin!"

"I don't believe you!" I exclaimed.

"You and your cousin are here, are you not?" Eblis replied with a sneer. "Tell me Caleb, what is it that you feel?" he asked focusing his attention once more on my cousin. "Fear of the unknown, perhaps? Vengeance for thy father's death? Jealousy and anger for being cast aside by the Board of Governors? Confusion over the fact thy God has deserted you here this evening? You are simply a beleaguered soul who has lost his direction!" Eblis explained, culminating with an evil chuckle.

"Ben! The Lord's Prayer!" Caleb called out. I waited for him to begin and joined in.

"*Our Father which art in Heaven, hallowed by thy name...!*"

"Enough of this foolishness!" Eblis howled stopping our recital. "Caleb, I can give you anything you desire! The position on the Board of Governors can be yours!"

"'*...For God cannot be tempted by evil, nor does He tempt anyone!*'" Caleb replied, standing firm.

The grin began to disappear from Eblis' face. "Caleb why do you seek me?"

"To destroy you and put an end to your sinister meddling in the town of Lynn!" Caleb pronounced boldly.

Eblis studied the determined look in Caleb's eyes. "No! You've come to make a deal," the demon shoemaker suggested. "Allow me a moment of thy time to explore how you may orchestrate my departure from Lynn."

"No!" I shouted. "Caleb, do not listen to this monster!"

"I'm not fond of riddles, demon!" Caleb proclaimed. "Explain yourself! What do you mean a moment of my time?!"

"Exactly that, a moment of your time. I want you to take a walk with me to discuss a proposal I have, and should you accept that proposal, then you have my word that I shall vanish from this wretched little town of yours."

"And should I not accept your proposal?!"

"I'm certain you will not be able to resist it; however, if you do decline, then I believe we are at an impasse. And thus I will continue to peddle my *soles.*"

"Caleb! Let's leave here now!" I plead.

My cousin suddenly appeared confused as he breathed heavily and twisted his head back and forth from Eblis to me; but when Caleb made the move to step from out of the triangle and toward the demon, I could contain myself no longer and withdrew the pistol out from inside my breeches. Nervously I pointed the weapon at Eblis and shaking violently placed my finger on the trigger and pressed. The pistol exploded with a flash and the musket ball accelerated out of the barrel; but to my amazement the flight of the ball slowed dramatically and seemed to nearly stop and hang in mid-flight as it moved toward the intended target. It glided along on the remainder of its trajectory, floating in air as if it were a feather being drawn toward the demon. When the ball finally neared the dark shoemaker, Eblis slowly reached out and grabbed it from out of mid-air with his left thumb and index finger. He squeezed, forcing the metal ball to disintegrate into powder and calmly brushed its remnants from his hands.

"Have you not been witness to my powers on more than one occasion?!" Eblis growled. "Why do you think it is that the two of you are still alive?! Surely I could extinguish your life with the ease of snuffing out the flame of a candle!"

At those words from Eblis I quaked with such fear that the pistol fell from out of my hand. Nevertheless I found the courage to continue to warn my cousin. "Caleb, we should leave here now!"

"Benjamin, I have grown tired of thee!" Eblis clamored and then thrust both of his arms in my direction. The motion of his arms coincided with a tremendous rush of wind that struck me with such force that I fell backwards onto my back. When I found the strength to prop myself up by my hands into a sitting position, I became horrified to discover that six large hissing serpents now surrounded me. The rattle snakes corralled me with purple forked tongues shooting in and out of their mouths in my direction, threatening me with gaping mouths that brandished large fangs. Petrified, I could not move a muscle.

"Caleb, on my command these serpents will strike and Benjamin will die from the poison they will inflict!" Eblis described. "Or you can walk with me! The choice is yours!" the demon added, and then turning his back toward us, he began pacing in the opposite direction. As he walked, a large dark sphere materialized before him in his path and upon reaching the sphere Eblis spun around and called out, "Join me, Malik!" before turning again and stepping inside the dark sphere, where his figure gradually vanished as he moved deeper inside.

Caleb gave me a look of desperation steeped in fear—a look I had never seen on my cousin's face before. He obviously recognized my predicament and realized his actions could save me. I wanted to cry out and warn him, but I dared not speak at the risk of agitating the serpents. Without uttering a word, my cousin followed the demon shoemaker into the eerie dark portal and vanished. At that moment one of the serpents hissed and lunged at me and I screamed, closing my eyes in anticipation of the painful bite; but I felt nothing. And when my eyes opened, I found the serpents had disappeared and my cousin laid next to me face down on the soil.

"Caleb! Caleb!" I called out, shaking my cousin and rolling him over on his back. I looked around and realized that Eblis and the eerie black sphere were gone before refocusing my attention on my cousin. "Caleb!" I called again. As Caleb slowly opened his eyes and began wheezing to catch his breath, I was taken aback by his appearance.

His clothes were wrinkled and dust-covered, with oily and disheveled hair, and his face appeared weathered and sunburned with parched lips; but the most bewildering feature was the thin beard that covered his neck and lower face, as though he had not shaven in a week.

"Ben," he began with a dry, scratchy delivery. "The serpents...are you all right?!"

"Yes...where did he take you?"

Caleb avoided the question. "How long was I gone?"

"An instant."

"What do you mean? I feel like I haven't eaten or slept in a week! What do you mean an instant?!"

"Caleb, a moment after I watched you disappear in that sphere, I closed my eyes as a serpent prepared to strike me and when I opened them, you were here next to me!" I described with disbelief. "It was but an instant!"

Caleb sat up and coughed. "Let's get out of here, Ben!"

"Caleb, where did Eblis take you!? What did you see!?" I asked, rising to my feet.

My cousin sighed. "There was so much, Ben. I need to digest it all."

"What of the proposal!?" I continued.

"Now is not the time," Caleb explained as I helped pull him to his feet.

I looked my cousin in the eye. "Caleb, did you make a deal?!"

My cousin sighed. "No..." he said quickly and began gathering up the objects we had brought with us, placing them inside one of the small sacks.

CHAPTER 37

eptember, 1774

S After our encounter with Eblis, I began to notice how Caleb seemed to be avoiding the subject of that strange evening. I longed to learn just what exactly had occurred between my cousin and the demon shoemaker; but since Caleb made no attempt to broach the subject, I decided to wait for him to approach me. For I didn't want to appear intrusive, convincing myself that he needed time to come to terms with the incident. In the meantime I nervously awaited the next act in our scary duel with Eblis; although surprisingly the calendar days for the remainder of the month of July and August passed uneventfully. And although I welcomed the peace, I sensed it was merely the calm before the storm.

I had seen nothing of Eblis since the night at the cove with Caleb, and Darcie had not shown her face either. I found it unusual how Caleb continued to delay his return to the congregation in Simsbury and remain in Lynn. And even though we were both temporary boarders in Jamesina's home, our paths began to cross less and less as though my cousin was purposely trying to sidestep me. As the days moved further away from that macabre evening, my cousin's reluctance to share his experience alone with the demon began to evolve into what he claimed to be a loss of memory in reference to the entire evening. I became increasingly frustrated with Caleb's avoidance of the subject and rather suspicious as well; although I questioned whether or not I was being selfish for harboring such feelings.

The one very bright constant in my life proved to be how fast my romantic relationship with Samantha had blossomed. We became inseparable, seeing one another on a daily basis and the fact that Master Kerstland rehired me—this time as a shoemaker and not a journeyman—delighted Sam. There was no more talk of cowardice as Sam fed my ego with sweet compliments and we even began to discuss a future together. She breathed life into my every day, giving me the strength to rise above the gloom and hopelessness that had plagued me for so many years. Certainly the threat from Eblis was still very much prevalent, but my fondness for Sam had presented me with a tangible objective in life.

Still shy of my twenty-first birthday, I had already been witness to more strange happenings than I could have wished upon my greatest enemy—each one seemingly more bizarre then the last with the potential to alter the course of any young individual's existence. Yet the turning point in my life came not at the hands of a sinister act orchestrated by supernatural forces; but rather it came as a result of an unfortunate accident.

It was late September and I had just begun to breathe a sigh of relief in the realization that the historically dark autumn month, in which young girls had disappeared from off the streets of Lynn, was about to pass without incident yet again, when I got word that Samantha had severely injured herself from a fall from her horse. The accident had occurred at her grandfather's farm and I quickly rushed off on horseback to be at her side.

I arrived in such a distraught state that I don't remember what person gave me entrance to the farm house nor do I recall even entering the home. And when I stepped through the doorway of the bedroom where Sam lay motionless on the bed, I am uncertain whether I acknowledged the salutations given to me by the small group of family members who had been drawn to Samantha's bedside. What I do remember was the hush that fell over the room as I entered, and the unsettling sight of my love lying peacefully on the bed face up. Her eyes and mouth were closed and one would think she laid deceased if not for a slight rhythmic rise and fall of her chest with each delicate breath.

I stepped up to the bedside and stared at her for a moment before turning and catching the eye of Emery Kerstland. "What is her injury?" I asked.

"She struck her head when falling from the horse, Ben," Kerstland replied somberly. "She hasn't regained consciousness."

"When will she?"

Kerstland delayed his response before adding, "It's very serious, Ben. The doctor doesn't think she will recover."

It took me a moment to digest the gravity of his response. "But she's breathing!" I exclaimed grasping at hope.

"But her brain is not functioning," Kerstland uttered with barely a whisper. "There is no telling how long she may linger in this state," he added, forcing the painful reality from his lips before drooping his head. Samantha's mother began to weep and had to be led from the room.

I turned back toward Samantha and grabbed her hand. I held it tight wishing that my touch might spark her to awaken; but she remained non-responsive and it was then that I too began to weep.

A short time later, after gathering my composure, I left the farm on horseback and began what I was sure to be a gut wrenching journey back to Lynn filled with melancholy and emptiness; but in my despair I remembered Rachel. I felt that if anyone could bring me comfort in this dark time, it would be my friend and her positive demeanor. So I steered my mare northward to Swampscott and by late afternoon I had arrived at the home of the Goodes.

Dinah permitted me entrance to the home and in minutes Rachel appeared in her wheelchair surprised to see me. My lips began to quiver as I explained the reason for my sudden visit, revealing Samantha's dire situation with a somber and unsteady delivery. I could feel tears welling up in my eyes and when Rachel began to weep, I followed suit. My friend beckoned me with outstretched arms and I stepped up before her wheelchair, leaned over, and we embraced, sobbing.

The next thing I knew, Rachel and I were in the parlor sitting beside one another—she in her wheelchair that was set adjacent to the upholstered chair that I rested upon. Dinah had illuminated several candles in the room as the fading afternoon sunlight streaming in through the windows had begun to shrink from the parlor, and we were no longer weeping. In light of the tragedy that had befallen Samantha, my friend suggested that we pray together and she opened her Bible—the one that I had recovered as we fled the witches coven that night in the forest.

"Ben, this is from Luke," she said and began to read the passage with her soft soothing voice. *"Meanwhile, all the people were wailing and mourning for her. 'Stop wailing,' Jesus said. 'She is not dead but asleep.' They laughed at him, knowing that she was dead. But he took her by the hand and said, 'My child, get up!' Her spirit returned and at once she stood up. Then Jesus told them to give her something to eat."* Rachel paused and began flipping through the pages of the Bible until she found what she was looking for. "Here Ben, I believe you may find comfort in these words," she pronounced, passing me the book.

I held the book with both hands and began to read the psalm Rachel had selected, *"The troubles of my heart are enlarged: O bring me out of my distresses. Look upon my affliction and my pain; and forgive all my sins."* My voice fell away as I finished the passage and I lowered the book.

"Ben, what is it?" Rachel asked.

"The passage I just read...it's Sam who needs our prayers. Not me. She is the one near death."

"Romans says: *"We do not know what we ought to pray for, but the Spirit himself intercedes for us with groans that words cannot express."*

"I'm sorry Rachel," I remarked. "I respect your deep devotion to the Bible but my love lies helpless and dying; yet all I am armed with are...are mere words!"

Rachel placed her right hand on my right arm. "Ben, before God can hear you, He must believe you! You must believe in yourself and have faith in God! The Book appears as only words to the unbelievers. It's not magic Ben...it's faith," she proclaimed and gently lifted my right arm, bringing it to my chest with my open palm pressed against my beating heart. "It's what's in here," she emphasized tapping my palm against my chest. "You must open your heart. Paul says: '...the righteousness of God is revealed...by faith."

I sighed and turned the pages of the book randomly until I found the words of John and read aloud. *"Let not your hearts be troubled. Believe in God; believe also in me."*

"Ben," Rachel called out softly. "What are you feeling?"

"What am I feeling? What do you mean?"

"When you read those words, what is it that moves you?"

"I...I don't know. I respect them; but I'm not sure that I feel anything?"

"Ask God to help Samantha."

"Yes...of course," I replied and began leafing through the Bible in search of the right prayer.

Suddenly Rachel reached out and placed her left hand on the book, preventing my continued search. "Do not use the Book. Ask him with your heart," she encouraged with a delicate smile. "There are two types of prayers—guided with the words of scripture, and spontaneous prayer; but your spontaneity must be sincere and genuine."

I sighed and closed my eyes.

"Benjamin," she called out and I opened my eyes. "Ask him aloud, in front of me."

I nodded and paused to gather my thoughts. "Dear Lord...I ask for your assistance in saving our dear friend...and my love, Samantha Kerstland. She is in a grave situation and I fear that without your assistance..."

"Benjamin," Rachel interrupted. "What are you feeling?"

"To be honest with you, Rachel, I'm feeling frustrated by your constant interruptions."

"I'm sorry, Ben. But you need to be real. Your response seems rehearsed like you have repeated it over and over again in your head a thousand times."

"I'm confused..."

"What are you feeling?!" Rachel pressed, no longer with a delicate tone but a biting one that began to probe my soul.

I became restless from Rachel's line of questioning and no longer felt comfortable in a sitting position. I needed to stand and so I arose from my chair and paced back and forth with small steps. "I feel...I feel lost, Rachel."

"Talk to God, Ben."

I frowned and lifted my head to the ceiling. "Lord..." I began.

"Ben," Rachel interrupted again with a comforting smile. "Why do you look to the ceiling? Don't imagine God is above us and a thousand miles away. Speak to Him as you would to me here in this room, for He is here with you! In fact Benjamin, He is closer to you than I am to you seated in this room, for He is inside you! Open your heart!"

My frustration with Rachel began to wane and I suddenly appreciated my friend's guidance, for at that moment I felt deep admiration for her spiritual wisdom. I took a deep breath, returned the smile, and began to pray with spontaneity and with genuine feelings—expounding feelings that I would not have associated with prayer, but rather the words associated with a personal interaction.

"I feel lost dear Lord...abandoned," I began. "My heart aches for Samantha...she doesn't deserve to die!" I paused to look down at Rachel who nodded affirmatively, encouraging me to continue. "If anyone should be punished, it tis I. I have allowed my fear to bring the people close to me in contact with dark forces," I continued, thinking of Caleb now, as well as Rachel; although in my sudden explosion of prayer I was careful not to reveal too much of my relationship with Eblis, aware that Rachel was not privy to much of that chapter of my life. Suddenly I was without words.

"I sense anger," Rachel interjected softly, filling the void of silence.

I thought for a moment. "I am angry...my love lies dying," I replied, now filled with grief again at the thought of Samantha. "I want to believe in You my Lord...for I know I need You!" I exclaimed, directing my thoughts back to God. "If there is anything I could to do to bring Samantha back to this world and end her steady decline, please show me what it may be! Dear Lord! I am at your command!"

My talk with God grew more impassioned and personal as dusk set over the Goode residence and I sensed that Rachel was satisfied with the direction my praying had gone; for she didn't interrupt again until informing me that Dinah had prepared dinner. She invited me to stay for dinner and through the night, although I thought it best to return home to Jamesina so as not to worry her. But I returned the next day and the day after to pray with Rachel. We would begin our prayer session by taking turns reading from the Bible before offering our spontaneous prayers. When I finished I would set out on horseback to Samantha's grandfather's farm to spend the remainder of the day at her side. The doctor assumed that since my love's unconscious state prevented her from eating or drinking, it was only a matter of time before she expired. So I continued to pray and hope.

In praying alongside Rachel over the course of those two days, for the first time in all the prayer sessions I had shared with Rachel, I felt alive—reenergized—as if a dark corner of my soul had suddenly been illuminated. But more than anything else, I found the inner peace that enveloped me to be the most exhilarating aspect of my spiritual journey, and I hungered for more solitude conversations with God as my appetite for such reverent discourse became insatiable. And I still hoped and prayed for a miracle.

On the third day since I had begun my prayer sessions, I arrived at the farm after spending part of the morning praying with Rachel in Swampscott. Although prayer had brought me much inner strength, I feared the worst when I entered the bedroom and approached Samantha's bedside. My presence had afforded Sam's parents the opportunity to take pause from their vigil and exit the bedroom, leaving me alone with my love. The sight of her resting motionless on her back in the same position since the moment she had been brought into the room, appeared to me as a fate so unjust for an individual who, from the moment I had first met her, pulsated with an endless supply of energy. I reached down and laid the palm of my left hand over top of her left hand and dropped to my knees at the bedside. Gently I released my grip and lifted my hand from hers and brought it together with my right hand interlocking my fingers in prayer as I shut my eyes and began to pray silently.

Suddenly a soft voice uttered, "I love you." My heart raced as I was certain I had heard another voice speaking to me and with my eyes still closed I tried to identify the voice. *Was this the voice of God...or of an angel?* I thought perhaps I had imagined it when to my amazement I heard it again. "I love you," the voice repeated. I opened my eyes and to my astonishment I saw Samantha with her head turned in my direction. Her eyes were opened and she smiled. "Ben, I am thirsty," she added with a parched, weak voice.

I jumped to my feet, bending over to slide my arms around her shoulders and back so as to gently lift her upper body. I pulled her toward me in a gentle embrace and we kissed softly, before I carefully lowered her back onto the bed.

"Ben, my head hurts and I feel so stiff," she said raising her right arm and bringing her hand to her forehead.

"Sam, you've been unconscious for days!!"

Sam seemed surprised by the revelation. "It's as if I have been dreaming. I could hear voices...my mother and father...and yours Ben. It was so comforting," Sam uttered with a strained voice.

"Water...I will get you water!" I remembered, jumping up and hurrying from the room. My quick exit alarmed the Kerstlands who were seated in the adjacent parlor.

"Ben! What is it?!" Emery Kerstland gasped, rising to his feet.

Still trying to grasp the stunning development, I stopped and gazed at Samantha's father with what I'm sure was a dumbfounded expression. "She needs water!"

Kerstland looked confused. "What?! Who?! Samantha??!"

"Yes! Yes! She is awake!!" I announced with excitement.

Samantha's parents and grandparents burst by me like the wind as they made their way toward the bedroom where Sam lay and I hurriedly rushed to retrieve some water from the well.

The remainder of the afternoon was filled with immense joy and happiness as the farmhouse came alive with praise and thanksgiving. Sam seemed to grow stronger as the day progressed and I found I couldn't take my eyes off of her, which she acknowledged several times with a playful scolding.

Before too long the day had slipped away from us and soon dusk began to settle in on the farmhouse. Reluctantly I bid everyone good-night as I needed to return to my aunt's house at a late hour; but I did not leave before giving Sam a long, tender kiss on the lips filled with a passion that reflected my deep appreciation for her and for life in general.

I set out on horseback for Lynn realizing the need to share the wonderful news with Rachel and to thank her as well for giving me the strength through faith and prayer to cope with Samantha's fate; but as the sunset quickened I knew the good news for Rachel could wait until the morning. Yet there was one other to thank and that couldn't wait. As I reached the edge of the farm property, I brought my mare to a stop and gazed out at the fiery horizon of the clear sky at dusk just about the tree line and I prayed, thanking the Lord for His intercession in the day's blessed events.

CHAPTER 38

oston – October, 1774

B It had been one month since Samantha's accident and her recovery was nothing short of remarkable as she exhibited no lingering effects from her head injury. Thus I agreed to accompany Sam and her sister Muriel to Boston one bright and chilly Saturday afternoon in late October so that they might enjoy a few hours of shopping in the busy port city, in preparation for Muriel's spring wedding. The crowded roads were bustling with throngs of people moving with purpose up and down the cobblestoned city streets, negotiating fellow pedestrians and horse drawn carriages as was customary for a Saturday in autumn.

Not wanting to be dragged about the multitudes of shops in tow of two women who have the compulsion to explore every good or ware that is within sight, I bid my female companions goodbye and set out on a mission myself; for I decided to drop by Davern's shop and say hello to my friend and former employer. I left the ladies to shop on Beacon Street and headed toward Kings Street—the location of Davern's shop.

As I traversed the narrow thoroughfare of Kings Street, I found myself in front of the Massachusetts State House when, from my vantage point across the street, I recognized a familiar stature climbing the stone steps toward the front door of the government building. I stopped to gaze at the figure who wore a long dark coat and a circular wide brimmed hat and as if he had eyes in the back of his head, he stopped his ascent on the stairs and slowly turned in my direction. Our eyes met and he flashed that sinister grin; for it was Eblis. *What was he doing at the State House?* The demon tipped his wide brimmed hat in my direction, turned and continued his movement until he disappeared inside the front door.

I gathered my composure and resumed my walk; although my thoughts were now preoccupied with Eblis. The sight of the demon unnerved me and my imagination began to spin wild speculation on what sinister purpose might have brought him to the seat of Massachusetts government, when suddenly I found that I had arrived at the door of Davern's shop. My thoughts had been so consumed by Eblis that it was though my feet found their way to my former residence without the assistance of my head. But I was disappointed to learn that Davern happened to be out of town that day visiting a friend in Winchester, and so I stood outside the shop for a few minutes gazing at the flurry of pedestrians clad in their drab colored garments broken on occasion by the bright red uniform coat of a British regular. As I pondered my next move I became enthralled by a conversation between two elderly men standing in front of me. Their age was reflected by their raised voices bespeaking of poor hearing and I had no trouble picking up the dialogue that centered on news of the Continental Congress in Philadelphia which had dominated the gossip of Lynn's shoemaker shops in recent weeks. The old men's discourse revealed that the Congress had adjourned this past week with a pledge to work toward a peaceful resolution with the Crown; but at the same time it called on the colonies to continue their boycott of British goods and warned colonial militias to be prepared to defend their towns should violence erupt.

The old men finished their conversation and when they parted ways moving in opposite directions, my eyes became focused on the tavern across the street where I had once met Nigel Higgins—the expert in the origins of names—and I wondered if by chance I could find him again. I crossed the street, entering the sparsely crowded establishment and just inside the doorway I stood peering about the patrons brooding over their tankards of ale as if it were an elixir, before I spotted Higgins seated alone at the same corner table where I had first laid eyes on him.

I moved directly to the bar, purchased a glass of rum which I carried with me over to the table where Higgins was seated, and before he could raise his head in my direction, I placed the glass down in front of him. He stared at it for a moment before reaching for it—as a rat goes for a piece of cheese—placing his right hand around the glass just as I brought my right palm down over the rim of the glass, holding it steadfast to the table.

Higgins lifted his bloodshot eyes to me. "You look familiar," he blurted.

"Benjamin Pratt," I reintroduced. "We've done business before."

"Hmmm..." Higgins replied pulling his hand away from the glass which I still covered with my palm. "Then you will remember it is four names for a bottle of rum."

"It was three before," I replied quickly. "So you cheated me out of a name the last time we met?"

The rosy cheeked man chuckled, which produced a slight cough. "So this here beautiful glass of rum is for one name?"

"It is."

"All right man, I am in a good mood today. What's the name?" he surrendered.

"Malik."

"Malik?" Higgins repeated with a quizzical frown. "I must admit, Malik is a name I have not heard before."

I slid the fingers of my right hand around the glass of rum and lifted it from the table, causing Higgins to eye it as though it were an expensive jewel.

"Then I guess our business here is concluded," I said.

"Hold on now...so quick to give up," Higgins remarked. He reached inside his ruffled jacket and from an inside breast pocket he pulled out a tattered, yellowish pamphlet, placing it down on the table before him. "Sometimes I need a little help," he added with a grin and began leafing through the pamphlet, running his index finger up and down the lines of ink as he moved from page to page. "Yes...here it is. Malik."

"Go on," I encouraged eagerly.

"Malik...it looks to be the name given to a Persian or Egyptian male and means King. In Arabic it is referred to as al-Malik meaning The King and Lord of the Worlds."

"Lord of the Worlds—worlds plural?"

"Yes, worlds. Wait there is something else here under Malik," Higgins revealed. "There is another meaning. According to the Quran —the Mulsim Holy Book—Malik is referred to as the wicked angel who guards the gates of hell."

I was speechless and slowly set the glass of rum down on the table in front of Higgins.

Higgins quickly retrieved the glass and raised it, bringing the rum near his lips, pausing. "I hope this Malik isn't a friend of yours?" he warned, throwing back the rum.

Just after dusk that Saturday, Muriel, Sam, and I returned to Lynn, and after dropping the two sisters off at the Kerstland residence, I continued on to my aunt's home. As I unhitched the horse from the chaise and secured the beast for the night in the small stable behind the house, my thoughts were deeply troubled by the meaning of the name Malik and confounded by why Eblis and Darcie had used the name with Caleb.

I hurried inside to bring my cousin the news of the name's meaning and immediately found Jamesina seated on a rocking chair in front of the burning hearth. She rocked slowly and steadily back and forth knitting from a large ball of red yarn that rested in her lap, and appeared very much at ease, humming as she worked the yarn into the shape of a sock with two long needles.

"How did you and the sisters enjoy Boston today?" she asked acknowledging my presence with a glance and a warm smile before returning to the task at hand.

"It was a lovely day, Aunt Jamesina; although I cannot understand a woman's obsession with exploring every item for sale. It's exhausting."

Jamesina chuckled.

"Is Caleb in his room?" I asked.

Jamesina ceased her rocking and needlework and raised her head in my direction. "Did he not tell you?"

"Tell me what?"

"He's left today for Connecticut."

"He's returned to his congregation in Simsbury?" I asked.

"No. He's bound for New Haven. He's been reassigned to the Second Congregational Church there. The new congregation will be closer for him. I was certain he would have told you; for he's been accepted to Yale's Board of Governors."

My stomach turned.

"It seems that a vacancy appeared on the board after an unfortunate accident took the life of one of its members. Poor soul. Caleb received the letter last week."

I remained speechless.

CHAPTER 39

ecember, 1774
It had been two months since last I had seen or heard from my cousin when one mid-December afternoon I retrieved the mail from the post rider and was surprised to find a letter from Caleb. The correspondence was brief and asked simply that I travel to New Haven to visit him, emphasizing that it was a matter of urgency. Aside from the brevity of the letter, the other clue into my cousin's distressed state of mind was his penmanship—for his letters always exemplified a beautiful, meticulous writing style; but the scraggly penmanship in his latest correspondence reflected a painful, unsteady hand.

I asked Master Kerstland for a few days off from work and started out on horseback southwest toward Springfield by way of the Old Bay Road. The journey was slow, hampered by a frosty December chill in the air; although the rural landscape proved picturesque with a forest blanketed by a recent light snowfall. The farther one traveled west of Boston and the Atlantic seaboard, the more desolate the frontier, and aside from several stray farms, I encountered few dwellings on the road until reaching the banks of the Connecticut River, where a great many mills of all varieties began to appear strategically located to harness the power of the river. The appearance of this industrial activity indicated that I neared the village of Springfield.

Arriving in Springfield at dusk, I was eager to find lodging for the evening in order to rest and continue the remainder of my journey to New Haven in the daylight of the following day. The lone establishment was the Prosser Inn, a brick structure trimmed in wood and painted white, located on the outskirts of the village. I checked into my room on the second floor and returned to the taproom, which was located adjacent to the front parlor with the intent of grabbing a bite to eat aside the warmth of the large hearth. Finding myself alone in the taproom, I retired to a small circular table near the burning fireplace, having just ordered food and a tankard of ale from a pleasant woman who I assumed was Mrs. Prosser, when suddenly a man burst in through the doorway.

The thin stranger appeared to be a man of medium height with ruby hair resembling the color of scotch, pulled back from his forehead and tied into a ponytail with a ribbon at the back of his head. With a flushed face he breathed heavily and quickly glanced about the room before approaching in my direction, and oddly without saying a word he plopped down in the other seat across from me at my table. I was very surprised by his actions, considering that I had not given him any semblance of an invitation to dine with me, and by the fact that there were a number of empty tables at his disposal.

"Excuse my interruption but I haven't time to explain," he uttered quickly. "Your name?"

"Benjamin Pratt."

At that moment, two British regulars stepped through the doorway. From my position at the table I faced them and they stopped and threw a suspicious glare in my direction.

"And so that is how it all ended, Benjamin!" the stranger seated across from me suddenly blurted out. "Interesting story would you not say?"

I realized what he was doing and decided to play along. "Yes...quite a tale."

"I must introduce you to her sometime," the stranger continued.

The British regulars slowly approached the table and stopped beside it.

"Samuel Adams?" one of the soldiers called out.

The stranger looked up. "Can I help you?" he asked.

I stirred with excitement at the revelation of the stranger's identity but was sure to maintain a stoic demeanor.

"Can you account for your whereabouts this morning?" the soldier pressed Adams.

"Well...I was travelling with my friend," Adams lied extending his hand outwards toward me.

"The Prosser woman says that only one of you has a room here at the inn for the night," the soldier countered.

"We have only just arrived," Adams explained. "We are both famished and decided to eat first before procuring a room," he added before looking at me. "Benjamin, did you not wait for me and get yourself a room already?"

"Yes...I misunderstood," I obliged.

Adams chuckled. "I was outside relieving myself at the privy pit. It was a long ride and when you have to go...well..."

The soldier studied Adams suspiciously before focusing on me. "And what is your story? Have you been travelling with this man?"

"Why...yes," I stammered. "It is as Samuel has described. My friend and I have been on the road all day," I interrupted. "We are bound for New Haven and I have procured a room for the evening."

"And you are?" the soldier inquired, now with an incriminating grin.

"Benjamin Pratt."

"Where is your home?" the soldier continued.

"Lynn, Massachusetts. I am a shoemaker in the employ of Emery Kerstland."

"Edward Rallings, a tax collector from Enfield was attacked this afternoon...tarred and feathered," the soldier described sternly. "He identified Sam Adams as the attacker. Benjamin Pratt, if you are lying about your relationship to this man, then in protecting a criminal, you are committing a crime yourself," the soldier threatened and waited for my response.

Adams said nothing and gazed at me with a sympathetic glare. I could sense the tension and desperation emitting from a man whose fate I held with my next response. I rose to my feet and stared the soldier in the eyes. "I tell you the truth that Samuel Adams is a friend of mine and we have been travelling together today. I feel badly for this Rallings fellow, but it's wrong for people to spout the name of Sam Adams with each act of stupidity against the Crown. Samuel and I certainly do not agree on politics, but our friendship is stronger than that. I swear to you that you accuse the wrong man in this incident."

The soldier studied my facial expression for a moment and apparently satisfied that I spoke the truth, nodded. "Very well," he remarked. "My advice to you, Benjamin Pratt, is to be wary of what friends you make." The soldier reached up with his right hand and touching the front of his tricorn, he tipped the hat in my direction and turned, giving a scowl at Adams, who, with head down, never returned the look.

The two soldiers exited the taproom and Adams and I remained silent. From my vantage point I could see out the front window and continued to stand at the table, watching as the soldiers mounted their horses and galloped away.

"They've gone," I said.

Adams looked up at me from the table and smiled. "You were very good, Benjamin Pratt," he said with a wily smile. "I admire your courage. I owe you."

"Did you tar and feather that Rallings fellow?"

Adams shook his head. "No. I was present, but there were others who performed the act."

I shook my head in shame, realizing how close I had come to being hanged. "Well, I must admit that even though I question your actions as a rebel, I am excited to meet you," I acknowledged as I returned to a sitting position. "Your defiant acts against the Crown have made you legendary; but I fear that you and your Sons of Liberty are playing a dangerous game."

"These are dangerous times," Adams countered with a smirk. "So you're bound for New Haven?" he asked, quickly changing the topic. "What attracts you to the port city?"

"My cousin. He is a minister there."

Adams' facial expression grew more quizzical with my response. "A minister? What is his name?"

"He is a minister of the Second Congregational Church. His name is Caleb Brown."

Adams sat back in his chair and his jaw dropped. "Caleb Brown? What a coincidence this is, for I have just come from the meeting-house in New Haven for the Second Congregational Church and have just met with Caleb Brown!"

I was stunned. "How do you know my cousin?!"

"We have...similar interests," Adams replied, choosing his response carefully.

"Similar interests?" I repeated. "Such as harassing the British in New England?! He is a member of the Sons of Liberty, isn't he?!"

"No, Benjamin. I assure you he is not. He is indeed very concerned about the political climate within New England and his wisdom has been instrumental in guiding those of us who want to see change; but he is not a member of the Sons."

"But he is part of the rebellion?!"

"Benjamin, the rebellion runs much deeper than just a group of men harassing British tax collectors. There are many roles to play. As for your cousin's role, I cannot say any more about this subject. I'm sorry."

"I had always sensed that Caleb was somehow involved in the rebellion," I revealed with a discouraging tone. "He is quite passionate about it."

"He is a courageous man, your cousin; but I am worried about him."

"How so?"

"His health, Benjamin. He is not well. He maintains that there is nothing wrong with him; but I beg to differ. He looks like he has aged quite a bit in a short period of time and that fiery spark that once gleamed from his eyes has gone out."

I was worried. *The urgent tone of Caleb's letter and his unsteady penmanship. Something is wrong.*

"I hope you find him in better health," Adams added rising from the table.

"You're leaving?"

"I had better procure that room, Ben," Adams said. "And I need some rest for I plan to be miles from Springfield before the sun rises."

I stood up and shook Adams' hand as he thanked me again for my ruse and bid me farewell before exiting the taproom.

JUST AFTER SUNRISE THE FOLLOWING MORNING, I ATE A WARM breakfast, with no sign of Adams, and left the Prosser Inn to continue my journey south on the Old Bay Road toward New Haven. Within a few hours I had reached my destination and it didn't take long for me to locate the meeting-house of the Second Congregational Church. The structure was a large, almost square-shaped building, painted white, with a steeped pitch roof running east to west. I did not know the address of a residence for Caleb for he had only given me the address to the meeting-house so I was hopeful to find him inside. After dismounting and hitching my mare to a hitching post outside of the building, I found a door on the western side of the meeting-house to be open and I stepped inside.

The large room in the interior was sectioned by box pews—square-shaped pews encased in paneling about five feet in height. Each box had a door and a smooth wooden bench positioned on two adjacent sides of a pew. A balcony hung over the box pews on the east, south, and west walls and a high pulpit was located on the north wall. The air was cool inside the building as a result of the December weather and a great number of glass windows allowed the rays of sunlight to illuminate the meeting-house. Sections of box pews were separated by narrow aisles, and believing I was alone inside the building, I began to pace about the aisles as though I were navigating a maze.

Suddenly I heard a human cough and stopped in my tracks to look about, but I could see no-one. "Hello?" I called out. Again I heard a cough. "Caleb?"

At the end of the aisle where I stood, a door to a box pew opened and a head appeared. "Ben? Is that you?" I recognized my cousin's voice and quickly resumed my pace, arriving at the box pew where I found Caleb seated alone, with both elbows at rest on his thighs and staring at the floor.

"Shouldn't you be in the pulpit?" I asked jokingly.

Caleb slowly raised his head and it was then that I could see what Adams had described. My cousin's disheveled shoulder-length hair was uncharacteristically untied at the back and hung down around a somber pale face, partially hidden beneath a scraggly dark beard. His glassy bloodshot eyes glared back at me with dark circles beneath each and my cousin's usually disciplined, stylish attire had given way to drabbed, rumpled clothing.

"I believe the pulpit is the last place I should be..." Caleb replied with a raspy, tired voice.

I sat down next to Caleb. "Cousin, what is it?! You don't look well!"

"I am not well," he answered before coughing again. "That is why I have asked you to see me, Ben. I am dying and I feel the need to bare my conscience to you. For I'm afraid that before too long the person you once knew will have vanished forever."

"What are you saying?! Are you ill?!"

"I have a malady that is incurable, I'm afraid," he explained with a defeated tone to his words. "I am losing my grip on reality and sanity. In the process, I am losing my soul. I am possessed, and with each passing day I sense a dark presence enveloping me, devouring me. Every day a little piece of the man you knew as your cousin dies," he described before coughing.

"What do you mean possessed?! Possessed by what...demons?!"

"Possessed with evil," Caleb replied grimly. "The pleasures and joys of life...my devotion to God and His church—they are gone. I have become an empty shell. My thoughts are now consumed by despair and a desire for vengeance."

"Vengeance for what?!"

"For life! My life has all been a clever ruse!"

"What has changed you?! It was the meeting with Eblis back in September, was it not?! The night at the cove!"

"Yes..." he said with disdain.

"When the two of you disappeared, where did Eblis take you?!"

"On a walk through time," Caleb remembered. He coughed again and took a deep breath. "I witnessed my birth...born during a witch's coven! Benjamin my mother..." he paused to find strength. "My mother was Bridget Campbell!"

"Bridget Campbell?" I repeated, not recognizing the name.

"Remember the name on the grave marker in the cemetery near my father's plot?! The name in my nightmare—Bridget Campbell!"

"What?! This is madness! What do you mean when you say you saw your birth at a witch's coven?!"

"Bridget Campbell...my mother...was a witch?! My given name that night was Malik!"

Malik...the wicked demon who guards hell. "No! It can't be true!"

"I am a bastard child—the illegitimate son of a demon who impregnated Campbell!" Caleb continued. "I tell you I was born during a witch's coven and during the birth my mother died! Eblis showed me this! I witnessed it as if I were there in person!"

"What you say is lunacy! Caleb you're delusional! It is clear that the strain of your new position on the Board of Yale and your devotion to your congregation is taking its toll on you! Not to mention your involvement with the rebels..."

"Rebels?"

"I met Sam Adams. He told me that you advise his rebel group!"

Caleb paused for a moment and stared beyond me. "Yes...my connection to the rebellion is important for the dark one." Suddenly my cousin appeared to be racked by pain as he gripped the sides of his head with both hands and leaned forward facing the floor. He grimaced before letting out a deep moan.

"Caleb! What is it?!"

My cousin remained hunched over, staring at the floor and breathing heavily. "He reminds me of who's in control," Caleb replied with a strained voice.

"Who is *he*?!"

"The dark one..." Caleb revealed with exasperation. "Ben, let me explain to you how I was able to acquire that position on the Board of Governors," he said, sitting upright and raising his head to look me in the eyes. "The vacancy opened after the sudden death of a member. In witnessing the dark powers of Eblis that night back in September, I realized that my Christian faith was no match for his wickedness. At that moment I had given up and I allowed my ego to impede my judgment, promising Eblis that should a vacancy open on the board, I would accept the position only if he pledged to stop preying upon the villagers of Lynn."

"You lied to me! You told me you had not made a deal with the demon!"

"Yes. I lied. I have lied to many men over the past several months!"

I felt anger but it was tempered by a deeper concern for my cousin's well-being. "But Caleb, the vacancy on the Board of Governors was mere coincidence!"

Caleb shook his head. "I'm afraid not, Ben. The board member's heart stopped beating in the presence of a cat whipper. He was purchasing new shoes, Ben! And I've learned the cat whipper was Eblis!"

I was stunned. "It is unbelievable!"

"Believe it!" Caleb growled. "It is true! Look at me, Ben! I am no longer your cousin...I was never really your cousin! After my birth, I was left in the forest to be found by Edward Brown, and raised in the Brown household as a Christian! My rapid ascendency in the ministry has been orchestrated by demons! It has all been a diabolic demonic plot!"

"But why?! Why does Eblis want you on the Board of Yale?"

"The board has influence! Eblis is seeking to extend his reach using me as his vehicle!"

"Vehicle for what?!"

"There is a revolution brewing! There will be war and death! It breaks the commandment *Thou Shall Not Kill*! There will be many souls for the taking on both sides!"

Suddenly my cousin grimaced and cried out in pain again. His eyes rolled back in his head and he shook violently before collapsing onto his side, sprawled across the bench. Instinctively I dropped to my knees and bent over to look him in the face that appeared jaundice, drenched with perspiration, and I placed my hands on each of his shoulders shaking him. "Caleb! Caleb! Caleb!" I called out. My cousin opened his glassy, bloodshot eyes, producing a long ghastly moan as though he were a wounded animal and I pulled him into a sitting position and shook him some more. "Caleb, you must resign from the board and return to Lynn with me!" My cousin moaned again and closed his eyes, breathing heavily. "Caleb, you must resign..." I started to repeat.

"I heard you Ben," my cousin replied, slowly opening his eyes. "It matters not anymore, for I am a product of a demon seed! I am changing with each passing day! My destiny has been forged for me and soon I will be Malik and Caleb will be gone!" my cousin forewarned, dropping his head in a display of humiliation.

"No! There must be something that can be done!" My pain for Caleb's suffering had given way to intense anger and I rose to my feet. "I will not stand by and watch as Eblis destroys everything I have loved! The demon has used me as well, as a means to get to you! Don't you see cousin, if all is as hopeless as you say, why didn't Eblis go directly to you?! He made contact with you through me!"

"What is your point?" Caleb asked listlessly.

"My point is that you had changed! You may have been the product of a demon seed, but your upbringing and Christian faith allowed you to move away from your wicked roots...it has given you armor to fight that which is evil! Eblis could not break through that armor without help...without me!"

Caleb thought for a moment and shook his head. "No, Ben. Don't blame yourself. Save yourself!" He reached up and grabbed hold of my left arm and gripped it tightly. "There may be a way to defeat Eblis... and to protect yourself from me as well."

"What are you saying?! I am not going to destroy you!"

"Listen to me!" he growled. "When I am no longer Caleb, I may be a threat to you! You must protect yourself!" he exclaimed, pausing to be certain he had my attention.

"Go on..." I replied with deep sadness.

"Do you remember the Englishman I told you about...Graeme Barnett?"

"Yes...vaguely."

"I have recently received correspondence from Barnett. He is arriving in the colonies to visit friends in February and has promised me that he will look you up. He does not know my situation...I have told no-one what I have told you today. But I am convinced that if there is anyone who may have a method to protect you from this evil that grows and surrounds you, it is he," Caleb explained with intensity. "Promise me you will meet with him!"

I sat back down in the pew and looked my cousin square in the eyes. "I promise...cousin," I replied and embraced Caleb with both arms. "Caleb...I love you!"

CHAPTER 40

ynn – February, 1775

L Christmas and New Years had passed without much celebration. In fact the traditional peacefully-crafted Christmas message delivered from the pulpit of the meeting-house was laced with angry references to British meddling in the affairs of American lives. It appeared as though the days of lengthy God-fearing sermons and celebratory holiday gatherings were but memories now, and the rhetoric of conflict on both sides of the Atlantic, coupled with the presence of British regulars in New England, foretold of an ominous aura to the coming New Year.

Caleb did not return home for the holidays, which I certainly understood; but his absence brought much disappointment to Jamesina. I did make certain that she was welcomed into the Kerstland home on Christmas Day where I spent time with Samantha and her family. Although plagued with guilt, I did not want to worry my aunt about Caleb's condition or predicament, and so I refrained from revealing to her the conversation I had with my cousin back in New Haven. In fact I told no-one.

As for my mother, Samantha and I did journey to Falmouth for a few days to spend some portion of the holiday with her. She and her Aidan appeared happy and content and my mother clearly seemed thrilled with my new love as well. On our return journey from Falmouth we spent a day with Rachel, exchanging gifts and pleasantries with our good friend who revealed her father's holiday plans to take Rachel with him to Europe for a few months—they were to return to Swampscott in April.

While the Kerstland family began planning for Muriel's spring time wedding, the love between Samantha and myself continued to develop and I made certain to thank the Lord for her recovery with each passing day. Now I found myself praying deeply for my cousin as well. God had answered my prayers with Samantha, but I knew that Caleb's condition called for extraordinary measures and I wondered if God was up to the task.

My steady employment with Kerstland and the growth of my relationship with Samantha painted a portrait of a stable world full of wonderful possibilities for me...on the outside; but on the inside I was still very much tormented because of the recent developments with Caleb and his connection with Eblis. I believed beyond a doubt that the demon had used me to get to my cousin, and I realized time was running out before Caleb would be completely consumed by evil. He needed my help but I needed assistance, and so I anxiously awaited the arrival of Graeme Barnett.

I told Sam nothing of my concern for Caleb or my anticipation of the arrival of the Englishman; but she knew me all too well and could sense that something bothersome preoccupied me. I continued to reassure her that it was nothing, which added to the burden of my guilt.

The month of January seemed to last a year and then February came, but each passing day brought no sign of the Englishman. I began to wonder if Graeme Barnett really existed. *Maybe the Englishman had changed his mind about traveling to the colonies or perhaps the threat of conflict had forced him to reconsider such travel? Maybe it was the evil persona of my cousin trying to keep me hoping futilely for someone who did not exist, while Caleb slowly died? Was I being used again?*

Midway through the month, colonial gossip began to spread news that the British Parliament had declared the colony of Massachusetts to be in a state of rebellion, and on the twenty-sixth of the month, British forces landed at Salem in an attempt to capture the arsenal there but were repulsed by a large crowd without any casualties.

It was on the following afternoon, the twenty-seventh of February —just as I was beginning to give up hope that Barnett actually existed

—when a slender man, with average height walked into Kerstland's shop from out of the frigid cold. He wore a long gray wool coat and a dark tricorn set atop a white periwig that formed a ponytail in the back that hung down past his shoulders and was tied by a large black bow. A round pair of spectacles rested half-way down a long pointed nose and his weathered, but clean-shaven face appeared very angular, traversed with many wrinkles that told me he must have been at least three decades older than I.

The stranger found me alone in the shop, sitting at a work bench working with my awl and a pair of leather soles that I had pressed against a lasting jack. "Good afternoon," I welcomed.

"Good day to you," he replied with a strong English accent that piqued my interest. "I am seeking a fellow by the name of Pratt."

"I am he," I replied eagerly.

"And who is your cousin?"

"Caleb Brown."

"Then I have found the right man. I am Graeme Barnett."

With excitement I rose from the bench and quickly approached Barnett with my right hand extended. "It is a pleasure to meet you," I announced as the Englishman politely took my hand.

Barnett returned the handshake but said nothing. He looked me over carefully, studying me as though he were a teacher evaluating his pupil.

"I was beginning to doubt you would come," I added.

He chuckled. "It seems as though I have been riding on horseback in this wretched weather all day."

"Where are you staying?"

"In Concord," Barnett replied. "Is there some place we can go that has privacy?"

"We are alone here at the moment."

"Yes...but we may have much to discuss and it needs to be completed without interruption," he described glancing around the shop. "This is a business establishment and it appears to be attached to a home, so I am guessing we may not be alone for long."

"Very true. *Newhall's Tavern* is several blocks from here and there are rooms that are used for private gatherings," I enlightened. "It's midday so I am guessing such a room should be available."

"Splendid. I shall give you some time to clean up and get your operation here in order. Shall we meet at the tavern, say, in one hour?"

"Yes. I will meet you there."

I ARRIVED AT THE TAVERN AT THE AGREED UPON TIME AND QUICKLY located Barnett who found a semi-private room in the back of the establishment. The small windowless area had a doorway with no door attached and was enclosed by four walls. I joined Barnett, sitting down opposite him at a circular wooden table that was large enough for four patrons, and from our vantage point through the open doorway we could see the bar counter that set aside the large burning hearth located across the tavern. Soon the proprietor, Talbot Newhall, arrived at our table and we exchanged salutations as he illuminated a candle at our table and brought us two tankards of ale. After the tavern owner retreated from the room, Barnett and I raised our tankards and clanked them together. "Cheers," the Englishman called out and with the toast each of us took a gulp of the beverage before returning our mugs to the table.

I took a moment to examine the Englishman who had removed his long wool coat and tricorn, and was now fussing with the tight sleeves of a fine pale wool jacket with turned down collar. He ran his fingers delicately along the narrow silver braid of the jacket, and once satisfied that he was comfortable, sat back in his chair and lifted his eyes to me.

"This is my first time in America," Barnett explained leaning forward in his chair. "And the timing of my arrival seems to have been somewhat ill-conceived with such tensions running high in the colonies. I am surprised by the great number of the King's soldiers in the city of Boston. It looks like a war zone."

"It may soon be a war zone," I countered.

"Hmmm...yes, let's hope not," Barnett commented and sat back in his chair. "So tis you who battles a demon...aye?"

"May I ask you, when exactly did my cousin write you?"

"I believe it twas in September. Why do you ask? Has your demon suddenly disappeared? It is often the case, you know."

"What do you mean?" I inquired, somewhat taken back by the statement.

"What I mean is that most of the troubled souls who seek out my advice in such matters as the occult find how suddenly there emerges an explanation for their strange goings on, or it is soon discovered that they are simply mad to begin with, and thus they end up wasting my time," Barnett enlightened with a cynical grin. "Of course, there have been those few incidents where I have happened upon a sincere individual with convincing physical and mental anguish bespeaking the torment that characterizes demonic possession, and I pity them," he said fussing with his tight sleeves again.

"Why do you pity them?"

Barnett sighed. "Because unfortunately they have become privy to the battle between good and evil. It is a battle that rages every day. For while most mankind moves through life in a haze, oblivious to what is really happening around them, these unfortunate souls are thrust into the heat of the conflict witnessing it firsthand," the Englishman divulged and leaned forward, peering at me with a wrinkled brow. "So tell me, young man, am I wasting my time with thee... or have you been chosen to receive my pity?"

"If so few of those who seek your advice waste your time, then why travel over three thousand miles across an ocean to see me?" I pried. "What makes you believe my demonic encounter to be true when we have never met or corresponded?"

Barnett chuckled. "You flatter yourself, Pratt. I have not ventured to this bloody continent for the sole purpose of establishing validity to your demonic tale. I have other reasons to be here in the colonies; however, I am indeed here in Lynn today to seek you out on behalf of your cousin. Caleb is a good man and I owe him a favor. If your cousin is convinced that there are demonic forces plaguing you, his word is good enough for me."

"And my cousin wrote to you this past September?"

"Yes...you seem obsessed with the timing of my last correspondence with Caleb?" Barnett questioned with a hint of frustration. "I apologize if it has taken me until now to reach you, but it takes time to get one's affairs in order before making a seven week journey across the Atlantic, and it indeed can be an expensive proposition as well. I have been here in the colonies for some time visiting family since my arrival. I'm sorry to say that your obsession with demons has not been a priority for me being here."

"No, the timing of your arrival is not an issue," I made clear. "I do appreciate you making an effort to seek me out while on your trip. I am only trying to understand when my cousin felt the most recent need to reach out to you. There was a troubling incident that occurred in August that Caleb has been dealing with, so the fact that he wrote to you in September tells me that his concerns for me occurred directly after the incident."

"I'm sorry to hear of this," Barnett offered earnestly. "I am here in the colonies for only a week longer and I had hoped to see Caleb."

"I'm afraid that may be impossible, for he is New Haven as we speak."

"I see," Barnett acknowledged. "How may I be of help to you? Benjamin, is it?"

I nodded.

"Then Benjamin, tell me your problem," Barnett encouraged and sat back in the chair with arms folded across his chest.

"As you are aware," I began, leaning forward with both of my arms resting on the table, "I have been—how did you put it—ah yes, privy. I have been privy to the battle between good and evil; for a demon has tormented me for some time. The situation is grave now and it is necessary that I destroy this demon once and for all. My cousin believes that you possess information on how I can finish this monster."

Barnett reached for his tankard of ale and brought it to his mouth, taking a gulp, before returning it to the table. "Benjamin, why do you feel as though the task of destroying this demon has become your responsibility?"

"Because I believe I may be the reason for its presence in Lynn. It has used me to get to Caleb."

"Explain what you mean by...*get to Caleb?*"

"I believe Caleb to be possessed and it is at the hand of this demon!" I revealed my tone now full of passion. "I suspect, as does Caleb, that my cousin's ministry has been the prize sought out by this dark creature! As a man of the cloth, Caleb's influence has a long reach across New England, especially in such rebellious times as these!"

Barnett said nothing for a moment and I sensed that he was still analyzing me and had yet to be convinced by my accusation. "I'm surprised to hear that you may believe Caleb to be possessed? Your cousin is such a strong pillar of piety," the Englishman announced. "His last letter to me did nothing to arouse any suspicions on my part. The topic of the letter focused solely on his concern for you and your demonic problem. He wrote nothing of himself. Granted, the letter was uncharacteristically short in length, but the tone did not seem out of the ordinary."

"Things have changed."

"Hmmm...perhaps I should alter my plans and make an effort to see your cousin?" Barnett pondered. "Your concerns about his demonic possession trouble me." The Englishman brought the hands of his right finger to his chin. "I am confused though. Why wouldn't Caleb ask to see me directly, if, as you say, he claims to be dealing with demonic possession himself?"

"He feels his situation is hopeless. He has told me this," I revealed.

"That is very sad," Barnett uttered.

"Caleb is tormented by the same demon which haunts me," I disclosed. "More the reason for me to destroy it!"

"Benjamin, this demon of yours...is it in human form?"

"It is. He calls himself Eblis—the name of a djinn."

"Ah yes," Barnett replied with raised eyebrows indicating he was impressed with my use of the tern for the demon. "I remember my conversation with Caleb. He did mention the name of Eblis—the most powerful djinn within Islamic mythology," Barnett recalled. "I imagine you are a Christian?"

I nodded.

"Is there anything unusual about the physical characteristics of Eblis? Any strange markings on his body that you know of?" Barnett asked.

I thought for a moment. "His eyes--one eye is blue and the other is brown."

"That is interesting," Barnett remarked. "Do you know why this demon—Eblis—is in Lynn?"

"In addition to what I have told you about using Caleb as an outlet to spread his wickedness, I believe he is stealing souls...as crazy as that may sound," I explained.

"Not crazy at all; although I find it interesting that you use the term steal."

"How do I stop him?!" I pressed anxious to learn what advice Barnett could give me. "I do not possess his powers! He could certainly strike me down in an instant! Caleb has told me that you may be wise in the ways of how to battle such dark forces!"

"I am only the messenger, Benjamin, and not the warrior," Barnett cautioned, "for I do not possess all the weapons that will be needed."

"What sort of weapons?"

"All in good time. Now, why do you suppose Eblis hasn't struck you down?"

"As I have said, he has used me to get to Caleb," I reminded him. "I have led my cousin down a dark road because of Eblis..." I added, and paused abruptly to avoid divulging the disturbing truth about my cousin's birth. I reached for the tankard of ale and took a swig, before continuing. "I have a debt to repay Caleb. I must destroy this demon and free my cousin, and myself, and lift the pall of evil that shrouds the town of Lynn!"

"It is quite a task," Barnett cautioned, hitting me with a dose of reality.

"Yes...and I am afraid that it may be impossible," I said with discouragement. "I have nothing to compete with the powers of Eblis."

Barnett leaned forward again and stared deeply into my eyes. "Do you have faith in God?"

"I believe in God. I know He saved the love of my life; but I will admit, my faith wavers."

Barnett sighed and removed the spectacles from his nose. "Then I am afraid I am wasting my time with you," he said leaning back in his chair again. He breathed on both sides of the glass spectacles and wiped them clean with a linen napkin. "Caleb gave me the impression that you would be stronger than what I am hearing from you. If what you have told me is true, then you are up against very dark and dangerous powers," he added placing the spectacles back on his nose. "One cannot do battle with such evilness without the proper armor. That armor Benjamin, is faith—deep, unwavering faith. There can be no room for doubt."

I grew irritated. "I tell you that I have known this demon for years! I have watched him suck the life out of Lynn and the demon grows more powerful with each passing season! Give me the weapons to fight Eblis and I promise you I will find faith! Even within the sinful village of Lynn, where faith is weakened; for it's as though God has abandoned the town! I have seen Eblis desecrate the inside of a meeting-house with his presence, unaffected by praise and worship of God!"

"Then the meeting-house you speak of must have been unclean—awash of sinners and bereft of true faith," Barnett reasoned.

"How can a house of God be unclean?"

"Because it is a house of the material god."

"I don't understand?"

"Of course not," Barnett responded callously. "Benjamin, show me your devotion to God, so that I may know that what I am about to reveal to you is not to be wasted."

"Show you? How can I show you?"

"Say a prayer for me. Recite your favorite Bible passage from memory—one that brings you the most peace and comfort."

"I am not convinced that merely reciting a prayer is an indication of faith!" I exclaimed, rapidly losing patience with Barnett. "A very good friend of mine recently taught me that prayer is a spontaneous conversation with God which is achieved through the heart and not only by the memorization of words! I opened my heart to God with my own words and He gave life to my love!" I explained and rose from my chair. "Perhaps it is *you* who have wasted *my* time!" I implied, beginning to doubt the credibility of the Englishman. "I don't understand how Caleb could have been wrong about you?! Rest assured that I will pray for your soul and I shall do it with a sincere conversation with God!"

"Sit down," Barnett demanded.

I looked at Barnett and scoffed.

"Sit...down...Benjamin," Barnett repeated with a slow annunciation of each word. Reluctantly I dropped back into the chair. "Your dramatic little display has convinced me, Benjamin. I sense a fire within you fueled by a faith waiting to be unleashed! You will need that fire to grow tenfold before encountering the demon! And I do admire the conviction behind your personal approach to prayer. I was merely testing you."

"Testing me?!" I exclaimed. "I am not one of your insane clients who jump at the sound of unexplained noises in the night!" I growled and reached across the table to grab hold of Barnett's right arm with my right hand, pinning his appendage to the table. "I have been through a hellish journey that continues to haunt me and what I have experienced and witnessed has all been very real! Do not try my patience by testing me!"

If I didn't have Barnett's attention or confidence in the validity of my demonic experience before, I certainly had it now; for the Englishman appeared somewhat startled by my display.

"Calm down, Benjamin," Barnett implored. "It is apparent that you need me...I am willing to help you."

I released a hold of his arm, which he recoiled rather quickly, and I took another swig of ale from the tankard. After I had swallowed I apologized. "Forgive my actions, but the stress..."

"I understand, Benjamin. And more importantly, I believe you."

I took a deep breath. "Tell me Barnett, what is your field of expertise?"

Barnett adjusted his jacket and cleared his throat. "I am a student of chemistry, metaphysics, theology, and occult philosophy," he described boastfully.

"The occult—such as black magic and witches?"

"Yes."

"Have you yourself ever seen a demon?"

"No...but I have seen those who claimed to have been possessed by a demon, and I have probably unknowingly looked one or more demons in the eye; for they walk amongst us, as you are aware."

"Yes," I agreed. "My demon lives, breathes, and walks the streets of Lynn just as any other man who makes his home and works here."

Barnett did not respond but studied me from across the table. I detected that our conversation had reached a point where the Englishman had to make a decision whether to proceed with revealing to me his recipe for destroying the demon, or to bring our discussion to an end. He turned his head to the right and to the left as if he were making certain that no-one was near enough to hear. Then he leaned forward resting both elbows on the table.

"Benjamin, in addition to faith, the other weapon you will need to combat the demon is *gnosis*—the Greek word for knowledge," Barnett revealed, his voice lower now.

"Knowledge? Knowledge of what?"

"The truth. You must listen carefully to what I am about to explain to you and at the same time you must open your heart and mind to it," Barnett advised. "For only then will your deep faith prevail over the forces of evil."

"You have my attention."

"Good. Dark forces have been at work on this planet since the dawn of human civilization in an effort to steer man away from a blissful eternal life. As a Christian, I am certain you are familiar with the concept of heaven?"

"Yes, of course," I admitted. "It is a place above the stars where good souls go to live eternally with God after death."

Barnett produced a coy smile as if he found my answer infantile. "Human culture is strong, Benjamin, and religious dogma is a great example of this strength; for religion is a product of culture. The culture of the Christian Church has been very successful down through the centuries at promoting the concept of heaven as you have just described, and with it the idea of eternal life; however, there is a better description and one that I believe to be the correct one.

"In my many years and travels across Europe, Asia, and North Africa, I have stumbled upon a variety of fascinating, yet controversial ideas that challenge our understanding of the material and supernatural world. Their concepts, cloaked in mystery and protected by small secret orders of individuals scattered around the globe who have passed the knowledge down from one generation to the next, offer what I have come to believe is the truth to what can be described as the real spirituality and destiny of man. But it is a dangerous truth for it challenges the existing order and fundamental beliefs of established religions."

"I'm not sure I understand?"

"You will and you must," Barnett emphasized. "Throughout my travels I have amassed a great deal of knowledge plucked from ancient documents of the three great monotheistic faiths—Judaism, Christianity, and Islam. I have been very fortunate to set eyes on and study many of these documents, particularly since their existence is a closely guarded secret."

"How were you able to see them?"

"Mostly through chance; but in some cases the sincerity behind my genuine interest in such matters is easily apparent and has been successful in opening doors. There is a bond that connects those who believe deeply in similar ideas," Barnett alleged. He reached for the tankard and took another gulp of ale. "Five hundred years ago, Fakhr al-Din al-Razi, a Muslim theologian and philosopher proposed the theory that there exist multiple worlds within the universe, and even suggested that there may be multiple universes," he explained, setting his tankard back on the table. "What does Genesis say about creation, Benjamin?"

I thought for a moment. "*In the beginning God created the heaven and the earth...*" I recited and paused. "I don't recall the exact wording of the text that follows."

"*In the beginning God created the heaven and the earth. And the earth was without form and void; and darkness was upon the face of the deep. And the spirit of God moved upon the face of the waters...*" Barnett rattled off flawlessly.

"You know your scriptures well," I acknowledged.

"*And the earth was without form and void; and darkness was upon the face of the deep,*" Barnett repeated. "Have you ever thought about what is meant by *the deep* within that passage?"

"No...not really."

"*Heaven* is the reference to the universe and *the deep* refers to its expanse and wonder," Barnett illuminated.

"What does all this have to do with Eblis?"

"Everything," Barnett implored. "The cataclysmic event that created the universe..."

"Created the universe?" I interrupted, puzzled by that idea.

"Yes, Ben. Everything has a beginning. *God created the heaven and the earth.* Heaven is reference to the universe."

"I understand but you described it as cata..." I stammered.

"Cataclysmic."

"Yes...that sounds like a violent term."

Barnett smiled, obviously slightly amused by my limited vocabulary. "It is violent. Benjamin, what I am about to tell you is not my own opinion, but a theory built upon the ideas of many others who base their understanding on ancient documents and oral narratives originating from different cultures and different faiths from around the globe. These individuals maintain their anonymity because of the threat of reprisals by powerful religious and political leaders who recognize the damage such a theory could do to the age-old hierarchy of organized religion."

As I listened, I began to wonder if Barnett's philosophical description of what he saw as the problem was too grandiose for the likes of the small town of Lynn. *Of all the places in the world, why Lynn?* And then I remembered Caleb and his terrible predicament. And I remembered what my cousin had said about the possibility of war erupting in the colonies. *Maybe soon Lynn and the other colonial towns will no longer be regarded as quiet American havens known only to the locals.*

I realized that Barnett had paused. "I am listening," I reassured him.

"As I was saying...," the Englishman continued. "...the cataclysmic event that created the universe, whether by accident or by design, has its roots in energy." Barnett hesitated turning to look through the doorway. I followed his eyes and realized he fixed them on the burning hearth across the room. "Benjamin, do you see how the embers have broken away from the burning log?" he asked, turning his attention back to me. "The embers will eventually burn out and grow dark unless returned to the center of the fire. In the same way, at the time of the universe's creation energy exploded outwards comprising the building blocks for the heavens. This energy is composed of two parts—positive energy which shares attributes of the creator diety..."

"*And God said let there be light...*" I interjected.

Barnett nodded with enthusiasm. "Yes, Benjamin. But the second aspect of the energy is negative energy—a dark force if you may. Let us return to the embers as an example. Just because an ember may grow dark away from the fire doesn't mean it can't still be a source of energy. Many early peoples and ancient beliefs have a strong metaphysical connection to light and dark as synonyms for good and evil. In Exodus, for example, darkness is one of the final plagues God unleashes upon the Egyptians, and in Genesis we find God separating light from darkness on the first day. Within the Muslim Quran, individuals who do wrong are destined for an eternity spent in ice cold darkness. Even the Chinese symbols Yin and Yang represent dark and light, and the ancient Greek deity name Erebos means darkness. In fact the Greeks describe Erebos as one of the first five beings in existence born from chaos."

"Chaos?"

"Yes...the cataclysmic event," Barnett continued. "The explosion of energy at the creation of the universe produced chaos. *And the spirit of God moved upon the face of the waters.* By *waters* the Bible is not referring to the seas of the earth, but rather it is a reference made to describe the chaos of energy, devoid of form, abounding across the universe at its inception. Thus the battle between light and dark, good and evil, is a battle between positive and negative energy that has its roots at the beginning of time."

My head was spinning now and full of questions? "How can such information, if it is true, threaten religion?" I asked. "How can it threaten the Christian Church? As you have said, light and dark are part of the Christian faith and found in the Bible!"

"Religions are structured around and manipulated by cultural beliefs," Barnett answered directly. "Culture is strong Benjamin, and the great religions have been subject to and molded by the customs and traditions native to various regions around the world. The foundation for salvation still exists, but it has been buried beneath cultural rubble. Upon such rubble religious hierarchies have been built and they are nourished and sustained by culture. To put it simply, the Church doesn't want to be told that they lack the whole story—that they are missing the most important part."

"What part of the story is missing?" I probed.

"The institutions of religion and the hierarchies they have created, all have their foundation with the rigidity of early human tribal roots," Barnett explained. "Thus they have unwittingly become a road block to eternal life."

"I'm confused," I acknowledged. "So what is the path to eternal life?"

Barnett produced a satisfying grin. "It is simply knowledge of our place in the universe, and using that knowledge to live a life guided by faith and morality. Humans are the highest life form on the planet and in addition to the size and development of our brain we are blessed from birth with positive energy—energy passed down from the Creator."

"How is such energy recognized?"

"It is recognized by our deeds and our faith. The energy is our souls Benjamin. The goal of our existence is to find our way home—back to the source of the positive energy."

"Back to God?"

"If that term pleases you, then yes...God," Barnett conceded. "However, the cultural complexities that work to make people try hard to recognize differences and encourage people to identify those differences as weaknesses, cloud the pathway back to the Creator."

"But Jesus preached of heaven, and not about a source of energy returning to the Creator," I countered.

Barnett took another drink of ale from his tankard and set the mug back down upon the table. He took a moment to reach up with both hands and adjusted his periwig before gazing back at me, and produced a modest grin as though he were about to reveal his most surprising secret. "One of the most revealing documents I have encountered in my travels..." he began. "...is a Greek text that I came upon within a Coptic Egyptian monastery. In the text, Jesus refers to an energy force within us all that needs to be set free."

"In which Gospel does Jesus say that?"

"The Gospel of Truth."

I was confused. "I'm not familiar with that Gospel?"

"How many Gospels are there?" Barnett asked.

"Four. Matthew, Mark, Luke, and John."

"Actually there are twenty-seven and maybe more," the Englishman revealed with a tone of arrogance. "The early Church selected the works of Matthew, Mark, Luke, and John to be official books of the Christian faith. In the second century, Iranaeus, Bishop of Lyon in France, wrote a treatise that attacked many of the earlier written works whose ideas differed from those of the established Church. These additional writings were branded as works of heresy and efforts were made to destroy them. But some have survived."

"Why did the Church want to destroy them?"

"Many of the early documents rejected by the Church tell a different variation of the story than what the Gospels of Matthew, Mark, Luke, and John profess," Barnett revealed, his speech becoming more excitable now.

"Are you saying Matthew, Mark, Luke, and John were wrong?" I questioned.

"No. Just that their perspective may have been different," Barnett clarified. "Some of the other works reveal Jesus to be a messenger whose mission was to enlighten mankind to the idea that the spark of divinity lies within us all. Thus anyone can be divine if they acquire true knowledge of the Creator. The goal is to make our way back to the Creator, which is the source of all positive energy in the universe. The world in which we live is a flawed world created by a material god that attempts to lure the positive energy in a direction away from the Creator. For example, within the same document where Jesus preaches of an energy force within us, there is a passage describing how Jesus laughed at the disciples for praying to the destructive god that created the world."

"This is all very fascinating; but I still don't understand the connection to Eblis?"

"Eblis is a product of the dark, negative energy! The demon who torments you is a servant of the material god!"

"Then the material god is Satan?"

Barnett nodded.

"And if what you say is true, Satan—as the material god—would be the Earth's creator?"

"Perhaps, Benjamin. I suspect that positive and negative energy manifest itself differently in every corner of the universe." Barnett's eyes began to light up and he leaned forward. "Imagine that the Creator is attempting to reclaim the positive energy that was thrust outwards at the universe's creation, but a dark force, taking advantage of the chaos, is working to prevent this in an effort to acquire supreme power of its own, in competition with the Creator. So within our corner of the universe the dark force creates Earth as well as most life on the planet in an effort to entrap the positive energy. The Creator counters by creating man—an intelligent creature blessed with positive energy and who, with proper guidance—from a messenger such as Jesus—can transmit that positive energy back to the Creator. But the demiurge..."

"Demiurge?"

"Yes...it is a name that is often used by the ancients to describe the dark one," Barnett enlightened. "The demiurge is aided by a legion of archons or demons, which prey upon man's weakness for material and bodily pleasures, entrapping him while on Earth. Although man is gifted with positive energy from the Creator, he is a product of the chemical composition of the Earth and thus susceptible to the whims of the architect, Satan. Then in death, the demiurge may steal man's soul—his positive energy—so that it can be transformed into negative energy enhancing the power of the demiurge."

"Then Eblis is an archon and the demiurge the architect—father and..." I paused. "Father and son—s...o...n. And not s...u...n—the meaning of Cyrus!"

Dusk had fallen and although we had no window in our room, through the doorway we could see a great many shadows of objects as the tavern had grown darker and the fire in the hearth more intense.

Barnett turned toward the doorway and yelled for the bartender. Talbot Newhall acknowledged his call and appeared within the room a few seconds later.

"My good man, would you be so kind as to fetch me a piece of parchment, a quill pen, and inkwell," Barnett asked.

Newhall nodded and left the doorway.

"Tell me Barnett, if one is possessed and consumed by dark forces, is there a chance he could regain the positive energy and make the transformation from evil to good?" I asked.

"It tis a good question," Barnett acknowledged. "I would like to believe so, for the source of the energy remains the same. What changes is only how that energy is used. The purpose of the fire in the hearth is to bring warmth and light into this room; however, in the wrong hands that fire could burn this building to the ground."

I pondered his answer in silence for a moment.

"You're worried about Caleb, are you not?" Barnett deduced.

"Yes."

"If Caleb is indeed possessed then the positive energy that once guided his existence has transformed, thus it may be able to transform again."

"Yes, you're right! Then maybe there is a chance!"

"But Eblis may have a powerful hold over Caleb," Barnett cautioned. *If he only knew.* "You may have to defeat the demon first before addressing your cousin's situation."

"If there are demons among us, where are the angels?" I inquired with a tone of frustration.

"Perhaps they are in here," Barnett offered lifting his right index figure to the side of his head. "And in here," he added bringing the index figure to his chest.

I recalled my prayer session with Rachel and how she had performed a similar action. "Perhaps," I agreed.

Before Barnett could respond, Newhall returned with the items the Englishman had requested and set them down on the table in front of him. Barnett thanked him and the tavern owner exited the doorway leaving us alone again.

"You mentioned that in confronting the demon it is necessary to be armed with faith and knowledge," I interjected. "Knowledge of what? The knowledge that everyone has the power to be divine?"

"Yes, but also knowledge that the earth was created by the demiurge. Such an admission of humility infuses one's positive energy! This counters the power of the archon which preys upon man's ignorance and obsession at placing mankind at the center of the universe, or at the forefront of whatever religion he chooses to worship!"

Barnett dipped the quill pen into the small pewter container of ink and began to write on the parchment. "There's more," he explained as he continued to write. When he had finished he replaced the quill in the inkwell and sat upright, looking at me again from across the table. "Benjamin, listen to me carefully. You must confront Eblis directly, and if your faith and knowledge is strong, it should allow you to temporarily weaken the demon; but Eblis needs to be *distracted* from his objective!"

"Distracted...how?"

"It would depend upon the situation. If Eblis has directed all his powers at confronting you, then you must find a way to deflect his attention, for he needs to be distracted to break the continuum of dark energy. And of equal importance is that *you must not be distracted* and stay focused on the task at hand. If you allow your faith and concentration to be compromised, then the power of the demon will strike you down. Is this understood?" Barnett emphasized and waited for my response.

"Yes...I understand. And then what?"

"At the moment you do accomplish that distraction, you must recite these words," Barnett instructed, sliding the piece of parchment across the table in front of me.

I read silently what Barnett had written before looking up at the Englishman. "Where is this from?"

"The first passage is from the Gospel of Truth and the second is a Coptic spell," Barnett illuminated.

"What will happen when I have recited the phrases?"

"The demon's power will temporarily be crippled and the physical shape of the demon will be reduced to air flow that can be captured and concealed inside a container," Barnett described. "That is why it is crucial that you confront the demon when it is not in its human form, but in a supernatural state. The human form of Eblis will never fit inside a container."

"A container? What size?"

"Any size," Barnett shared, shrugging his shoulders. "But the container must have an opening in which to capture the air flow and a means to conceal it."

"A cask?"

"Yes...a cask should work."

"Surely the power of the demon will unfasten the lid or burst the cask!" I surmised with a tone of doubt.

"Fill the container with sand. The sand will displace the dark energy, reducing its power," Barnett instructed. "The spell should also limit the demon's power and the symbols you must carve on the outside of the cask before you encounter Eblis, will assist in keeping it a prisoner for eternity, as long as the container remains sealed and undamaged."

I glanced down at the parchment and noticed Barnett had drawn three symbols beneath the lines he had written. As I viewed them, the Englishman described each. "They are the three monotheistic symbols: The Jewish Star of David; the Christian fish; and the Islamic crescent moon. All three religions worship the same Creator and when combined these three symbols will serve as powerful guardians over the captive demon."

"Are you serious?!" I exclaimed. "What madness! Am I to believe that a powerful demon with supernatural forces can be reduced to air flow and captured and concealed within a wooden cask?! Does there exist any records to suggest this might actually work?!"

Barnett took a deep breath. "None that are documented; but the method I have described is a thousand years old."

I scoffed and sat back in the chair, exhausted from Barnett's philosophical explanation, and now exasperated by the improbability of the solution.

"Benjamin, you must understand that you navigate uncharted waters," Barnett reasoned, sensing my frustration. "But what other choice do you have? Trust your faith and use the wisdom you have gained tonight. Have faith in the positive energy you have been blessed with. It is stronger than the dark energy and when you realize this, you will find your God," he advised with a serious tone.

"Tell me Barnett, with this knowledge that you possess, have you found God?" I countered. "Perhaps together we could fight Eblis... surely there exits strength in numbers?"

"I am afraid I would only be a burden to you, Benjamin. I do not have all of the weapons needed to fight the demon; for I do not have strong faith," Barnett explained. "I am a man of science and reason, and I lack the discipline and spirituality that you appear to possess. Faith draws much of its power from innocence, for the world is a dark and corruptible place. My soul is contaminated as a result of my travels and the sinister influences I have encountered. I am here not as a warrior, but only to teach with the hope that my work will allow my positive energy to find its way back to the Creator."

I was confused. "What makes you think I possess strong faith?! I have challenged my cousin's religious approach in dealing with this demon all along!" I explained. "I continue to question my faith with every step I take!"

"I meant what I said about self-reflection in trying to locate the angels among us," Barnett expounded. "I sense you may be a special individual, and that may be another reason Eblis has targeted you. You already had the faith, Benjamin...I have given you the *gnosis*."

"God help me..."

CHAPTER 41

Night had fallen over Lynn by the time Benjamin and Barnett had concluded their discussion and said goodbye. The trip from Lynn to Concord would take Barnett many hours to complete, so the Englishman decided to wait until morning and travel the route in daylight. He stayed overnight at Newhall's Tavern; although the establishment was not equipped to serve as an inn, but Newhall did have a spare room and for a few extra pounds, the tavern owner could be persuaded to rent it out.

The following morning, after enjoying a hearty, hot breakfast prepared and served by Mrs. Newhall, Barnett set out on horseback for Concord. The sun remained hidden behind an ashen overcast sky swept in sections with darker shades of gray and the Englishman could see his breath in the cold air as his mare trotted along the narrow road that was blanketed by a dusting of snow that had fallen overnight. A few miles west of Lynn, the road wound through a thick forest of bare trees with dark limbs and branches trimmed in white by snow.

The forest was quiet, broken only intermittently by a snort from Barnett's horse and the rustling of branches by a slight frigid breeze blowing directly at him, forcing the rider to lower his head as a means of lessening the bite of the frosty gust. At one point the Englishman was surprised when he raised his head to see a horse and carriage stopped alongside the road some distance ahead of him. As he drew near the vehicle he noticed a man bent over the rear wheel of the carriage struggling to try and lift the wheel from out of a ditch.

Barnett brought his horse to a halt alongside the closed carriage. "Can I be of any assistance?" he offered.

The stranded traveler dressed in a wide-brimmed, circular top hat and a long dark wool coat did not look up, but continued to work at trying to free the wheel. "Slid off the road in this wretched weather!" he grumbled.

Barnett took a moment to glance inside the carriage window as he dismounted his steed, but could not see deep enough into the dark compartment, and he stepped over behind the carriage next to the stranded stranger. "Let me help you try to move the wheel forward," Barnett offered.

The stranger stood up and turned to Barnett. "Do I detect an English accent?" he asked.

Barnett saw that he was a young, well-dressed gentleman with a bronze complexion. "Yes, you are correct..." Barnett paused in mid-sentence.

"What is it?" the stranger asked with a smile.

"Your eyes...one is blue and the other brown..." Barnett realized and then gasped. "You're Eblis?!"

"Do you have any spells to cast my way, Barnett!" Eblis sneered.

Barnett took two steps back and turned for his horse as the carriage door flung open and the assistant Patch leapt from the vehicle clutching a large knife in his right hand. Before Barnett could pull himself up on the horse, Patch was on him. In one swift motion he grabbed the Englishman, spun him around, and plunged the blade deep into Barnett's chest. The Englishman did not feel the blade at first, only the pressure of Patch's arm against his chest. When Patch withdrew the knife Barnett could feel the sharp pain increase rapidly and he watched the blood spurt from the wound and saturate the white snow at his feet. He began to lose consciousness as the blood continued to pour from his body and fell face down to the snow. In a few minutes he was dead.

Patch lifted the body and tossed it inside the carriage before joining Eblis who had already climbed the perch and had hold of the reins to the horse. With a snap of the reins the carriage pulled away.

A brief but heavy snowfall later that morning buried the bloody evidence in the road and Barnett's horse wandered aimlessly back into Lynn by early afternoon. The Englishman was never seen again.

CHAPTER 42

I pondered my conversation with Barnett for two weeks, realizing Caleb had been correct to call the Englishman eccentric; for his philosophical and spiritual theories and obsession with positive and negative energy were wasted on me. I refused to accept his assessment that I had been gifted with strong faith and decided to focus mainly on Barnett's method to capture the demon; although I doubted it as well. Yet, as the Englishman had pointed out, what other choice did I have? Reluctantly, I made my decision and felt it necessary to confide in Sam. If something were to go wrong, I wanted her to know the truth, and so on a chilly, but bright Sunday morning in mid-March, I found the opportunity to open up to my love on our walk home from the religious service. I told her everything...about the night Caleb and I encountered Eblis at the witch's coven...about Caleb's demonic roots and his gradual transformation...about Barnett's theory of light and dark forces and the prospect of divinity for all humans...and about the method of how to capture Eblis. If she hadn't witnessed the demon herself the night she and I spied on the witch's coven, I think she would have thought me mad as Barnett. Surprisingly, and most importantly, she agreed that I needed to destroy Eblis, if not for Caleb's sake, then for ours. Sam loved me and I loved her, and if we were to finally live a life together in peace, I had to free myself from the demon. No matter how preposterous Barnett's method for trapping the demon sounded, *I had no other choice.*

The question now became where and when to confront Eblis? I realized that to simply challenge the demonic shoemaker to a duel on a date of my choosing was foolish and unrealistic. I could certainly summon the demon using coral, black candles and a fig branch, as Caleb had, but I feared the use of Darcie's method of black magic might put me at a disadvantage. *I didn't want an invitation...I wanted a confrontation.* Barnett had made clear that Eblis needed to be distracted and the demon had to be present in a supernatural state. Thus I valued the element of surprise.

One morning I found myself alone in the Kerstland shoe shop staring out the window and across the street at the Hassett enterprise. I did not hear the door to the kitchen open and was pleasantly startled when I felt a soft kiss on the back of my neck. I smiled and turned around to find Sam dressed in a blue gown with beige lace apron, trimmed at the top by a white lace neck kerchief. She looked lovely and I placed my hands on her hips, pulling her in closer for a firm kiss.

"You're scheming on how to confront Eblis, aren't you?" Sam guessed aloud as she pulled away, breaking the interlocking of our lips.

"Yes," I replied with a sigh, releasing my grip on my love and turning back toward the window. "We need to know the future—where Eblis is going to be at a specific moment."

"Well he is still playing the part of a shoemaker, is he not?" Sam inquired.

"Yes," I replied with piqued interest in my voice.

"Then he must still be filling orders...which is a terrifying thought," Sam deduced.

"Of course!" I stated with excitement spinning back around toward Samantha. "That's it Sam! I need to see Eblis' book of orders and learn where a future shoe delivery will go! Then I can be at the location ahead of the demon!"

"You're going to break into one of his outbuildings?" Sam asked with concern. "Don't you remember Ben what happened the last time we went snooping around that monster's lair? Patch nearly killed you!"

"Yes, and later with Caleb, we were attacked by Daniel," I remembered. "Despite those close calls, I still must see the book. I need to be able to get in and out of there quickly."

"Yes *we* will."

"What do you mean *we?*"

"I'm going with you," Sam announced confidently.

"No. It could be dangerous."

"Exactly! That's why you will need another pair of eyes!" she insisted. "Besides, how do you intend to get in and out of the outbuilding quickly with the door being fastened? If you break the door down, someone will hear you."

"How did we manage to get inside the first time?" I asked, trying to remember.

"The picklock. The lockmaster Oliver Purvis had left his picklock here in the shop," Sam recalled.

"Yes, that's right! If I only had a picklock..."

"You do," Sam revealed. "Did you ever return the picklock to Purvis?"

"No, I don't think so?"

"That's right, you didn't. You gave it to me to hold onto, Ben. And I still have it," Sam disclosed with a smile.

"After all this time?! It's been years!"

"I thought it may come in handy one day," she replied, still smiling.

"Well, my love, today's that day," I said and turned back to the window. "Let's see what is in that book of orders."

Sam rushed off to her bedroom to retrieve the picklock before rejoining me in the shop. After closing up the workshop, she and I casually made our way across the street and down the side alley adjacent to the Hassett residence until we found ourselves behind the house. There the ground of the backyard was spotted with patches of snow still protected from the sun's rays by the cooler shadows of buildings, stone walls, and tree trunks. We wound our way around the stark mulberry trees until arriving at the first of three ten-footers as Sam handed me the picklock. I quickly worked at opening the outbuilding door, while she stood watch, combing the area for any sign of Eblis, Patch, or Daniel.

Before long I picked the lock and we quietly gained entrance into the ten-footer. The outbuilding was as I had remembered—dark, cold, with corners encased in cobwebs, dusty shelving, and a collection of dust-covered shoemaking tools littering long workbenches. Immediately I rushed to the rear of the ten-footer and approached the shelving, scanning each narrow wooden shelf for the book of orders, remembering how I had failed to locate it the last time I entered the outbuilding with Caleb; but I attributed that to my confrontation with Daniel and our hurried departure, hoping my luck would be better this time around. And then I saw it—the long book with leather binding. I felt a rush of adrenaline as I opened the book, and didn't need to say anything to Sam who rushed to my side when she heard my breathing slow. Together we turned the pages deliberately, pouring over the names of dozens of Lynn residents from Adrian Lyttleton to the Reverend Sparston.

"Ben, why do you think the demon masquerades as a shoemaker?" Sam asked, staggered by the list of buyers of Eblis' shoes.

"Lynn is a town of shoemakers, therefore it has become easy for Eblis to blend in," I explained. "And I believe the shoes to be a manner of entrance into individual lives—everyone is in need of *soles.*"

I continued to examine the list and as I ran my finger down the page, reading the names silently to myself—all of which were assembled chronologically around orders and deliveries—I shook my head in bewilderment.

"What is it?" Sam asked.

"All the names on this list had ordered and received shoes from Eblis and many that I recognize are now dead or missing," I replied.

"But I remember us discussing this when first we laid eyes on this book," Sam recalled. "Why does this surprise you?"

"I just don't understand it? Think about it Sam, the sudden arrival of Eblis to Lynn preceding these strange deaths...the fact that this property has mulberry trees that produce berries—berries that leave stains on a missing girl's shawl...an outbuilding that doesn't appear to have seen any activity in ages...a book of orders that lists the names of deceased residents of Lynn! So much evidence! Why hasn't the law taken action against Eblis?!"

"Constable Dixey tried and he was killed."

"But there have been other constables and now a sheriff. Has the law suddenly abandoned this town?"

"Maybe they are afraid," Sam surmised. "You and I have never said anything to anyone about what we saw at the witch's coven, with the exception of Caleb. We were afraid. Maybe Lynn has been reduced to a demon-fearing lot of people as opposed to God-fearing."

I turned toward Sam with a curious look. "No...I believe God-fearing is right; for Barnett mentioned how the material god created the Earth," I offered. "Maybe the Englishman isn't so crazy after all?"

"Ben, while you were away all that time in Boston, my father would share conversations with me that he had with the various constable's who would come and go in Lynn. Do you know that most, if not all of the victims in the series of strange occurrences in Lynn were residents who had done something wrong?" Sam explained.

"Something wrong?" I inquired.

"Yes. Many of the names on this list of orders are people who committed immoral acts at some point in their past or present," Sam educated me. "It's as though Eblis is punishing them for their sins. Perhaps the residents of Lynn not only fear Eblis, but welcome his presence?"

"What are you saying?"

"Maybe Eblis is cleansing the town of...of bad people?"

I turned to look at Samantha. "Anna Hood, Abby Becker, Melissa Sheehan...are you saying they were bad?"

"They are not on this list."

"But Eblis had something to do with their disappearances...I'm sure of it," I said boldly. "The demon once left a clue for me revealing the death of Melissa—one as sweet as honey! And he marked my Bible with the names of all three...in blood!"

Sam sighed. "It is strange."

"Sam, I have questioned myself about why these people in this book of orders were selected by Eblis as you have. In fact I have thought about it for years and after listening to Barnett I believe I may have an answer. I don't believe Eblis is passing judgment on people. He delights in their faults...he feeds off of it; for he's a demon who is only focused on stealing souls—energy—for the purpose of gaining power. All of these victims have been weakened enough by their own immorality to allow Eblis to prey upon them. He may bait them with guilt, but it is only a method to further weaken their faith, so that the demon may capture their souls before each individual seeks forgiveness in an attempt at rebuilding a connection to the Creator.

"No matter their sins, everyone has the right and ability to restore their positive energy; but the window is narrow for those weakened by immorality. One should not give up on such individuals because of past indiscretions," I preached. "No. Eblis is not cleansing the town, he's preying upon it! Lynn is not the same place it was before the arrival of the demon...you know this to be true. Suspicions run high and such mistrust can give way to *wrath*."

"One of the seven deadly sins," Sam reasoned.

"Yes. Eblis is removed from legal prosecution because he has the entire town under his spell, simply because they suspect one another and they fear justice at the hands of Cyrus Eblis; although the demon's justice is merely a ploy to acquire their souls!"

"That is very interesting, Ben; but what about Anna, Abby, and Melissa?" Sam challenged. "If they were not weakened by immorality, how do you explain their disappearances?"

"I don't believe Eblis personally harmed them," I offered. "Remember, the demon not only feeds on immorality, but breeds it. I believe Eblis has directed those who did harm the three girls. Someone else is behind their disappearance," I suggested, redirecting my focus on the book and turning another page. "Hmm...There is a new order here," I announced and read it aloud. "Five hundred military boots for General Thomas Gage?! Eblis has a contract with the British army?!"

"Five hundred *soles* Ben!" Sam exclaimed. "That is five hundred *souls* as in spiritual *souls*!"

"Sam, look!" I directed, pointing my finger at more writing on the middle of the page below the order for British military boots. "There is a list of twelve names here—all females who are due to receive a new pair of damask shoes on April nineteenth!"

"Next month."

As I studied the notation, I noticed how all twelve names were connected by one long line of ink that extended across the page to one solitary name set aside on the right. The lone name was Darcie.

"Sam, remember at the witch's coven how you identified one of the thirteen witches in addition to Miss Darcie!" I prompted. "What was her name?!"

Sam thought for a moment. "Price...Charity Price!"

I scanned the list of names on the left side. "Here she is...Charity Price! These are the witches!"

Sam cast an eye over the page. "Ben, there is something written beneath Darcie's name," she spotted.

"Yes...I see," I acknowledged and leaned in closer to the book to decipher the scrawled entry. "It reads...sacrificial rite...the twelve and the lamb."

"Why do you think Darcie's name is set across the page from the other twelve?" Sam asked.

I pondered the notation for an instant before looking up from the book and at Sam. "He's going to kill them at the witch's coven!" I deduced. "Darcie is going to lead them there! Apparently Eblis has no more need for these twelve women other than to capture their souls! Their time has come!"

"What do you believe is meant by sacrificial lamb?"

"Lamb?" I paused and then my heart began to race. "Oh God!"

"What is it, Ben?!"

"That night at the witch's coven, Darcie referred to Rachel as the lamb...her name means lamb! They plan to sacrifice her the night of April nineteenth!" I was sickened by the thought. "When is Rachel due to return from Europe?!"

"Early April."

"The notation references a sacrificial ritual which I'm certain will take place at the witch's coven," I assumed. "We have our next order for soles, Sam. I will be waiting for Eblis at the coven!"

CHAPTER 43

ew Haven, Connecticut – Sunday, April 16th, 1775

N Thirty minutes had passed since the Sunday service had ended and Caleb was still sharing pleasantries with members of his congregation outside the front of the meeting-house. After he said goodbye to the Coughlin family he turned to re-enter the building, certain he had gratified all those who wanted a word with the preacher, when he noticed a tall, well-dressed man standing off to his right.

"Master Arnold," Caleb identified, inviting New Haven's druggist, bookseller, and trader in West Indies goods to approach with a smile and extended hand.

"Reverend Brown," Arnold acknowledged as the two men shook hands. "I can't tell you how wonderful it is for Margaret and I to see the improvement in your health. Only a month ago you looked weak and pale during the service and we could barely hear your strained voice. We had been very concerned; but now we are relieved to see that your recovery has been nothing less than remarkable."

"Thank you," Caleb replied. "How is Margaret and yours sons?"

"They are well, thank you. They were all in attendance at the service today and I have sent them on home ahead of me, for I was hoping to have a word alone with you," Arnold stated with a coy grin.

"I see," Caleb said, turning his head from side to side to see if anyone else lingered about. "Let us converse inside," he offered as he turned and stepped toward the meeting-house door, grabbing the handle, and pulling it open. He held the door ajar for Arnold who respectfully removed his tricorn and stepped inside ahead of Caleb.

Once inside the meeting-house, Caleb pulled the door shut behind him and turned toward Arnold. "What say you, Benedict?"

"Your sermon today—I enjoyed its message," Arnold praised. "What was the passage from Corinthians you quoted?"

"This is what the Lord says to you: 'Do not be afraid or discouraged because of this vast army. For the battle is not yours, but Gods...," Caleb recited from memory.

"Yes...don't be afraid," Arnold pronounced. "Well that vast army just may be coming soon. My sources in Boston tell me General Gage is prepared to use all necessary force to halt the buildup of colonial arms. I fear he may attempt to seize another arsenal as the redcoats did at Charleston back in September."

"Is your militia prepared?" Caleb asked.

"Yes. We are ready to protect any of our arsenals in Connecticut and are committed to rush to the aid of any of our friends in Massachusetts or Rhode Island," Arnold assured.

"What can I do for you then?"

"I have a shipment of French arms arriving from the West Indies later this week, but I sent word for it to arrive in the port of Salem," Arnold described. "I fear I am under the suspicion of the customs officials in New Haven and so I have had to divert the shipment. I need to get word to our friends in Salem and I was hoping you might assist me."

Caleb reached out and placed his right hand on Arnold's shoulder. "Of course, Benedict. As it so happens I am bound for Lynn tomorrow and will pass through Salem."

"Thank you, Reverend."

"Be careful Benedict, trust no-one for there are many loyalists among us," Caleb advised. "Give my love to Margaret."

"Yes, Reverend," Arnold promised as Caleb led him to the door, pulling it open for him.

"May God be with us," Arnold proclaimed.

"Yes...yes. May He be with us," Caleb agreed and closed the door behind him.

Caleb fastened the door from inside the meeting-house, sighed and stared at the wood. Slowly he lowered his head and pressed his forehead against the door.

"Quit your sulking, Malik!" a deep voice called out from behind him.

Caleb sighed, pulling his head away from the door and slowly turned around to face the boxed pews of the meeting-house. From his vantage point, the preacher could see the man in dark clothing and a circular wide-brimmed hat seated in one of the pews facing him.

"Just when I think thy transformation is complete, you have a moment of weakness!" the man barked.

"Eblis, you needn't be here!" Caleb called back.

"Oh, but I do! After all I am your mentor!" the dark shoemaker exclaimed, followed by a sinister laugh.

Caleb felt a sudden surge of pain streak up from the spine and into his head, doubling him over as he moaned.

"You're just not quite there yet, Malik! But I am pleased by the development in thy transition," Eblis remarked with a wide ,grin. "I can feel your progress, for as your dark energy grows, so grows mine!"

The pain subsided enough for Caleb to right himself. He could only stare back at Eblis, void of emotion, breathing heavily.

"Well dear preacher, your sermons truly seem to inspire the masses," Eblis continued. "This Benedict Arnold acquaintance of yours is full of fight."

"Arnold is loyal to the cause," Caleb blurted barely above a whisper.

Eblis laughed again. "Man is only loyal to himself, Malik. Take thyself for example. If it were not for your selfish desire to be a member of the Board of Yale, you would not have struck an agreement with me and thus delayed thy destiny!"

"I had no other choice when I learned I am a product of a demon seed!" Caleb retorted with a tone of regret. Suddenly pain racked his head again and the preacher grimaced before stumbling to the floor on both knees.

"Malik! Are you listening to me?!" Eblis called out.

From his position kneeling on the floor, Caleb slowly raised his head in the direction of Eblis as the pain began to fade. "I'm listening..." he wheezed.

"On your travels to Lynn tomorrow you are to stop in the town of

Lexington and use your oratory talents to convince the militia leader, a pleasant fellow by the name of John Parker, that it is imperative for his men to defend their properties and hold their ground against any British aggression," Eblis instructed. "Only last week did I visit the sleepy little village of Lexington—a community of farmers wanting to play soldiers."

"Why were you in Lexington?" Caleb inquired, panting.

"Why Malik, to deliver *soles, of* course," Eblis replied with a sinister smirk.

"Soles? There must be troubled and tainted souls everywhere," Caleb said with disappointment.

"There are indeed sinful people in every corner of the map," Eblis validated with glee. "But my selection is not restricted to them. Oh, no, Malik. Not only to them; but I need to start somewhere, and the weak and confused are the simplest prey. My power grows with each acquisition and soon, with thy help, I shall not need to discriminate!" he concluded with a devious sneer.

Caleb grimaced, recognizing the evilness behind the demon's words, but the fiendish grip that held sway over the preacher, left his reaction numb. All Caleb could do was respond to his master as does a minion. "Lexington is out of my way, as I am bound for Salem tomorrow," he explained.

"Then adjust your course!" Eblis growled.

Caleb sighed.

"Just do what I say!" Eblis commanded. "Is this understood?"

The vanquished preacher nodded.

"Soon you will have your war!" Eblis announced. "And I will have my souls..."

CHAPTER 44

L ynn, Massachusetts, Early Morning – April 19th 1775

...He pulled tight on the horse's reins and the beast stopped and whined, kicking high into the air with its front two legs. It was then that I noticed the noose at the end of a rope swinging from a tree limb high above. Quickly pulling myself into a sitting position, I began a backwards crawl but my escape stalled when my back collided with a cold, stone object. I spun around to discover a headstone with the inscription concealed behind a thick layer of dust. Frantically I worked at brushing away the dirt to reveal the name of...Samantha Kerstland... I gasped and sat up in bed. "Samantha! No!" I cried out, staggered by the revelation of the identity on the headstone within my nightmare. *Why Samantha?! I must protect her!* As I continued to digest the alarming disclosure in my dream, I glanced about my bedroom, which had been dimly lit by the light of a full moon penetrating the window. I realized it to be still very early as the sun had not yet begun to rise. *A full moon. There shall be another full moon tonight. Ideal for a witch's coven...and a sacrifice.* I turned and dropped my legs over the side of the bed and sat on the edge of the mattress facing the window. *I fear today may be the worst day of my life...*

LEXINGTON, MASSACHUSETTS – A FEW HOURS LATER

John Parker realized the young preacher from New Haven was correct, for Caleb Brown had visited him the day before and told him to beware of a potential British military operation in the vicinity of Lexington. The military expedition was confirmed by three colonial messengers—Paul Revere, William Dawes, and Samuel Prescott—who awakened Parker in the middle of the night with the news. Now at the crack of dawn, the colonial farmer and elected captain of the militia assembled seventy-seven armed men on the village green blocking the road to Concord. With both the rising sun and the full moon still visible in the sky overhead, Parker and his untested colonial militia were nervously awaiting a British army that numbered nearly seven hundred, commanded by Lieutenant Colonel Francis Smith. Acting on orders from General Gage, Smith's army was to seize the weapons and ammunition located at the colonial arsenal in Concord, but it had to pass through the village of Lexington to get there.

A detachment of light infantry, under the command of Major John Pitcairn was sent ahead of the British column of soldiers and arrived at the village first. At the sight of the armed group of Lexington farmers on the green, the advancing British halted their march and under orders from Pitcairn, quickly formed a defensive posture opposite the Americans, breaking into companies, loading muskets and fixing bayonets. The pompous major rode his horse in full gallop toward the colonists and paraded the animal up and down the unsteady line of minutemen, harshly demanding they lay down their arms and disperse. But amidst the yelling and confusion that ensued, a shot was fired from an unknown source and all hell broke loose as the colonists and British regulars began to exchange musket fire. When the smoke cleared, eight colonists lay dead and ten wounded. The British infantry awaited the arrival of the bulk of Smith's army and they continued their march on to Concord—*many of the regulars wearing new military boots purchased from the manufactory of Cyrus Eblis.*

LYNN

Still wrestling with my recent nightmare, I met Samantha on the beach that morning near the rocky promontories of Great and Little Nahant. Earlier in the week I had asked Master Kerstland for the day off from work, and Sam and I made plans to meet on the morning of the nineteenth to discuss our strategy for the evening, which involved disrupting the witch's coven in order to protect Rachel and force a confrontation with Eblis in his supernatural state. We chose the Lynn coastline as a rendezvous site to be certain that we would be discussing our plan alone, realizing our plot was certainly doomed if word of it should leak out. Despite weeks of brave talk, I had not yet fully committed to the plan, still questioning the sanity of Barnett and thus harboring many reservations about his methods for confronting the demon; but now, because of last night's dream, things had changed.

Originally Sam had offered a convincing argument to allow her to accompany me to the gathering of the daughters of black magic, built around the assumption that the situation seemed extremely dangerous for one person, let alone two. At first, I vehemently resisted this notion out of danger for my love, although Sam's persistence and logic wore me down.

So I told Sam of my dream and how it revealed the name on the headstone to be hers. I could sense initially that the nightmare genuinely frightened her, but her stubbornness supplanted her fear and she insisted that we needed to be together. However, even though I realized Eblis could strike her down from anywhere, I wanted her nowhere near that witch's coven; but my impassioned Samantha would not take no for an answer. Our impasse produced a heated verbal exchange as we went back and forth over the subject for some time. Realizing at one point that the morning had slipped away from us, I finally gave in and agreed to a compromise. The agreement would be that I would journey to the witch's coven in the woods of Swampscott as planned, but rather than stay in Lynn, Sam would travel to Swampscott to remove Rachel from danger before joining me at the coven. I remained disappointed with the decision, but I knew Sam's determination, and I knew that no matter what we may have agreed to, her strong will would not permit her to stay behind. Thus I reasoned that if I gave her a purpose, she would be satisfied, and most importantly she would be away from the witch's coven.

CONCORD, MASSACHUSETTS—LATE MORNING

Just before noon, Lieutenant Colonel Smith's army arrived in Concord and began searching for weapons in various homes and businesses. Forewarned of the British approach, local residents had hidden much of the weaponry, shot, and gunpowder in a variety of locations and thus the soldiers could only find gun cartridges stored away in the village meeting-house, along with three massive cannon capable of firing twenty-four pound shot buried behind the tavern of Ephraim Jones. The British quickly went to work smashing the trunnions of these cannon so they couldn't be mounted. In their attempt to destroy the gun cartridges by burning them, the British erroneously set fire to the building and the flames began to spread to nearby homes. In the meantime, the soldiers threw a quarter of a ton of musket balls they had uncovered, and over a hundred barrels of flour and salted food into the millpond, intensifying the ire of the local inhabitants.

The Concord militia, led by its captain, James Barrett, watched from a secure location in the wood and atop a hill overlooking the village. And while the British continued their destruction in Concord, colonial militia from Lexington and western towns and villages joined Barrett's men until the American militia force had grown to a size of over four hundred.

LYNN

Although I realized the witch's coven would not convene until after dusk, I decided it best not to linger about my aunt's home throughout the day, for I feared that to do so might cause her to grow suspicious. So I grabbed my Bible, my uncle's sword, the Damascus blade, and the parchment that contained Barnett's sacred phrases, Coptic spells, and religious symbols, and set out on horseback. My first stop was at the Wrigglenecke grocery where I purchased an empty wooden cask and a forty pound bag of sand, and from there I headed off in a northeasterly direction toward Swampscott. I traveled with no sense of urgency as the springtime weather was agreeable and with the knowledge that I had more than enough time to arrive at the witch's coven well before sunset.

As I guided my horse on the leisurely trot through the familiar coastal landscape, my mind was fixated on the task at hand. I felt truly petrified when pondering what evening may produce and what tomorrow might bring, or if there would even be a tomorrow if I failed in my mission, and at several points along the route, I nearly surrendered and turned the horse around. Barnett mentioned that my faith and confidence needed to be tenfold what I had exemplified before confronting the demon, and at the moment I felt as though I had little faith and no confidence at all. However, what boosted my courage over the course of those long afternoon hours in anticipation of nightfall, centered on the realization that I held the fate of Samantha, Rachel, and Caleb in the palm of my hands...and perhaps the population of the town of Lynn.

Occasionally I would pause along my journey to stop, dismount my horse, and take refuge beneath the shade of tree, using the opportunity to read from the Bible or pray spontaneously to the Creator for protection and wisdom. At these moments I gave much thought to what Barnett had professed about the messages revealed within the other gospels that he was so adamant existed, in addition to the standard four, and to his conclusion that the spark of divinity lies within us all. Such thoughts did much to rally my confidence; but just as suddenly, I would study the wooden cask in my possession and regress, wondering how mad I must be to believe that I could capture the demon in such a container. *Such an act would truly be divine.* Nevertheless, as the Englishman had reminded me that night in *Newhall's Tavern*, I had no other choice and the time would soon be at hand. I decided to wait until arriving at the location for the witch's coven before carving the three religious symbols into the lid of the cask, and I would not fill the cask with sand until I absolutely necessary, since I realized that the weighed down barrel would prove cumbersome.

My deliberate journey to Swampscott not only produced periods of deep reflection, but also afforded me the opportunity to help free my mind of details and scenarios of what might unfold when I finally did confront the demon. So at intervals along the way, I dismounted my horse and unsheathed my uncle's sword to practice the fencing move Caleb had taught me, not in anticipation of using the weapon, but in an effort to quell my nervous energy. *If only the duel with Eblis could be so promising.*

As I continued traveling northward, there were several moments where I encountered solitary riders on horseback galloping furiously in a southerly direction, moving at such a pace that they needed to secure their tricorns to their head with one hand lest their hats blow away. It did not occur to me at the time that something major was unfolding in Lexington and Concord.

CONCORD—*EARLY AFTERNOON*

Observing the smoke from the burning fires in the village, Captain Barrett led his militia force, now numbering over four hundred, down the wooded hillside and onto the road leading into Concord. Two British light infantry companies that together barely numbered one hundred soldiers, took up position on the North Bridge spanning the Concord River. When the companies saw the superior numbers of the approaching American militia, the British fired their muskets, instantly killing two Americans and wounding five. At the sight of their fallen comrades, the militia began to return fire upon the soldiers, killing three and wounding thirteen and producing such panic within the British ranks that the companies abandoned the bridge, retreating until they had regrouped with Lieutenant Colonel Smith's army. Surprised that his two companies deserted the North Bridge, Smith and three officers galloped on horseback to assess the situation at the overpass. From a safe position behind a wagon they observed the size of the militia and after a tense standoff that lasted for nearly a quarter of an hour, the lieutenant colonel made the decision to order his men to retreat back to Boston.

LYNN

After meeting with Benjamin along the beach, Samantha did not return directly home but instead rode out to her grandparent's farm. There she rode Savior hard in full gallop around the fenced corral in an attempt to reduce her anxiety, as well as to free her mind of her worried thoughts and images of what nightfall may hold in store.

By midday she had returned to Lynn and was somewhat surprised not to find either her father or Wright inside the Kerstland shoe-making shop, considering it particularly odd since Ben had the day off.

"Mother!" Samantha called as she wandered through the empty shop, relieved to undo the top button of her gray waist-seamed riding jacket.

Her mother burst through the doorway from the kitchen.

"Samantha! Where have you been?!" she asked with distress; but before Samantha could answer, her mother had deduced from the riding jacket, buckskin tight fitting breeches and long black boots that her daughter had been riding. "Were you at your grandparent's?"

"Yes. Where is father? Why is the store empty at this hour?"

"Oh...it has been a very strange afternoon!" her mother enlightened, wiping her hands nervously with the apron that she had tied around her waist. "Something is going on, Sam! There is word of fighting between British soldiers and the militia in Concord! Blood has been shed! People have died! A call went out for assistance and your father and Wright joined dozens of other men of Lynn and have rushed off to Concord! I pleaded with him not to go, but his stubbornness would not hear of it! I am very worried about him!"

"Oh my word! That is frightening!"

"And your sister...I expected her back hours ago! Have you seen her?" her mother inquired.

"No. Where did she go?"

"I sent her on an errand to obtain cloth, but she hasn't returned!"

"Perhaps she is with Roman?"

"No. I ran into his mother out in the street just a little while ago and Roman also has heeded the call to arms!"

Samantha turned away from her mother and moved toward the front window of the shop with her eyes fixed on the Hassett shoemaking establishment across the street.

"I'm worried about her!" Samantha's mother exclaimed.

Samantha looked back at her mother. "I will search for her! I'm sure she is fine...probably consoling or being consoled by someone because of today's events," Sam offered.

"Oh...my bread! I have bread in the oven and I can smell it beginning to burn!" her mother blurted. "Thank you Samantha, and please be careful. It is such a dreadful day!" she assessed and disappeared into the kitchen.

Quickly Samantha grabbed an awl and a half-moon shaped shoemaker's knife from off one of the workbenches and slid them inside the pockets of her jacket. Her intuition told her that she best begin her search for her sister by exploring the Hassett shop, for she realized with the incredible news of a battle raging in Concord and the knowledge of the commencing of a witch's coven later that evening, anything was possible.

Samantha exited the shop and briskly made her way across the street where she surveyed the front of the Hassett establishment. Peering through the window she could see that that shop, as usual, remained dark and decided to explore the ten-footers behind the building. She moved down the alley adjacent to the Hassett shop and slowed her pace when entering the backyard. Cautiously she approached the first of three outbuildings; but before she could reach it, she was startled by the appearance of Daniel who bolted from out of the ten-footer farthest from the house. The crazed young man did not see her as she quickly darted behind the trunk of a mulberry tree and hid there watching him sprint across the yard, carrying a bright blue bonnet in his hand. His destination was the backdoor of the Hassett shop and when reaching it, quickly disappeared inside. "Muriel's bonnet?!" she thought, her heart racing faster now. She decided to forego an exploration of the first and second ten-footers and instead began moving briskly toward the third ten-footer from which Daniel had emerged, using the mulberry trees for her stealth.

Upon reaching the third ten-footer, she discovered two unsettling facts—the windows of this outbuilding, unlike the previous two, were painted black, and Daniel had left the door to the ten-footer ajar as if he intended to return soon. Hurriedly, she slipped through the open doorway and into the outbuilding expecting to find it completely dark; however, the room was partially illuminated from a flickering glow eerily ascending from a large square opening in the floor. Set behind the opening was a trap door connected to iron hinges attached to the floor boards that had been thrown open. Aside the opening laid a rolled up carpet that apparently concealed the location of the trap door when closed.

Samantha approached the opening warily and when just above it, peered down to see that a flight of narrow wooden steps were assembled directly beneath the opening that led down into a subterranean room. Slowly she stepped onto the steps with both feet and began her descent, stopping when her head passed beneath the floor. At this point, she balanced herself on the stairs, and stooped down to look around the room. At first glance she noticed a long wooden table set with three burning candles in its center resting next to a circular tinder box, and as she looked away from the table over to one side of the room, she gasped when she discovered her sister seated on a wooden chair. Muriel had been gagged with a piece of cloth around her mouth and each of her limbs were bound by rope to the arms and the legs of the chair. At the sight of Samantha, Muriel, who was fully clothed and conscious, began to squirm excitably within the confines of the chair.

Samantha rapidly finished her descent and when both feet left the last step, she hurried across the wooden floor over to her sister, quickly untying the gag at the back of her head and pulling the cloth from out of her mouth. "Hurry Sam! He will be back!" Muriel blurted.

"I know! I know!" Samantha replied as she pulled the shoemaker's knife from out of her jacket pocket. "What was he doing with your bonnet?!" she inquired as she began to use the blade to cut the rope that bound her sister's right wrist to the arm of the chair.

"He mumbled something about a trophy!" Muriel revealed. "He said he was going to place it with the other three!"

Samantha paused from cutting the rope. "The other three?!" she repeated in an inquisitive tone laced with trepidation. She raised her head and looked across the room. Situated at the far wall Samantha focused on an area of the floor that was without floorboards, and slowly rested the knife gently in Muriel's lap, leaving her sister's side to begin a pace in the direction of the far wall.

"Sam, please! He will return soon!" Muriel pleaded.

Samantha ignored her sister, curious by the lack of flooring at the far end of the room, and she paused at the table to pick up one of the burning candles. As she lifted the candle she noticed that the top of the wooden table was covered with ruddy discoloration that she guessed were blood stains, and began moving in the direction of the far wall holding the candle out in front of her to use the light as her guide. Samantha had noticed the strong pungent odor that hovered about the area as she stepped from the staircase, but in approaching the far end of the room, the caustic air became almost overpowering. She grimaced, ceasing her advance when she observed how the exposed dirt floor was arranged in three slight mounds of earth. A number of stones—none larger than the size of an adult hand—were strewn about, indicative of the rocky New England soil, and a spade rested in the corner of the far wall. Reaching the mounds she stopped and held the candle low to the earth before shuddering at the sight of a small human hand, blackened from deterioration, protruding out from the dirt mound.

"Three mounds for three bodies!" Samantha deduced with a look of horror. "Anna, Abigail, and Melissa?!"

Suddenly, the room exploded with a thud and Muriel screamed. Samantha whirled around and saw Daniel positioned on his knees at the base of the steps after having jumped from the top step into the room. Quickly he stood up and darted toward Samantha who dropped the candle and reached into her jacket pocket to find the awl. The candle flame extinguished when it hit the floor, bringing darkness to that corner of the room just as she withdrew her hand from her pocket clutching the sharpened shoemaker's tool. She held her right arm outstretched and went to swing the pointed awl at her attacker, but he struck her arm first with such force that Samantha lost her grip on the instrument and it flung from her grasp. She collapsed back-wards to the floor violently and was rendered winded for a moment, gasping for air as Daniel dropped to his knees and straddled her waist. Samantha recovered her breath but now felt her attacker's firm hands around her neck squeezing it tightly, and she struggled to breathe once again. She choked and squirmed in an attempt to pull Daniel's hands from her neck, but his grip was strong. Suddenly she released her right handed grip on his wrist and reached out with the free hand to probe the floor. It was then that she found the stone. Gripping the rock in the palm of her hand she found the strength to lift the stone and swung it at Daniel's head. The stone struck her attacker at his left temple and as his eyes rolled toward the back of his head, he slumped over unconscious onto the floor, falling to the left of Samantha.

Samantha coughed, gasping for air and sat upright dropping the stone. The only sound she could hear was that of her sobbing sister and she slowly pulled herself to her feet and approached Muriel. "It's all right!" she reassured, in between deep breaths.

When Samantha was once again standing beside the chair that confined her sister, she lifted the knife from Muriel's lap and finished severing the rope that bound her right wrist. She moved to begin cutting the rope that bound her left wrist when suddenly she paused.

"What is it?!" Muriel whispered.

Samantha held her index finger to her own lips and raised her head, rolling her eyes to the ceiling. Her sister could hear the footsteps above them.

Muriel began to sob again as Samantha quickly lifted the cloth from off the floor at the side of the chair and placed it back into her sister's mouth. Muriel fought this action, pulling and tugging at Samantha's arm with her free hand.

Samantha grew angry. "Your right hand is free! Here, let's place the knife underneath you!" Samantha whispered as she slid the blade beneath Muriel's petticoat and on the seat of the chair. "I need to gag you again to make it seem your bondage is unchanged! It is for your own good!"

Muriel, now understanding her sister's strategy, reluctantly nodded her approval and Samantha quickly tied the gag at the back of her head. Next she wrapped the severed rope back around Muriel's right wrist so it gave the appearance that her arm remained fastened to the arm of the chair.

As the sound of the footsteps stopped above the square opening in the ceiling, Samantha darted over to the other side of the room and retrieved the stone she had used to defend herself against Daniel, before crawling beneath the table. She listened as the steps began to creak from the weight of the man descending them, although from her position, she could not distinguish his identity; but Muriel could clearly see that the man who stepped from the last stair was Patch.

When Patch had reached the floor of the subterranean room he stood slightly hunched with a bewildered look as he gazed at Muriel's predicament tied to the chair. As he turned he saw the body of Daniel resting on his stomach and began a slow pace toward the motionless young man, passing the table with not so much of a glance beneath it. When he stepped up to the body, Samantha dashed out from beneath the table and charged Patch from behind; but before she could strike him with the stone, Patch—sensing danger—spun around swinging his left arm and striking the woman across the face with the back of his fist. Dazed by the blow, Samantha tumbled to the floor.

Patch located a supply of rope in one corner of the room and quickly went about the task of tying Samantha where she lay, binding her wrists together as well as her ankles. Still stunned by the force of being hit in the jaw, Samantha put up little resistance. Muriel sobbed as she watched Patch complete his task of binding her sister, and attempted to discern at what point she could safely retrieve the knife she sat on to free herself; but she realized that any sudden movement would surely be noticed by Patch.

The one-eyed assistant to Cyrus Eblis pulled a large knife of his own out from inside his jacket with his right hand and held up Samantha's bound arms with his left. Muriel's sobbing evolved into a hysterical motion of moving her head from side to side at the sight of Patch holding the knife to her sister. Using the blade, he cut the sleeve of Samantha's chemise at the right arm below the elbow, pulling it from her and placing the garment around her mouth as a gag, before tying it into a knot behind her head. Samantha fell back to the floor on her side and Patch rose, turning toward Muriel before pacing toward her. As the confined woman stiffened with fear, Patch checked the binding of her left wrist to be sure it remained secure to the chair before moving to her right side. Just as he reached down to place his hand on her right arm, he was distracted from a moaning sound emerging from the far end of the room and looked up to see Daniel staggering to his feet, rubbing the side of his head. He left Muriel's side to approach the dazed man.

Muriel breathed heavily, relieved that her free right wrist had not been exposed and watched Patch assist the unsteady Daniel, who continued to battle the effects of being bashed with the stone. Samantha was also cognizant now and she remained positioned on her side looking up at the two men standing near and above her.

Patch placed his left arm around Daniel's shoulder and began to address him directly. "You're a fool, man! By trying to feed thy craving for the blood of young women you risk jeopardizing everything our master has assembled to this point!" Patch scolded. "The dark one overlooked thy appetite for the first three lasses, but you have been careless with this one! You have even been foolish enough to have snatched her off the street in daylight! Our prince is so close now...the hour is nearly at hand when the dark one will be all powerful! Soon he will be finished with that Pratt fellow and his destiny will be fulfilled!"

At the mention of the name of Pratt, Samantha and Muriel exchanged worried glances.

"But Daniel, you've become a burden to our master!" Patch continued as Daniel dropped his head in shame. "There can be no more mistakes!" the one-eyed man added and suddenly with his right hand still grasping the knife, plunged the blade deep into Daniel's stomach. The young man gasped from the piercing pain and when Patch withdrew the blade, Daniel grew faint as blood quickly saturated his shirt and he collapsed to floor with his final breath.

Patch leaned over and cleaned the blood-stained blade by rubbing each side against Daniel's jacket, before returning the knife inside his own jacket. He turned toward the sisters. "I've got to leave you now lasses to assist the dark one. So don't cha run away, now," he snickered with an evil grin. "When I return I'm going to have some fun with the two of you!" he added with a creepy laugh before extinguishing the two remaining candles on the table. The room grew dark and the sisters could hear the weight of Patch on the creaking steps as he ascended the stairs, followed by a loud thud from the door closing overhead.

Clearly in shock by the sequence of events, Muriel could only shake violently and stare into the darkness. After several minutes had passed, Samantha grew concerned by not hearing any sign of movement from where her sister sat; for she could not see her in the darkness, nor could she call out because of the gag. Rolling over onto her stomach, Sam used her elbows to slide in the direction of Muriel across rough floorboards that tore away at her clothing and exposed skin; but her determination would not be denied and soon she was tapping her head against Muriel's ankle. The tapping worked and quickly Muriel went about the task of retrieving the knife hidden on the seat beneath her as she removed her own gag. Next, with probing fingers, she reached down at her feet and touched her sister's face, pulling the gag from around Samantha's mouth before freeing her own left wrist and ankles.

"Muriel, can you find the table?!" Samantha asked, breathing heavily.

"I think so."

"We need light!"

The frightened woman rose from the chair, gingerly stepped over her sister, and carefully maneuvered across the dark room to where she visualized the table was located. Upon reaching it, Muriel ran her fingers across the tabletop until locating the round tinderbox, which she opened and blinded, set about the task of striking steel and flint to produce a flame on the cloth. When the feat had been accomplished, she applied the flame to the candlewicks of both candles that rested on the table and turned to view her sister on the floor. Returning to Samantha, Muriel used the knife to free her from her bindings before helping her sister to her feet. Muriel trembled as they both hugged and wept in one another's embrace.

"Are you harmed?" Samantha asked.

Muriel could not find the composure to speak and only moved her head up and down to indicate she was all right. Samantha brought her right hand to her own face and massaged her jaw that still stung with pain as her sister gasped at the sight of Daniel lying face down on the floor in a pool of his own blood. "Don't look!" Samantha commanded, reaching up and physically turning her sister's head away from the grisly scene with her hand. It was then that Samantha noticed the awl lying on the floor behind the table and remembered how she had lost control of it when Daniel had struck her. She left her sister and quickly walked over to retrieve the sharpened instrument. "Let's leave here!" Samantha advised, delicately removing the knife from Muriel's shaking hand and slipping both tools into her own jacket pocket. Samantha grabbed her sister's hand and together they began climbing the stairs. Upon nearing the top step they paused, and in unison they pushed up on the heavy wooden door, throwing it open. Cautiously surveying the dark, quiet ten-footer, they found no-one and emerged from out of the opening.

"I fear Ben's life is in danger!" Samantha revealed to Muriel, who remained traumatized and unable to speak. "Ben believes he is setting a trap for Eblis, but Patch's comments make me think the trap is being set for him! I need to warn him!" she proclaimed before looking Muriel in the eyes. "I'm taking you back to the house and you can wait for father and Roman to return! I need to get to Ben before Eblis does!"

ON THE ROAD BACK TO BOSTON—LATE AFTERNOON

Lieutenant Colonel Smith ordered the British army in Concord to begin the twenty mile return trip to Boston and by late afternoon they arrived in Lexington; but not without much hardship. The colonial militia had grown to over one thousand and had harassed the British retreat since Concord, killing over three dozen British troops.

Both Smith and Major Pitcairn were wounded and unable to command by the time the British army arrived in Lexington, and the loss of two of their top commanders added more confusion to a military retreat that was rapidly running out of ammunition, and growing increasingly frustrated with an unseen enemy that engaged in a military style of shooting at the British from behind trees, stone walls, and houses.

The fighting intensified and grew deadlier on the road from Lexington to Boston. By the time the British reached the Massachusetts capitol, the colonial militia—recruiting from towns and villages in every corner of the colony—had grown to over four thousand. The united colonial effort to seek revenge against Smith's army had inflicted over three hundred casualties on the British with nearly one third of that number dead.

Most alarmingly, with the outbreak of the Battles of Lexington and Concord, the Americans now had their war for independence, and Cyrus Eblis had his *souls,* with the promise of more to come...

LYNN

Jamesina tilted the wooden water bucket over her daffodils and water poured from its neck as she shared her backyard garden with the shadows of late day. But as she moved on to water her crown imperials, she noticed the sudden appearance of a new shadow and turned around quickly, gasping at the sight of Caleb standing aside the well.

"Caleb!" she exclaimed with excitement and relief. She paced toward the preacher and embraced him tightly, burying her head in his chest. Caleb remained silent and returned the hug, but it was not a strong one and Jamesina detected a lack of emotion from her son.

"Did I frighten you?" Caleb asked.

"Yes...a little perhaps. With the terrible news of the events today trickling in by the hour, everyone's nerves are on edge," she explained. "What do you make of all this fighting in Lexington and Concord?"

"What do I make of it? It's war."

"Oh, how terrible," Jamesina lamented. "I'm just relieved at this moment to see you standing here before me, knowing you have not run off to the battle as many others have done this day."

"I suspect some will not be returning home," Caleb offered stoically.

"What is the matter with you, Caleb? You do not seem yourself today," she observed.

Caleb ignored the question. "I've come to see Ben, and stopped by the Kerstland shop first, but it was closed. Has my cousin run off to Lexington and Concord?"

"No. He left here this morning before news of today's events arrived in Lynn," she explained. "I believe he mentioned something about traveling to the Goode residence in Swampscott, probably to visit his friend, Rachel."

Caleb pondered the information for a moment, saying nothing.

"Caleb?" Jamesina inquired, confused by his silent demeanor.

"Then I am bound for Swampscott," Caleb replied. "Good to see you, Jamesina," he said and turned to walk away.

"Jamesina?!" she repeated with ire. "You're using my first name now?! I am your mother!"

Caleb slowly turned back toward Jamesina. "Woman, you are not my mother! Your husband and your brother should have left me in the woods to die that day they found me!" he replied with a tone of anger and resentment.

"How can you say such a thing?!" Jamesina cried out.

"Edward would be alive today if he had not been so weak and sympathetic to care for a crying infant!"

Jamesina gaped, stunned by Caleb's insensitivity. In her anger she moved to strike him with her fist against his chest but suddenly stopped, frozen with a look of terror. "Your eyes! Caleb, your eyes! One is blue and the other brown! Like that monster...Eblis!"

Caleb took two steps backwards and spun away from Jamesina, moving quickly through the garden and toward the backdoor.

CHAPTER 45

The Goode residence — Swampscott, Evening, April 19th, 1775

Samantha's arrival to Swampscott coincided with the last glimmer of sunlight at dusk, and she slowed her horse Savior's gallop to a trot upon noticing the open chaise parked outside of the front door of Rachel's home. What seemed strange to her was how the carriage's shafts rested on the ground unattached to any horse, for no animal could be found. Samantha guided her mare to the front of the house beside the chaise, dismounted, tied the reins to a hitching post, and approached the entry way of the house, seeing that the door had been placed slightly ajar. Reaching inside her pocket, she pulled out the shoemaker's knife, clutching the blade in her right hand, and delicately pushed open the front door with her left, stepping inside. The entry hall was well-lit with burning lamps and she decided to explore the parlor situated to the right of the entry-way. Holding the half-moon blade of the knife out in front of her, Samantha found the parlor to be illuminated and immediately noticed Rachel's sedentary wooden wheelchair positioned beside a round wooden table that had been set with a flagon of tea and two pewter cups and spoons.

At the back of the parlor was another door and Samantha slowly opened it, discovering it led into the kitchen. As she stepped around the corner of a counter, Samantha beheld a body lying on the floor resting on its side next to a wooden rolling pin. She rushed over to the body and instantly identified Rachel's servant, Dinah.

Bending over Dinah, Samantha noticed that the woman still breathed and began to shake her. "Dinah! Dinah!" she called out.

Dinah grunted and moaned, slowly opening her eyes instinctively reaching for the back of her head. Samantha assisted her into a sitting position, resting her back against the counter.

"Dinah! What happened?! Where's Rachel?!"

Dinah moaned again, rubbing the back of her head with her hand. "I had left her in the parlor with that woman..."

"What woman?!"

"An old woman, the chandler from Lynn."

"Darcie!" Samantha deduced.

"Yeah...Darcie. I think that was her name," she recalled, wincing. "She claimed she was bearin' important news for Rachel on the behest of Benjamin. They was restin' in the parlor after I had fixed them some tea and I was returnin' to the kitchen for sugar and honey. Next thing I know I felt a painful thump on the back of my head, and must of passed out on the floor!"

Samantha lifted the rolling pin from off of the floor. "I think she hit you with this!"

"That wicked woman!" Dinah exclaimed before moaning again from the pain shooting through the base of her skull.

"Where is Master Goode?!"

"He journeyed to Boston this afternoon. I had thought he would have been back by now; but I guess he's held up there."

"Come, we need to find Rachel before it's too late!" Samantha instructed rising to her feet and replacing her knife in her pocket. She leaned over and grabbed Dinah's wrists and helped pull her into a standing position.

Arm in arm, Samantha assisted Dinah from the kitchen, through the front parlor, and into the entry hall, where she swung the front door open wider.

"Dinah, did the woman arrive by chaise?"

"Yes," Dinah replied still rubbing the back of her head. "Both of them."

"Both of them?!"

"There was a driver...he wore an eye patch."

Samantha gasped. "You're lucky to be alive!"

"Do ya think they are still in the house?" Dinah asked.

"No. The horse to the chaise is gone!" Samantha offered, staring out at the horseless carriage. Suddenly off to her right, she caught a glimpse of a faint light in the distance, moving across the clearing in the front yard. "Look!" she pointed in the direction of the light.

"They're moving toward the cliff!" Dinah determined and with a groan slumped down into an entry hall chair, continuing to massage her head.

"Dinah, you're in no condition to move! You need to stay here and wait for the return of Rachel's father!" Samantha advised.

Dinah nodded with a grimace and Samantha exited the home. She quickly unhitched Savior and mounted the horse, steering the mare in the direction of the faint lantern light; although she remained careful to travel through the adjacent woods and not across the clearing so as to remain undetected.

THE COVE—OUTSIDE OF SWAMPSCOTT

I started to feel that something was not right. Darkness had fallen and I had been perched on the stone-covered hill overlooking the cove for several hours awaiting the arrival of the witches; but aside from soaring bats at dusk, a curious raccoon, and a herd of foraging deer, I remained alone. With the loss of sunlight, the evening had grown considerably cooler and the fact that I remained sedentary in attempting to remain hidden, enhanced the effects of the chilly night on my body. *The witches should have been here by now...it's after dusk. Have I missed something? The date in the book of orders was the nineteenth. Everything for the coven ceremony should have been in place by now...* And then it dawned on me. *They are to sacrifice the lamb—Rachel. Perhaps the witches are bringing the coven to her?!* I had convinced myself that I was in the wrong location and quickly descended the hill to my horse and mounted the mare, setting off in the direction of the Goode residence with the hope I was not too late.

SWAMPSCOTT—OUTSIDE OF THE GOODE RESIDENCE

Samantha followed the lantern's light to the edge of the cliff.

When the light had ceased its movement, the brave shoemaker's daughter tied her horse's reins to a tree and carefully began a nervous pace through the wood in the direction of the lantern's glow. She held the knife out in front of her with her right hand as she vigilantly darted from one birch tree to the next, using the trunks to conceal her approach. When finally she had reached the tree-line at the edge of the woods, Samantha remained hidden behind a large pine and observed the scene before her.

About thirty rods from the tree-line and only about half that many from the edge of the cliff, Rachel sat on the ground with her back slumped against a large fallen oak. Samantha's friend appeared unconscious with her eyes shut and her head hanging, resting her chin in the dark green triangular kerchief that was draped around her neck and tied at the front with a large knot. A black horse stood with its reins fastened around the trunk of a birch and Darcie stood next to Rachel with her back to the tree-line, working at removing black candles and a pewter mug from inside a burlap sack and setting them on the fallen timber as though she were setting a table. The wind blew steadily from the direction of the cliff's edge, setting the witch's long gray hair to flight, and the faint sound of ocean waves breaking over the rocky coastline below the cliff revealed to what lofty depth the crag dropped to the shoreline below.

Darcie's actions with the candles convinced Samantha that the witch was setting preparations to hold the coven of witches right there at the cliff's edge. *Where is Patch?* Guardedly she scanned the dark forest around her and despite her inability to locate the eerie man Samantha realized if she were going to act then it had to be now. With a deep breath she burst into the clearing running toward the fallen oak gripping the knife in her raised right hand. Darcie detected her movement and whirled around now clutching a small squared lead container in her right hand, moving to hold it above the unconscious Rachel.

"Stop!" the witched cried out, bringing her left hand to the container and quickly unscrewing its small cap.

Unsure of what diabolical substance the witch possessed inside the container, Samantha abruptly halted her approach only a few rods from the two women. "How can I be sure you haven't killed her already?!" she called out.

The witch snickered. "She is merely asleep—the result of a strong opium potion I have concocted; but rest assured, the lamb will awaken soon, for she is needed as an active participant in our ritual!" Darcie sneered.

"Then what is it you threaten her with?!"

"Oh, I don't threaten the lamb, my dear, for her fate has already been determined. I threaten thee!" the witch addressed pointing at Samantha with the bony index finger of her left hand. With her right palm she gently shook the open lead container, moving the container away from its position above Rachel and carefully poured a drop of the liquid onto the fallen timber. The spot where the drop struck the wood began to sizzle and burn as a puff of smoke rose above it. "This be acid, my darlin'!" she revealed, snickering once again.

"You're a beast, old woman!" Samantha exclaimed taking a step forward.

"Take one more step, and I will be sure to scar the both of ya!"

"How do you plan to kill the others?!"

"Why, whatever do ya mean?" Darcie questioned with phony ignorance.

"The other twelve witches! They are being summoned here so you can take their lives tonight!"

Darcie flashed a wicked smile as though she were impressed with Samantha's deduction. "Thou is indeed a most clever lass!" she acknowledged and then pointed to the pewter mug that rested on the fallen oak. "The daughters shall honor thy prince tonight with the greatest gift—thy souls! They shall drink poison hemlock from the cup!"

"Unknowingly I'm sure!" Samantha replied.

Darcie snickered. "They be a devoted lot; but sometimes they need...assistance...in thy worship, lest they weaken!" the witch added and wailed with laughter.

The combination of Darcie's shrilling laughter and the howl of the wind prevented Samantha from hearing the approach of Patch from behind her. With the swiftness of a striking serpent the one-eyed man wrapped his left forearm around Samantha's throat and held his knife to her cheek with his right hand. "Drop the knife!" he demanded.

Samantha could feel the sharp point of his blade pressing against her face and slowly she opened her palm, allowing the shoemaker's knife to slip from her grasp and fall to the ground.

Patch removed his arm from around her neck, grabbed a large lock of her hair and pulled hard, jolting Samantha's neck backwards. He held on to her hair, pulling her to the ground into a sitting position and straddled Samantha, still with a grip of her hair so that her face was raised to the sky and his blade pressed against her neck.

"Do not kill her!" Darcie exclaimed. "We shall offer her up with the lamb and honor the dark one with two special sacrifices this evening! The prince will be pleased!"

Patch removed the knife from her neck and released hold of her hair.

"But we shall prepare the pretty thing for the sacrificial offering by marking her!" Darcie decided with a sinister grin. "A few drops of acid from my container should do the trick! Hold her down! I want to christen her face!" Darcie shouted and raised both arms to the sky with a menacing look of delight as if invoking and invisible force.

Samantha struggled with Patch, who had placed his knife aside on the grass, and was using both hands to press down on her shoulders and hold the young woman steady, as she lay flat to the ground on her back.

With arms still raised, Darcie continued to clutch the open lead container of acid in her right hand and moved to take her first step in the direction of Samantha and Patch; however the witch failed to notice that the effects of the opium-laced tea on the unconscious prisoner resting on the ground beside her had worn off. As Darcie lifted her right foot, Rachel reached out and grabbed the sinister chandler's right ankle. The witch lost her balance and stumbled forward; but in her attempt to remain upright, Darcie lost a grip on the lead container. The canister flipped upside down and the acidic liquid poured down upon the sleeves of both arms of the witch as well as on the front midsection of her black dress. In seconds the areas of her garment that had been splashed with the acid began to dissolve and soon the caustic liquid was boring through her skin.

When Darcie cried out in agony, Patch raised his head to look in the witch's direction, lessening his grip on Samantha's shoulders. His prisoner seized the opportunity to reach into the pocket of her jacket and retrieve the awl with her right hand. Gripping the handle of the awl, Samantha stabbed Patch's left thigh with the sharp instrument and pulled it out. He wailed with pain, releasing his hold on Samantha and stepped over her. Dropping to his knees, the sinister assistant reached for his knife on the ground, extending himself in a direction away from Samantha who had now rolled over and was on her knees as well. Patch found his weapon just as Samantha leaped toward the evil assistant and plunged the point of the awl deep within the side of his neck, puncturing the jugular vein. Stunned, she let go of the awl and quickly rose to a standing position. Patch gargled with blood that began to fill his mouth and spill over his lips. Instinctively he pulled the awl from out of his neck, causing his blood to spray outwards like a leak in a dike. Within seconds, Patch—saturated in blood—lost consciousness and fell face down onto the dark, saturated soil.

Samantha could not bear the gruesome sight of Patch's blood soaked body and bent over to vomit, spewing the contents from her stomach on the ground. Then she heard Rachel's chilling scream and turned to see Darcie—her garment still smoking from the burning acid—dragging the handicapped girl across the ground. The witch moaned with great pain from her wounds as she gripped Rachel's triangular kerchief, and was using the article of clothing to pull the girl, positioned on her back, toward the edge of the cliff. Rachel gasped for air as the taught kerchief choked her, and at one point brought her hands to the knot in an effort to pull it away from her skin.

Samantha began a sprint toward the witch and Rachel, but by this time Darcie and her prisoner had reached the edge. Samantha could only watch with horror as the witch, who had stopped, gripped Rachel's kerchief with two hands. Standing only inches from the edge of a fifty foot drop, the horrid woman mustered up every ounce of strength in her frail body, pulling on the garment to toss the girl over the cliff; but at that very moment Rachel found success in undoing the knot of her kerchief. The garment was pulled free of her neck by Darcie who now struggled to maintain her own balance as her momentum shifted the upper half of her body over the edge. The witch rolled both arms in a desperate attempt to halt her motion but could not and disappeared over the side of the cliff. Rachel watched as Darcie's figure descended rapidly, but closed her eyes just before the evil woman smashed face down against the boulders along the shoreline.

Samantha hurriedly reached her friend and fell to her knees to lift Rachel. The two women embraced and wept for a few moments before pulling apart and wiping the tears from their own faces.

"Are we safe now?" Rachel asked, sobbing.

Samantha swallowed hard and sighed. "Not yet, I'm afraid. I need to help Ben—he is in danger! Come...I must get you back to your house and then go to him!"

"No!" Rachel exclaimed. "There isn't time! I want to be with you!"

Samantha realized they had no time to argue. "All right! We need to hurry!"

"Where is he?"

"The cove where the witches meet!" Samantha replied. "Hopefully he has realized there is no coven there tonight and is bound in this direction! Perhaps we can reach him before Eblis does!"

SWAMPSCOTT—THE GRAVEYARD

I had my horse moving briskly; although not in full gallop as it was difficult and dangerous to let her out on such a narrow, winding path through the woods, when I came upon the graveyard. Here I had to slow the mare's pace so it could meander around the headstones safely. The sunlight was completely gone now and the light from the full moon cast eerie shadows across the resting places of the dead. Still early in the spring, the stark branches of budding trees had yet to leaf out, adding a spooky aura to the landscape, and as if I didn't need anything else to frighten me on this disturbing eve, I came upon the massive oak that dominated the graveyard, remembering the broken headstone that marked the resting place of the pirate captain. As I passed the tree, I turned to gaze upon the buccaneer's grave before being suddenly startled by my horse's abrupt halt. The animal whined and jerked its large head, refusing to advance even as I kicked its sides with both feet. Staring straight ahead, I could see nothing on the ground that would be a reason for the horse to be frightened; but then a white wisp of mist suddenly appeared from out of nowhere only a few rods in front of the horse, and several feet off the ground. The vapor began to spin slowly before me, as if it were being molded by an unseen force, until materializing into the image of a boy. It was Jordan, my brother.

Slowly I dismounted and stood beside the horse staring at the flittering transparent image of my brother before me. It was as I remembered when first encountering the apparition—the eyes were opened but his face was expressionless with mouth closed.

"Jordan!" I called out. "Why do you haunt me?!"

The apparition did not reply but slowly lifted its right arm and pointed off to my left. I followed the direction of its extended index finger and realized it was pointing at the large oak tree; but what began to unfold beneath the oak quickly caught my attention. I watched with amazement as the earth in front of the broken headstone began to move—slowly at first, and then violently as the ground appeared to be pushed upwards. Next, my astonishment erupted into terror with the appearance of skeletal fingers and hands pulling away at the earth from beneath. Suddenly a swiveling human skull came into view and in seconds a full skeleton appeared after it had used both hands to propel itself up and out of the hole, and into a kneeling position aside the grave. The demonic assemblage of bone reached back down into the hole, retrieved a large rusted cutlass, and quickly sprung to its feet, facing me. Raising its sword, the skeleton set its bony legs and feet in motion, taking a few steps in my direction, and broke into a sprint, rushing toward me. I turned to look at the apparition of my brother, but it had faded from view and I quickly moved to my horse, hurriedly pulling the sword from the sheath slung over the animal's back. I spun back around holding the blade out in front of me as the skeleton drew near; but I darted away from the horse, seeking shelter behind a narrow stone monument that rose from out of the ground at a height slightly smaller than mine.

The skeleton reached the monument and we danced around it for a few moments, stabbing at each other unsuccessfully while attempting to dodge one another's blades. Terror fueled my adrenalin, although I began to grow exhausted from the futility of our duel. I decided to dash away from the monument, but in my haste tripped over a headstone and fell face down to the ground. The skeleton, which was on top of me now, moved to stab me with its cutlass, and I quickly evaded the strike by rolling over. The blade of the skeleton's sword stuck into the soil just long enough for me to rise up into the fencing position Caleb had taught me before the creature could regain control of its weapon. With my body slightly turned and knees bent, I extended my sword out before me with my right hand as the relentless skeleton charged me. The demonic human remains swung its sword at my head, and I blocked the strike with my blade. With our swords locked together, I stepped in closer to the creature and used the strength in my sword hand to push its cutlass in the direction of the sky, and in one swift motion brought my weapon down, spinning completely around to finish the move by running my blade through its rib cage. With momentum bursting, I forced the impaled skeleton backwards until driving the creature over a headstone. The skeleton crashed to the ground on its back and I withdrew my sword from its midsection; although the duel continued as the possessed set of bones frantically swung its sword at me from its position lying on the ground. Avoiding the skeleton's blade, I leaped in the direction of its upper body, and in the same motion landed a firm kick with my foot to the skull of the creature, separating it from the rest of the skeletal structure.

I halted my sword play when realizing the skeleton—still on its back slicing its sword in the air haphazardly—had been blinded with the separation of the skull. So I dropped my sword to the ground, picked up a large tree branch and began pummeling the bones with the wood until smashing its rib cage and breaking both arms. The creature's cutlass fell silent and so I dropped the branch, retrieved my sword and approached the skull. Using the tip of the sword, I snared the skull through its eye socket and lifted the bony head from the ground flinging it in one swift movement and sending it into flight in the direction of a flat headstone, where it smashed into pieces upon impact.

Exhausted, I bent over with both hands resting on my knees and gasped for air before hearing a slow clapping sound rising up in the distance from one corner of the graveyard. I righted myself and turned in the direction of the clapping to view a man dressed in black with a circular, wide-brimmed hat leaning against a headstone. I didn't need to be able to see his facial features to discern it was Cyrus Eblis.

"Bravo! Bravo!" Eblis called out.

I ran to my horse, returned the sword to the sheath and worked fast to retrieve the empty cask and bag of sand from off the back of the animal. I pulled the Damascus blade and the Bible from out of a burlap sack and slid both items inside the waistband of my breeches, before positioning the bag of sand over my right shoulder and tucking the wooden cask under my left arm. I turned to see that Eblis had begun a slow, haughty stroll across the graveyard in my direction.

"So Benjamin, we meet again!" Eblis called out arrogantly, maintaining his pace. "Somehow I sense this may be our final meeting!" he added with a devious chuckle.

I gave my horse a hard slap on the backside and it whined and trotted away from me. Not knowing what may transpire, I didn't want the horse to be in harm's way nor did I intend for it to impede my mission, so I thought it best to send the animal off, realizing it wouldn't wander too far without me.

"Thou ignores me?!" Eblis continued, obviously annoyed by my silence. "It appears that you are preoccupied, my friend! Benjamin, you should have realized by now that you cannot run from me!"

Refusing to acknowledge Eblis, I examined the graveyard around me searching for the largest and widest headstone, when in the center of the cemetery I located a sandstone monument shaped like a church steeple—wide and square at the base but narrowing as it rose, with a spire at the top. It would do, and I darted in its direction.

At the sight of my flight, Eblis stopped his pace, raised his right arm and extended it in my direction. Suddenly, when he opened the fingers of his right hand, a bolt of lightning—originating from within his palm—streaked across the graveyard and struck the ground in front of me forcing the earth to explode where it impacted. The force of the explosion knocked me to the ground on my backside and caused me to lose control of the cask which collided with the hard earth, forcing the lid to separate from the barrel. I pulled myself up, gathered the lid and sand bag and attempted to retrieve the cask from off the ground when a second explosion of energy a few rods from where I stood, startled me and prevented me from regaining the barrel. At that moment, I decided it was best to seek shelter behind the steeple-shaped marker and ran over to it, positioning myself behind its eastern side as Eblis resumed his approach from out of the west. *Surely he could have destroyed me with the bolt of energy! He's toying with me!*

When Eblis saw me disappear behind the monument, he stopped

again. "So we are playing games now?!" he called out, obviously annoyed. "You have witnessed my power which has grown considerably since this day began! Benjamin, I find it ironic how when we first met you carried a cask, and here we are in what may be our final meeting, and once again you are burdened by the wooden barrel! What be its purpose?! Surely you are a fool to heed whatever outrageous idea the lunatic Englishman Barnett threw at you! He was a silly old man who buried himself in manuscripts filled with lies and wasted his days away in search of elusive glory! An occultist...philosopher...theologian...Ha! He fooled you Benjamin! He was nothing but a little, insignificant man! As are you!"

I listened to Eblis from behind the monument, helplessly staring at the barrel that lie a short distance from me. *I need to regain possession of that cask! Surely he could blow it into splinters of wood with another blast of energy from his demonic hand!*

"And yes Benjamin, you heard me correctly!" Eblis continued. "I speak of the daft Barnett in past tense! He's dead! I was with him when he died!" he revealed. "He claimed to be able to unlock the secrets in which to combat me?! Why, the imbecile couldn't even save himself!" he added with a menacing laugh. "Hiding behind the monument will not protect you from me, Benjamin!" Eblis explained. "All that it does is to delay the inevitable, and holdup our arrival to the witch's coven that meets as we speak!"

I continued to stare at the cask. *How can I retrieve it?! Maybe I should just recite the spell! But then what can I capture him in?! I am doomed without that cask!* I pulled the Damascus blade out from inside the waistband of my breeches and carefully carved the three symbols of the monotheistic faiths in the top of the lid—the Jewish Star of David, the Christian fish, and the Islamic crescent moon. After completing the third symbol, the curly maple handle of the blade grew very hot in my hand—so hot that I had to drop the burning knife to the ground. Then I watched with alarm as the blade melted before me, until all that remained of the dazzling instrument was a puddle of steaming water.

"And Benjamin, it matters not anyway, for certainly Rachel has been sacrificed by this hour!" he assumed with more laughter.

The mention of Rachel's name stunned me. I was mortified by his words. *Could it be true?! Maintain your focus, Ben! No distractions!* Suddenly

I saw my horse trotting from out of the woods at the edge of the graveyard; but it was not returning alone, for directly behind the animal appeared Samantha on horseback with Rachel seated bareback behind her, with both arms joined around Sam's waist. Our eyes locked and I could tell immediately that my love could see me.

"There was no sacrifice, Ben!" Samantha called out, invalidating Eblis' claim. "Rachel is here with me! No witch's coven! Darcie and Patch are both dead!"

Eblis' face turned red as fire and he bellowed with the growl of ten lions.

"Samantha! Take shelter!" I warned.

Suddenly the graveyard was whipped into a tempest—stray branches swaying and debris being tossed around as if a cyclone had touched down. The wind stung my eyes as I continued to try to maintain my vision of Eblis from behind the monument; but a column of blue light appeared, engulfing the body of the demon shoemaker and his frame began to fade from view. I decided to seize the opportunity to retrieve the cask, but the wind had now blown it farther from my location, to a point where it rested wedged in between two headstones that had been set very close to one another.

Rachel slid from Sam's horse and now took cover behind a monument, but my love remained atop her Savior. The rolling cask had caught Samantha's eye before it became wedged and I sensed she understood my predicament as she yelled a verbal command sending the mare into a gallop, steering the animal in the direction of the barrel. My heart pounded furiously as my attention shifted back and forth from the sorcery surrounding Eblis, to watching my love bouncing atop her horse as it galloped across the graveyard.

The column of blue light vanished and where Eblis once stood, materialized the beast, appearing larger than I remembered from my first encounter with it. The sight of the grotesque monster with human arms, hands, and legs, combined with two large wings at each side, two cloven-feet, a horned head, and a short, thin tail protruding from its lower back, terrified me as much as it had the first time. With bowed posture, the hairy behemoth with a face of a wild boar, opened its frothing mouth and roared, exposing four large fangs among its teeth. *Eblis was now in his supernatural state!*

Sam could not help but look upon the beast herself and I could see her horrified expression with mouth gaped. The howl of the wind masked her scream although my love had the presence of mind to look away and continue the desperate ride.

Recognizing that time was of the essence, Sam closed in on the cask and without slowing the horse she slid slightly from her saddle to the right of Savior and leaned down low. As she drew near the cask, Sam reached out with her right hand and grabbed the barrel, gripping the rim of the open container. Clutching the pommel with her left hand, she pulled herself back in the saddle and pulled on the reins to turn the galloping horse in my direction. Sam and the horse passed me without breaking stride and my love tossed me the cask, which I caught with both hands.

Seething with rage, the beast watched Savior gallop across the graveyard and extended its hairy arm in the horse's direction. The monster opened its fingers, releasing a bolt of lightning from its grainy palm that struck a headstone just in front of the horse. The headstone exploded into pieces of sandstone startling the mare, which pulled to an abrupt halt. The animal whined, rose up on its hind legs, and kicked its front legs wildly, high in the air. Sam lost her grip on the reins and was thrown from the horse, crashing to the ground.

I cringed at the sight of Samantha lying motionless face down on the grass. "Sam! Sam!" I cried out. Sam did not move as the roar of the beast brought my attention back to it, and I realized it began to lumber in my direction. *No distractions! No distractions!* Hurriedly I worked to fill the container with sand. As I did, I turned back to look at my love and noticed she was now moving, slowly trying to lift herself from off of the ground. She appeared dazed as she struggled to her knees, when I saw a black horse gallop from out of the woods in the direction of Sam, carrying its male rider. As the fury of the wind continued to hammer the graveyard, I found it difficult to identify the strange rider, who, upon reaching Sam, dismounted and picked her up, placing her in the saddle. She slumped forward as the rider steadied her with his left hand and swung himself up and onto the back of the horse, squeezing himself into a position on the saddle behind her.

The beast watched the rider with interest as well. "MALIK!" it growled, revealing the rider's identity.

Caleb! No! Not now! I completed filling the cask with sand and from inside the Bible pulled out the parchment that Barnett had written on.

"MALIK!" the beast bellowed again. "Thou does honor me with thy presence! Kill the bitch!" it directed.

I trembled at the terrifying command and watched Caleb stop his horse beneath a large branch of a maple tree. Sam was still dazed, slumped over and resting on the neck of the stag when my cousin threw a rope over the limb above him. *What is he doing?!* Caleb grabbed the end of the rope that dangled over the branch and tied a not, pulling on the twine to tighten it. Then I shuddered at the sight of a noose at the other end of the rope.

"Caleb! NO!!" I called out, but my cousin did not acknowledge my scream.

I began to weep. *No distractions! No distractions!* I stepped out from behind the monument and placed the open cask at my feet in front of me. In my left hand I held the lid to the barrel and in my right I held the parchment. I had placed myself in a defenseless position directly before the beast, which now towered over my frame with a height easily three times my own, only ten rods from me.

The beast growled and hissed at me, confronting me with a tongue lashing laced with profanity.

Shouting above the howling wind and the beast's profanity, I began to read from the parchment. *"I am the perfect day..."* when suddenly my voice grew silent and my throat began to burn as if an unseen force squeezed it.

The beast, assessing my situation laughed and began to spout more profanity. When it spewed out the last of its vulgarity, it decided to address me one final time.

"Thy spells are futile!" the beast barked. "Did you really think you could successfully challenge me and defeat me?! I control thy tongue now and soon I shall crush thee once and for all, Benjamin! It tis the end for you and thy friends! But before I strike you dead, I want you to watch thy love as she swings from the branch of the tree!" it hollered with a brusque, frightening tone. "And pay heed to whose hand holds the rope!"

Immediately I remembered my dream and Samantha's name on the headstone. *Caleb is the dark rider that chased me through the woods?!* I began to weep harder now gasping for air as the beast snared me with an invisible stranglehold. I was losing control. The demon monster roared with laughter and I didn't want to, but I watched, as from his perch on the back of the horse, Caleb finished securing the rope to the tree and reached up to grab the noose. Sam continued to rest in her position situated on the saddle, slumped over on the horse's neck.

"Samantha! Samantha!" Caleb called out, shaking her from behind with both of his hands placed on her shoulders.

Samantha opened her eyes and turned slightly to see Caleb behind her. The minister concealed the noose from her view. "Grab hold of the horse's reins! When I yell for you to ride, do not turn around but take the horse to Rachel! Do you understand?!"

Samantha, still slightly dazed, nodded and turned away from Caleb.

Caleb then placed the noose around his own neck and hollered, "Ride!"

Samantha gripped the reins and kicked hard at both sides of the horse and the steed set off in a gallop. With the rope around his neck, Caleb was pulled from the horse and hanged from the tree, gasping for air and kicking wildly.

"MALIK!!" the beast cried out, enraged at the sight of Caleb swinging by his neck from the tree branch.

At that moment, the burning sensation in my throat subsided. *Caleb had distracted the beast!*

"Eblis!" I called out, remembering Barnett's emphasis on gnosis and humility. "I believe you are an archon in the service of the architect of this world, and that my flesh and bone is forged of your wicked hand! But servant of darkness, my soul belongs to the Creator and tis His light that draws me home!"

The beast growled with an intensified fury and I began to read with a confident voice—first from the Gospel of Truth...

"I am the perfect day, and in me dwells the light that does not fail!"

And next the Coptic spell...

"And when they take my soul to the place of the light
The great and powerful archon
Who is full of anger, the successor of the archon of outer darkness
The place in which all forms change
Who is powerful
Who is spread out upon the way of the midst

Who carries off the souls by theft
When they take my soul to that place
I will reveal the mystery of their fear
So that the archon will be powerful no more
I will reveal to them Eblis!..."

AT THE CONCLUSION OF THE SPELL I HELD THE LID UP IN THE AIR and in the direction of the beast so that it could discern the three religious symbols. Suddenly the monster emitted a high pitch shrill as does a wounded animal and the creature became engulfed in a bright light—so bright that I had to shield my eyes with the palm of my right hand. I could no longer see the beast through the intense brightness and with a violent whoosh, the light was sucked into the cask at my feet. When the illumination had disappeared, I quickly sealed the barrel with the lid and stepped back. The cask rocked back and forth violently for a minute or two before coming to rest. The tempest ceased as the branches returned to their sedentary positions and debris quietly fell to the earth, bringing a lull to the graveyard.

Breathing heavily, I looked over at the tree where Caleb hanged and I could see that Sam had guided my cousin's horse beneath him so that his body now rested on the back of the steed as she worked at pulling the noose from around his neck. I ran to my horse, mounted the animal and joined Sam beneath the branch, assisting her in removing the rope. Caleb's eyes were closed and I supported his body that lain limp in the saddle, before we carefully slid him from the horse and onto the ground. My cousin was dead.

Standing over Caleb's corpse, Sam and I shared a firm embrace filled with a sense of relief, gratitude, and melancholy. We pulled back away from one another as she gazed down at my cousin. "I'm so sorry, Ben!" she grieved, tears welling up in her eyes.

We embraced again.

"Are you hurt?!" I asked.

"No. And you?!"

I shook my head.

"Praise God!"

"Yes...praise the Creator!" I replied. "The spell worked, Sam! It worked!"

"It worked because of you, Ben! You were strong! You stood up to the demon and your confidence and faith defeated it!" she acknowledged.

"I could not have done it without you, Sam! I love you!"

"I love you too, Ben!"

My eyes dropped to Caleb and I bent over and lifted his cold hand. "And I couldn't have done it without you either, my good cousin. Thank you."

I stood up and hugged Sam once again. "Rachel?" I remembered, and we turned together and rushed over to our friend, still hidden behind the headstone.

Upon reaching her, we dropped to our knees and embraced in one great hug, weeping together, when suddenly I could hear the whisper of my name; although my friends did not produce a reaction and I was convinced they could not hear it. Nevertheless, I lifted my head from the embrace and looked beyond our huddle to see the appearance of three apparitions hovering above the ground several rods away. I slowly rose to my feet, still staring at the specters in awe as their identity came into focus and I recognized the three—my uncle Edward positioned in between my brother Jordan and Caleb. All three spirits were locked arm in arm and staring in my direction, with smiles and a genuine expression of tranquility illuminating their faces. Next, as if on command, all three raised their heads to the sky. I watched as from high above the trees, a bright beam of light streamed down from out of the heavens and engulfed all three specters. In a flash, the beam of light was drawn back up into the black sky, carrying the three apparitions with it. Radiating with a feeling of peace, I dropped back down to my knees and returned to the trinity.

CHAPTER 46

alem, 1831
     Benjamin Pratt sat back in the church pew and took a deep breath, while at the same time carefully assessing his son. Joshua Caleb looked astounded with lips slightly parted and eyes wide opened.

"Father, it is a fantastic tale!" Joshua acknowledged.

"Do you believe it?"

"Should I?"

The old man chuckled. "Yes, my son, you should. As I said before, my experience with Eblis was only known by three people—myself, Rachel, and Samantha—your mother," Benjamin explained before reaching for his cane and using the staff to assist him to his feet. "Rachel's funeral today has given me the opportunity to share the story with you, my oldest child."

"But father," Joshua began, still seated in the pew and looking up at his father now. "You haven't told me what became of the cask—the one that contained the demon?"

"Ah, yes, the most important part of the story...for you, that is," Benjamin divulged. "For if something should happen to me, then the responsibility becomes yours."

"What do you mean...responsibility?"

"Come with me," Benjamin instructed and stepped out of the pew.

He shuffled his way in the direction of the church altar with Joshua close behind.

Benjamin climbed the marble steps of the altar, leading his son to its center and stopped at the diamond-shaped sandstone that was set in the marble floor in front of the altar table.

"Do you remember, Joshua, the well on our property back in Tarrytown, New York?" Benjamin asked.

"Yes. As I recall you filled it in."

"And for good reason. I buried the cask in that well, but after your mother's death I began to search for a more permanent location for the barrel," Benjamin enlightened, resting the tip of his cane on the center of the sandstone. "The cask is now buried beneath this stone," he revealed. "It is wrapped in chains with a padlock and set in cement. The key to the padlock lies at the bottom of the Hudson River."

"It is here?!" Joshua was surprised. "How were you able to convince Father O'Brien to bury a cask beneath the altar?"

"Remember, I once owned the land that this church is built upon, and so it became a tradeoff for donating the land to the Catholic Diocese."

"But wasn't the priest suspicious of a cask wrapped in chains?"

"The cask was set in cement before being brought to the church for burial," Benjamin explained. "With Caleb and Barnett in mind, I had a biblical passage engraved on the cement and expressed my wish to have the monument buried beneath the altar."

"Which passage?"

"From Colossians...It reads, *See to it that no one takes you captive through philosophy and empty deception, according to the traditions of men, according to the elementary principles of the world, rather than according to Christ*," Benjamin recalled from memory. "Father O'Brien did think it odd that I would want to bury it, rather than have it exposed above ground for all to read, and to this day I do suspect that he assumes there is more to the story of this monument; but a deal is a deal, and the good priest has never questioned me. Thus the demon rests here."

Joshua stared down at the sandstone. "It is amazing to think what great evil lies buried beneath a house of worship."

"And the responsibility you have, my son, is to see that it remains here," Benjamin stressed with a serious tone.

Joshua looked at his father with a sobering expression. "Yes...father."

Benjamin patted his son on the back and smiled. "It is a befitting ending, wouldn't you say?"

"How so?"

"The demon attempted to use the church as an instrument of its sinister activity," Benjamin recalled, pounding the stone three times with the end of his cane. "And yet here we have the archon Eblis set to spend eternity inside a Catholic Church."

THE END

ABOUT THE AUTHOR

A native of Pittsburgh, Pennsylvania, Mark is a 1982 graduate of St. Bonaventure University where he studied journalism and received a Bachelor of Arts degree in communication. In addition to harboring a passion for writing, his love for history and education encouraged him to pursue and receive a Masters of Arts and Teaching degree from the University of Pittsburgh. At present, Mark brings his enthusiasm for history to the classroom as a Social Studies teacher for the Seneca Valley School District in Western Pennsylvania, where he teaches the subjects of AP World History and Honors United States History to sophomore and freshman students respectively. One of Mark's many other interests, rests in the penchant for telling stories. His knowledge of history, coupled with a curiosity for understanding and appreciating the affinity for all religions as well as the power of faith, provided the inspiration for *The Soles of Cyrus Eblis*.

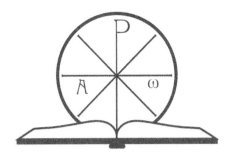

St. Polycarp Publishing House

CPSIA information can be obtained
at www.ICGtesting.com
Printed in the USA
LVHW110754040219
606285LV00007B/38/P

9 781947 707801